ASHES REMAIN

By Gwendoline SK Terry

Danethrall Trilogy
Danethrall
Rise to Fall
Ashes Remain

ASHES REMAIN
GWENDOLINE SK TERRY

TWO RAVENS PUBLISHING

Copyright © 2022 Gwendoline SK Terry

All rights reserved.

ISBN-10: 978-1-7339996-4-9

This is a work of fiction. Names, characters, places, and incidents either are the products of the author's imagination or are used fictitiously. Any resemblance to actual persons, living or dead, businesses, companies, events, or locales is entirely coincidental.

www.gskterry.com

In memory of
Tony Hartwick
21ˢᵗ June 1980 – 23ʳᵈ September 2019

Horror covers all the heath,
Clouds of carnage blot the sun.
Sisters, weave the web of death;
Sisters, cease, the work is done.

The Fatal Sisters
Thomas Gray

CONTENTS

PROLOGUE 1
CHAPTER ONE 8
CHAPTER TWO 15
CHAPTER THREE 28
CHAPTER FOUR.. 44
CHAPTER FIVE 51
CHAPTER SIX.. 66
CHAPTER SEVEN 72
CHAPTER EIGHT 87
CHAPTER NINE 97
CHAPTER TEN 110
CHAPTER ELEVEN 119
CHAPTER TWELVE.. 130
CHAPTER THIRTEEN 146
CHAPTER FOURTEEN 152
CHAPTER FIFTEEN 160
CHAPTER SIXTEEN 169
CHAPTER SEVENTEEN 182

CHAPTER EIGHTEEN 194

CHAPTER NINETEEN 200

CHAPTER TWENTY 210

CHAPTER TWENTY-ONE 218

CHAPTER TWENTY-TWO 232

CHAPTER TWENTY-THREE 243

CHAPTER TWENTY-FOUR 249

CHAPTER TWENTY-FIVE 263

CHAPTER TWENTY-SIX 271

CHAPTER TWENTY-SEVEN 280

CHAPTER TWENTY-EIGHT................................ 291

CHAPTER TWENTY-NINE 303

CHAPTER THIRTY...311

CHAPTER THIRTY-ONE 316

CHAPTER THIRTY-TWO......................................322

CHAPTER THIRTY-THREE................................. 331

CHAPTER THIRTY-FOUR 345

CHAPTER THIRTY-FIVE......................................353

CHAPTER THIRTY-SIX 365

CHAPTER THIRTY-SEVEN 374

CHAPTER THIRTY-EIGHT.................................. 380

CHAPTER THIRTY-NINE.....................................389

CHAPTER FORTY...398

CHAPTER FORTY-ONE 403

CHAPTER FORTY-TWO 419

CHAPTER FORTY-THREE 424

CHAPTER FORTY-FOUR 427

CHAPTER FORTY-FIVE 431

CHAPTER FORTY-SIX 445

CHAPTER FORTY-SEVEN 462

ASHES REMAIN

PROLOGUE

NORTH SEA
Late Spring, 886

"NOTHING CAN KILL a man if his time hasn't come, and nothing can save one doomed to die."

The black waves surrounding my ship mirrored the midnight sky almost perfectly. I was the only person awake, my crew and passengers fast asleep. Everything was calm and quiet, the occurrences from just a few days ago temporarily forgotten. I turned my gaze from the star-laden sea to the withered faces of those near me, dirt and blood dried upon their skin and clothes. In just a few hours they would wake, ripped away from the evanescent serenity sleep blessed them with.

Njörðr the god of seafaring seemed to have taken pity on us. Even the ocean god Ægir, his wife, Ran, and their nine daughters seemed to have turned a blind eye to us, granting us safe passage across the seas from Britain to our home in the Danish lands.

So many had died …

I squeezed my eyes shut and eased a sigh through my pursed lips. The past year had gone by in a haze of blood and death. From the summer of 885 until just weeks ago, we had suffered horrendous losses from our failed siege on Paris. What was meant to be an easy victory turned into a bloodbath. After our bloody defeat, we went to the town of Gipeswic in the Kingdom of the East Angles to recuperate, but that was not meant to be …

I could still feel the heat of the blazing Danish homes singe my skin as I dashed past them, clutching my children as we pressed through the panicked crowds to the harbour. Anglo-Saxons rushed into the throng, beating and killing the innocent Danes who fled from their burning abodes.

Thankfully, most of my crew escaped the riots of Gipeswic relatively unharmed. Now slumped in rows clutching their oars, they rested. Strangers were huddled about my ship too, injured men, broken families, women clutching children to their breasts, orphans shivering alone on the wet floorboards, their families slaughtered by the Anglo-Saxons. All of them sought sanctuary on my ship, wanting to get as far from the hate-filled Anglo-Saxons as they could. My eyes burned with sadness at the sight of them, but there were no tears left in me.

A sound beside me stole me from my thoughts. Æsa, my only living daughter, whimpered in her sleep. Her delicate face screwed up and indiscernible words slipped from her lips. Before I could move to comfort her, my eldest son, Young Birger, who was asleep beside her, woke enough to pull her against him.

Immediately her cries quietened, the furrows in her brow eased and her frown slackened. She burrowed against him, his presence expelling her nightmare immediately. A ragged sigh tumbled from Young Birger's lips and he fell back to sleep, his own body and mind fatigued by what had happened in Gipeswic.

I gazed at my children. Hidden beneath furs with only their heads sticking out, Young Birger, Sander, Æsa and Einar were clustered together on the ship's rough, wet floor. The cool breeze tugged at their golden hair, the fair hair they had inherited from their father ...

Even in the silvery light of the moon, I could see their cheeks whipped red from the salty sea winds, their faces wilted by sadness. They had lost so many loved ones over the past two years, their darling sister, Alffinna, our dear thrall and friend, Caterine, who had cared for my children like a second mother, their grandparents, my husband's parents Freydis and Alvar, and now their father, my beloved husband, Vidar ...

Vidar ...

My hands curled into fists and my ragged nails dug into my palms. Damn the Kingdom of the East Angles! Damn me for *wanting* to return to that place! I could feel my husband's last kiss tingle on my lips as though he had only just placed it there, but he had not. Vidar had died days ago on the shore of Gipeswic, killed by an Anglo-Saxon – my countryman – thanks to the riot incited by my own brother, Beric.

I hadn't seen my homeland, the Kingdom of the East Angles, for twenty years. When I was just a young girl, the Great Heathen

ASHES REMAIN

Army flooded my lands, burning homes and slaughtering all in their path. I had been lucky for my life had been spared. Rather than taking me as a thrall, my captor, Birger Bloody-Sword, adopted me and raised me as his daughter. For the past twenty years I had lived in Denmark, believing my whole blood family were dead. Little did I know that one of my seven brothers had survived.

After besieging the Franks at Paris, and losing miserably to them, Vidar took me back to the East Angles, took me back to my old village, to lift my spirits. By chance, I met a childhood friend, Guthlac, who had survived the Great Heathen Army's attack alongside my brother – news that shocked me to the core. Guthlac told us Beric might be stationed in Gipeswic with King Alfred's *fyrd*, for Beric was a soldier now.

We travelled to Gipeswic immediately, and I met another soldier there, Theodric Holt. I had not recognised him at the time, but Holt had been a thrall owned by my husband in Roskilde, Denmark. Holt had escaped many years ago and somehow managed to return to the East Angles. He hadn't recognised me either and, swayed by my sadness, he helped me find Beric.

Reunited, my brother and I were elated, but time had changed us both in such drastic ways. Beric sought to kill every last Dane in vengeance for our family. Stupidly, I told him of my Danish husband, my Danish children, my Danish adoptive father, in hope that he would make an exception, that he would love me, his sister, that he would love his niece and nephews. Maybe in time he would accept my Danish family, even if he couldn't forgive what the Danes had done in the past ...

I had been wrong – again, I was naïve, and my naivety had given me foolish hope. Time had hardened my brother's heart to stone, he was consumed with a loathing for the Danes so dark and strong that not even I, his long-lost sister, could overcome it.

"Aveline is dead! Had I known you were a traitor like Guthlac, I never would have met you. Leave this place and never return, do you hear me? Otherwise, you'll be killed like your Danish kin!"

Those had been the last words my brother had said to me after twenty years of separation. In his rage at my revelation, Beric disowned me, he stormed into the darkness and set aflame the homes of Danes settled in Gipeswic. Beric slaughtered Dane after Dane – Beric started the riot that led to my husband's death.

I should never have returned! Sentimentality had made me want to visit my homelands again and Vidar made that wish come true. Vidar had supported me through every wish, whim or want. He was my guide, my absolute, my protector. He didn't want me to return to the Kingdom of the East Angles in fear of losing me to my previous life, but he took me back there regardless of his fear, just to make me happy.

Vidar had been everything to me.

Our romance began when I was just fifteen and lasted over fourteen wonderful years, six of which we were married. The years had been difficult, but our love burned brightly through all storms – battles, wars, the deaths of our loved ones. We stood beside each other, constant and devoted, but thanks to my ridiculous sentimentality, thanks to my foolish naivety, I returned to the land of my birth and led Vidar to his death.

I hadn't known Vidar was doomed to die, but the Allfather had been right – nothing could save him. I had dreamt of a long life together, a blissful marriage that spanned decades, but that did not come to pass. Of course, it hadn't – Vidar was a Dane and Danes died young, they fought, they raided, they battled, they died.

But Vidar's death ... It was my fault.

I didn't even try to beg the gods – the Christian one nor the Norse pantheon – to return Vidar to me, for I knew they would not.

When our daughter, Alffinna, had been killed, her death almost destroyed me. I sank into a depression so immense, I never thought I would escape it – and part of me didn't want to. I couldn't bear even the light of day. Even when I slept, I saw Alffinna being killed before my eyes over and over again, helpless to stop it, unable to turn back time and bring my daughter back.

In desperation, I travelled across Denmark in the dead of winter to find a völva, a seeress and witch, rumoured to be powerful enough to speak to the gods. I almost died reaching her, but I arrived at her door and through potions and rituals, she sent me to the spirit realm.

ASHES REMAIN

I met the Allfather, the One-Eyed One, Odin, in the spirit realm. He told me that nine deaths had been sacrificed so that I might have a second life as a Dane. Those deaths had been my parents, six of my brothers and Mildritha – an Anglo-Saxon woman from my village who had protected me on the ship that took us from Britain to Denmark. After Mildritha's death, I was alone among the Danes – she had been the final link to my previous life as an Anglo-Saxon.

The Allfather said that sacrificing nine more lives would grant his blessings on my children. My children would live long, honourable lives and my sons would gain glory in battle and eventually die honourable deaths. I promised immediately, not weighing the consequences of that vow. I didn't want to watch another of my children die.

Five of the lives the Allfather requested had been taken before I'd even had the chance to make that promise to him, Birger, my adoptive father, Estrith, a thrall and dear friend, Caterine, Alffinna and Freydis. With Alvar and Vidar, the Allfather had seven of his nine sacrifices. Only two more lives were left to sacrifice, and I didn't know when or who would be taken.

Had I known that Vidar would be sacrificed, would I have made that vow to the Allfather? For the sake of my children, would I have made that same promise? Did it even matter whether I had agreed to the Allfather's terms? I had not agreed to the nine lives sacrificed for my second life as a Dane, nor had I agreed to the five lives that were sacrificed *during* my life as a Dane. The gods were cruel and fickle, they did as they desired and bestowed blessings only on a chosen few.

Perhaps I could have requested Vidar be excluded from the sacrifices?

Hot tears brewed in my aching eyes, I screwed them shut, refusing to let them fall, and released my breath from my pursed lips in quiet sputters. I couldn't think like that, I couldn't let these thoughts lead me into darkness. I couldn't go back in time and change anything, I couldn't – no matter how much I wanted to, I couldn't.

"That which is worth having is worth sacrificing for." The Allfather had said. "… A second chance at life – escaping death! – *that* is something great and deserves a great sacrifice! These lives paid for that, for you, for this life you live now, whether you chose it or not. Nine deaths paid for you to *live* as Aveline Birgersdóttir, not to *die* as Aveline Eadricesdohter."

"How am I meant to live with the guilt? With the burden of their deaths resting on my shoulders?" I had demanded.

"You honour them. You live the greatest life you can in respect to them." The Allfather had replied.

Whether you chose it or not ...

I had agreed to the Allfather's terms to protect my children. I had agreed for him to take the lives of my dear ones for the sake of my children. Whether I agreed or not, those lives would still have been taken from me, but I *had* agreed ... I had agreed to Vidar's death and nothing could bring him back to me. Now I had to honour him, and all those who had died for the sake of my damned promise. I had to live the greatest life I could, in respect to them, and I would.

The love Vidar and I shared had burned strong for almost fifteen years, now Vidar was dead. Never would I be so naïve, never would I trust so easily, never would I make a promise so thoughtlessly – not even to a god – and never would I return to the East Angles. Vidar always considered every option, always looked at an issue from all possible angles before making a decision. I did not, I was too emotional, too brash, too given to nostalgia and sentimentality. Never would I be that way again.

"The death of your daughter has shown you an agony more painful than anything you'll ever know." The Allfather said. "You can choose to let that pain destroy you, or you can draw wisdom from it. You can accept, as hard as it is, that death is a natural part of the cycle of life, and you can draw strength from the knowledge that nothing will ever hurt you as much as this has. Or you can kill yourself now and end the pain. Which do you choose?"

I had chosen to live. I had chosen to accept the tragic death of my daughter, I had chosen to embrace the pain of her death and let it strengthen me. My family would never be whole after Alffinna's death, but I had come to accept that.

With Vidar's death, I knew that agony once more, and I would have to draw wisdom from it as I had from Alffinna's death. I would strengthen from it, I would live the greatest life I could, to honour Vidar and all those who died because of me, but I would *never* be naïve again.

I rubbed my eyes with the heels of my hands and turned away from the star-sprinkled waves. I gazed at the occupants of my ship. These people, my crew, the poor displaced men, women and children, I gazed at my own sweet children curled on the wet ship floor. These were my responsibility.

I couldn't change the web the Nornir had woven for me on their tapestry of life, but I *would* be great enough to earn the ability to change the direction they wove to suit me – *not* to suit the cruel, fickle gods.

With Vidar dead and my sons too young to take his jarldoms themselves, I would take them myself. I would lead my warriors to victory – careful, calculated victories. I would protect my people from armies and enemies, I would be the best leader I could, just as Vidar was. I would make Aros and Roskilde thriving market towns like the great town of Ribe. I would do everything for my children to succeed, for the Allfather's prophecy to come true.

I would make Vidar proud, until the day I would meet him again in the afterlife.

CHAPTER ONE

OBOTRITE SETTLEMENT
Autumn, 886

SEARING PAIN TORE through my lungs with each rasping breath. Exhaustion weighed down my aching arms, my calves throbbed, and sweat stung the bloody cuts and open wounds scattered over my body. I couldn't rest though, it wasn't over yet.

Bodies littered the ground, both young and old, their blood seeping into the earth. The soft rattling breath of those not yet dead was audible among the corpses. I carried on walking step by heavy step, glancing over those that still clung to life. They posed no threat, from their wounds I knew they would die soon enough.

The tiny broken bodies of children, their pale cheeks stained with tears, were cradled by their mothers or siblings. My heart ached at the sight of them, but I trudged past them all the same and made my way to the nearest log house in search of survivors.

Inside the Wendish dwellings, I kicked aside stools, children's wooden toys, spinning tools and broken dishes scattered across the floor. The homes had been ransacked already and my men had turned their attention to the church in the centre of the Obotrite town. While they collected their plunder, I crept about the town to slay any survivors who might be hiding, thankful to be alone regardless of my gruesome mission.

I shoved open the door to the nearest house and entered it, lifting my sword, *Úlfsblóð*, in front of me, ready to cut down whoever might be hiding in the shadows. So far, all the small windowless single-roomed houses were dark and silent, empty of people or filled with corpses. This house was no different, there was no one to slay here. The corpses of the presumed family, an old woman, man, a younger woman and two small children, were piled beside the brick oven in the corner of the little log home.

A shuddering breath sputtered from my cracked lips. I clapped a hand to my burning chest, feeling a thick glob of mucus leak down the back of my throat. I spat onto the ground – my saliva was red with blood. I wrinkled my nose and stumbled out of the house, letting the door swing closed behind me.

The next dwelling, a dilapidated shack of a home, stood far in the distance, clutched tightly by a wild tangle of overgrown brambles and weeds. I wondered whether the place was even inhabited considering its dire state, but I couldn't leave it unchecked. With a shallow, wheezing sigh, I trudged towards it, my legs trembling and arms aching.

I tried the lock. It was stiff, but with a little wiggling it lifted, yet the door still wouldn't open.

"Damn it …" I grumbled quietly.

I lifted *Úlfsblóð*, my muscles tight and sore, and rammed the door with my shoulder. Bruised from slamming against so many doors, I winced, unable to stop myself from crying out. Thankfully, the door swung open when I rammed it a second time, sending it clattering against the wall.

I almost gasped aloud when a cat skittered across the room yowling, whipping past my legs at lightning speed. I managed to control myself, paused in the door frame, listening.

No sound … No scuffle of feet in the dirt floor, no sharp intake of breath, no whimper. I glanced over my shoulder and watched the ginger feline plunge into a thicket across the way before I slipped into the dark abode, the door creaking shut behind me.

Flames danced in the oven across the room, lighting the sparse area with an eerie glow. The only furniture inside the house was a mouldy straw bed covered in a tattered blanket, a low table with a bowl half-full of cold stew sat upon it, and a cupboard storing whatever else belonged to the dweller of this pitiful hovel. But for the overgrown vegetation slowly consuming the house, it was not any different to the other houses in this poor village.

Thump!

Úlfsblóð slipped from my trembling, sweaty fingers and landed on the packed-dirt floor. I stared at it, at the long red stains on the double-edged blade, at the filthy handprint marring the pale antler hilt. I reached for it, but my aching legs and back would not bend. Instead, I fell to my knees, collapsing on the floor beside it.

Rather than reach for my sword, I drew my hands onto my lap and stared at them. My palms were small and my fingers slender, but they were red and black with blood and dirt, filth caked beneath each nail. My cramping muscles would not allow me to hold my hands out flat without pain tearing through them.

I forced myself up, flinching and groaning as I stood. I staggered to the oven where a wooden bucket of water stood, my sword forgotten on the floor behind me. I eased myself down beside the bucket, my joints popping and cracking, and dipped my hands into the lukewarm liquid.

Wishing for a chunk of lye soap, I scrubbed and scrubbed, watching the paleness of my flesh gradually reappear as the filth washed away, fouling the once-clear water. My hands were finally clean, but there was still dirt beneath my nails. I pulled my utility knife from my belt and–

"Argh!"

My head pounded and ears rang – it took me a moment to realise I was flopped over the upturned water bucket. The water pooled over the ground, soaking my skirts and turning the dirt floor to mud. I glanced over my shoulder to see a skinny, scruffy man wearing threadbare clothing – one of the damned Wends! He held *Úlfsblóð* in his quaking hands. The bastard had struck me with the pommel of my own sword! That was his mistake – he should've stabbed me when he had the chance.

The Wend barked something at me in his language. I eyed him groggily, this house must belong to him for his clothes were as shabby as the dilapidated dwelling.

"Give me my sword." I rasped, delicately touching the knot that had sprung up from where the fool had struck me.

The Wend couldn't understand me. He barked at me again. His eyes were wide and sweat poured from his brow. The knuckles of his skinny, trembling fingers were white from the tightness of his grip around *Úlfsblóð*'s filthy hilt.

With a flick of his head, he signalled me to stand.

Slowly I rose. I stepped towards the Wend, glancing from his terrified face to *Úlfsblóð*. He shuffled aside, nodding his head at the door, barking anxious words at me.

"I'm not leaving without my sword." I said regardless that he apparently could not understand the Norse language.

ASHES REMAIN

He started yelling, shaking my sword in a manner I assumed meant to threaten, put the fear and panic in his eyes betrayed him. I stepped closer, he was less than an arms-length away from me.

"Give me my sword." I said.

The Wend's temper was running short. He yelled at me again, Úlfsblóð held across his chest. Though he was becoming more animated, I wasn't afraid – from the closeness I was standing to him, he couldn't stab me, he'd have to swing to truly harm me and in doing so, he'd leave his torso unprotected.

"Give me my sword." I growled.

Finally, the Wend swung.

He lifted Úlfsblóð to his shoulder and in that moment, I plunged my utility knife into his stomach. Úlfsblóð clattered to the ground. The Wend gawped at the small knife sticking into him, my hand clasped around the short wooden handle.

He was frozen in shock, I stabbed him again. Blood oozed from the little wounds, and his tunic muffled the wet snap of his skin as my metal blade pierced his flesh and perforated his organs.

I managed to gore the Wend twice more before he recovered from his shock. He punched me, hard. A white light flashed before my eyes, stealing my vision for just a moment. I guarded my face with one arm while stabbing wildly at him, the blade piercing him over and over. Still the Wend beat me, but he was tiring quickly.

I could not take many more punches.

I threw myself across the room, landing in a pile on the floor. The Wend glared at me, his face deathly pale, blood streaming from his belly. Our eyes locked briefly then dropped to Úlfsblóð at his feet. He reached down to grab it, but I dove at him, tackling him to the ground. The Wend cried out and I sank my knife into his neck. I felt the knife ricochet against his bone, sending shudders through my arm. The Wend yowled but he silenced quickly. His body dropped.

I disentangled myself from the Wend and heaved him over to retrieve Úlfsblóð. A soft gurgling sounded from his throat as I shoved his body aside. I crouched beside him and grabbed a fistful of his black hair. His dark brown eyes darted in their sockets. I pulled his head back, dug my knife's blade into the soft flesh of his neck and slit his throat, the tender flesh snapping and releasing a cascade of blood. His gurgling intensified, his body spasmed violently then he fell still. Dead.

"I can't believe you hit me with my own sword," I grumbled as I sheathed *Úlfsblóð*. "Fucking bastard."

I did a quick search of his body, but I found nothing, just as I expected. The man had nothing. There was not a single thing of value on his person or in his home – the clothes on his back seemed to be the only clothing he owned.

My eyes drifted over the wounds in his stomach, the wounds I had given him. He had only tried to defend his home, tried to save himself from the horrifying fate his village had suffered at the hands of raiders. That was what we were, my army of Danes and me. We were raiders, we were killers …

I squeezed my eyes shut tightly and tried to swallow down the emotion knotted in my throat. I turned my back on the Wend, left his dilapidated dwelling and made my way to the church in the centre of the settlement.

I squinted up at the sun in the middle of the clear sky. We had made good time, at this rate we could arrive back in Aros by evening meal. I needed to go back home, I needed to be with my children. I had been away from them for far too long.

Out of the four of them, my eldest two had come to war with me, both boys old enough to fight. My youngest children, Æsa and Einar, were still far too young, and I had left them in my hall back in Aros, safe with my thralls, Melisende and Rowena, and my friends, Guðrin and Borghildr, watching over them.

In the Norse world, boys were considered men at ten years of age, but were not able to fight in battles until at least the age of twelve. Young Birger, my eldest son, was old enough to actively participate in expeditions at almost thirteen years of age. I had fought beside Young Birger in Francia shortly before his twelfth winter. He was an excellent warrior and a highly capable archer.

Sander had seen that battle, but he had been too young to fight. He was forced to remain at camp or huddle by the mast of our longship with the women and children whether he liked it or not. He was still too young to actively participate, but since he would see his tenth winter and thus become a man in just a few months, I allowed him to attend the expedition, to view and learn from it.

ASHES REMAIN

We had not fought soldiers nor besieged an entire city like Young Birger had for his first combat experience. No, we had slaughtered unarmed monks, nuns and abbots, plundered their abbeys and monasteries, killed unarmed villagers or those equipped with rickety farming tools, but it had been enough to whet Sander's appetite for war.

My army and I had been raiding the Wendish lands for two months. I hadn't seen Æsa and Einar for *two months*. This settlement was the last of our expedition. It belonged to a tribe of Obotrites, also known as Polabian Wends, not too far from the East Francian border. Some Wends were Christian, like those of this settlement, while others worshipped Wendish gods.

I did not know their gods, nor did I care. We had come to plunder, to ravage their lands for gold and goods and we had been victorious – though the villagers of this settlement had been poor, their Christian church was not. We would return home this very day, our arms filled with riches, sacks of grains and other foodstuffs, though there was nothing more I wanted than to embrace my children again.

I was halfway to the church when I spotted a small group of warriors marching towards me. There were six of them in total, all wild and bloodied and grinning.

"Any survivors, Jarl?"

"Not anymore, *nei*." I replied.

"Are you alright?" Jan asked, gazing at me with concern in his sapphire eyes.

"*Já*, I'm fine." I shrugged. "Did you load the plunder?"

"That we did, Jarl." Domnall beamed through his bushy ginger beard, his light blue eyes sparkling. "I've my eye on a few trinkets I think Guðrin will like."

"I'm glad to hear that." I smiled warmly to the giant fiery-haired Dane. "She will have whatever you want to give her."

"Borghildr might not be happy with what I've found." Ebbe chuckled.

"Not another concubine, man?" Hallmundr rolled his eyes. "Borghildr will kill you if you bring another home!"

"I'll have her, I've seen the woman – she's a fine-looking thing." Lars piped in.

"*Enough.*" I said firmly. "No one is having her, she'll be put in with the others and sold at the market, just as I ordered before we came here. Keep your silver, but the thralls *will* be sold."

"It's probably for the best." Ebbe said with a shrug.

"*Já* it is," Einarr the musician said. "If you keep bringing home these concubines, Borghildr will make a eunuch of you."

"You should see the tits on this thrall, though." Ebbe winked, earning laughter from his companions.

"Come on, we'll talk about the thrall's tits on the ships." I said, rolling my eyes at him. "Is everyone set to leave?"

"That's why we came to find you." Domnall said. "The ships are loaded and the crew ready. We just have to get on Storm-Serpent then we can head back home."

"Good." I said. "Let's go."

"*Já*, Jarl Aveline." The men nodded.

Ebbe, Domnall, Hallmundr, Lars and Einarr swiftly turned and started towards the bay where our three huge dragon-headed warships, Sea-Wolf, Oak-Blade and Storm-Serpent, were bobbing on the calm waters. Jan didn't move, though. He blocked my path, his eyes locked on me, his great muscled arms crossed over his chest.

"What is it?" I asked.

"You're wheezing and there's no colour in your face." Jan said. "Where are you hurt?"

"All over, Jan, I've just been in a battle." I scoffed, bumping him with my shoulder as I started after the others.

"Do you want some wine?" Jan asked, walking beside me.

"I'd kill for some."

"No need, I already have." Jan grinned. "The casks are on Storm-Serpent for us to enjoy."

"You *are* good to me!" I laughed.

"I do my best."

CHAPTER TWO

AROS, DENMARK

MY HALL BUZZED like a hive, swarming with townspeople. Sitting in my highbacked chair holding Einar, my youngest child, I watched the crowd. There were warriors grimy with dirt and blood, reeking of the salty tang of sweat and sea, their wives or lovers draped over them, glowing with pride. Children clung to their fathers' legs, and elderly men and women grinned at their sons and grandsons, proudly grasping their warrior's strong shoulders with gnarled hands. Faces glanced at me with admiration and pleasure, their cheeks flushed by mead and ale, their arms filled with gold and trinkets.

"The spoils are divided, are you all satisfied with your lot?" I asked, examining each warrior in turn.

"*Ja*!" My warriors cheered, clutching their trinkets or raising their horns.

"Good, you have earned them." I smiled. "An entire season of battle and we have come out victorious! I congratulate you, my men. I am proud of you all."

"Odin was with us!" A warrior exclaimed, holding his silver chalice in the air.

The young, mousy-haired warrior was answered with a resounding roar of agreement, other warriors lifting their tankards and cups high, too, in honour of the gods.

"And why would he not?" I called over the enthusiastic din, ignoring the bitter pang that struck my heart at the warrior's excited words. "You all were powerful, strong, merciless – you were everything a fine warrior worthy of Valhalla ought to be, and more!"

Another great cheer shook the walls of my hall.

"But do not give the gods *all* the glory, my friend." I smirked, pointing at the young warrior. "*You* were the ones who proved yourselves today – *you* were the ones who earned each and every victory we have gained this season. I am thankful to have the honour to fight beside you – as are the gods, I am sure! More so, I'm thankful to not be fighting against you." I added with a laugh echoed around the room by all those grinning faces. "Now go to your homes, all of you. Take your riches, enjoy your wives, play with your children. There will be a feast here tonight, to celebrate *you*." I lifted my horn of mead in the air. "*Skål!*"

With a rousing exclaim of '*Skål!*' every man and woman brought their horns and tankards, and even glittering golden church chalices, to their lips and downed the contents. Mead, ale and beer dribbled down bearded chins accompanied by gruff chuckles and trill giggles. The townspeople's happiness was infectious and noisy, but they finished their drinks and did as I bade, gradually filtering out of my hall.

We had returned to Aros that morning from our fruitful raiding expedition in the Wendish lands. We had fought hard, attacking farming village, market town and monastery alike, and hadn't lost a single man. Each of my warriors held in his arms chalices, pyxes or crucifixes made of silver and gold. We had seized countless purses of coin, gems and jewellery – both silver and gold, casks of wine, livestock, furs and sacks of wheat, barley and oats – all kinds of marvellous plunder to keep and to sell.

The hall became deafeningly quiet in the townspeople's absence. I released a sigh, my ears ringing from the quiet, and kissed the top of Einar's head, glad to have my family together again. I shuffled Einar higher up my lap and turned my gaze to Æsa, Sander and Young Birger who were happily digging through our mountain of spoils.

Æsa's hands were heavy with rings, and bracelets slid up and down her wrists clinking when she moved. Sander kept piling necklaces over Æsa's head, much to her delight, and Young Birger was sitting nearby, laughing at the sight of them.

As Jarl of Aros, I received the biggest share of the plunder, though I had been more than generous with my men. My share would be added to the rest of my riches. My wealth would not just be spent on finery, it would be used as rewards for loyalty, presents to sweeten alliances, gifts to persuade opposition into allies. I would pay for building supplies and labour to improve and expand the towns I ruled, to fund raids and war, to arm my warriors, to build a bigger, better fleet and to mend our existing ships. Should it ever happen, my fortune would pay to mend Aros or Roskilde if either of my towns were attacked.

In just a few years, my riches would pay for Æsa's *heiman fylgia*, dowry, when she wed, the *mundr*, bride-price, and the *morgen-gifu*, morning gift, for each of my sons' future wives, and when I died my riches would become my sons' inheritances.

"Would you like to pick something from the pile?" I asked, pointing at my other children and the mountain of chalices, jewellery, coin and crucifixes.

"*Nei.*" My four-year-old son replied stoutly.

"What would you like then?" I chuckled at the serious expression on Einar's face.

"Where's Jan?"

"Jan? He's busy at the marketplace." I replied, caught off-guard by his question.

Einar stared at me disappointed, his fingers fiddling with the embroidered hem of his sleeve. A sigh fell from his lips and I kissed the top of his head.

"Jan will be back soon, my love." I soothed. "Why don't you look through the pile and find something for him?"

Einar stared at me with reluctance.

"Come now, my love. It would make Jan so happy to receive a gift from you." I urged.

"Fine." Einar grumbled.

"While you look, I'll wash and change." I smiled as Einar slipped off my lap and trudged over to his siblings.

My smile vanished the moment Einar's back was turned. I ran a hand through my greasy, knotted hair as I watched him reluctantly pick up a chalice.

Einar had grown close with Jan since Vidar's death. When we moored our longships in the harbour this morning, it was not me or Young Birger or Sander who Einar dashed toward first, but Jan. Einar immediately begged Jan to play with him, explaining with almost unintelligible speed everything he had done while we were away raiding, wanting to share every detail with Jan. Though I wouldn't voice it aloud, I was jealous, jealous of the attention Einar gave Jan, but I didn't fault my son. Einar was searching for a father figure now his own father was gone.

"Your bath is ready, Jarl." Melisende said, appearing beside me.

"*Þakka fyrir.*" I said to my Frankish thrall.

I made my way to the kitchen slowly, grazing my fingertips along the posts that ran down the centre of the hall, supporting the roof. The posts were painted white with quicklime and at the top of each were gorgeous images carved into the wood. Across the room, my Anglo-Saxon thrall, Rowena, was already busying about tidying, sprinkling ashes on spilt drink puddles and sweeping the unsettled dirt of the floor.

I paused and watched my children. Young Birger and Sander were laughing at Æsa, who was spinning in circles, the gold and silver she was laden with jangling noisily. A sharp pang struck my heart at the sad sight of my youngest son, Einar was standing beside the pile of plunder half-heartedly examining the different shining pieces, frequently glancing between the spoils and the great door of our hall.

I dropped my head and turned away, continuing to the kitchen. I didn't know where Jan was – he had run off soon after we had unloaded the ships, his portion of the loot already in his chest on Storm-Serpent. Apparently, he needed to speak to someone at the marketplace – who that someone was, I didn't know, and I didn't bother to ask.

Though I wasn't concerned about where Jan was or what he was doing, Einar was, desperately. It broke my heart to see my youngest child so worried, but I knew when Jan came to the hall Einar would be elated and happy, back to the cheery child he normally was. This happened every time Jan was absent, there was nothing I could do but assure Einar that Jan *would* return.

"Would you like help undressing, Jarl?" Melisende asked as I entered the kitchen.

"*Nei, þakka.*" I smiled. "I'll call should I need you. Do tell me when Jan arrives, though."

"Of course, Jarl." My Frankish thrall nodded before leaving me in solitude.

ASHES REMAIN

Steam rose enticingly from a large wooden tub beside the fire pit in the centre of the kitchen. Upon the hot vapour was the aromatic fragrance of lavender, lending me a sense of calm. I inhaled it deeply, eager for my first hot bath since I'd gone off to raid. The skirts and hem of my gown were stiff with blood, sweat and dirt, and though I'd washed my face and hands, I still reeked of the salty brine of seawater and the fetid stench of death from those I'd slaughtered.

Since we'd returned to Aros, no one had time to wash or change, too excited to see our families and divide up the plunder. It was finally time for me to wash away the foul smells and filth of battle and settle into my home.

Folded neatly on the scrubbed tabletop near the bathtub were clean clothes, a linen sheet to dry with and a basket filled with a variety of soaps. I began the ordeal of stripping my filthy clothing from my body, starting with the blood-splattered tortoiseshell brooches on my dress.

Slowly I unpinned the brooches fastened to the straps of my apron gown. Between them was a string of gorgeous glass beads, amber, scarlet and gold in colour. My adoptive father, Birger Bloody Sword had gifted me these brooches when I was a young girl. A small smile lifted one corner of my mouth as thought of my dear Birger. I laid the beads and brooches gently on the tabletop and continued to peel my stinking clothing from my body.

Glad to be free of the grimy garments, there was only one thing left on my naked body: around my neck hung a simple silver ring tied to a long thin black leather thong – Vidar's wedding ring.

I never removed the necklace. I wore it as I slept, as I bathed, as I battled. As Vidar lay dying, he bade us take his sword, bow and arm bands to his sons, and the Mjölnir pendant he always wore to his daughter. Our friends Hallmundr, Domnall and Einarr retrieved these items from my husband's body while Jan forcibly carried me to the ship.

One of our three companions had retrieved Vidar's wedding ring for me – I did not know who had and I hadn't asked, but I was thankful. Upon my finger I still wore the engagement band and wedding ring Vidar had given me years ago, and around my neck, tucked beneath my clothes, hung Vidar's ring.

I took the basket of soaps and set them on the ground beside the tub. I climbed into the bath, avoiding the heated stones at the end of the tub, a low purr of delight rolling in my throat. The bite of the heat warmed me to my bones, turning my pale flesh red as I sank lower into the water, my every ache and throb soothed at once. I leaned back to soak my tangled hair and my scalp burned, but I didn't care – this was my first hot bath in months and, scalding or not, I was going to enjoy it for as long as I could.

Carefully I wiped the film of grime from Vidar's ring underneath the water with my fingers until it shone silver once more. As I cleaned the black leather thong, my mind drifted to the expedition in the Wendish lands.

It was the first raid I had led as Jarl of Aros. It had been bountiful, not just for the spoils we had returned home with. I had solidified my people's faith and trust in me. Whatever doubts they might have had in my leadership were wiped out by the success of this expedition. I had proven to them I could lead them in battle, that I could fight alongside them, that I would not fail them. Not a single member of my crew had died nor been terribly injured, and all of them had returned home far richer than when they had left. I had earned my people's confidence, I had their trust, and most importantly, I had their loyalty.

The face of the young, mousy-haired warrior whirled in my mind.

"*Odin was with us!*"

Nei, *Biólan Koðránsson*, nei, *he was not*. I thought bitterly, staring at the smoke-stained ceiling beams. *I did not see him there – do not give the One-Eyed One an honour he doesn't deserve.*

I had met him, the one called the Allfather. Sat on a great wooden throne, his great hands curled around the roaring wolves carved into the chair's arms, his one piercing blue eye scrutinised me. His other eye socket was empty, the lid sewn shut. He had been vast, not old yet not young, intimidating yet comforting. His laugh had been loud and warm yet sent shivers down my spine. His great muscled body was clad in indigo, fine leathers and shadow, his snow-white beard braided loosely. He had been a friend, had made promises to me, but he had also kept a secret from me that I could never forgive him for.

ASHES REMAIN

Nothing can kill a man if his time hasn't come, and nothing can save one doomed to die ...

The One-Eyed One could have warned me, but he didn't ...

An invisible fist squeezed my heart. I sank deeper into the tub, my eyes stinging with tears I wouldn't let fall. I breathed in, out, in, out, calming the rage seething inside me.

The lavender scented steam was thick and warm, swirling through my nostrils and dancing down my throat. Clasping Vidar's ring, I let the bath mist lead me into a stupor. I listened to my heart beating in my ears, steady as a drum, listened to the deep, slow breaths gently fall from my lips. Gradually memories and thoughts slipped away. My grip on the ring lessened, until finally my mind was clear.

"Aveline?"

I woke with a start. I didn't know how long I had been sleeping, but the bath water had chilled considerably. I sat up in the tub and the cool air rushed over me, creating goosebumps over my flesh.

"What the—" I gasped.

With a few long-legged strides, Jan, still dressed in his filthy expedition clothes, made his way to me and crouched down beside the tub, a mischievous grin playing on his lips. A hot blush burned on my cheeks, I folded my arms over my breasts, my long, thick chestnut curls clinging to my body, concealing most of me from Jan's view.

"I tried to stop him, Jarl—" Melisende stammered from the doorway, pale-faced with horror.

I waved a hand wildly at her and she vanished quickly.

"What are you doing in here? I'm having a bath!" I snapped.

"I can see that." Jan grinned. "Melisende said you wanted to know when I arrived. She offered to announce me, but I thought I'd announce myself." His wicked grin was replaced with an innocent smile, but I knew better than to fall for it. "Can I pass you the soap?"

"Hand me that linen. I'll not talk to you while I'm unclothed." I growled, very conscious of my nakedness under his sapphire gaze.

Jan let out a dramatic sigh, shrugged his shoulders and fetched me the linen. I snatched it out of his hands and held the folded fabric against my chest.

"Get out of here! We'll speak when I'm dressed."

"You seem irritable, is there anything I can do to relieve your stress? I could rub your shoulders – or wash your hair?"

"Had you been any other man, Jan Jötunnson, I'd have your head cut from your body!" I snarled.

"Surprisingly, that's not the first time I've been told that." Jan mused, strolling towards the door.

"Better yet, I'd do it myself!" I shouted after him, watching him disappear into the main room.

"I'd prefer it if you did!" Jan called back wickedly.

I sighed, relieved that he had left but shocked he'd dared to enter while I was bathing in the first place. I couldn't help but chuckle as I tossed the linen back onto the table. Damn that Jan! He dared to do anything and almost always managed to get away with it. He had always been cheeky and forward, but with the newfound closeness of our relationship, I had to become accustomed to his mischievousness and his love of crossing boundaries.

Over the months, Jan's and my friendship strengthened, we became much closer than ever before. Bonded by grief, since Vidar's death, we were there for each other always. Jan became my rock, my support, the person who kept me standing while my life fell apart around me. But for the children, Jan was the one person in the world who grieved for Vidar as I did.

Vidar was ripped from our lives so suddenly, and despite his own sadness, Jan stepped up and became such a major role in my life. It was so hard for me to keep myself together and simultaneously be there for my children. Jan helped not just me, but the children through their grief as well. Jan was by my side through it all.

When Alffinna died, I failed my family. Swallowed by my own sorrow, I left Vidar to struggle through his grief and at the same time guide the children through theirs while I wallowed selfishly alone. I swore never to do that again – I would be strong, I wouldn't fail them again.

But I had never imagined I'd lose Vidar. I couldn't fathom a life without him – I thought he'd be with me through everything, and when he was killed, I had no idea how I could keep my vow when I was just as devastated as our children.

ASHES REMAIN

That was where Jan came in. I confided every secret, every emotion, every thought in him and only him. Every day since Vidar's death, Jan visited to make sure the children and I had eaten. He played with them, went hunting and trapping with us. He wouldn't leave the hall until the children were asleep, and when he went to the shipyard he always took the boys along.

Jan filled the place Vidar had left, becoming a father-figure to my four sweet children. He held them and listened to them when they were sad. He shared tales of Vidar's life with us, Vidar's childhood long before I'd ever stepped foot in the Danish lands, to keep Vidar's spirit alive and bright in the children's hearts. He made the children happy, and in turn, Jan made me happy, too.

I grabbed the lye soap and lathered my body and hair with it, washing myself as quickly as I could in the lukewarm water. Soon enough, I stepped out of the bath, water streaming from my clean body, and hurriedly dried myself and dressed.

I emerged into the main room dressed in a gorgeous forest green gown, the sleeves and neckline embroidered with silver, red and blue thread. I smelled far better than I had in months. Indeed, I even felt lighter, as though the filth and blood dried to my body had been weighing me down. I was free of that burden ... Until the next expedition at least.

"I apologise, Jarl, I–" Melisende started, still flushed with embarrassment.

"It wasn't *your* fault, I know." I interrupted, staring pointedly at Jan.

Jan grinned innocently, sipping his tankard of honey mead.

Melisende pulled a chair out from the table for me, opposite Jan, and I sat in it, still glaring at Jan. Leather thongs and an assortment of oils and various sized combs were laid out upon the table in front of me. My thick, matted chestnut curls hung like soggy rat tails to the small of my back, leaving a dark sodden patch on my gown. Behind me, Melisende lifted my hair over the back of my chair and set to work detangling my hair with her fingers, grunting and gasping at the state of it.

"You needed me, Jarl?" Jan asked brightly.

"Have you seen Einar yet?" I asked as Melisende took one of the combs and picked at a particularly snarled lock of my hair.

"*Já*, we played for a while before I came to see you. He gave me the most wonderful chalice."

"I'm glad to hear that." I smiled. "He missed you earlier."

"He's a great boy." Jan grinned. "All of your sons are, and Æsa is a wonderful girl. Einar reminds me of you, he's sweet, sensitive, kind."

"*Þakka fyrir*. Not the words one usually uses to describe a boy, but I appreciate it." I laughed.

"A man must be strong, resilient and brave, but he must also be generous and aware of others. If my son has just a fraction of Einar's heart, I would be proud." Jan said warmly.

Jan's son … Jan had not seen his son, Thórvar, for four years. Jan had been raiding for a few months along the coast of Francia and during that time, his wife, Thóra, took their son Thórvar and left. She left a message for Jan with a neighbour and the message was simple, Jan could keep all their money, possessions and property and she would not ask for a single thing, but she was taking Thórvar. She bade Jan not to follow them and said she and Thórvar would never return to Roskilde. Thóra gave no reason as to why she was deserting Jan, she just left. Jan had searched desperately for them for years, but to no avail.

"I'm sure your son is every bit as wonderful as Einar." I assured with all the sincerity in my heart.

Jan shrugged. drained his mead and hailed Rowena over to fetch him another. She hurried away, Jan's cup in one hand and a broom in her other. We sat in silence as Melisende dedicatedly combed my hair and coated my curls in sweet smelling oils.

I tried to imagine what Thórvar would look like now, but all I could conjure was a miniature version of Jan. Unfortunately, Vidar and I never had the chance to meet Thórvar – in fact, I had never met any of Jan's children.

I lived in the Kingdom of the East Angles when Jan was married his first wife. After her death, he brought many women into his bed, thralls and Danes alike. Over the years, Jan had conceived four children between four thralls, and one legitimate child with his second wife.

The two daughters he'd conceived in the two years after his wife's death had died shortly after their births. After Jarl Erhardt had taken me as peace bride and forced me to Aros, Jan conceived a child with another thrall, a son he'd named Jarðarr. Unfortunately, Jarðarr had drowned in Roskilde Fjord soon after his third winter, a tragic accident.

Jan met his second wife, Thóra, at Vidar and my wedding. He quickly conceived a child with her and married her, and the bitch abandoned him after their son saw his second winter. Two years after Thóra vanished, Jan had taken a thrall named Fríðr and gotten her with child. She, like his first wife, died giving birth to his stillborn child. He named his daughter Jóra and she and Fríðr were laid to rest in the burial grounds at the heart of Aros.

The gods seemed to toy with Jan. The Nornir had cursed him with a life of loss – on top of the children, the wives and the lovers he had lost, Jan's eldest brother had died when Jan was just a boy and his mother had died birthing his youngest brother. Now he had lost Vidar, his closest friend.

Despite all the tragedy in his life, Jan always smiled, Jan always jested, Jan always laughed. I had only seen glimpses of his inner broken self in rare moments when Jan accidentally let his guard down, but on the battlefield, I saw his rage ...

Since Fríðr and Jóra's deaths, I hadn't seen Jan with a woman, not Dane nor thrall. I wondered if he had given up on the idea of marriage and fatherhood, a preposterous idea for most people but not at all an unreasonable decision for Jan.

Though I hadn't lost half as much as him, I had a small insight to Jan's tragedy, having lost my birth family, my adoptive father, my daughter, Alffinna, and my husband, Vidar.

As a widow, I was expected to remarry, but I could remain unwed for the rest of my life if I chose to, though that decision was critically ill-advised. Unwise or not, it was the decision I had privately made, and I supported Jan with every fibre of my being if that was a decision he had made, too.

"Anyway," Jan said, accepting his fresh mead from Rowena before she continued tidying. "I heard you gave a fine speech, honouring the men over the gods and all that."

I narrowed my eyes.

"What did you hear?" I asked, my voice low.

"You're fine for now, Jarl, no one is suspicious of you." Jan said. "*Do not give the gods all of the glory.* If the townspeople were not so elated, some might say you were speaking against the gods. Not something a jarl should do in any case."

"Are you *scolding* me, Jan Jötunnson?"

"Never, Jarl. I'm merely advising you." Jan said, raising his thick tawny brows at me. "As I said, the townspeople are delighted to be home with their families, so they have taken your comment in stride – in fact, they were thrilled you honoured them as highly as the gods. But I know you, Aveline. You must watch what you say."

"*Þakka fyrir*, Jan. I will heed your advice," I said levelly, though anger bubbled in my stomach. "But understand, my relationship with the gods is between them and me, no one else."

"I do understand," Jan said. "But you cannot have the townspeople know you're angry with the gods."

"I can be angry with whomever I want – the gods, the townspeople, *you*." I grumbled. "When I defeated those who challenged me after we came back from Gipeswic, I honoured the gods for my victory, didn't I? I slaughtered goats to the gods before setting sail to the Wendish lands, did I not? I celebrated Baldr at *Midsumarblót*, correct? You were by my side when I began organising *Vetrnætr* before we even left for this expedition. Did I not host *Sigrblót* when we returned from the East Angles, even though I was mourning my husband and father-in-law? Damn it, Jan! Didn't I do all these things?"

I slammed my fists on the table, sending the combs clattering away. I caught Rowena's nervous glance in the corner of my eye and felt Melisende pause, a lock of my hair still held in her fingers, the weight of the antler comb tangled in the strands. Jan gave no reaction, he simply gazed at me over his tankard, unblinking and expressionless.

"I have honoured the gods far more than they deserve!" I hissed. "I have continued honouring them for the sake of the townspeople, so do not come into my hall and reprimand me for asking my people to share in the triumph of *their* actions rather than give all of their hard-earned glory to the damned gods!"

ASHES REMAIN

My nails dug hard in my trembling hands, splinters of pain slicing through my palms, but I did not uncurl my fists and I did not break my fiery glare from Jan's cool sapphire gaze.

"*Já*, you have, Jarl." Jan agreed. "You have proved yourself to be a respectable, praiseworthy jarl, your people support you, they are yours. *But* – and I say this as your friend – the townspeople will love their female Anglo-Saxon jarl for only as long as you continue leading them to victory. That does not mean you are safe from being challenged again. You do not have Vidar here to protect you anymore, so be sure to watch what you say."

Before I could say another word, Einar and Æsa burst into the hall and threw themselves at Jan.

"Jan! Come outside with us!" Einar demanded.

Jan wrapped his arm around Einar, though his eyes didn't drop from mine. Æsa grabbed his arm and dramatically attempted to drag Jan out of his chair, much to Einar's amusement. I didn't laugh. I didn't smile.

"Off with you, Jan Jötunnson." I muttered.

"*Já*, Jarl," Jan muttered, allowing my children to lead him out of the hall.

CHAPTER THREE

THE FEAST WAS in full swing by evening time, my hall bursting with townspeople yet again. The delectable scent of sizzling pork and rich goat stews filled the air, made from the animals we had sacrificed to the gods at the beginning of the celebration. Trestle tables were covered with platters of roasted duck, goose and chicken, roasted vegetables and wild salad greens, a variety of fish that was dried, salted, pickled and smoked and plates piled high with bread and cheese.

Mead, ale and beer flowed from casks into cups, tankards and horns and were quickly guzzled down. Children ran about the hall together, pausing only to grab fistfuls of dried fruits or gulp down cold water or tangy buttermilk.

My crew had rested and washed during the day like I had, and the overwhelming stench of body odour and filth was replaced with the delightfully clean aroma of lye soap and oils made from flowers and herbs. I drifted about the hall with a horn of sweet honey mead in my hand, watching and listening, satisfied by the pleasure of my people.

Beside the fire a group were doubled up and howling with laughter in response to a particularly vulgar verse in a *flyting* – an exchange of insults, a popular drinking game. I chuckled at their happiness and spotted my friends, Guðrin and Borghildr, beyond the way. They laughed behind their cups, their cheeks rosy.

In quite the fantastic imitation, Borghildr's daughter Borgunna and my beloved Æsa were sitting beside Borghildr and Guðrin, cups clutched in their little hands, giggling together. Borgunna's black hair trailed down her back in plaits like her mother's, and Æsa's hair was plaited and pinned to her head like Guðrin's, for I could see no hair peeking out from beneath the kerchief pinned to Guðrin's head. Both Borghildr and Guðrin wore a white *hustrulinet* over their hair, the sign of a married woman.

ASHES REMAIN

I coiled a lock of my loose chestnut curls around my finger. Melisende had plaited the hair framing my face and pinned it back, leaving the rest freely flowing down my back. Unmarried maidens wore their hair loose and visible while married women tucked theirs away beneath kerchiefs. Despite my widowed status, I had continued to wear my *hustrulinet* until just recently.

During the past raid, my *hustrulinet* had been ripped from my head by a terrified monk who had tried to fight me as he fled from the monastery we were raiding. I won the fight and killed him, but not before he yanked the white fabric from my head. He had jerked the pins and they had scratched long deep cuts through my scalp. As my wounds healed, my *hustrulinet* had irritated them something fierce.

"Well, Aveline, don't take this the wrong way, but you aren't married anymore." Jan had said delicately a few days after the incident.

We had just slaughtered a farm and were loading the few spoils we'd seized onto Storm-Serpent. My scabs had been reopened by my *hustrulinet* pins during the brief battle. Rivulets of blood slipped down my face and the sweat of my scalp seeped into the wounds, stinging me painfully. Jan had helped clean my head up, dabbing my wounds with a wet rag.

"I know ..." I had mumbled.

Though I loathed to admit it, Jan was right, I didn't *need* the *hustrulinet* for I truly wasn't a married woman anymore, I was a widow. Despite that, I wanted to continue wearing the fabric over my hair just as I continued to wear my wedding band.

It had been weeks since then. The cuts had healed but my *hustrulinet* remained folded neatly in a chest near my bed. Was it a sign I was moving forward with my life or had I just become accustomed to being without it?

"Aveline!" Guðrin beamed, snapping me out of my thoughts.

I grinned back at her and slipped through the crowd to sit with them. Borghildr held her cup to me, showing me the gorgeous dark red wine swirling inside.

"I've never tasted a wine so delicious!" Borghildr exclaimed. "What is it – Arabic, Frankish?"

"Consecrated?" I shrugged as I accepted the cup. "I did not think to ask the monks where they got their wine before we killed them."

"Next time you should." Borghildr winked. "Such bold, sweet flavour! It's wonderful."

I sipped at the wine, immediately filled with a delightful warmth. The flavour was a rich, delectable mixture of sweet and tart with a fresh, sharp aftertaste. I had expected a dry grape wine from the deep red colour, but it was in fact a wild berry wine.

I had been fortunate enough to have tasted many wines throughout my lifetime – being the wife of a jarl and now a jarl in my own right, I had and could afford the luxuries of importing wine for my table. I didn't always purchase wine, however. During expeditions, we seized casks of wine from every monastery we raided, some to sell for a lofty price while the rest I shared generously with my townspeople during feasts.

"You're right, Borghildr, it's lovely." I said, smacking my lips in appreciation as I handed her back her cup.

"Monks usually make all the alcohol themselves in their monasteries," Domnall explained as he strode to the table, Hallmundr with him. "Wine, beer, ale, the lot. Monasteries have vast tracks of land to grow barley and grapes and all that. They keep wine for their masses and sell beer to pay for tithes and monastery upkeep."

Guðrin, Borghildr and I gawped at Domnall, our jaws hanging open, brows raised and eyes wide. Hallmundr snickered at our identical expressions as he sat across the table from us.

"I'm impressed." I remarked.

"What? I've been raiding for a long time, of course I've picked up some knowledge along the way." Domnall shrugged as he sat down opposite Guðrin, his wife.

"Is there space for me to join you, my love?" Ebbe interrupted, appearing behind Borghildr and squeezing her shoulders.

"As long as you've been behaving." Borghildr replied, kissing one of his fingers with wine-dampened lips.

"Of course, I have!" Ebbe exclaimed.

"You're drunk." Borghildr remarked, examining her husband through narrowed eyes.

ASHES REMAIN

Ebbe slipped his arms around her and brought her against him. "I have drank, but I am not yet drunk."

"That's a joke if ever I've heard one." Hallmundr scoffed.

"And how has your evening been, darling?" Guðrin asked Domnall. "Win any games?"

"Every game I entered," Domnall replied proudly. "Of course, I was matched with Ebbe for more than a few, which is why he's so addled by drink."

"You must stop before you make a fool of yourself." Borghildr scolded.

She tried to maintain her stern expression, but she could not hold back her giggles as Ebbe clumsily nuzzled her neck, his hands brazenly exploring her body as he did so.

"Then you should take me home," Ebbe suggested between kisses. "Guðrin will take care of the children – won't you, Guð? And *you*, my beloved, should take me straight home to bed!"

"You think I'll let you enjoy me when you're in such a state?" Borghildr scoffed.

"If you won't, there was a blonde I noticed earlier who might – she was lovely! Very well endowed." Ebbe grinned, winking at Domnall and Hallmundr. "She was tall, too, and dressed in a yellow gown, which was so tight over her bosom, I thought her brooches might pop off–"

"If you continue to speak about this woman – or *any* woman like her – I'll take you home and cuts your balls off." Borghildr snarled, her smile swiftly twisting into a scowl.

"Oh, come now Hild, that was a jest – you know it's *you* I want to enjoy!" Ebbe persisted, attempting to nuzzle her neck again.

"Get up, you're going home before I rip your slimy tongue out." Borghildr snapped, standing up and towering over her much shorter husband.

"You better do as she says, Ebbe," Hallmundr warned. "I've no doubt she'll slit you from neck to prick if you don't."

"I swear to all the gods I will." Borghildr vowed darkly.

Ebbe laughed, but stood up at once, swaying on his feet. He snaked his arm around his wife's waist and snuggled close to her. Borghildr allowed him to cling to her, though her broad shoulders tightened visibly, and disgust deepened on her face.

"*Góða nótt* to you all." She said stiffly.

Borghildr dragged her husband unceremoniously through the crowd, barking at their four children to follow as she spotted them. The children rushed to her and followed in her shadow as they left my hall, whispering between each other and giggling at the state of their father. Ebbe was too drunk to realise the world of trouble he was in with his wife.

"She'll kill him in his sleep one day." Hallmundr commented, watching them disappear.

"She wouldn't wait until he's sleeping," Guðrin said. "Borghildr is an honest woman, she'd make sure Ebbe sees it coming."

"Borghildr isn't afraid of a fight." Domnall agreed. "She knows she could beat him, she just chooses not to."

"Could you imagine that fight?" Hallmundr laughed. "It'd be over in a heartbeat! I don't know why Ebbe infuriates her so, even I would fear fighting that woman!"

"Do you remember when she caught him in *their* bed with that Swedish woman?" Guðrin said.

"The idiot invited her to join them when she found them." Domnall said, shaking his head.

"What about when he took her to market to help him pick out a concubine?" Hallmundr pointed out.

As Hallmundr, Domnall and Guðrin reminisced on the many times Ebbe had enraged his wife, I spotted Jan across the hall. He was chatting with a tall blonde, remarkably similar to the woman Ebbe had described, right down to the yellow gown and 'well-endowed bosom'.

Even from this distance, I could see a light blush on Jan's alabaster cheeks. The woman moved her sleek golden tresses over one of her shoulders and ran her fingers through it, subtly attempting to draw his attention to her cleavage, no doubt.

Despite how angry Jan had made me earlier, I was pleased to see him enjoying the woman's company. I hadn't seen him blush or flirt with a woman in a long time, and the gods knew Jan had quite a following of admirers.

"They're getting along well, aren't they?" Guðrin murmured.

"They seem to be, *já*." I replied, watching the two laugh together.

"It's about time Jan found a woman." Guðrin commented.

ASHES REMAIN

"It's about time Jan found *happiness*."

"Do you think it will last?"

I shook my head.

"I don't know if it will get further than this hall." I said.

"For his sake, I hope it does." Guðrin said, and I nodded in agreement. "What about you – have any men caught your eye? Perhaps while you were raiding?"

"*Nei*, Guðrin." I replied firmly.

"In time, my friend." Guðrin said, resting her head on my shoulder.

I dropped my gaze from Jan and his busty woman to the silver rings on my wedding finger. Romance hadn't crossed my mind since Vidar's death, other than my adamant decision not to pursue it again. Guðrin was a dear friend, she and Borghildr wanted what was best for me, but remarrying was not an option.

A woman must have a husband to protect her.

Had I not proven I could fend for myself? Not just in the last expedition, but when I returned to Aros and Roskilde as well. After announcing the deaths of Vidar and Alvar and my taking of their jarldoms, I'd been challenged by several men in each town, and a handful more over the six months since. I had defeated each of the contenders in one-on-one combat. I could protect myself.

A woman could not be a jarl.

Yet I was – the people of Roskilde *and* Aros had supported my decision to take up my husband's mantle. I may have been challenged so many times, but after proving I could hold the position, the townspeople rallied behind me and supported me.

A woman could not speak in court.

I had already successfully settled numerous disputes between my townspeople, and they abided by my rulings. When the time came for me to go to the annual þing, I *would* speak, I *would* be heard.

I had three sons, the heirs to my jarldoms. I had no use for romance, no need nor want for it. The only romance I longed for was that between Vidar and I, but I could never get that back.

"It's awfully hot." I commented, fanning myself with my hand. "I think I'll go outside for a moment."

"Would you like me to come with you?" Guðrin offered.

"*Nei*, but *þakka* my dear." I shook my head. "I'll be back."

Before I got to my feet, the music that had filled the hall came to an abrupt stop. The crowd parted to allow through a horde of men, who stopped before the two highbacked wooden chairs on the platform in the middle of the hall. There were perhaps twenty men, but I couldn't be sure from where I was sitting.

I rolled my eyes. Was this another challenger?

The leader, a tall, muscled man, fair skinned with long dirty blond hair and a cleanly trimmed beard, paused in front of the platform, seemingly admiring the two ornately carved chairs. He climbed onto the platform, running one hand over the chair that used to be Vidar's. My hands curled into fists as I watched him. Thankfully, rather than sit on Vidar's chair, the stranger stood between the two, one hand rested on the top of each, examining the crowd.

"My name is Jarl Borgulf Sveinsson of Lund. I have come to Aros in search of Aveline Birgersdóttir." The stranger announced.

"And you have found her," I called out, rising to my feet.

In silence I approached Jarl Borgulf. Beneath his crooked nose, his thin pink lips twisted into a smile. He didn't seem very old, maybe the same age as Jan, perhaps a little younger. I climbed onto the platform and the jarl took a step back, our eyes locked.

"What do you want, Jarl Borgulf?" I asked, sitting in my highbacked chair.

Jarl Borgulf stepped down from the platform and stood before me, far closer than I was comfortable. I wanted to move, but I didn't – I stayed still, glaring at him defiantly, almost daring him to come closer.

"News of Alvar the First One and Vidar Alvarsson's deaths have travelled far. I knew them both – we were kin for a time. Vidar Alvarsson was married to my sister for ten years." Jarl Borgulf said.

My heart dropped into my stomach. Of all the people to come to my hall, I hadn't expected the brother of Vidar's first wife. I caught Jan in the corner of my eye, shoving through the crowd. He paused at the edge, watching Borgulf carefully.

"Vidar was a brother to me for a long time." Jarl Borgulf paused and chuckled. "Do not look at me like that, Aveline, you have no need to fear, there were no hard feelings between Vidar's family and mine when he and my sister divorced."

ASHES REMAIN

I furrowed my brow and pursed my lips, not realising my shock was so visible on my face.

"My sister wanted to divorce him just as much as he did her. Theirs was an unhappy union, but thankfully she married well afterwards." Borgulf assured. "She was much happier with her second husband than she was with her first. Word has it that Vidar had the same luck, he was incredibly happy in his marriage to you."

"*Þakka fyrir*, Jarl Borgulf." I said slowly.

I did not care for his blatant flattery, but due to his peaceful introduction, it would be wrong of me to turn him away. I swallowed hard. I would be judged harshly for my inhospitality to someone who had shown no immediate threat to me.

"If you are a friend of my late husbands, then you and your men are welcome at my table."

***

AS THE EVENING passed, Jarl Borgulf's men gradually scattered around my hall, mingling with my townspeople, enjoying mead, food and music, and partook in the games. I kept a mental note of their whereabouts at all times. Jarl Borgulf strutted around my hall, impressing the men with his skill at games, boasting and wrestling, bone-throwing and dice. He charmed the women with his beautiful eyes and amorous comments, and he entertained all with his lewd poetry. I sat in my highbacked chair, a cup of wine in my hand, watching.

Vidar hadn't told me much about his first wife – and even less about her family. I knew she was from Lund, and they'd married when he was sixteen and she thirteen. They learned quickly into their marriage that they could not conceive a child and she immediately lost interest in sharing his bed.

Jarl Borgulf was correct, Vidar and his first wife had been unhappily married for a decade before they divorced, and that was that. I didn't know her name, who her father was, nothing. She was just a woman from Lund.

"It was inconsequential, a childless marriage that ended over a decade ago. Why would anyone say anything about it?" Vidar had pointed out.

"Then why are you telling me about it now?" I had asked him.

"Because you are to be my wife soon. I want no secrets between us, Aveline, and no omissions, only the truth – no matter how dreadful ..."

I slipped Vidar's ring out from beneath my dress and stroked the smooth silver. She wasn't important to Vidar and he wouldn't keep secrets from me. He hadn't told me about Borgulf because he probably thought he wouldn't see him again, and why would he? Why would I meet Borgulf? Why would I meet Vidar's former wife? She lived in Lund, a sea away, why would I ever find myself there? Why would it matter?

It matters because there are things about Vidar I will never know – things I will never be able to ask him, things I will only hear from the tongues of others, never from him.

I took a deep draught of my wine and tucked Vidar's ring back beneath my dress.

"Aveline, care to play a game of Hnefatafl?" Jarl Borgulf asked, appearing before me.

Borgulf held out his hand, presenting the Hnefatafl board set up on the table nearest me. I had been so lost in thought, I hadn't noticed him assembling the game. A few people, a mixture of his men and mine, stared at us eagerly, the stranger had challenged the jarl. I examined the thirty-seven game pieces, thirty-six warriors and one king. Twelve of the exquisitely carved warrior figures and the king were made of dark walnut wood, the rest were carved from whale bone.

"I haven't played Hnefatafl since Vidar died." I murmured. "This was his and my game."

"I didn't realise you had such an emotional attachment to the game." Borgulf said. "If you'd like, we don't–"

"*Nei*," I tossed the rest of my wine down my throat before stepping down from the platform. "It's only a game."

I wanted to be sentimental. I wanted to throw the board across the room and strike Borgulf for daring to ask me to play the game that was Vidar and mine. I hadn't even looked at the game since Vidar had died ...

No matter my feelings, I could not deny Borgulf a match – I would practically be yielding to him. Though he hadn't caused any trouble in the hours he'd been in my hall, I still questioned his motives for being here.

"Would you like to be the defender or attacker?" Borgulf asked.

"I will defend." I replied, sitting across from him.

Hnefatafl was a strategy game played on a square-shaped board. Mine was made of walnut wood with a grid of eleven squares by eleven inlaid with whale bone. There were five refuge squares on the board, one in each corner and one in the centre, distinguishable by the ivory patterns inlaid into the squares.

My ivory king and warriors occupied the centre of the board, my king in the middle with the twelve warriors arranged in rows around him in a diamond formation, protecting him on all sides. The attackers were placed symmetrically on the edges of the board, six on each of the four sides.

The objective of the attackers was to seize my king by surrounding him on four sides. As defender, I had to get my king to one of the four corner refuge squares. If a warrior piece became trapped between two of the opposing warriors, they would be removed from the board, seized by the enemy.

Each piece could move vertically or horizontally, but none could move diagonally, not even the king. The warrior pieces could move one or more squares until they were stopped by another piece or the edge of the board. Only the king could return to the central refuge square, the warriors were not allowed to occupy any refuge squares, but they could cross the central refuge square if the opposite side of it was empty.

"Please begin, Jarl Borgulf."

Jarl Borgulf smiled, studied the board for a moment then moved one of his warriors to the square next to a corner.

Of course, he guards the corners first ... I thought, rolling my lips together.

By barring the corners each with a diagonal line of three warriors, the corners would be impregnable. Borgulf would have to act fast, however – if I gained control of just one corner, his strategy would crumble.

Another strategy Borgulf could use as the attacker was to restrict my king's movement while approaching him with assassins or herd my king into an ambush. Forming a tight blockade around my pieces would be a good bet – making an unbreakable ring around my pieces would force a draw or hold off the attack for as long as possible in the hopes that I'd make a mistake. He could close in on my pieces, giving me just enough room to move one or two squares and thus place myself into a precarious position. As he closed in, he would force me to move and expose my warriors to capture, reducing my forces and leaving my king unprotected, or isolate him from defending forces – then all Borgulf would have to do is capture my king.

I took one of my warriors and moved him a few squares over to a different corner. I needed to have my warriors break through the gaps and passed the blockade. If I could keep the gaps open, I would have a spot to get my king to the corners. By getting my warriors past the blockade, Borgulf's warriors would be vulnerable to capture from behind.

Borgulf moved another piece.

We took our time silently and carefully studying the board, surrounded by the crowd of warriors, both Borgulf's men and my own. Einar had fallen asleep hours ago, but Young Birger, Sander and Æsa sat beside me, watching with wide-eyed interest. Occasionally Borgulf sighed or groaned dramatically for the crowd's amusement before moving his ivory warrior.

I stole glances of Borgulf on his turns, his forest green eyes were flecked with gold, like leaves dappled by the sun, and when he was concentrating, he would stroke his fine blond beard. There was a long skinny white scar, almost indistinguishable from his pale flesh, which ran down the length of his face on the right side, hidden beneath locks of his long blond hair.

"I must say, I've never played with a woman so skilled before." Borgulf said. "Vidar and you must've played together frequently?"

"We did." I murmured, watching him trap one of my warriors.

Borgulf removed my warrior from the board and placed the little carved figure to the side, watching me as he did so. I smirked. It didn't matter that he'd taken one of my warriors – capturing warriors was not a necessity to win the game. All I had to do was forge an avenue through his blockade and I would win.

"I played with Vidar at his wedding to my sister, and a fair few times afterwards as well. I was just a boy when he married her though. He wouldn't let me win, but he took it easy on me, recommending tactics and tutoring me as we played. As I grew older, he wasn't as lenient." Borgulf paused for a moment, stroking his beard and staring off briefly. "I don't recall ever winning against him."

"Did he try and distract you, too, or is that just a tactic you've picked up over the years?" I mocked, moving my warrior.

"I wouldn't do that!" Borgulf gasped, but he couldn't hold his façade for too long before he burst out laughing. "Where's your thrall? I need another drink."

Borgulf captured another of my warriors. After removing it from the board, he waved down Rowena, shaking his empty horn at her.

"Tell me about yourself, Jarl Borgulf. You came here to offer your condolences, which I appreciate, but you are still a stranger to me. I would like to know the man who once was family to my husband." I said, moving another warrior.

"And I would like to know you, too." Borgulf winked. "Ask and I shall answer, I will keep no secrets from you."

"You came to my hall with quite a following of men. I didn't realise it took so many to bring condolences to a widow."

"Ah-ha! You're not subtle with your suspicions, are you?" Jarl Borgulf chuckled. "I have my following to protect me on our journey – I never leave Lund in a party of less than twenty men. I am a jarl after all." Borgulf said matter-of-factly. "Now it is my turn to ask you a question."

I nodded. Borgulf moved his warrior.

"Who sits in your late husband's great empty throne now that he is dead? Have you remarried – perhaps you're betrothed?"

"I don't think my marital status is any of your concern, Jarl Borgulf." I replied stiffly.

"But it is, Aveline." He said. "Vidar was Jarl of Aros *and* Roskilde – no matter how briefly. Who is it that rules in his place now he's dead? Vidar's brother died when he was a boy, and his uncle and only male cousin died fighting with the Great Army twenty years ago. Vidar's sons are the only males of Alvar the First One's bloodline left, and they're too young to rule – they're not even of marrying age. So, who rules in Vidar's stead?"

"I do." I said simply.

"You? A woman?" Borgulf scoffed.

"*Já*, a woman." I smiled humourlessly, moving my warrior.

"That cannot be – a woman can't be jarl." Borgulf said, accepting a full horn of mead from Rowena.

"And yet it is, for I *am* the jarl." I said sternly. "The people of Aros and Roskilde swore fealty to me. In fact, this very feast is to celebrate our successful raid in the Wendish lands, a raid which *I* commanded. This woman jarl led her warriors to victory and filled their arms with gold, without losing even a single man."

"You lead them in battle? You fight beside them?" Borgulf gawped.

"*Já* – I lead them in battle, I fight beside them. Rules or no rules, Jarl Borgulf, I am jarl. I lead my warriors to glory, I kill our foes alongside them, and I rule – just as well as a man."

Rousing cheers of agreement rumbled around us. Borgulf glanced around at the men surrounding us – the men glowering at him. Rather than being intimidated, however, another stream of silky laughter poured from his lips.

"So, the rumours were true!" Borgulf said, moving his warrior. "I am impressed, *Jarl* Aveline. You are quite the woman – I see why my former brother-in-law was so taken with you. Beauty and bravery, eh?"

"*Þakka fyrir*, Jarl Borgulf." I replied flatly, trapping one of his warriors between two of mine.

Borgulf marvelled at me as I took his warrior off the board. It was the first warrior I had taken of his during the entire game, whereas he had a small pile of mine discarded beside the board. I held his warrior firmly in my palm.

"I am surprised but impressed. You must be *something* for two great towns to allow you to rule in a man's place." Borgulf continued, leaning forward over the gameboard. He moved one of his warriors, trapped yet another of mine and took it off the board. "I heard you defeated twelve challengers, too?"

"I commend the person you heard these rumours from, they are remarkably accurate." I said dryly.

"*Þakka fyrir*, I will tell them of your compliment." Jarl Borgulf winked. "However, no matter how incredible you are, I must ask why you feel entitled to hold this position?"

ASHES REMAIN

"*Excuse me?*"

Borgulf's gall and audacity infuriated me.

"Regardless of your peoples' support, being jarl is no position for a woman. A man would be far better suited for the position." Jarl Borgulf said, seeming not to realise his own impertinence. "You were lucky in the Wendish lands it seems, but a woman is no match in battle for a man, no match in strategy.

"In fact, as a woman jarl, you are turning both Aros and Roskilde into targets – everyone knows that women are the weaker sex. Defeating twelve men is a commendable feat, but one successful raid against some monasteries and a few poor villages does not mean you are strong.

"A town ruled by a woman suggests that it would be easy to conquer, it creates the assumption that the town has no men capable to rule it. Not everyone will hear rumours of your successes, Aveline, but *everyone* will hear these towns are ruled by a woman. You are inviting danger to your door. Do you understand?"

"I hear what you're saying," I scowled at him over the gameboard. "What do you suggest then, Borgulf?"

"I suggest you marry a man worthy of ruling in your husband's stead." Borgulf said, meeting my gaze.

I let out a short, bitter laugh, cocking and eyebrow up at him.

"Oh *ja*? And who would that be?"

"Me, of course." He said, leaning back in his chair with his arms crossed behind his head. "I've ruled Lund for a decade, I've defeated every enemy who has dared attempt to attack it. I have a fleet of forty ships and a vast army. I would be a perfect candidate to rule Aros and Roskilde, by your side."

"My husband has been dead for just half a year. You expect me to marry again so soon?" I demanded.

"Why not? Most women do."

"I have no interest in marrying again, let alone marrying *you*." I snarled. "The people of Aros and Roskilde trust in me to rule them, otherwise they wouldn't have bidden me their fealty. You insult not just me, but them as well–"

"That was not my intention," Borgulf said, enraging me further by speaking over me. "I merely wanted to tell you what impression a woman jarl makes."

"So, you suggest marrying me and taking my land, my people, my towns and settlements as a solution?"

"I suggest creating an allegiance between your towns and mine." Borgulf said. "Lund, Aros and Roskilde united through marriage! Vidar thought an alliance between Roskilde and Lund was a grand arrangement, which is why he married my sister."

I bit my lip so hard I could taste the copper of my blood. How dare Borgulf make such a callous statement! Did he really think a remark like that would sway me into accepting his proposal?

"By merging our lands and wealth we could become king and queen! Is that not enticing to you?" Borgulf pressed.

"*Nei*, not when the king is too concerned with meeting his own ends rather than paying attention to what is happening right beneath his nose." I glanced down at the gameboard.

While Borgulf was talking, I moved my king to one of the corners right in front of him. Borgulf looked down, his eyes widened. He scanned the board, making sense of where I had slipped passed him. He had been so concerned with taking my warriors that he hadn't noticed the gap in his blockade.

"What were you saying earlier, Jarl Borgulf? *A woman is no match in battle for a man, no match in strategy*. You are correct, I am not your equal, I am better. I have proven I can best you at strategy, do you need me to prove I can best you in battle as well?"

"*Nei*, Jarl Aveline." Borgulf smiled. "I would prefer to have you as my ally, not my enemy. I am disappointed in your answer to my proposal – you would be a remarkable wife."

"As *romantic* as your proposal was," I said sarcastically. "I stand by my decision. I would approve of an alliance of good faith between my towns and yours – *not* one involving marriage. Perhaps another time we could discuss this possibility?"

"I look forward to that day." Borgulf grinned. He drained the wine in his horn and stood up from the table. "Anyway, I think it's time my men and I leave you and your people to your celebrations. Until the next time we meet, Jarl Aveline."

"*Þakka fyrir*, Jarl Borgulf."

ASHES REMAIN

I stood up and the townspeople of Aros parted to allow Borgulf and his men passage to the doors of my hall. The music stopped the moment Borgulf and I rose from our chairs, and not a soul spoke. All eyes watched me glare at Borgulf. Those surrounding us as we played had certainly heard Borgulf's insults and his proposal. They had also heard my answer.

Perhaps Borgulf didn't notice the tense atmosphere or maybe his just ignored it as he happily called his goodbyes over the sea of heads between us. He waved at me with one hand, grinning jovially, and pulled the door open with his other.

"Oh, I almost forgot." Borgulf said, pausing in the doorway. "Aveline Birgersdóttir, you have been summoned to the þing. Word of your appointment as Jarl of Aros and Roskilde has reached all corners of the Danish lands, displeasing many by your blatant disregard of the law. Nine jarls will assemble at the þing place in Odense three weeks from today. You *will* attend and stand trial for your lawbreaking, otherwise Aros and Roskilde will face the consequences."

CHAPTER FOUR

JARL BORGULF AND his men's laughter was audible albeit muffled from behind the great wooden doors. As their voices disappeared, anxious discussion rang through the hall, my alarmed townspeople echoing my own trepidation ... I had been summoned. This did not bode well.

I knew the position of jarl was only for men, there had never been a female jarl. A woman could be a queen by marrying a king, a woman could be a jarlkona by marrying a jarl, but a woman herself could not rule in her own right like a man. From the moment I decided to take on my late husband and late father-in-law's jarldoms, I knew I would receive criticism, but to be summoned before the þing ...

Had my sons been older when Vidar died, I would've given the jarldoms to them without a second thought, but at their young ages, with hardly any experience at leading warriors, strategising battles, handling village affairs such as finances, judicial functions, overseeing supply inventory and harvest reports, I couldn't give them the jarldoms. They would be challenged by others immediately and lose everything. It was safer for them if I became jarl and ruled until they were older and wiser, regardless of the spectacle it caused. I certainly wasn't going to remarry and give my sons' jarldoms away to my new husband.

I wondered how many other jarls of Denmark took issue with me. There were far more than just nine, not including me, that ruled in the Danish lands. Were these nine that were due to judge me the only ones able to meet on such short notice or were they the only ones offended by a woman jarl? The þing was not usually hosted this time of the year, indicating the former ...

There had been many of my own men who had questioned my ruling. I had been challenged many times since returning from Gipeswic, but I had earned my place and earned the respect and support of my people. Woman or not, they knew I could rule as well as any man. I did not know which jarls would judge me, but I would prove to them my worth, just as I had proven it to my townspeople.

"I do not fear Jarl Borgulf nor his threats, and I certainly do not fear judgement at the þing." I declared loudly over the hum of conversation. "Have I not proven to you all that I am capable? Have I not proven to you all that I am worthy of this position?"

My people cheered, my heart lifted. I glanced over each encouraging face, my smile growing from the determination and loyalty shining in my people's eyes.

"I will meet these nine jarls and I invite you all to attend the þing with me, to stand by me! Together we will prove to them that I deserve this position – and that no stranger can enter my hall and insult me as Jarl Borgulf did today!"

My people cheered louder this time.

"I support you, Jarl Aveline." Hallmundr proclaimed, appearing beside me with a horn of wine in each hand. "I would be honoured to support you at the þing – and to wipe that cloying smile off Borgulf Sveinsson's face!"

"And I would be honoured to have you at my side." I gratefully accepted the drink and raised it into the air. "I would be honoured to have every one of you at my side! *Skål!*"

The sound of merriment returned to my hall and gradually all continued their games and drinking. I sifted through the crowd, pausing continually to smile and chatter with my townspeople, happily accepting the abundance of support they offered me.

"We support you, Jarl!" The young, mousy-haired warrior Biólan Koðránsson called.

Biólan was grossly inebriated, wavering on his feet. He would have fallen where he stood had it not been for Gísla, the pretty young lady he was clinging to. She giggled at him, her cheeks and eyes just as rosy and bloodshot as his.

Young Birger and his friend Yngvi, Domnall and Guðrin's copper-haired son, were sitting at the table behind Biólan, clumsy smiles stretched across their red faces. Sibba, another fair maiden sat across from them, she was identical to Gísla, but for the sprinkle of freckles on her fair cheeks.

GWENDOLINE SK TERRY

A silvery-haired boy named Galinn Johansson, perhaps fifteen years of age, had a stern look upon his pointed face and an arm wrapped the Sibba's shoulders. Yngvi was the same age as Young Birger, older by just a few months. Biólan was fourteen and the twin girls were about the same age as him.

Gísla clung to Biólan tittering like a bird and slurring kindly words of support – or at least that's what I assumed, for I couldn't understand most of what she said due to her drunkenness.

"*Þakka fyrir*, both of you." I smiled warmly. "I think it's time Young Birger and Yngvi helped you back to your home, Biólan. And Galinn, will you accompany Sibba and Gísla back to their home on the way to yours?"

"Of course, Jarl." Sibba beamed. "We enjoyed the feast! *Góða nótt!*"

"*Þakka fyrir*, dear. *Góða nótt* to you, too." I beamed.

Sibba slipped out from the table and wrapped her arms around her sister's waist, the two girls giggling together. Biólan's heart noticeably sank as he helplessly watched Gísla stagger away with her sister.

Galinn didn't say a word, he just grunted as he slipped out from the table. He was tall and skinny, already a head taller than me though he was more than a decade younger. His pointed chin was covered in a fuzz of pale hairs, hardly noticeable against his ghostly skin. Unlike the rest of his fair features, Galinn's eyes were black as coals and narrowed beneath his thick, knitted white brows.

"I look forward to your wedding next year, Galinn." I said as he skulked passed me. "Sibba is quite a sweet young woman, I'm sure she will be a dedicated wife."

"*Já*," Galinn grumbled. "*Góða nótt.*"

I scowled at the moody young warrior as he reluctantly followed his betrothed and his future sister-in-law out of the hall. I turned to Young Birger and Yngvi, who were arranging themselves on either side of the sorrowful Biólan.

"Bucket of laughter that Galinn, isn't he?" I remarked.

"Never mind him, *móðir.*" Young Birger smiled.

"He always has a gripe with somebody." Yngvi said, hoisting Biólan's arm over his shoulders for the third time – Biólan seemed to have lost control of his limbs in his ridiculous state.

ASHES REMAIN

"I'm glad to see you both haven't lost your minds on drink like our dear friend here." I said, accompanying them to the door. "*A man knows less as he drinks more and loses more and more of his wisdom.*"

"That he does." Young Birger said.

"I'm sad because Gísla is gone!" Biólan announced.

"Calm down, man, she's only gone back to her house." Yngvi laughed. "You'll see her again."

"The next time I see her, I'll ask her father for her hand in marriage!" Biólan decided. "I can't believe she let me hold her the whole night! To be deserving of Gísla's affection – the gods surely smile on me! Now I have coin and honour to my name, her parents cannot deny my proposal. And it's thanks to you, Jarl Aveline, for leading the raid that gave me my wealth! I'll have the woman of my dreams as my wife! Thank Frigg, Freyja and Odin!"

"*Góða nótt*, Biólan." I smiled, chuckling behind my horn.

Young Birger and Yngvi bid me goodnight and struggled to carry their drunken friend. Biólan stumbled a few times, but Young Birger and Yngvi prevented him from falling down completely before they managed to haul him outside.

I leaned against the doorframe, holding the oak door open with one hand, and watched the three stagger away, the cool breeze drifting about the bottom of my skirts. Biólan began a jarring romantic ballad about Gísla, which was thankfully cut short by a swift slap on his back by Yngvi, who scolded Biólan for being unmanly enough to sing a love song in public.

"Anything he bloody sings is bad, let alone what he's singing about." Young Birger laughed.

"I can't help it, I love her!" Biólan exclaimed.

"You say one more unmanly thing and I'll drop you." Yngvi grumbled. "I'll not be seen carrying a drunken wimp around."

I giggled, not doubting Yngvi for a second. As sweet as Biólan's song was, he would have to perform it in private, lest he be labelled *ergi*. Biólan thankfully did not continue his screechy, heartfelt ballad, luckily for everyone within earshot of him. The three young men disappeared into the night without another threat from Yngvi nor another melody from Biólan.

A few clusters of people dwindled outside the hall chatting quietly in the moonlight, cups and tankards clasped in their hands.

Many guests had returned to their homes, of those that remained, some were fast asleep where they had been sitting while others continued to enjoy the feast. They laughed and played games or sat together drinking and eating. Lars was singing, and Einarr the musician plucked a soothing melody on his lyre, accompanied by the steady, slow beat of drums and the drifting harmonies that poured from two or three bone flutes.

Tables were cluttered with empty tankards and plates with discarded meat bones and cold bits of food. Clean up tomorrow would be atrocious, but the hall had to be readied for another day of feasting – there were to be three nights of celebration in total.

I watched Melisende and Rowena whisk around the room serving drinks and tidying up. Many guests had brought their own thralls to serve them, and they too ran about my hall, sweat pouring from their brows, dark smudges beneath their sleepy, bloodshot eyes.

Perhaps I should buy another thrall? I wondered, imagining how much work Melisende and Rowena had cut out for them tomorrow. If I was to buy a thrall, I'd have to purchase them from Herra Kaupmaðr ... I sighed and sipped my wine. That would be a consideration for another day.

Herra Kaupmaðr was a famous merchant who visited Aros a few times a year. He was known for acquiring and selling the best quality items, from fabrics to glassware and jewels, strong, hardworking thralls from all across the world and much more. All merchants paled in comparison to him. Indeed, his byname, Herra Kaupmaðr, meant 'Lord Merchant' in the Norse tongue, and he truly was a lord among merchants. No one knew what his real name was, the eccentric nomadic little Swede kept that a secret.

Vidar and I purchased our Frankish thrall, Caterine, from Herra Kaupmaðr five years ago. She served us loyally for many years and became a loving friend. My heart still ached for her – she was killed a few years ago, alongside my daughter, Alffinna.

Before I had purchased her, Caterine had risked her life to save Sander from drowning when he was just a young boy. It was a bitter cold winter day and my family were visiting the market to purchase a thrall. Sander wandered off and no one could find him.

ASHES REMAIN

Little did we know, Caterine had fled the thrall platform after she spotted my four-year-old son fall into the cold, vicious waves.

We spotted her crawl out the sea like a bedraggled animal with our half-dead son in her arms. We rushed to the marketplace to get Sander and Caterine warm and dry, but Herra's men seized her and whipped her for leaving the thrall stand, even though she did it to save Vidar's and my son. Furious, I immediately bought Caterine and chastised Herra for his cruelty, refusing to purchase goods from him ever again.

Vidar allowed Herra to continue selling his wares in Aros – he *was* the greatest merchant ever known, with the highest quality goods, we *couldn't* ban him from Aros. I wouldn't shop with him or even visit the marketplace when he was in town. When we needed to buy from Herra, Vidar would go without me, but now Vidar was gone. I would have to swallow my pride and ignore my quarrel with Herra if I was to buy another thrall.

Sweat trickled down the side of my face. The roaring fire and heat radiating from my guests was suffocating. Lured by the breeze wafting through the open doorway, I drained the last of my wine, set the empty horn on the table and slipped out into the night.

***

THE RUSH OF crisp autumn air danced on my face and chest. I gulped it like it was water, not realising how muggy and hot it was in the hall until now. I dabbed my face with the hem of my sleeve, my fingers grazing the damp roots of my hair. Though I had escaped the heat of the hall, I hadn't escaped the noise.

I strode away from the hall, steering clear of celebrating townspeople, a desperate need for solitude driving me far from my hall. I didn't worry about leaving my children, Sander, Æsa and Einar were all tucked away in their beds. With Melisende, Rowena and the guests left in my hall, I knew they were safe. Young Birger was old enough to run about as he pleased, he'd go to bed when he was ready.

Soon enough, I passed through one of the gates in the wooden palisade surrounding Aros. I closed the great gate behind myself, shutting out the music and voices from my hall.

GWENDOLINE SK TERRY

Finally, I found a spot on the shore where none of the noise could reach me, where the sloshing of waves was the only sound to be heard. Upon the waves and seafoam danced the reflections of the scattered stars and the waning moon, which was slowly descending the blackened sky. In the distance I spotted three ships, Jarl Borgulf's assumedly. I collapsed to my knees on the soft sand, watching them disappear, my heart drumming in my ears.

Finally, they were gone.

The sea spray carried on the winds, sprinkling my face in droplets, like tiny tears.

I breathed in deeply.

I breathed out.

I breathed in.

With a tightness in my throat, I exhaled a shuddering breath and wept.

ASHES REMAIN
CHAPTER FIVE

I WATCHED THE waves kiss the shore and as they ebbed away, they left behind a delicate lace of ivory foam. I admired the fragile patterns, like the finest of needlework, but the bubbles popped quickly, and the beautiful lace disappeared. As swiftly as they had vanished, the waves came again and gifted the shore another evanescent offering, and the cycle continued.

As morning grew closer, birdsong erupted around me, carried on the breath of the gentle, balmy breeze. Ribbons of pink and orange stretched across the deep blue sky and a gull soared somewhere overhead as the sun peeked over the horizon.

Aros would wake in an hour, maybe less, and my solitary peace would disappear like the lace of seafoam. I rested my forehead on my knees, hugging my legs against my chest a little tighter, my skirts pooled about me, filthy with sand. An unseasonably warm day was rising, but inside me a bitter tempest brewed.

Though I told my people I didn't fear the þing, I *did* fear it, I *was* disregarding the law. A woman could not be a jarl, nor could a woman even speak at the þing. How in Midgard could I defend myself if I wasn't allowed to even speak? I would have to break that law and make them listen …

I would need to take as many warriors as I could to support me, to speak on behalf of me. Perhaps if my army of men defended my abilities, we could sway the laws – what was the þing for but settling legal disputes and law-making?

It would be difficult. How many warriors would be able to accompany me? It was harvesting time – if we did not reap the crops and ready them for storage soon, we would not have food for the winter. That would put my people at risk for starvation – if I couldn't keep food in my people's bellies then I did not deserve to be jarl.

I would find a way to complete the harvest, store the food and gather enough men to support me, without putting out my people. Herra Kaupmaðr would possibly be at the þing – if he were, I would purchase as many thralls as I could and immediately send them to Aros to be put to work.

I had three weeks – no, less than that. I owed my people two more days of feasting before we could work, we would have to take a few days to prepare for the journey, a full day and night travel there in the ships, plus a day for riding to the þing place from the harbour – perhaps we'd be allowed an extra day to set up camp as well? ...

Fourteen days. I had fourteen days to harvest as much as possible. If the crops rotted before they could be harvested, I would buy as many sacks of oats, barley, rye and salt to store in the silos as I could afford. I hoped we would not be gone for long, and I hoped the weather would hold out, but I couldn't be sure. If these nine jarls wanted to oust me, then keeping me at the þing long enough for my townspeople to suffer would be a good way of turning my people against me.

I wouldn't let them. I would give them three days to decide. I would leave whether they came to a decision or not. These nine jarls could strip me of my title and steal my jarldom away without me there to fight for it, but if that was what they chose, they would have to come to Aros and take my jarldom from me by force. I would not allow them to seize my jarldom without fighting for it.

Could I defeat these jarls? Nine armies versus my one? Between Aros, Roskilde and the men from my smaller settlements, I had a force to be reckoned with. But even with all my warriors, could we defeat *nine* armies? Would I be sentencing my men to death? They would die honourably fighting for me, but would it be worth it?

No. I couldn't let it get to bloodshed. Their armies would overwhelm mine. They would slaughter us, they would kill me. My children would have no protector and would be killed too, to avoid the risk of them seeking vengeance and claiming the jarldoms when they grew into men. I would not let them kill my children.

If I wanted to avoid bloodshed and surrendered my jarldoms, would these jarls just take them and that would be that? Or would they punish me further for my other lawbreaking? Perhaps I could convince them to fine me no matter how outrageous the sum? It would be better than being outlawed or killed for my crimes.

I rubbed my face in my rough hands.

I had to retain my position as jarl. I could not let my children lose their home, could not risk them becoming outlawed alongside me or subjected to slavery if the jarls took our riches. I had to convince all nine that I was worthy, that I was every bit qualified for the position I had taken up, that I was as good as a man.

In just three years, when Young Birger would turn sixteen, he would be old enough to marry and to rule Roskilde. Would he be strong enough to fight any adversity? Any challenger? Mentally, I believed he could, he could outsmart them. Physically? Young Birger was tall – already much taller than me at his thirteen years of age – *and* he was fast and strong, but there were many men who were bigger, stronger. He still needed time to grow, to gain muscle, battle experience ...

No, Young Birger would be fine.

Young Birger was Vidar Alvarsson's son through and through. Wise beyond his years, Young Birger was every bit as intelligent, sensible and strategic as his father was. Whatever adversity Young Birger would face, his people would support him. He knew his vulnerabilities but was smart enough to know how to counter them with his strengths. The devotion of his people was one of his many strengths and I had no doubt they would risk their lives for him. He was so much like his father, a constant reminder of the jarl our people had loved.

Though it was daunting to be in Vidar's shadow, though it was overwhelming to have so many expectations of him, I knew Young Birger would succeed. He would be the Jarl of Roskilde that Vidar was meant to be.

Sander ...

Sander wasn't yet a man – he wouldn't be a man until he'd seen his tenth winter. He was far too young to rule, not even old enough to marry. Just over six years had to pass before Sander could marry and take on the jarldom of Aros at the absolute earliest.

Would Sander be ready? He was well loved, but a troublemaker. His curiosity was admired by men, his boldness, his bravery – they were such sought after traits in the Norse world. Sander wanted to travel the furthest parts of the world, to sail to faraway lands never visited by Danes. Vidar was immensely proud of Sander's adventurousness, but a jarl that was absent too often from his jarldom would be easily deposed, regardless of the riches he brought back from expeditions ...

As significant as raiding and exploration were, Sander had not yet realised the importance nor formed an interest in learning the fundamentals let alone the intricacies of ruling a town and handling its affairs. Sander had not proved his maturity yet, he hadn't proved his competence for such an important role as jarl.

Sander may have looked like Vidar, but he lacked Vidar's calm and collective way of thinking. Sander had his head in the clouds, but I put that down to his youth. In time Sander would prove himself, but there was no way he could take on a jarldom just yet.

"You have proved yourself to be a respectable, praiseworthy jarl, your people support you, they are yours. But – and I say this as your friend – the townspeople will love their female Anglo-Saxon jarl for only as long as you continue leading them to victory. That does not mean you are safe from being challenged again. You do not have Vidar here to protect you anymore, so be sure to watch what you say."

Jan's words floated through my mind.

There were so many obstacles for me, for my sons. Jan was right, Vidar *wasn't* here to protect me anymore. Though there were always issues to face, obstacles never seemed as intimidating nor as complicated when Vidar was around. Of course, had Vidar survived the riots of Gipeswic, none of these problems would have arisen – I would not be jarl. My sons would be free to grow and learn, to gain their necessary experience in due course.

Unfortunately, that was not meant to be, and I had to stop dwelling on it. I had to stop dreaming of what the future might have been had Vidar not died, because he *had* died.

Vidar was dead.

Vidar was gone ...

I rubbed my eyes with my fists. Jan was right, I needed to take care with what I said and did. I was the only parent my children had left, I was their only protector. I couldn't put their safety at risk by making stupid decisions. I would need all the support I could get and do whatever was necessary to get it.

ASHES REMAIN

I hoped most of all that I still had Jan on my side.

I had never yelled at him like I did yesterday ... Jan and I had been friends for many years, but since Vidar's death, he and I had grown even closer. We had suffered the same loss, we mourned together, we comforted each other and shared memories of better times, we wept together. And now ... I snarled and snapped at him like a dog when all he had done was offer me sound advice.

I *was* angry with the gods, I was furious with them, but I didn't need to take my anger out on Jan. Jan was not just a dear friend to me, he was my last link with Vidar. Though they hadn't been related biologically, Vidar and Jan had been family.

Vidar had been raised as Jan's foster brother for a time, until Vidar's older brother died. Vidar was forced to return to Alvar the First One's hall and take his late brother's place, to ready himself for the day he would inherit his jarldom. Though I could reminisce with other friends who had been close to Vidar, it was not the same as remembering him with Jan. To hear Jan speak of Vidar – it was as though Vidar was alive again.

"How long have you been here, Aveline?"

My heart lurched in my chest, I had not heard the crunch of footsteps in the sand coming up behind me. I knew who the voice belonged to, but I was too tired to face him. I continued to stare into my lap, my eyes closed, my breath dancing in the curls trailed over my face.

"Vidar used to do that." I murmured.

"Do what?"

"Suddenly appear when I thought of him."

"You were thinking of me?"

"Maybe."

"I wonder whether that's a good thing or a bad thing." Jan grinned, sitting down less than an armlength from me.

"I shan't tell you, you must guess." I smiled.

"Then I don't want to know what you were thinking, it was probably bad." Jan snickered.

"*Nei*, nothing bad," I admitted, lifting my head to gaze at the waves. "I was just thinking."

"Anything I can help you with? Maybe talking about it would–"

"*Nei*, I don't even want to think about it anymore. I've thought far too much about it as it is." I said firmly, hastily adding, "*Þakka fyrir*, though, I appreciate your concern."

"If you change your mind, I'm here."

I finally turned to him. Jan was hunched over his legs, his elbows rested on his knees, picking at a broken nail on one of his fingers. He wore the same clothes he had on during the feast and his long tawny hair was a mess. Judging by the puffiness of his bloodshot eyes, I did not think he had gone to sleep at all.

"What are you doing here, Jan?"

"I came here to think."

Jan glanced at me from the corner of his eye, our gaze connected long enough for him to offer me a wink and a small smile before he returned his attention to the waves. The glow of the sun lit up his alabaster flesh and sparkled in his sapphire eyes. I lowered my gaze, spotting a flat, round pebble in the sand. I picked it up and brushed the golden grains away with my thumb.

"What are you thinking about?" I asked quietly, glancing between Jan and the pebble.

Jan shrugged his shoulders.

"Same as you, I suspect." Jan said.

"Before *he* appeared, you seemed to be enjoying the feast." I said, not wanting to discuss Jarl Borgulf. "That beautiful young woman in the yellow dress?"

"Ah, her? She was good company, nothing more."

"What was her name?" I pressed.

"Aveline, she's not important." Jan said firmly.

"Why not? Can't she become important in the future?"

"*Nei*, I don't want her to be."

"Was she boring? Was her voice squeaky?"

Jan laughed and turned to me, a warm grin spread across his face. Heartened, I returned his smile, glad that he did not resent me for how terribly I'd treated him earlier.

"Please, ask me about anyone else at the feast, but not her." Jan said, rolling his eyes dramatically. "She was not boring, but she was not to my liking. I admit, she would make a great bed companion, as long as she doesn't speak as much in bed as she does out of it."

"Ah, so her voice *was* irritating, wasn't it?" I smirked.

"*Nei*, it was lovely. Just ... Constant. Never-ending." Jan winked again. "No more of her, now – I can hear her babbling every time you mention her."

"Fine." I giggled. "Tell me, then, about Galinn."

"Who?" Jan paused thoughtfully. "Galinn Johansson, the half-Dane? That white-haired louse? The rat-faced bastard?"

"That's the one." I snickered.

"Well, there's not much to say about him," Jan said, to which I laughed. "From what I've heard, his mother is a Dane, and his father was a Norwegian. They lived here during Erhardt's rule and after Vidar took Aros, the half-Dane's father ran off, never to be seen again. His mother, Ósk Guðmundsdóttir, has been alone ever since, raising the boy alone. He is to marry next year, isn't he?"

"*Já*, he is. His mother was quite adamant about it – she wants him married as soon as possible." I replied. "She tried to get my approval to have him married a year earlier, but I refused."

"She has no one else to help tend their land. A wife for Galinn means help for Ósk."

"I wonder why she hasn't sought a husband for herself since Johann abandoned them. It would have been much easier for the two of them if Ósk had remarried years ago, rather than struggle alone for so long."

"Oh *já*, remarry, that would solve her problems." Jan grinned, reaching out and shoving me gently. "You know all the advantages of remarrying, don't you?"

"My husband *died*, he didn't abandon me." I grumbled, shoving him back. "Johann abandoned Ósk and Galinn. Instead of suffering for so many years, she should have remarried – the moment Johann turned his back on them, she should've sought someone better."

"Perhaps Ósk still pines for him? Perhaps she loves him? Perhaps she holds on to the hope that he might return?"

"I don't know, you have insight into Ósk's situation what with your wife abandoning you, so you answer those questions."

"Getting back at me for my comment?"

"I am indeed, *já*."

"You're very cruel, Aveline Birgersdóttir."

"Whatever I learned, I learned it from you, Jan Jötunnson."

"Why the sudden interest in Galinn, anyway?" Jan asked, leaning back onto his elbows and stretching his long, muscled legs out in front of him.

As Jan stretched, his joints popped audibly. I gawped at him for a moment, surprised by the loudness of his stiff joints.

"I'm getting old," Jan said in reply to my expression. "Carry on."

"Well, I met Galinn tonight – I've only ever seen him in passing before." I explained. "Even when Ósk came to me to arrange his marriage, she came to me alone. I was surprised by his absence, but I didn't ask about it. Come to think of it, I've spoken to her only a handful of times in the past. I don't know that family at all."

"Aveline … Galinn and Ósk are not thrilled with your ruling." Jan said slowly.

"What?" I frowned, surprised by Jan's revelation.

"Vidar was the reason Johann abandoned Ósk and Galinn. After Vidar killed Erhardt and came to Aros to seize Erhardt's jarldom, he gave the men here an ultimatum." Jan said. "They had the option to give fealty to Vidar or to die. Well, rather than be forced to decide, Johann fled Aros, leaving Ósk and Galinn.

"Their farm has not been doing well since Johann left. Over the years, Ósk had to sell all their thralls and a lot of their land to make ends meet. They have harboured quite the grudge against you and Vidar, blaming you both – and all of us from Roskilde – for Johann's departure and for ruining their lives."

Jan was correct, from what Vidar had said, when the battle calmed, he gave the adult males of Aros the choice, give Vidar fealty or die. Those that promised their allegiance to Vidar were spared, and those that did not were killed, just as Vidar swore would happen.

The women were offered a similar choice and given some leniency (if you could call it that) due to their gender, they could swear loyalty to Vidar otherwise they could choose to leave Aros, remain in Aros as thralls, or die beside their men. Those who remained loyal to Erhardt and refused to flee or subject themselves to thraldom were piled into Erhardt's hall and burned to death with their husbands.

It had been a bloody day. I understood why Johann had fled since he didn't want to pledge his loyalty to Vidar, but this was the

ASHES REMAIN

Norse world and fleeing was dishonourable for a man. He wouldn't be able to show his face in Aros ever again, not for fear of what *I* might decree, but what the townspeople who had known him might do to him. He was a coward in their eyes – it was better to die than to run away.

Ósk and Galinn must have lived in shame all these years – still live in shame – for Johann's cowardice ...

After taking Aros, Vidar had tried to prove to the townspeople that he was a just leader. He spent the following year rebuilding Aros, mending their homes from his people's attack, and he let them keep whatever they had during Erhardt's rule, and even shared with them land from those who had chosen to leave or had been slaughtered.

His generosity had won him most of the people. By the time I returned to Aros after a year of absence, I could not tell who had truly accepted him and who hadn't, for those who disliked Vidar wisely kept their genuine feelings secret.

My arrival, however? It had been frosty to say the least. The hollow smiles and the sideways glances as I walked down the streets ... I remembered their faces, their false kindness when they welcomed me at the celebration Vidar had hosted. I remembered the tenseness in the air. Their words were empty, and my stomach sank deeper with every lie. I wanted them to stop, to leave me alone, but I sat through it all until the very end.

They didn't trust me, they gossiped about me, they kept a façade of respect up for me when I was in Vidar's presence, but when I was alone, they eyed me with abandon, a few even spat at my feet.

I had been Jarlkona of Aros for the four years I had been married to Erhardt as his peace-bride. For me to return to Aros as Vidar's wife *and* Erhardt's widow ... They called me a snake, said I had pit Erhardt and Vidar against each other using seduction and feminine trickery. They blamed me for the deaths of their neighbours, friends and kin when Roskilde attacked them. They blamed me for the destruction of their town.

I had wept for weeks over the allegations circulating Aros about me. Although Vidar had done everything he could to remove any landmark or subtle trace of my previous miserable life in Aros – he had even built a new hall for us upon the ashes of Erhardt's, vastly different to that which had stood there before – all the tales and rumours reminded me of why I'd never wanted to return. Most of the townspeople knew the situation that led to my marrying Erhardt, they knew I had never wanted to be his wife, knew I'd been betrothed to Vidar when Erhardt stole me, so why were they accusing me of these heinous allegations?

In the late spring of 874, Erhardt and his warriors attacked Roskilde, the town belonging to Vidar's father, Alvar, while Alvar and his fleet were overseas fighting in the lands of Britain with the Great Army. Vidar hadn't gone to Britain, instead he and a force of warriors were ordered to remain in Roskilde to protect it against any enemy attack. Aros and Roskilde had been feuding for decades, and Erhardt had attacked it in the past – Alvar had always left a contingent to defend it ever since.

Unfortunately, Erhardt had a group of scouts survey Roskilde for some time. The moment Vidar travelled to Ribe to trade, Aros attacked Roskilde in the dead of night. Surprised and vastly unprepared and undermanned, Erhardt's men sprang onto the unsuspecting Roskilde and overpowered it with ease.

I was engaged to Vidar and carried his child when Vidar's mother Freydis was forced to give me to Erhardt as peace-bride for the safety of Roskilde. Only Vidar and I knew I was with child, and for the sake of our unborn son, we had to keep his existence a secret.

Vidar was forced to take Erhardt's youngest daughter as his wife in my place. It was not a choice Vidar wanted to make – no, Erhardt had vowed that if Vidar didn't take Ursula as his peace-bride, then Erhardt would kill me. If Ursula gave birth to Vidar's child, she would have a legitimate heir to the Roskilde jarldom – not to mention, she was a spy for Erhardt.

Vidar and I saw each other only once over the four years I was married to Erhardt. Vidar and Ursula came to meet Young Birger and congratulate Erhardt and me on our handsome son, a year and a half after Young Birger had been born. Of course, Young Birger was Vidar and my child, but no one could know the truth.

During the few weeks Vidar and Ursula were in Aros, Vidar and I conceived Sander during clandestine meetings under cover of night. Thank the gods, for I hadn't wanted to conceive any child of Erhardt's, though it sickened me that I had to pretend Vidar's children were Erhardt's.

The next time Vidar and I saw each other was *Midsumarblót* in 878, when Vidar killed Ursula and Erhardt and freed us from our bitter marriages and ended the feud between Roskilde and Aros for good.

Yes, Vidar had killed so many people during his attack. He had cut them down, burned them, banished them, and yes, he had done so in my name. Lives had been ruined.

"Don't worry, little fawn. It is always difficult to adjust to a new leader, especially after an ongoing feud as the one between Aros and Roskilde. These people are being forced to forget a feud that had gone on for decades, it will take time." Vidar had explained, stroking my hair as I wept into his arms one night. "They *will* forget, little fawn. And those that do not? Well, everyone has enemies, and I promise I'll kill anyone who tries to hurt you."

Vidar had been right, they had forgotten – or at least, they seemed to. Over the seven and a half years Vidar had ruled Aros, the people had come to love us. And those who harboured deep, unshakable hate for us? They were unseen, unknown.

There were bound to be a few people like Ósk who had not forgiven us and never would, but as long as she didn't cause trouble – as long as her son fought in the battles I led – what did it matter if they remained in Aros?

I had more faithful followers than I had enemies, I was sure of that, and if my opposers decided after all these years to rise up and take vengeance on me for what had happened in the past, I would be forced to kill them, and I would have my people's support.

"How did you come across all this information?"

"Ósk told me."

I gawped at Jan.

"A few years after Vidar seized Aros, I was drinking alone in the alehouse and I noticed that she was, too." Jan explained, a small smirk playing on his lips. "Not one to let a woman drink on her own, I sat with her. She was quite taken by her ale by the time I'd joined her and had no problem telling me exactly what she thought of me, Vidar, you, and all the other Danes of Roskilde who *stole this land from the good people of Aros*."

"I see. But we took Aros eight years ago – it's been how many years since you spoke to her in the alehouse?"

"Four, maybe."

"Did you tell Vidar?"

"Of course, I did. Vidar was unconcerned."

"Hmmm ... Perhaps she has moved on from her ill-feelings? She has been cordial to me, she bade fealty to me quickly and willingly when I became jarl."

"And what would you have done if she hadn't?"

I didn't reply.

"You can tell by Galinn's behaviour that he is still resentful towards your family. His mother is more skilled at disguising her bitterness than he is."

"How many others are bitter, Jan?"

"I can't be sure – remember, I was Vidar's righthand man, anyone who despises him and you, despise me just as greatly. Ósk's secrets were spilled by ale – others have a better hand on their alcohol than her. She is skilled at hiding her ill-feelings, but not when she's filled with drink."

"Every soul in Aros bade their fealty to me. Should any of them break their oath, I will slay them."

"Most will not break their oath, but I'd be careful about the þing, it might just be the moment they decide to let their true opinions known." Jan advised. "And you *must* slay them if they do. You must not be afraid to spill blood, Aveline, be it man or woman. If someone breaks their oath, you *must* make an example of them so no one else will think you weak and betray you, too."

"I'm not afraid to kill." I said, but cold fingers of anxiety crept up my spine. "Jan ... Young Birger and Yngvi were with Galinn this evening."

"Young Birger could easily defeat Galinn despite their age difference." Jan said confidently. "Galinn is emotional and short-tempered – he fights impulsively and doesn't consider his enemy, he just flails and bashes until he wins or loses. Young Birger is entirely the opposite, which makes him a better warrior."

"You think it will come to a fight between the two?"

"Possibly. Next week, next year, next decade perhaps. Who else were Young Birger and Yngvi with besides Galinn?"

ASHES REMAIN

"Sibba, Gísla and that Biólan boy."

"Ah, that's why they were together then. Galinn's betrothed to Sibba so he *must* follow her around at the feast. Sibba and Gísla are never separated, and right now Gísla has set her little heart on Biólan. Biólan is an idiot, but he has a great arm for throwing axes, spears and the like. He and his family are proud supporters of yours, a good friend for Young Birger to have."

"You know quite a lot, Jan Jötunnson." I remarked.

"Auða, Sibba and Gísla's mother, visits Heimlaug often. They gossip together while I work on the farm, and during evening meal Heimlaug shares all that gossip with me."

"What of Auða and her husband? I thought they were friendly with me, are you going to tell me now that they are both against my rule, too?"

"*Nei*, Auða and Hvítserkr are very fond of you, for all I know at least." Jan said. "And I'll tell you a secret, Auða isn't pleased with the match between Sibba and Galinn, but Hvítserkr arranged it with Johann years ago.

"Even though the match is not beneficial for them and Auða and Hvítserkr's views differ from Ósk and our absent Johann's, Hvítserkr won't break it – he gave his word that Sibba and Galinn would be married, and that's that. Sibba is infatuated with the boy anyway, for whatever reason – perhaps his pretty white hair."

"Urgh!" I groaned. "How was Vidar so calm all the time? When he told me of situations like this, he said so in such a manner that I wasn't concerned. He already seemed to have everything under control."

"That was just Vidar." Jan shrugged, sitting up and crossing his long legs. "He was quite a man."

"*Já*, he was ..."

We were silent for a while. As the moments trickled by, Jan shuffled closer to me and pulled me against him in a one-armed hug and I let him. I rested my head against his shoulder, silently grateful for his embrace. Though I could not know for sure who supported me and who didn't, I knew that Jan was on my side, and that comforted me enough. Wordlessly, we watched the sun rise over the waters, lost in our own thoughts.

The cry of roosters pierced the air, reaching us over the sloshing of the waves. The dull sound of the wakening town drifted to us, but neither of us made any attempt to get up. We sat together, clinging to the peace and quiet. A whirlwind of thoughts and emotions thundered inside me, but I was sick of talking about it. I just wanted peace.

"Earlier ... I'm sorry I hurt you. It's just – I just want you to be aware, to be cautious." Jan said quietly. "Vidar was a kind man, a strong man, but he was a fearsome warrior and had no qualms with exacting punishment on those who needed to be punished.

"When he took Aros, he took it with fire and blood. He intimidated his surviving enemies into submission – all those people from Aros who pledged their loyalty to him, who gave oaths not to take vengeance for Erhardt, they did so because they feared Vidar and they feared the consequences of their betrayal. He was a mighty jarl, everything a jarl should be.

"During his rule, Vidar was just, he was generous. Yet some still saw him as the fearsome warlord who slaughtered their kin and their neighbours. Others saw Vidar as a man avenging his lover, exacting the revenge he rightly deserved to take. Vidar was not cruel like Erhardt, but he was still a force to be reckoned with. Now he is gone, and with you being jarl ...

"They accepted you because you were Vidar's wife – because they expect the same fierceness from you that they saw from him. Had Vidar been less intimidating, less generous with his riches, the survivors of Erhardt's Aros would have plotted against him.

"You face the same challenges Vidar faced – but you're at a disadvantage because you're a woman, you're instantly seen as weaker. You cannot fail your people, you *cannot* commit even the smallest of mistakes – it only takes a single drop of poison to injure, and it only takes a single word or action to destroy a reputation.

"With every challenger you defeated, and between Francia and the Wendish expedition, you've shown them you're more than capable. They may not have trusted you at the beginning, but most of them do now. You *must* continue, you must work harder. You must expect that your enemies will try to overthrow you, you must always keep one eye open.

ASHES REMAIN

"I know there aren't enough of Erhardt's supports hidden in Aros to overthrow you, otherwise there would have been a traitor sitting in Vidar's chair upon our return from the East Angles, or even an attempt to kill you while in the Wendish lands. Despite this, you cannot get comfortable, enemies *are* out there."

"I know, Jan." I mumbled dismally. "I know."

"Anyway, enough of all this serious talk. I have something for you." Jan said brightly.

"What?" I gawped up at him.

"You will find out soon enough." Jan grinned. "I've been working on something for you – a gift."

"What? Why? What is it?"

"You'll see – it arrives today."

"When?"

"It should be here any time now. Shall we go back to the hall and find out?"

GWENDOLINE SK TERRY
CHAPTER SIX

"THERE IT IS." Jan said, bouncing on his feet.

A wagon rumbled up the road, creaking and groaning, pulled by two ruddy-brown oxen yoked together. The oxen were massive, broad-chested with huge shoulders, wide foreheads and long sharp horns. Clouds of dirt puffed about their hooves and the wheels of wagon as the beasts trudged towards the hall dragging their mysterious load. Steering the oxen was Lars, switch in hand and beaming like a fool.

What in Hel could this gift be that requires oxen to pull it? I wondered as another wagon pulled up behind Lars. This one was pulled by a single ox that fiery-haired Domnall steered.

"*Móðir*, Jan, what's going on?" Young Birger asked, stepping out of the hall carrying Einar on his hip.

Jan and I had marched up the shore towards my hall, (rather, Jan marched, and I scurried excitedly ahead of him), but hadn't made it inside before the rumble of the wagons and oxen stopped us in our tracks. As loud as thunder in the clear, bright morning, I assumed the noise had woken my sons. From the doorway of the hall, bleary eyed, they peeked through their tousled hair at the wagons, both still dressed in their nightclothes.

"It's a surprise." Jan beamed.

Sander and Æsa appeared in the doorway. All four children craned their necks to see what was on the wagons. The whole of Aros seemed to be awake now, townspeople poked their sleepy heads out of their doors and stared at the scene unfolding before them. Lars stopped the oxen in the centre of the wide dirt road, his wagon positioned so the rear was facing the burial ground, so we still could not see what was inside.

The burial ground was a large square of green in the heart of Aros situated opposite my hall on the other side of a wide dirt road, one of three that stretched from shore to shore across the

ASHES REMAIN

length of Aros. A few grave mounds were situated on the green, but for the most part, we used the space to cremate our dead.

There was a single wooden grave marker standing upon the green – a crude crucifix made by Young Birger when he was a boy. The cross marked Caterine's grave. She had been Christian, so after her tragic death we buried her in the Christian manner – the first and only Christian buried in Aros.

Domnall stopped his wagon in front of us, and inside we saw a variety of logs and rope. Young Birger's icy-coloured eyes widened. He examined the planks and the logs, glancing at the ropes then back to the wood, before turning to Lars's wagon.

"Jarl, Young Birger, children." Domnall nodded to the children and me, flashing us a mischievous wink.

"What are you making, Jan?" Excitement peppered Young Birger's words.

"You'll soon see." Jan grinned.

"Hallmundr, Ebbe and the others are coming now." Domnall said.

"Are any of you going to tell us what it is you're doing?" I demanded. "What is all this?"

"With all due respect Jarl, it's a surprise." Lars grinned as he approached us.

"The next person who says *it's a surprise* is getting cut through with my sword." I grumbled.

"Young Birger, come with me, you can help." Jan said.

"I can help too!" Sander exclaimed.

"Come on then!" Jan laughed.

Sander scrambled after Jan. Young Birger set Einar on the ground and rushed off after them to Domnall's wagon. I watched my sons' faces light up as Jan whispered something to them from behind his hand. Domnall and Lars joined the three, and together they began unloading the ropes, logs and planks of wood.

"What are they doing, *mumie*?" Einar asked, winding his arms around my legs and staring at them.

"I have no idea."

Soon enough, a crowd had formed. Hallmundr, Ebbe, Einarr and three other burly men from the town had come to assist Young Birger, Sander, Jan, Lars and Domnall with whatever was in the other wagon. They leaned the planks diagonally from the back of the wagon to the ground, forming a long ramp, and at the end of the ramp they arranged the logs horizontally with a foot or two of space between each.

Multiple times townspeople asked me what they were doing, and all I could do was shrug my shoulders in reply. While Jan worked, I had Melisende and Rowena bring out a trestle table and set it with dried fruit, cheese, bread, buttermilk and mead, for many people (including myself and the children) hadn't eaten breakfast yet, too overwhelmed with curiosity.

Soon enough an impromptu town gathering had formed, women in the village assembled a morning feast. They brought out cauldrons of hot stews, leftovers from the feast the night before, and set up yet more trestle tables and covered them with dishes of nuts, great steaming pots of hot oatmeal and porridge, bowls, spoons and more. A large group of men were aiding Jan, my sons and their group, and finally, the surprise was revealed.

Three rows of men spread out behind the wagon, Jan, Einarr and Hallmundr heading them with eight men each behind them. They held ropes presumably attached to whatever was inside the wagon. Young Birger and Sander were hanging from the sides of the wagon, while Lars was standing inside it.

"Pull!" Young Birger called out.

Immediately the three rows of men began to pull. The wagon groaned and yowled as the men tugged the massive object forward, scraping the wooden floor with a raucous din. The men pulled and pulled, their faces red from the strain of tugging whatever it was. Townspeople craned their necks and gathered closer, attempting to peek at the thing in the wagon.

The mob of townspeople gasped, with an almighty tug, a wicked crack ripped through the air as the wagon fractured under the weight of the *thing* as it slid vertically down the wooden plank ramp and onto the logs. It was a gigantic rock, a granite obelisk perhaps two metres in height. It was somewhat rectangular in shape, the base was flat and the top tapered to a point.

"Why are they moving that boulder there?" Æsa asked.

"I have no idea." I replied blankly.

ASHES REMAIN

I couldn't turn away from the huge block. The massive rock rumbled as the men hauled it over the logs that creaked unnervingly as the granite slowly rumbled over them. The logs rolled beneath the granite as the men pulled, and every now and again, the men would pause while Lars and Young Birger took a log from the back and slip it in front of the granite to roll it further forward.

It took a while, but finally, the granite was seemingly where Jan wanted it, for he shouted out, "S*tǫðva!*" and all the men stopped. They wiped the sweat that poured from their brows, sodden tunics clinging to their bodies. Others had stripped off their upper clothing completely, dripping and gleaming with perspiration. All were red faced and panting from their exertion, but all wore expressions of concentration: their task was not yet complete.

Jan and Young Birger strode over to the oxen, who were contentedly chewing cud, and unhooked their yoke from the wagon. Young Birger tried to lead the stubborn beasts by the rope but Jan, who had taken up the switch, had to strike the headstrong creatures on their rears a few times to get them to move. Young Birger led the beasts in front of the granite. Jan took the rope from him, and Young Birger slipped between the beasts, patting them affectionately and murmuring to them.

The block's pointed end was facing me while the flat base was directed towards the oxen. Ebbe and Hallmundr tied ropes around the upper third of the granite, then secured the ends of the rope to the oxen's yoke. They were going to pull the granite up! Everyone watched wide-eyed as Ebbe and Hallmundr nodded to Young Birger and Jan. Jan nodded back, then ordered the oxen to walk.

"*Já, bragða*, that's it – keep moving!" Young Birger called to Jan.

The large, heavy beasts plodded forward, dragging the granite up on to its base. It was *terribly* slow, careful work, Jan inched the oxen forward, wary in case the granite might tilt to one side and fall. Jan wanted the granite to stay vertical – he wanted it to stand on its flat base, the pointed end aimed at the sky. With bated breath I watched the granite stand and, as it lifted off the ground, I realised the flat face of the granite that had rolled over the logs was carved with multiple images and runes painted in various vibrant colours.

"*Stǫðva!*" Young Birger exclaimed.

Jan stopped the oxen, a beaming grin lighting up his face. The granite block was standing upright on the grass. Domnall, grinning too, patted the granite, then tried to shove it and sway it. The granite didn't shift even slightly, it was stable, they'd done it! The men cheered and Domnall proceeded to untie the ropes from the granite, two other men quickly aiding him, while Young Birger slipped out from between the oxen to stand with Sander and admire the rock.

Once the rope was unfastened from the granite, Hallmundr led the oxen back to the wagon while Jan strode over to me. The moment Domnall had removed the ropes, the townspeople swarmed around the obelisk, admiring the colourful images carved into it, gasping and chattering amongst themselves.

"Your surprise, Jarl." Jan smiled, offering me his hand.

Silently I placed my tiny hand in his huge one and let him lead me to the granite. The crowd immediately parted for us. I examined the exquisite images carved deeply into the rock. One was a warrior armed sword and shield fighting a wolf – the Norse god Víðarr and the wolf Fenrir perhaps? The wolf was painted dark grey but for its glaring red eyes, and the warrior was painted completely white, except for his blond hair and blue eyes and the red blood on his blade.

There was also a gorgeously detailed longship carved into the granite. Its hull was low and there were lines carved along the side of the ship marking the planks. The stems were long, the back ending in a point that arched over the ship whereas the front stem held a dragon head. The longship carving was so fantastically detailed, with thirteen shields hanging on the gunwales and thirteen oar-holes just beneath the shields. There was even a side-rudder and the rig showed the mast, yard, sail and stays. The longship was painted golden-brown and the sail was grey ... It looked like Storm-Serpent.

Framing the images was a ribbon filled with runes. At the beginning of the ribbon was a beast's head and at the end was a simple swirl. The ribbon was white, but the grooves of the ribbon's outline and the runes were painted in a vibrant shade of red. I followed the runes, reading the carved message:

ASHES REMAIN

Jan Jötunnson raised this stone in memory of Vidar Alvarsson,
Father of Birger, Sander, Æsa, Einar and Alffinna,
Husbandman of Aveline.
There was no greater man than him.
He met his end in the west.

I touched Vidar's name, traced each rune with the tip of my finger, the grooves cut into the stone painted red, like blood …

"Do you – do you like it?" Jan asked in a small voice.

It took a lot of effort, but I tore my eyes from the runes and looked up at Jan. He stared at me anxiously, his brow was knitted, and a frown turned down the corners of his rose-coloured lips. I opened my mouth, but no words came out. Jan's gift had rendered me speechless.

"The Swedes make runestone memorials for their dead. They use granite for most of the runestones, so I did the same." Jan said. "It took a while to source the best granite, and even then, I had to chisel the front and the base to get them as flat as I could, it took a lot of time to get the granite just right. Vidar's stone had to be as big as possible, and I wanted the images and runes to be unmistakable. It had to be flawless, for him."

No matter how hard I tried, I couldn't swallow down the knot wedged in my throat. Instead, I flung myself at him, gripping him against me tightly, my face buried in his tunic. I heard Jan's sharp intake of breath, surprised at my abrupt embrace. He rested his hands on my back before drawing me against him, so close I could hear his heart race in his chest and his breath dance in my hair.

"Does this mean you like it?" Jan grinned.

I gazed up at him with tear-filled eyes and nodded.

"It's wonderful," I managed to mumble. "*Þakka fyrir.*"

CHAPTER SEVEN

I WIPED MY brow with the sleeve of my dress and threw my aching body into a chair as far from the roaring firepit as possible. Harvesting was far from complete, but we were doing well. In just three days I would have to travel to the þing place, and I wanted as much done as possible before I left.

Immediately after the three days of feasting had ended, I travelled to Roskilde and shared the news of my summons with my people there. I managed to rally a large following of men to support me at the þing. In total, I had four hundred men accompanying me to the þing between both the towns and all the settlements under my power – a huge number to be sure.

The jarls might not listen to me, but they would see the great number of my men and hear what they had to say. Four hundred men should be enough to sway them … The rest of my men would remain at home and tend to the fields and farms.

With that done, I immersed myself in preparations for winter. Though the thralls had taken the brunt of the work in the fields, every townsperson was busy preparing for the coming winter. I had spent the past week dashing about the village, tallying the harvest stores around Aros. I had sent Jan to Roskilde to act on my behalf, tallying their stores and organising their preparations, and to find out what Roskilde needed aid with.

After tallying, I spent my time spinning, carding, weaving and sewing, salting and smoking fish and meat to keep over the winter months with the other women of the town.

A lot of livestock, those too old to endure the coming harsh cold, had been slaughtered. I kept a large herd of sheep on the mainland, watched over by a family I had hired, while my ewes and lambs were kept in a paddock behind my hall. Normally Norsemen kept their livestock penned inside their homes, but as Jarl, I could afford the luxury of a barn to keep my animals outside.

ASHES REMAIN

Growing up in the Kingdom of the East Angles, my family had been sheep farmers. After Birger Bloody Sword had taken me away to Denmark, he purchased sheep for me to raise in our little home in Roskilde. Half our home was for us, the other half was sectioned into pens for our flock. They stank, they were noisy, but the heat their bodies generated kept us warm during the winters.

When Vidar and I took Aros, Vidar had gifted me huge pastures and doubled my herd. I continued to raise my sheep and continued to name them. Vidar used to tease me for naming my livestock, but he had teased me affectionately. He used to refer to each sheep by their specific name, for he knew them all.

I looked down at my skirts, a few strings of fat I had trimmed from the meat clung to my dress and dark splatters of blood soaked the blue wool. My hands were crimson, too – I seemed to be drenched in blood all too often these days ... It wasn't human blood staining my clothes this time but the blood of my sheep – I had to cull almost half of the herd Vidar and I had raised together.

Like a sudden gust of wind, a deep sigh fell from my lips. I wiped my palms on my skirts, dirtying my dress even further, and stood up, shaking the thoughts of Vidar out of my head.

Vidar was frequently on my mind – indeed, our children were spit images of him and reminded me of him every time I set my eyes on them. I glanced at them from across the room, Young Birger was carving a longship from a hunk of oak and Sander, Æsa and Einar were playing by the fire with their toys.

Young Birger and Sander were their father through and through, from their golden hair and bronze skin to their icy blue eyes. They'd also inherited their father's height, Young Birger was far taller than me, and Sander was the same height as me already. Vidar had towered over me, the top of my head had come up just below his chin – I had no doubt that in just a few more years, Sander and Young Birger would tower over me as well.

Æsa had my amber eyes and pale skin, but her hair was white-blonde, much like Vidar's mother Freydis. Freydis had been a beautiful woman, tall, regal and elegant, with meadow green eyes and almost white hair. Æsa was already so similar to her grandmother in mannerism as well as looks.

Einar was still just a young boy so I could not determine whether he would inherit Vidar's height or mine. He was the only one of Vidar and my four living children to share some features with me. Einar's hair was golden like Vidar's, but it was wildly curled like mine, and he'd inherited my amber eyes.

Only one of Vidar and my five children had looked like me more than Vidar, and that was our late daughter, Alffinna. She'd had my amber eyes, my chestnut curls, and she had been as pale as moonlight. Alffinna had been dead for two years now.

We didn't talk about Alffinna much. Einar didn't remember her well at all, but Young Birger did, as did Sander. Æsa had a vague recollection of her younger sister, but unfortunately, she remembered Alffinna in death more than she remembered her when she was alive.

Alffinna's death had been terrible. She had been killed before she had even reached a year of age, an innocent victim caught in the middle of a blood feud – the feud between Jan and Thorn Arnsteinson, the brother of Jan's second wife, Thóra.

Years after Thóra had left Jan, her brother, Thorn, arrived in Aros seeking vengeance, convinced that Jan had murdered Thóra, which Jan had most certainly not done. Vidar had decided they would settle their feud with a *hólmganga*, a duel of honour, and the first man to draw blood would be the winner.

Jan had defeated Thorn, and Thorn was supposed to give up his demand for vengeance. Of course, Thorn didn't do that, so certain in his conviction that Jan had murdered his sister. He spotted my thrall, Caterine, who he'd mistake as Jan's lover. Despite losing the *hólmganga*, Thorn was desperate to take his revenge and struck Caterine – who was holding Alffinna – with his blade.

The blade slashed through Caterine's neck and across her chest and slit Alffinna's throat. Caterine's body collapsed to the ground, Alffinna with it.

I had scooped my baby up and tried to cover her wound to stop the bleeding, but the gash was too deep. Alffinna shrieked and writhed in my arms, before she stopped, dead.

Vidar had avenged her immediately, strangling Thorn, crushing Thorn's throat in his hands, while our baby daughter bled to death in my arms. Vidar, Jan and Young Birger slew all of Thorn's men.

ASHES REMAIN

Vidar and Young Birger had never told me what had happened that day – nor had I asked. Young Birger had been a few months away from his tenth birthday when he had killed for the first time – too young to take a man's life, but old enough to avenge his sister's death. Though at the time I had focussed on nothing but my dead daughter in my arms, I was proud of Young Birger for avenging her, though I wished he'd never had to.

My hands trembled at my sides. It was stifling inside the hall, the air was so thick with smoke and heat I could hardly breathe. I crossed the room and stepped out through the large oak door hoping the autumn air would cool me down.

There it was.

Directly in front of the hall, bright and colourful, standing tall at the edge of the burial ground like a sentinel, the runestone loomed before me. A constant reminder of the husband and daughter I had lost. The moment I opened the door, I could see nothing but that huge, towering monument.

Drawn to it, my feet began to move. I couldn't stop myself even if I tried. Every time I opened that damn door the runestone pulled me to it. At first, I loved it, I still appreciated Jan for creating it – it *was* a wonderful memorial to the greatest man I'd ever known. Yet with each passing day, a sadness grew inside me. Jan had raised the runestone so Vidar's life would never be forgotten, but all it did was remind me that Vidar was dead.

> *Jan Jötunnson raised this stone in memory of Vidar Alvarsson,*
> *Father of Birger, Sander, Æsa, Einar and Alffinna,*
> *Husbandman of Aveline.*
> *There was no greater man than him.*
> *He met his end in the west.*

I read the runes over again and again, my heart racing faster with each word. I traced my fingers over the blood red carvings, laid my hand on Vidar's name ... The runestone was a beautiful gift, but it haunted me.

Vidar had been killed in the spring of 886. It had been seven months since then ... Most young widows would be searching for a new husband by now, if they weren't already remarried. A woman needed a husband for survival, for the money or loot he brought home and for physical protection, just as much as a man needed a wife to produce heirs and manage their home and farm.

Life expectancy wasn't fantastic, either. Most adults didn't live to see their sixtieth winter, in fact they usually died between their thirtieth and forty-fifth winter due to disease, battle or, in women's cases, childbirth. Even children weren't spared from the tragedy of an early death – almost half of all children died commonly from disease or hunger before they saw their seventh winter. Seven months was a long time with all those factors considered.

Not long enough for me to heal from Vidar's death, though. Seven months wasn't long enough for my heart to stop aching – a lifetime wasn't long enough for me to move on. I didn't want to hurt, to ache for Vidar and Alffinna. Raiding allowed me to release my anger at the Norns for cutting their lives short. Young Birger, Sander, Æsa and Einar kept the smile on my face and happiness in my shattered heart, my duties as jarl distracted me from thinking about my late husband and daughter, but now in front of my hall was a massive runestone reminding me of them every day.

I didn't want to forget Vidar and Alffinna. Selfishly, I just didn't want to think about them every moment of the day, I didn't want to miss them, to hurt, to wane and become an empty husk of the woman I was. I didn't want to collapse into that dark hole of sadness like I had after Alffinna's death … I had failed my children then, I had almost wasted away, so distraught and stricken by grief.

But Vidar had pulled me out of it. He had taught me to remember our daughter, and to live for our other children. Vidar had helped me, but now he was gone … Try as they might, no other man would ever be able to do the things Vidar could. No other man could help me the way Vidar had. Vidar was my safety, my tranquillity, my defender. And he was gone …

I closed my eyes and rested my brow against the cold stone, picturing Vidar in my mind. As clear as day I could see him, his dazzling ice-blue eyes twinkling with mischief, a smirk playing on his full pink lips. His bronze skin glowed, his long golden tresses tied back with a leather thong, strands drifting behind him on the breeze like beams of light almost haloing his head. I remembered the roughness of his hands as he caressed me, the warmth of his skin as I held him, the beat of his heart against my ear as we embraced.

Inhaling slowly, I remembered the smell of him, his natural scent mingled with strong lye soap, the scented oils he'd run through his beard and hair ... If I concentrated hard enough, I could almost hear him say my name.

"*Little fawn ...*"

I smashed my fists against the monument, my heart racing in my chest. Why did Vidar have to die? Why did the Nornir weave this fate for us? Why did they give us a dazzling love, a beautiful family, a wonderful life together, just to rip it all apart? Damn the Nornir – damn the gods – damn them all!

"Aveline, are you alright?"

I lurched backwards and spotted Jan standing a few paces away from me. He was frowning, his arms crossed over his chest. I gulped hard and dropped my hands from the runestone.

"What's the matter, Aveline?" Jan asked, taking a few steps closer to me.

I shook my head and swallowed, trying to dislodge the knot in my throat.

"I'm fine." I lied. "Come to the hall and tell me about Roskilde."

***

"IF ROSKILDE KEEPS up its progress, the stores will be filled to bursting by the time the first frost arrives." Jan said, settling himself at my table. "The fields are bountiful, thank the gods. They could do with more thralls for field labour, but the townspeople are getting along with what they have.

"Before I came here, I went to the mainland to see how the work was going there, and so far, so good. Depending on how harvesting goes after the þing, we may want to send twenty or so thralls from Aros to Roskilde. Aros has a good yield and is reaping it quickly, but Roskilde is booming with crops. Unless they get more labour to aid the harvest, much will rot in the fields by the time winter arrives."

I was hoping that having Jan tell me about his trip to Roskilde would draw my attention from the emotions storming inside me.

It didn't work. Although I heard Jan's words, I wasn't truly listening to him.

Jan didn't seem to notice for he continued relaying the goings on of Roskilde and Aros in full detail. He pulled a variety of tally sticks from his satchel and spread them over the table. He held them up one at a time and pointed to the notches, informing me which stick tallied the item, meat, fish or crop from which family.

I nodded along, catching every few words. Too restless to sit, I slowly paced the room, my arms crossed over my chest. At some point Rowena appeared before me, a cup of mead in her hands. Upon sight of me, her brows drew tight over her round, searching eyes. I accepted the cup, offering her a small, brief smile.

"It's fine – I'm alright." I whispered in Ænglisc.

Rowena's frown deepened, she didn't believe my lie. Regardless, she didn't press. She returned to the kitchen to continue pickling fish and salting pork, the odours of the tangy vinegar and briny fish were so strong, not even the pungent smoke of the many firepits burning in the hall could conceal the stench.

I closed my eyes and brought the mead to my lips, the sweet flavour dancing on my tongue. Vidar's kisses always tasted like this, honey mead, his favourite drink …

All of a sudden a dizzying nausea clutched my stomach and my whole body shook. My cup fell from my shuddering hands and thudded on the packed-dirt floor, mead splashing over my boots.

"Aveline!" Jan jumped to his feet.

The room spun, I wavered, holding my arms out to balance myself. I tried to stagger to the table, but I hardly made three steps before my legs gave way. With seemingly one swift movement, Jan caught me just in time. He held me against him, the only thing keeping me standing.

My heart hammered against my ribs so hard I thought it might burst. I struggled for each gasping breath and a cold sweat drenched my body. Powerless, I closed my eyes and drooped against Jan, the scent of sea water on his tunic filling my nostrils. His heart pounded just as fast as mine, I focussed on it, listened to the *thump-thump-thump*, his warm breath dancing on my hair.

The soothing rhythm of Vidar's heart had always calmed me …

ASHES REMAIN

I ripped myself from Jan's grasp and stumbled to the table, my eyes clamped shut. I gripped the tabletop, tried to focus on the solidity of it, but the whole world seemed flipped upside down.

Jan's shadow blanketed me, blocking out the light from the fire behind us. He crouched down beside my chair and the light cast over me again. Still Jan didn't say anything, he didn't reach to touch me, he sat on his heels, his stare weighing heavily on me.

Every part of Aros and Roskilde reminded me of Vidar, I couldn't even speak of Francia or the Kingdom of the East Angles without thinking of him. Before setting off on a voyage, I inspected our ships, following Vidar's steps exactly. In my mind, I heard Vidar's voice as I enquired about each ship, examining the mast, sail and rudder, the yearly repairs and the moss, animal hair, tar and tallow that filled the spaces between each plank.

There was not one thing I did in this damned place that didn't remind me of my late husband, that didn't remind me of the gaping hole in me caused by the death of him.

I couldn't even be comforted by Jan without thinking of Vidar. Jan was my closest companion and as much as I appreciated his friendship, as much as I enjoyed his company, it didn't feel right to be sitting together, just the two of us. Vidar was missing – it had always been the three of us but for those brief few years when Jan lived in Roskilde with his wife and son.

"Damn the gods …" I murmured as I caught my breath.

Jan placed his hand on my back.

"I'm here, Aveline." Jan said softly. "If you need me, I'm here."

***

THE UNSEASONABLY BALMY weather had quickly soured into the usual bitterness we expected this time of year. The wind had picked up, the mild warmth replaced by the bite of coldness, the days had grown shorter. I tugged my cloak around me, hoping the weather might warm up later on. It was still early morning, the sun had only risen two hours ago.

The ground was strewn with dry brown and faded gold leaves, crunching beneath and flittering about the hooves of our horses on the chilly wind. Hiding among the leaves were conkers fallen from horse chestnuts, snapped twigs and tree roots. A few fiery scarlet and yellow leaves clung to spindly tree branches, but the blustering wind sought to dislodge them all.

Three ships from Roskilde bobbed on the rolling waves of the fjord, anchored a little way from the docks, their raven banners flapping wildly in the salty wind. The ships were filled with people, the crew sat at their posts, ready to row to Odense.

Three ships from Aros, the warships Storm-Serpent and Oak-Blade, and a *karfi*, cargo ship, named Wind-Rider, were moored to the docks. Storm-Serpent and Oak-Blade were fully manned and loaded with passengers.

For the past two hours, my men strode across the gangplanks loading Wind-Rider with horses, trunks of belongings and cooking implements like pots, dishes and cutlery, sacks of food and mead, wooden beams and folded woollen tents that we would be camping in during our stay in Odense.

Some women were accompanying their men, bringing with them merchandise and wares to sell at the þing. Privately I wondered how many merchants or customers would be in attendance considering the haste in which this gathering had been organised.

I shook my head, trying to clear away the anxiety that ebbed into my mind. For now, I did not need to think of the þing, I needed to organise my people. Once we were on the water, I could consider what might happen there and form a plan to tackle each possibility, but not until then.

"*Móðir*," Young Birger called.

He trotted over to me on his beautiful red mare, Frár, with Einar sitting on the saddle in front of him. Smiling, I waved at them. Einar's cheeks were red and glowing from beneath his fur hood.

"*Mumie!*" Einar grinned, reaching for me.

I took his gloved hand in mine and kissed it.

"How is it looking?" I asked.

"Well, *móðir*, very well," Young Birger beamed. "We're almost set to leave."

"I'm glad to hear that," I replied. "I intend to set off shortly."

"Would you take Einar?" Young Birger said. "I need to get Frár onto Wind-Rider."

ASHES REMAIN

I nodded, took Einar by his waist and, with Young Birger's help, carefully removed him from the saddle. Einar's furs made his small form bulky, but I managed to set him on my hip. Einar held onto me, his legs clamped around my waist. He gripped a fistful of my coat in one of his hands and patted Frár with the other.

"Galinn asked permission to join us." Young Birger said, shifting forward in his saddle now Einar was off.

"Oh? I thought he wanted to stay here and help with the harvest?" I commented as nonchalantly as I could.

"He came to me early this morning as I was saddling Frár. He was dressed ready to leave at that very moment, carrying his pack and everything. He asked if he could come along after all and I didn't see harm in it."

"There isn't," I agreed. "Will Ósk be attending?"

"*Nei*, someone must take care of their farm. They still have a lot of preparations to take care of before winter."

"Before you load Frár, go to the hall and find three sturdy thralls. Take them to Ósk and tell her they are to aid her with her winter preparations while Galinn is away. Tell her – and the thralls – if she needs more labour, she must only go to the hall and fetch more. I want her ready our return – they have seven days."

"That's kind of you, *móðir*." Young Birger remarked admiringly.

"Off with you now." I said. "Do hurry, as I said before, I want to leave as soon as possible."

Young Birger nodded. He nudged Frár in her sides, tugged the rein to direct her around and cantered off towards the hall. I appreciated Young Birger's compliment, but I was far from being kind – gifting her the use of three thralls was not out of the kindness of my heart but a selfish action.

I remembered what Jan had said – that Ósk and Galinn did not approve of my being jarl. Perhaps if Galinn spoke against me at the þing, I could use the fact that I sent thralls to help his mother while we were away as evidence of my kindness, and as a tool to damage his reputation. Who is dishonourable enough to speak against the person who gives aid to his lonely mother?

"Are we ready, *mumie*?" Einar asked.

"*Já*, almost my love." I kissed the top of his head.

I carried Einar to the shore, our feet slipping on the wet, sludgy sand. I set him down near the dock that Storm-Serpent was tied to, and he hurried ahead of me, racing up the trembling planks.

Hallmundr and Ebbe were standing at the edge of the dock, watching the final few people and trunks board the ships. Sander was leaning over the side of the ship with Ebbe and Borghildr's three raven-haired sons, calling out to Hallmundr and Ebbe, peeking over the shields propped onto the gunwales of the ship. Before Einar could scurry up the dock on his own, Hallmundr scooped him up by his waist and held him under his arm like a sack, much to the boy's delight.

"Jarl," Hallmundr and Ebbe greeted me brightly.

"Is everything set?" I asked, grinning at Einar squirming in Hallmundr's grip.

"*Já* Jarl," Hallmundr said. "We just need this lot to get on and we can depart."

"Is Domnall on Wind-Rider already?"

"That he is, Jarl. He's waiting for word to load the gangplank." Ebbe said.

"Not yet, I have one more thing to load—"

"Aveline," I looked over my shoulder and spotted Jan striding towards us. "I saw Young Birger heading towards the hall, did he forget something?"

"He's running an errand for me." I answered. "He'll return shortly. When he and his horse are on Wind-Rider, we can depart."

"*Já*, Jarl." Jan nodded.

"Fetch Domnall, please. You both must be with me while we slaughter the goats." I said to Jan, who I had assigned as captain of the ship, Oak-Blade, and Domnall as captain of Wind-Rider.

The men agreed, Ebbe and Hallmundr strode up the dock to Storm-Serpent, where Hallmundr finally released Einar, safe on the longship. Jan, however, hadn't moved.

"What is it?" I lifted my eyebrows at him.

"We're with you, Jarl." Jan said out of the blue.

A fierce whirlwind raged in my stomach all morning, but the determination blazing in Jan's eyes burned away a lot of my anxiety. Four hundred men and women were ready to voyage to the þing and defend me, to fight for me to keep my title.

ASHES REMAIN

We were ready.

It had been seventeen days since I had been summoned, I had waited seventeen days to make this journey – it was time. It would take a full day and night to row to Odense, plus a day on foot to reach the þing grounds – less if we took minimal breaks, but considering how large a force we were, I didn't know how much time we could cut off ...

"*Þakka fyrir.*" I nodded, feeling a blush form on my cheeks.

With that, Jan turned and marched towards Wind-Rider to fetch Domnall. Soon enough, the two men strode down the gangplank and the dock, across the shore to where three goats were tethered by ropes to a post. As they dragged the goats across the shore to me, Young Birger appeared on Frár, the horse galloping happily over the sands, sure-footed and swift. My eldest son waved to me as he dismounted at the dock by Wind-Rider – Frár would be kept with the other animals and cargo on the *karfi*.

"The goats, Jarl." Domnall presented, a beaming grin peeking through the bushy red hairs of his beard.

"*Þakka fyrir,*" I smiled.

We returned to the edge of the fjord closest to Storm-Serpent, Jan and Domnall dragging the stubborn animals towards the water, the goats were afraid of the loud, crashing waves, jerking and flinching at the activity around them. The flock of wives that waved from the shore to their husbands on the ships approached us, standing a little way back from Jan, Domnall, the goats and me.

From a leather sheath hanging from my belt, I pulled my knife. I held it up to the sky and Jan brought forward the first goat, while Domnall struggled to keep the other two nervous goats from bucking and fleeing.

"Hail Njörðr,
Lord of the Vanir,
God of Wind and Seas,
Bountiful god, prosperous god,
God of Seafaring, Defender of Sailors,
Tamer of Winds and Calmer of Waters,
Father of Freyr and Freyja.
We gift you this goat
And ask for a swift journey in return.

GWENDOLINE SK TERRY

We honour you, Njörðr."

With that, I stood over the goat, grabbing the rope collar tight. I pressed the blade of my knife to the soft flesh goat's throat, just below its blocky head, with all the strength I could muster. I drew the knife swiftly across, slicing through skin, muscle and tendon, I could feel the heat of the goat's blood through my gloved hand as it poured from the wound. The animal screeched for only a moment before its body fell limp.

Jan dropped the tether of the dead goat and retrieved another goat from Domnall. The goat bucked and fought, rearing at the sight of the dead goat. It seemed to know what was coming …

"Hail Ægir!
Lord of the Ocean,
Mighty Brewer,
Generous Host of Ægirheim,
Husband of Ran, the Lady of the Sea,
Father of the Nine Waves,
We gift you this goat
And ask for a safe journey in return.
We honour you, Ægir.
We honour you, Ran.
We honour the Nine Waves."

Again, I approached the goat, stood over it, took its collar and swiftly sliced its neck open. Blood gushed over my gloved fingers, my blade dripping red. Jan dropped its body on the shore again, both the goats' blood seeping and staining the sands scarlet. Domnall brought forward the final goat, it fought so hard, both men had to hold onto it.

"Hail Odin!
Allfather, One-Eyed One,
Ruler of Valhalla,
Lord of the Æsir,
God of Wisdom and Battle,
Warrior and Wanderer,

ASHES REMAIN
Knower of All Things,
Husband of Frigg, the Allmother.
We gift you this goat
And ask for your blessings on our journey.
We honour you, Odin."

For the final time, I grabbed the remaining goat's rope collar and gripped it tight. It flailed and flipped, but Jan and Domnall held it tight. The moment my blade sliced its throat, the goat emitted a raucous cry. I continued on, panting and groaning, digging the knife into the goat's throat.

With a swift jerk, the struggling beast managed to pull away, its blood spurting all over my skirts. I grunted, its screeching wails piercing my ears. My fingers were still wrapped tight around the rope collar, I dragged the goat towards me with an almighty heave and shoved the knife into its neck, ripping the blade swiftly across and cutting its throat wide open.

Finally, the animal fell to the ground, dead.

"We dedicated these animals to the gods. Hail!" I shouted, grimacing at the bloody state of my skirts.

"Hail!" Jan, Domnall and the crowd replied, the ritual ended.

A group of women approached me as I cleaned the knife's blade on my sodden skirts, the blue wool splattered in dripping blood. Between them, they collected the dead goats and carried them up to the shore, to be cooked and shared with the townspeople, as most animals were after sacrificing them.

"You alright there, Jarl?" Domnall asked.

"It's time to board the ships." I grumbled.

Domnall and Jan nodded before the three of us headed to our designated ships. Upon the dock, I heard Jan, his voice slightly muffled by the howl of the wind, ordering his men to remove shields from the gunwales. I made my way up the dock barking orders to my crew, the wooden structure swaying somewhat under foot, and crossed the wobbling gangplank onto Storm-Serpent.

All my warriors were in position by the oars, the women and children arranged at the mast, sitting on trunks or musty old blankets on the damp floor. Everyone was ready. I spotted Einar,

Æsa and Sander sitting with Borghildr and her raven-haired brood, three sons and one daughter, closest to the mast.

Borgunna, Ebbe and Borghildr's only daughter, was Æsa's dearest friend. They were cackling together over something, while Sander and the two eldest boys were having a very vivid conversations, their arms waving about, laughing just as hard as the two girls. Ebbe and Borghildr's youngest son and Einar were sitting at Borghildr's feet playing with some small wooden horses.

"Are you ready?" I asked the children, who cheered in reply.

"I am too, *móðir*." Young Birger said behind me.

I grinned.

"Frár is loaded?"

"As is the gangplank."

"Excellent. Let's set off." I strode down the ship to the rudder, which I would man as captain, and barked orders to my crew, "Remove the shields! Untie the lines! It's time!"

Once rowed far enough into the fjord and away from the land, the wind had picked up tremendously. By luck, it was blowing to the south – the direction we wanted to go. The oars were set down and the masts of the six ships were hoisted upwards, immediately the six ships soared over the water.

Were the gods on my side? Perhaps. The fierce north-wind would cut the time it would take to reach Odense immensely, we'd be able to set up camp earlier and I would be able to face these nine jarls ready and prepared.

Or were the gods gifting me favourable sailing conditions so they might watch my fall sooner? If the north-wind continued to blow as harshly upon our return to Aros, it would take us a long time battling it to reach our home, not to mention the north-wind was usually a sign that a cold winter was coming. Would snow be coming soon? We hadn't finished harvesting or preparing for the winter yet, it was still too soon for snow.

I glared up at the sky, my lips curling into a grimace.

"Damn you," I murmured. "You fickle monsters."

CHAPTER EIGHT

THE LONGSHIPS BOUNCED on the churning waters, the icy waves crashing against the hull. The wind whipped across the beams and rigging, bulging the sail, and propelling us forward at such a speed my face and hands stung, and my ears rang. Tossed so viciously, the planks of the clinker-built longships shrieked, and the vessels tipped steeply left and right, a terrifying and exhilarating experience all at once. Everything held tight, as I knew it would, for these ships had been masterfully crafted. The only thing we had to fear was the will of the gods.

Thankfully, the raging sea did not take us. We rowed up Odense Fjord, passing many variously sized islands, their sandy shores hidden beneath the roiling waves. Forests of elm, oak, hornbeam, and beech were scattered around the lands, rising from long prickly grass, their brittle leaves and arching branches battered by the winds.

We arrived safely on Fyn, one of the largest islands inhabited by the Danes. The þing place was a few hours ride from the shore. Beneath the leaden sky, everything was devoid of colour, the great crowns of the trees had lost their lustre – the autumn leaves were muted not copper or gold as they were meant to be this time of year. The grass was dull, and the tall wild bushes were merely shaggy clusters of stems and branches, skeletons of the beautiful vegetation they once were.

I would've liked to have visited Odense on a brighter day, to see its landscape in its true glory, not this shadowed, colourless sight before me now. The bitter cold had robbed autumn of its colour signifying an early winter. I turned my gaze to the bay. The weathered docks were dangerously indistinguishable from the steely water. I spotted a dockyard on the bank, a few half-built ships perched on the muddy ground, lengths of masterfully hewn wood piled at the foot of a cluster of birch trees.

GWENDOLINE SK TERRY

I shielded my eyes from the spray of the water and peered at the land, the village of Odense was small – it was just a settlement, not even a town, but it was famous for the devout Odin worshippers who lived there and maintained the sacred þing grounds in the name of law, honour and the gods.

My ships were moored to the docks. Wind-Rider's crew unloaded the horses and chests of belongings, while the people on Oak-Blade and Storm-Serpent disembarked. Half the crew from each ship remained onboard, scooping buckets of water from inside the ships and tossing it overboard.

I strode into the little seaport, my clothing soaked from the hellacious journey, my wet skirts heavy and slapping about my legs. Soon enough, I found the head of the settlement, an old silver-haired man named Óðalríkr. I paid Óðalríkr handsomely to keep my ships safely on land, away from the choppy waves. Ours were not the only ships in Odense, there were at least twenty others.

It took a few hours for all three of my ships to be dragged inland. Óðalríkr was kindly (perhaps because of the ridiculous sum I'd paid him), he ordered his men to help unload Wind-Rider and pull my three ships ashore, docking them safely beside his own, while the twenty other ships were left rocking precariously on the waters with nothing but lines tied to the posts of the docks keeping them from capsizing.

"A woman jarl is bizarre," Óðalríkr said, as I mounted my ash-grey horse, Stjarna. "But considering the masses gathered here to support you, I'd wager you're just as good as any man."

"*Þakka fyrir*," I smiled.

"When you return, your title will be secured." Óðalríkr said, nodding knowingly. "There's a reason why the Nornir weaved this trial into your tapestry. Odin doesn't give his blessings freely, one must earn them. This is your chance to prove yourself and become something no other woman has before."

"*That which is worth having is worth sacrificing for, and that which you must sacrifice for is worth having absolutely.*" I quoted the words the Allfather had spoken to me though this man didn't know that. I hadn't told anyone but Vidar what the Allfather said to me. "I've been given trouble alright, but I intend to return here triumphant."

"We will make a sacrifice to the gods for you." Óðalríkr beamed.

"You show bias for me, Óðalríkr." I smiled.

"These men would not follow you here if you were not worthy. You have received the Allfather's blessings before, that much is obvious, otherwise you would not be here. You are a warrior, *já*? You have fought with your men?" He asked, and I nodded in confirmation. "You know the runes? You know how to speak to the gods? How to conduct the sacred blóts?"

"*Já*, I do. I know all of these things."

"Of course, you do, you wouldn't be jarl without that knowledge." Óðalríkr laughed. "You have Odin's blessings, Jarl Aveline, and so will you have mine. I'll show bias for the one that Odin favours. I see his messengers are here to make sure I do."

He pointed behind me where a pair of ravens were perched on the gnarled branch of an old oak tree. I smiled at the twinkle in the old man's eye as he gazed at the birds.

"Tell your master, we hear him." I called to them, noticing the white swirl in one of the raven's eyes.

Óðalríkr made a noise of delight – probably pleased I'd acknowledged the ravens rather than rolled my eyes. I passed him a final smile before I nudged Stjarna in her flanks with my heels. We trotted down the length of the procession my people were forming, making sure they were ready to leave. After checking on those at the very end of the procession, I galloped to the head, ready to lead my people. Jan and Domnall were there, waiting for me. I announced we were ready to go, Domnall brought his curved horn to his lips and blew through it, one long, deep blast. Chatter amongst the people ceased instantly.

It was time.

"*Þakka* again, Óðalríkr." I called. "We'll be back in three days."

"And you will return victorious!" Óðalríkr shouted. "Odin is with you!"

***

ÞING PLACE, DENMARK

I HADN'T EXPECTED the þing place to be as bustling as it was. Even from a distance, we could spot the ocean of pitched canvas tents, smoke streaming from countless blazing fire pits, a multitude of vending stalls and stands, and makeshift pens filled with livestock to be sold.

Jan and I shared a surprised glance between ourselves as we approached the Place, intrigued by such a large gathering on such short notice. Obviously, the local people were taking advantage of the situation – perhaps they thought that with ten jarls gathered, supported each by their own large retinues, there might be a lot of coin to be made.

Faces turned to stare at me, whispering and muttering behind hands, eyes wide with fascination. I knew what they all were thinking, a woman at the head of such a large procession of warriors and supports? The rumours were true! A woman jarl …

I held my head high and slowly made my way through the throng, seldom making eye contact with those about me. I may have looked haughty, perhaps I even looked contemptuous, but I didn't care. I couldn't trust a single face in the crowds – who knew which of them supported me and whom were against me.

We pushed through, ambling slowly on our horses, the wheels of carts and wagons in the middle of the procession roiling in the dirt roads created by the heavy foot traffic. Everywhere merchants were peddling their wares, women thrust fabrics and freshly baked bread into the crowds, attempting to lure customers with the quality of the materials and the delicious aromas of the food. Brewmasters were selling kegs and casks of ale and mead, various scents permeating the air from their stands.

Of course, we even found Herra Kaupmaðr. I paused in front of his grand stall, glaring at him from over the heads of his customers. Herra caught sight of me, staring at me excitedly as he presented his wares to the eager horde.

Pots of pungent spices lined his table along with casks of salt and bottles of oil and wine. He had ceramics, terracotta amphorae and pottery, rolls upon rolls of silk, richly designed fabrics, brocades, linen and woven cloth. He had expensive perfumes and dyes of colours I had never seen before. And, standing at the end of his stall on a platform were his thralls. Five women and five men, all gorgeously exotic with olive skin and thick black curls springing from their heads, their eyes as black as coal.

ASHES REMAIN

"–Silks from the lands to the East! Spices from the Arab lands, and beautiful thralls from *Miklagarðr*!" Herra announced, pointing at or lifting items as he listed them off.

"*Miklagarðr?*" I pondered aloud, dragging a long-forgotten memory to the forefront of my mind. "That's ... Constantinople, the great fortressed city far south of the Norse lands."

"It is, indeed, my dear Jarl Aveline." Herra grinned.

He was visibly surprised and impressed by my knowledge – as I was astonished by his remarkable hearing. A normal man wouldn't have heard my quiet words over the din surrounding us, but Herra – with his faults and his strengths – was not a normal man.

"The city is over a thousand years old and has been known by many names during its time, due in part to the many ancient peoples who have taken it in the past. Five hundred years ago, the city was renamed *Constantinople* after the death of the Roman Emperor, Constantine the Great."

Herra Kaupmaðr turned to the large crowds thronging him, enthralled by the wisdom the eccentric little merchant shared.

"As our wise and wonderful Jarl Aveline said, *Miklagarðr* is a great fortressed city." Herra continued. "Not only is it the largest and wealthiest city in the world, home to magnificent palaces, towers and domes – but it is famed for its defences! Layers of walls surround the city both on land and sea, varying in elevation, with palisades and moats in between! It is almost completely surrounded by sea, but for one side, and there they built huge walls. Why, the city is practically impregnable!

"Needless to say, the product from this town is unparalleled by anything else in the world!" Herra grinned. "And luckily for you all, I have been to the city, and I have acquired as many goods as my ships could carry, so that *you* might be able to own for yourself one of the wondrous items from the Great City!"

I tilted my head and rolled my lips together. I had heard of Constantinople only once before, many years ago, from a thrall who had come from those lands. Though I had never seen it, the thrall had explained the city to me in rich detail, I could picture the shining place in my mind, its tall buildings and vast, sweet-smelling gardens bursting with flowers like roses and snapdragons.

I shook my head, departing my mind from my memories. I nudged Stjarna in the flanks and continued on through the crowds.

"Jarl! Jarl Aveline!" Herra called, leaving his men to handle the sales. "Jarl!"

I hesitated, unsure whether I wanted to speak to the Swede.

"Aveline, Herra is calling you." Jan said.

I rolled my eyes, let out a blustering sigh and grudgingly stopped. Jan made my decision for me it seemed. I didn't want to explain myself to him – I purposely ignored his quizzical expression – instead I stopped and let the merchant approach me.

I had not spoken to Herra for many years … I knew I would have to swallow my pride and make peace with him at some point, I had put it off for as long as I could. I supposed if there was any time to reconcile it was now when I needed the support of as many as possible to defend my title.

"Jarl Aveline, I give you my sympathies for the death of Jarl Vidar." Herra said, bowing low to me. "I know he sits at Odin's side now. I apologise for not offering my condolences sooner."

"*Þakka fyrir*," I said stiffly, eyeing the gaudily dressed little man.

Herra Kaupmaðr's short figure was wrapped in garishly colourful billowing silks and a cloak made of mink, ermine and sable pelts. His clothing was edged with marten fur from the tops of his thick leather boots to the hems of his tunic and otter skin gloves. His wiry saffron hair peeked out beneath his bulky marten fur hat, and the strong scent of lye soap oozed from him, the stuff he used to bleach his mane. He did not bleach his beard, though, it remained orange like amber, his natural colouring.

Given the right amount of time and payment, Herra Kaupmaðr could find anything on earth. He was the richest and most famous merchant in all the Norse lands – so rich I was sure if the nomadic old Swede decided to settle, he was wealthy enough to be a king.

"It's been a long time since I've been lucky enough to lay my eyes on you, Jarl Aveline." Herra said. "Last we spoke I angered you and I've not had the chance to apologise to you. I apologise for not seeking you out sooner to make amends. Shortly after the – ah – *situation*, Jarl Vidar explained to me that my behaviour towards the thrall disturbed you greatly – he also advised me to let you approach me rather than the other way around.

ASHES REMAIN

"I took his advice, but, forgive my brazenness, with the amount of time that has gone by, I didn't know if you'd contact me. I'd like to take this moment not just to offer my condolences, but to apologise as well. I never intended to affront you, dear Jarl."

"What's done is done, Herra." I replied coldly. "That was years ago, the thrall has since died."

"*Já*," Herra replied, nodding solemnly.

He knew what had happened to poor Caterine, and Alffinna, too, his grave expression said as much. Many had flocked to the hall to give their condolences to Vidar and me – though I hadn't been in any state to receive anyone or do anything for that matter, Vidar and our children had done that without me. My mind was focussed on nothing but Alffinna during that time.

I remembered a few comments made between my children, the townspeople, between Jan and Vidar – the latter two remarking on Herra's absence in a quiet moment together, but I had heard it. At the time I hadn't cared, but now I did. For Vidar to be the one to tell Herra to keep his distance … I didn't know how I felt about that. I glared at Herra as he allowed a few polite moments of silence to pass before he continued.

"Despite your feelings towards me, Jarl, I want you to know I support you and your cause."

"You're going to become very unpopular here with that opinion." I stated, noticing a man behind him spit in my direction.

"The odds may be against you, Jarl, but the gods are not."

"Oh *já* – you know that do you?" I asked dryly.

"Of course! The gods only favour the brave." The merchant beamed, before adding with a wink, "Besides, no one can strike a quarrel with me – I'm Herra Kaupmaðr!"

***

WE MADE CAMP away from the other tents. There were broad clearings on three sides of our encampment, the fourth side facing the other tents. We were close enough to join any festivities at night but far enough away in case we might need to make a hurried exit. I didn't expect too much trouble, (I hoped not, at least), but it didn't hurt to prepare for the worst.

GWENDOLINE SK TERRY

Standing in front of my tent, I examined the people passing by, absentmindedly stroking Vidar's wedding band. I'd left my tent for fresh air, feeling stifled inside the woollen walls of the temporary abode. Giggles drifted to my ears from behind me where Sander, Æsa and Einar played with Borgunna and her younger brothers. Young Birger was with his friends a few tents down.

Night was falling, breath fell from lips in frigid plumes and fires roared in simple braziers, filling the chilled air with smoke. People stood around rubbing their hands and talking together in groups. Though laughter echoed about the grounds, the air was heavy with tension. I saw how the other jarls' retinues glanced at me and my camp. They mingled with each other, leaving distance between them and my people. Even those who were drunk did not socialise with my men nor even hurl insults at them, to my surprise.

A crowd nearby broke apart to allow a man through. He approached me like a shadow slipping through the twilight, I couldn't see his face.

"Aveline, it's nice to see you again." Jarl Borgulf called.

"I didn't realise it was you." I said, cocking my brow at him.

"You might not have noticed me, Jarl Aveline, but it wasn't difficult to notice you. You made quite the entrance."

"What do you mean by that?" I barked.

"Barging through the marketplace as though you were a queen."

"Is that what my adversaries are saying?"

"*Já*, it is."

"What a compliment they pay me if they thought I looked *queenly* riding through a few stalls and stands." I replied sarcastically.

"Oh, how I missed your wit!" Jarl Borgulf said, his smile permanently in place. "I was wondering when you'd appear here."

"You gave me three weeks, I'm precisely on time."

"You are indeed." Borgulf chuckled. "Would you be kind enough to invite me into your tent? It's rather chilly out here."

"What do you want, Jarl Borgulf?" I said, rooted to the spot.

"I wanted to see how you were, find out how your preparations for tomorrow are going. Tomorrow is the day you defend your title after all! You must be nervous to say the least."

Tomorrow. So, my trial would begin immediately ...

"What time am I to appear before the jarls?"

ASHES REMAIN
"Noon. Is that enough time for you to ready yourself?"
"I've been ready since the moment I was summoned."

***

"WHAT DID HE want?" Jan asked, appearing beside me as Jarl Borgulf sauntered off.

"I'm to defend my title at noon tomorrow." I replied, watching the jarl join his people, a cup of drink thrust into his hand.

"Tell me what you want me to do and I'll do it."

"Be ready."

I had expected a full day and night to ready myself, though of course I should've known my trial would take place promptly. I'd had three weeks to prepare for this, three weeks to imagine every argument these jarls might hurl at me and formulate a rebuttal for each one. I had obsessed over everything, I was as ready as I was ever going to be and yet ... The moment was here.

I took a deep breath.

"Borgulf said I made *quite the entrance*." I grumbled.

"Not only did everyone see *you*, Aveline, but they saw your retinue as well. None of the jarls brought as many people as you." Jan said – unfortunately he didn't succeed in reassuring me.

"The numbers of those who oppose me are far greater than those who support me." I murmured.

"Where is this doubt coming from? It doesn't matter how many of them there are. You *are* Jarl of Aros and Roskilde – *your* people wouldn't have accepted you if they didn't have complete faith in you. Every warrior assembled here to support you *will* give their lives for you. Don't doubt yourself – and don't doubt them."

I turned to Jan, wide-eyed. He had spoken with such fierce confidence, my heart stood still. He was right – of course I knew my men were here to support me and yet, when Jan said that – *how* he said it ... I had nothing to fear.

I reached out and placed my hand over Jan's heart, feeling the faint beat of it against my palm. Jan rested his hand on my shoulder, squeezing it gently.

"I hope it won't come to that." I said. "It heartens me to know you're ready and willing, though."

"I'm honoured to fight beside you and I'll be honoured to die supporting your cause." Jan said.

"I won't die for this." I scoffed.

Jan's brows shot to the top of his face.

"I won't die for this, because it will not come to battle." I grinned. "As you said, I *am* Jarl of Aros and Roskilde – nine men cannot take that from me and they won't convince my army to change their minds. When we leave in three days, I *will* still be Jarl of Aros and Roskilde."

Jan beamed at me.

"By the gods, you will be, Aveline."

ASHES REMAIN
CHAPTER NINE

"I AM AVELINE Birgersdóttir, and I am here to defend my title!"

"Women shall not speak at the þing!" Jarl Lingvi Gunnarsson of Viborg bellowed. "Did the Lawspeaker not just state the laws? *Only a freeman shall speak and cast his vote in the þing. A freewoman cannot bear witness nor speak at the þing.*"

"As Jarl of Aros and Roskilde, I *will* be heard, regardless of my sex!" I scowled, hot fury pulsing in my veins.

"You are not a jarl yet, Aveline Birgersdóttir," Jarl Lingvi retorted. "That is for *us* to decide!"

It took every ounce of strength I had to not rip my sword from its sheath and run it through the damned jarl in front of me. The assembly had begun only a short while ago, the Lawspeaker had recited the laws following which the jarls introduced themselves.

The nine jarls were sitting on ornately carved chairs in a row, each with two men, their advisors, standing behind them. The Lawspeaker stood a few paces from the jarls, dutifully maintaining a stony face throughout the proceedings. People crowded in front of the jarls in a sort of semi-circle, leaving a healthy distance between the jarls and themselves. I stood in that empty space for no chair was offered to me.

Jan stood on my right, Young Birger and Sander on my left, my younger children behind me with Borghildr, Ebbe, Domnall and the others. My warriors surrounded the rest of the crowd forming a wall of men around the people, assumedly unable to see much transpiring between the jarls and me. Obviously Lingvi had assumed Jan was beside me to speak on my behalf, for my sons were not yet old enough. Despite the law, as Jarl of Aros and Roskilde, no one spoke for me – I *would* speak for myself.

"Vidar Alvarsson is dead. Alvar the First One is dead." I said as calmly as I could, glaring at Lingvi. "Aros and Roskilde are both without jarls until the sons of Vidar Alvarsson come of age. As the widow of Vidar Alvarsson and the mother of his heirs, I lay claim to his jarldoms. The warriors of Aros and Roskilde will attest to my worthiness. I've fought beside them, I've spilt the blood of our enemies *with* them. Do not refuse me because I am a woman, for I have fought with as much honour and bravery as any man!"

"That does not change the fact that you *are* a woman," Porsi Hard-Bone, Jarl of Heiðabýr, said matter-of-factly. "And women *cannot* become jarls nor speak at the þing by law! Lawspeaker, recite the laws of which Aveline Birgersdóttir is breaking!"

"*A woman is prohibited from participating in political activities. She may not become a jarl, she may not be a judge. A freewoman cannot bear witness nor speak at the þing.*" The Lawspeaker recited.

"You have broken each law!" Porsi exclaimed.

A handful of the jarls sitting beside him nodded and mumbled their agreement.

"Furthermore, you are a foreigner. Man or woman, why would we allow a foreigner to rise to such a rank?" Jarl Lingvi added.

"Rich coming from you, Jarl Lingvi. Your mother was Frankish, was she not? Why were *you* allowed to rise to such a rank when you are only *half* Dane?" I asked, a wave of snickers and giggles passing through the crowd.

Lingvi glowered at me, his hands balled into fists. Beside him, Jarl Borgulf leaned forward in his chair and stroked his beard, chuckling. He seemed to be the only jarl amused by my taunt – Lingvi certainly wasn't.

Three of the nine jarls politely hid their smiles behind their hands, whereas Lingvi and the four other jarls glared at me. They were visibly outraged by my snide comment and brazen attitude, how dare a woman stand before them and speak for herself.

The idea of a female jarl, especially one who was seeking to obtain *two* jarldoms, was terrifying for them. I controlled a vastly bigger army than many of theirs (especially Jarl Lingvi's), of course they were threatened by me. That's why they called me here.

"Why do you allow this woman to speak?" A man called out from the crowd.

I scowled at him. I didn't recognise him – he must've been from one of the other jarl's retinues – perhaps Lingvi's considering his anger seemed to match Lingvi's own …

"Do not concern yourself with what's between my legs, it's none of your business." I snarled at the man. "As Jarl of Aros and Roskilde, I *will* speak."

"You impertinent creature!" Jarl Lingvi spat. "You exhibit your disregard for the law so shamelessly! Were your husband here, I wonder what he would make of your insolence?"

"Were my husband here, Jarl, *we* wouldn't be."

Laughter rippled through the crowds once again.

"Is this all a joke to you?" Lingvi demanded.

"Not at all, Jarl Lingvi." I replied. "What I do find funny, however, is that you won't grant me permission to speak at my own trial! *You* summoned *me* here! I stand before you ready to defend my title, yet you try to silence me every time I open my mouth!"

"If you want to speak here, woman, then you must find a *man* to speak on your behalf!" Jarl Lingvi snapped.

"My husband is *dead*, my sons are not yet old enough to speak at the þing and I have no living male relatives." I growled. "Regardless that I have not a single man to speak on my behalf, I am jarl, I demand to speak for myself."

"You are asking for special treatment." Jarl Askold of Ribe said.

"I am not." I replied firmly. "I am asking for *equal* treatment. I am a jarl like you nine standing here in front of me, and I demand to be treated the same. I have led my men into battle, I have spilled blood with them, I have honoured the gods – I have done *everything* my equals have done. Why must I be treated differently because I don't have a cock between my legs?"

"I'll give you a cock between your legs!" Someone in the crowd heckled.

"Silence!" Bellow Jarl Lingvi, pointing into the crowd.

"I am Jarl of Aros and Roskilde, I need no one else to speak for me." I continued unperturbed.

"You do not have the title yet, woman." Jarl Lingvi remarked.

"Say that to the four-hundred warriors who have come here to support my claim–"

My men interrupted me, their cheers deafening, echoing brilliantly across the clearing in which we stood. I didn't try to conceal my pride at their deep resonating shouts, nor did I try to silence them. I basked in the glory of their din, before raising my hands to silence them. Immediately the noise ceased.

"–I would've brought hundreds more, Jarl Lingvi, but you chose harvesting time to summon me, a most inconvenient time for all involved, I'm sure." I said, privately taking pleasure in the vein throbbing on Jarl Lingvi's broad brow. "By refusing to hear me, Jarl Lingvi, you refuse to hear the voices of my people. Aros and Roskilde *will* be heard, and they support my claim to my late-husband's jarldoms, regardless that I am a woman."

"Then pick one of your loyal supporters to speak on your behalf!" Jarl Lingvi roared over the din of my men's ovations. "You were summoned here to answer for breaking the law, you are accused of claiming a man's title – now you demand to speak at the þing as well? I will not have the laws so blatantly disregarded!"

"Our laws *will* be respected. I demand this trial be adjourned until you can find a man to speak for you. We will listen to what the men of Aros and Roskilde have to say – but we will hear it from a man's tongue – not yours."

"Do you not hear them? My warriors are here, shouting for their Jarl! As their Jarl, it is my duty to speak for them and I will *not* relinquish that duty!"

"Which is why a woman cannot be jarl! If you cannot speak for your people at the þing, how can you be expected to undertake every other duty a jarl must assume? A woman simply isn't suited for such a position!" Lingvi argued.

"There is a simple solution to all of this." Jarl Borgulf interrupted, standing up from his chair. "You wish to retain your position – of course you do, who wouldn't? – and you wish to speak at the þing. The simplest thing for you to do would be to remarry."

My jaw dropped, a red wave of fury crashed over me. The cheek of him! How dare Borgulf suggest such a thing – and in front of so many people! How dare he embarrass me like this in front of my people, the other jarls and their retinues!

"Find a man or jarl that your warriors would support. If he is unchallenged, he would make an appropriate husband for you. He would take on your late-husband's jarldoms and you would become jarlkona – not jarl, but you will still retain the privileges and wealth of your high station. When your sons come of age, they could inherit the jarldoms should anything happen to their stepfather, your new husband. You would also have a man who could speak on your behalf at the þing."

The other jarls nodded in agreement.

"You know your men well, do you, Aveline Birgersdóttir?" Jarl Askold Hófsson of Ribe asked.

I nodded, unable to speak from the rage blazing inside me.

"Then you should know who is worthy to choose for your husband." Jarl Askold said. "Jarl Borgulf is correct, that would be the simplest solution to all of your problems. You would no longer be breaking the law by holding a man's position and you would have a man to speak at the þing whom might convey whatever issues you could possibly have.

"I propose that, should you agree to these terms by this time tomorrow when this trial reconvenes, we will forgive your impertinence and show mercy to you for your transgressions against the law." Jarl Askold said. "You will still be subjected to punishment for your open disregard to multiple laws, but your punishment would be lenient in return for your cooperation."

Jarl Askold was not unkind – his green eyes gazed at me unblinking, beseeching me to consider the option they had offered me. I could not appreciate it, however, for even their very suggestion reeked of defeat for me. *I* was jarl. I refused to relinquish my position, no matter who to.

"And if I don't, Jarl Askold?"

"Then the offer for mercy will be rescinded. You better have a man here to speak on your behalf tomorrow." Jarl Lingvi replied.

"Finding a suitable husband should not be difficult for you." Jarl Borgulf urged. "Between Aros, Roskilde and all your settlements, you have of the largest armies. Men will be clamouring to become your husband considering what you have to offer them! You will be able to make a fine match indeed."

"Whether you like it or not, Aveline Birgersdóttir, you must swallow your pride and realise that this is what's right for you to do." Jarl Mats Olafsson of Alabu said matter-of-factly. "Being a jarl is simply not a suitable position for a woman. I understand that you have fought beside your men and headed a *single* raid so far, but no matter how successful that raid was, a woman just doesn't have the fortitude or disposition to lead battle after battle, raid after raid. You were lucky once, but the chances of lightning striking in the same place twice are few and far between."

"There are places for women and men, women are supposed to stay and run the household while the men must battle and fight." The Jarl of Kaupmannahǫfn said.

"What do you think you'll gain from battle? A place at Odin's table? Unfortunately, dear woman, that is a place for men and men alone. You are more likely to become a Valkyrie than sit beside Odin!" The Jarl of Vorbasse scoffed, his round eyes protruding from his plump face.

"I seek to retain my position for the sake of my sons and the sake of my people while I'm alive." I spat. "What happens after I die is of no concern to me – the gods can do with me what they like when I am dead."

"Think of your sons and your people, then, while you weigh your options." The Jarl of Kaupmannahǫfn said. "Do you people need an obstinate woman with high opinions of herself, or do they need a man with the strength, build and power to lead them and protect them?"

"I—"

"Silence!" Jarl Lingvi bellowed. "We will reconvene tomorrow at noon. Have your decision ready by then, Aveline Birgersdóttir."

***

AFTER JARL LINGVI postponed my trial, I shoved through the crowds and returned to my tent, where I had been fuming ever since. Young Birger had slipped in at one point to let me know that he and his younger siblings were going to spend the afternoon in Ebbe and Borghildr's tent before disappearing.

Outside darkness was falling, the scent of meat drifted on fire smoke. The chill of the cold evening crept in through the gaps of the woollen tent walls, but the rage boiling inside me protected me from the chilly touch of air.

No one had dared enter my tent. I could hear voices outside, my people conversing about what had transpired, wondering what my decision would be. Luckily, from what I had heard, my people seemed to agree with my decision, they supported my right to the jarldoms despite me being a woman. Of course, if any had disagreed, they would've been foolish to admit it outside of my tent, but I held to the hope that my people supported me, every one of them.

Jarl Borgulf ... Damn that man. How dare he suggest I marry? How dare he! His blatant attempt to usurp control of my jarldoms was shocking, he infuriated me by proposing to me in my hall three weeks ago, and now he announced that idea in front of eight other jarls and all their men? Advertising me as an advantageous widow available for acquisition! What was I – a prize sow?!

"Urgh!" I snatched a cup from a low table and hurled it across the tent.

The cup hit the woollen wall with a feeble thump, falling to the ground and rolling a short way on the canvas covered floor. The anticlimactic noise only enhanced my anger. Just as I prepared to kick the nearest chest with all my might, Jan poked his head through the door flap.

"Aveline?"

"What do you want?" I demanded, dropping my skirts – I'd hitched them up over my knees to kick the chest.

"I was wondering whether you'd reached a decision regarding your trial." Jan said, slipping into the tent.

"*Nei*, I haven't." I grumbled.

"They're interviewing your men out there – asking them their opinions on you and your rule." Jan said. "You'll be pleased to know that everyone is giving quite illustrious accounts on your behalf."

I *was* glad of it – I was pleased my men were defending me. And yet ... All at once, exhaustion crashed over me. I dropped myself onto the wooden chest and held my face in my hands, groaning. Jan strode across the tent and crouched beside me, I could see his arms resting on his knees through the gaps in my fingers, his hands entwined together, his long tawny locks cascaded over his shoulders. Slowly I looked up at him, his sapphire eyes exuding concern.

"This whole trial is ridiculous."

"I want to beat Jarl Lingvi within inches of his life." Jan said.

I couldn't help but grin.

"He's an insufferable pig." I remarked.

"Were he actually a pig, I'd have slaughtered him and cooked him for my evening meal by now."

"I wouldn't waste the effort, I'm sure his temper has rotten him to the core."

"You're probably right, but I would so enjoy seeing him roast on a spit." Jan said, gazing off wistfully for a moment. "Still, we have to deal with the swine."

"I don't know what to do, Jan. That Borgulf bastard wants my jarldom, I know it. That's why he suggested I marry." I sighed, rubbing my face in my hands again. "He proposed to me back in Aros, before he summoned me."

"You don't want to marry him." Jan said firmly.

"I realise that," I said. "What do you know of him?"

"Honestly?" Jan said, standing up. "I met him when I was a child, just before Vidar's first wedding. I didn't see him much, but for the wedding itself and the few occasions he and his father visited Roskilde. He really isn't a bad man, his reputation is good, Lund is successful under his control from what I've gathered, but he's the same smarmy arse as when he was a boy."

"I don't care to marry a smarmy arse."

"I'm glad to hear it."

He was quiet for a moment, he crossed his arms over his chest, pursed his lips and drew his brows together. Did he want to say something? What was holding him back from saying it – whatever *it* was?

"Aveline, if you married Borgulf you'd be a queen, you know this right? He – he could be beneficial to you." Jan said slowly. "He doesn't just rule Lund, he has numerous settlements under his power, too."

"He says he only has an army of five hundred." I replied.

"His immediate army from Lund is five hundred, *já*. I spoke with his men last night and this evening and I understand he has far more than that he can call on should he need to. He's coy – he doesn't want to tell everyone everything. The eight other jarls – they're all on the same side now, but what of when they decide to attack each other? Everyone ought to keep at least a few secrets." Jan said. "Of course, that could be drunken talk, all lies and spectacle to make their jarl look more powerful than he is, but even with five hundred, between the two of you, your army would crush most enemies in its wake."

"What of *his* sons? Does he have any that stand to inherit his jarldom?" I asked.

"Yes, two I believe."

"And their ages?"

"Old enough to speak at the þing."

"If I married him, his sons would inherit the jarldoms before Young Birger and Sander could – my sons would be robbed of their birth rights."

"Which is why you shouldn't marry him. You should know what you stand to gain if you did, however." Jan said.

"Say I married Borgulf, I would become a queen and he a king – but when Borgulf dies, his sons would inherit his jarldoms, *including* Aros and Roskilde. His sons would not want to relinquish nor split a *king*dom. My sons would have to fight them. They should not have to fight to get what is rightfully theirs, only defend it." I said. "I don't care to become a queen, Jan, I just want to look after Vidar's jarldoms until my sons can rule them."

"I understand and I agree. You shouldn't marry Borgulf."

"I still need to make a decision – after how today went, things aren't looking good. But for bickering, they wouldn't listen to me." I grumbled. "How will I convince them to hear me tomorrow? I refuse to have a warrior speak on my behalf and I plan to reject their terms of remarrying."

"Perhaps marry a man without sons?" Jan said.

"I don't want to remarry at all, Jan!" I snapped. "I don't want to agree to their terms and have every jarl under the sun banging at my hall doors proposing to me! I don't want my sons to lose their jarldoms, I don't want any of this!"

"What about me?" Jan asked quietly.

"What about *you*?" I barked angrily.

"Marry me, Aveline." Jan said, taking my hands. "By marrying me, I will safeguard Aros and Roskilde for Young Birger and Sander, I will speak on your behalf at the þing, I will stop the jarls from punishing you. You'll be jarlkona only in name – you'll still rule Aros and Roskilde! If nothing else, by being betrothed to me, no man will come harassing you with marriage proposals. You'll be safe, I can protect you, I can protect the children, just as I promised Vidar I would."

I stared at Jan, shocked and appalled by his suggestion – his *proposal*! I couldn't speak – I couldn't think!

"I – I know it's sudden, Aveline. I wouldn't have suggested it if there were any other way – as you said, I don't know how else to resolve this situation. Unless we can change the laws, they *can* punish you for acting as a man and taking up the jarldom, and for speaking at the þing. Lingvi is determined to punish you for it – marrying me might be the only way to lessen the punishment and let you keep your jarldom."

Jan swallowed audibly. His grip lessened, I ripped my hands away, curling my arms around myself, an abrupt chill taking over me. I shuddered – was that the coolness of the night I was feeling, or did Jan's suggestion of marriage make my blood run cold?

"I'll leave you to consider it." Jan mumbled, rising to his feet. "Find me when you've made your decision, no matter how late. I want to help, Aveline. I want to protect you and the children."

I stared at the ground, listening to his soft footfalls as he slipped out of my tent.

***

A LONG TIME ago, before Vidar and I began a relationship together, I entertained the idea of marrying Jan. When Vidar had first introduced me to Jan as a suitor, I had been entranced by Jan's handsomeness and height, his strapping muscles, his sparkling sapphire eyes and mischievous grin. I had been further enchanted by his witty humour and unremitting confidence, impressed that he never seemed arrogant even though he held himself in such high regard.

Although I was thoroughly charmed by the giant Dane, I rejected Jan – and the two other suitors I'd been matched with. I was secretly conducting a relationship with a thrall at the time, I couldn't admit to the affair, but I couldn't accept marriage proposals *because* of the affair.

I hadn't known until many years later, but Jan had been enamoured by me and asked Vidar for my hand in marriage that very night. Vidar had denied Jan's request to wed me, admitting his love for me to Jan. Months after that night, my relationship with the thrall had ended and Vidar was forced to reveal his feelings to me when I told him I wanted to marry Jan after all.

That had been so long ago – fifteen years ago …

When Vidar revealed his true feelings for me, I immediately didn't want to marry Jan anymore – I hadn't felt any love towards him to begin with. I simply recognised that, of the men I'd been offered, Jan would make the best husband. It was Vidar I had wanted even then, not the thrall, not my suitors, not Jan.

Really, I had told Vidar I wanted to marry Jan to force Vidar to admit his feelings for me. Vidar and I had grown close over the time he'd watched over me while my adoptive father was at war overseas. Vidar had been fiercely jealous of my relationship with the thrall after he'd discovered it, leading me to believe Vidar might feel something for me regardless that I was well below his station, and even though he had never admitted any sort of romantic feeling to me during the time we'd spent together. I hadn't assumed anything would happen between us … I was happily wrong.

Though I didn't love him, Jan was special to me, and he had been exceptionally important to Vidar. Jan was Vidar's foster brother and dearest friend – he was my companion, the only other person in the world outside of my children and I who felt the relentless agony of losing Vidar.

"Jötunnson, my friend, my bróðir, you must take care of Aveline, you must take care of my children, you must love them as I do. Protect them! Take them home for me, Jötunnson."

Yes, Vidar had asked Jan to protect us, to protect me and our children, upon his death. I knew Jan was just trying to live up to his promise to Vidar, but marrying Jan? That … No. By marrying another man, I felt I was betraying Vidar's memory.

But … Perhaps I shouldn't have been so shocked. Jan must have felt obliged to take on Vidar's widow. That sort of arrangement was acceptable, after their brother's death, unmarried men would take on their brother's widow, honourably keeping her and her children safe in his brother's memory.

Though they didn't share blood, Jan and Vidar were brothers. As my husband's brother, Jan and I had formed a strong friendship with each other. Since Vidar's death, Jan and I had mourned together, we depended on each other.

When grief took Jan, he would come to me for solace, and when grief took me, I would weep on his shoulder. Together we struggled through our sorrow, our hearts heavy, a piece of ourselves permanently missing, but we motivated each other to take on the day, to continue despite our anguish. Jan was my right hand, my advisor, my constant support, and I was his. Jan did as Vidar had requested and loved our children as though they were his own – he and Einar especially had formed a bond so like a father and son's.

If I was to marry, Jan would be the ideal man to wed. He proposed to me with noble intentions, to save me from endless proposals from jarls seeking to dig their claws into my jarldoms, to save my jarldoms for my sons to eventually inherit, to protect me. Jan was on my side, he was fulfilling his promise to Vidar.

His only living child had been gone for four years – we had no proof the boy was even still alive. So long as I didn't bare any of Jan's children, the chance of his only legitimate son returning in years to come and challenging Young Birger and Sander for the jarldoms was slim.

I shuddered. The idea of baring Jan's children just as shocking as Jan's marriage suggestion. The idea of baring anyone but Vidar's children was appalling to me, but the idea of baring Jan's? No, that was too much. I couldn't think like that – I couldn't share Vidar and my bed with another man, not with Jan, not with anyone.

I was trapped. My jarldom, my sons' inheritance, was on the line. I was reluctant to marry only seven months after the death of my husband, but I had to realise the bigger picture, these nine jarls wouldn't let me speak tomorrow, they didn't want me to keep my title. Remarrying was the easiest option and of all the men that could be offered to me, Jan would be best.

ASHES REMAIN

Jan's proposal was not a romantic gesture, it was simply a friend offering me help – why was I so opposed? Vidar was dead. Vidar *wanted* Jan to protect me, he wanted Jan to love our children as though they were Jan's own. So many widows remarried – many soon after the deaths of their husbands. I really wasn't betraying Vidar – how could you betray a dead man? And yet ... Why did it feel like I was betraying him just by considering marrying Jan?

What were my other options? Do as the nine jarls command and remarry or ... What? I would have to fight them. I knew I would, which is why I brought so many warriors to begin with. If I decided to reject their judgement, blood would have to be spilt. Though I had singularly brought the most men, the nine jarls' armies merged were much larger than mine. The chance of me winning was slim. Following the jarls' commands was not just the easiest option, it was the only one.

"Damn it, Vidar," I whispered, tears burning in my eyes. "Why did you have to die?"

CHAPTER TEN

I OPENED THE flap to my tent, greeted by the many faces of my men waiting outside for me. I wore my finest gown, blood red with intricate designs embroidered in silver thread on the hems, neckline and sleeves. Pinned to my front were my tortoiseshell brooches, beads hung between them, and, as always, tucked beneath my dress was Vidar's ring hanging on its leather thong.

My chestnut curls cascaded loose to my waist, and I'd made my face up with jet black kohl smeared over my eyes and red berry stain on my lips and cheekbones. With thick black boots on my feet, a bearskin cloak pinned over my shoulders with a larger brooch, and my sword and daggers sheathed at my hips, I looked every bit a warrior queen.

I was ready to face the nine jarls.

This was the first time I had left my tent since noon the previous day when my trial was postponed. My children had meekly entered my tent that morning, bringing with them food and water for me. I had thanked them, mustering as much cheer as I could in attempt to dispel their unease in my presence.

"Have you reached a decision, *móðir*?" Young Birger asked.

"*Já*" I nodded, stroking Æsa's hair, her head resting on my lap.

"What is it?" Sander asked.

"You shall have to wait and see." I grinned though inside ice ran through my veins.

"Don't be bothersome, Sander – *móðir* has good reason to keep it from you." Young Birger chided before another word could fall from Sander's wide-open mouth.

"I spent all night considering every option. It might not be the happiest decision, but it is the right one." I said softly.

"Jarl?"

Jan stuck his head through the flap of the tent.

"Your warriors have assembled." Jan said.

ASHES REMAIN

I nodded and rose to my feet, my children flocked to my sides. Jan hesitated. He looked as though he wanted to say something but didn't. Much to my relief he disappeared. I knew what he wanted to say, I hadn't given him an answer yet to his proposal. He would find out soon enough ...

Together my children and I exited the tent. I gazed at my men, each face filled me with pride and doubt. They all expected me to make the right decision – of course, that's why they agreed to my being jarl in the first place. They believed in me, they had faith in me. Was giving up my title to a man the right thing to do? Was it in the best interests of my people? Did I truly think of them when I argued to keep my title, or did I just think of myself and my sons? Any decision I made did not just affect me and my and children, it affected every townsperson under my rule ...

I should've made a grand speech, a motivational monologue to rouse their spirits and ready them for what was to come, but I couldn't. Words failed me. I eyed them all then bowed my head.

"It's time." I announced then marched through the labyrinth of tents, ready to meet my fate.

***

"WHO HERE SPEAKS on behalf of Aveline Birgersdóttir?" Jarl Lingvi demanded the moment my men and I were assembled.

Again, my men flanked the crowd, a column of them forging a path through the horde, making an exit for me should I need it. Briefly I mused – the games of *Hnefatafl* had aided my strategy making. The defender must force a gap in the attacker's blockade so the king could escape ... I was the king and my defenders had made the gap. Just like the game-pieces, my army was dwarfed by the attacker's numbers.

Jan appeared beside me. We glanced at each other briefly before turning to Jarl Lingvi. I watched Lingvi and the other jarls ogle Jan, their eyebrows raised, muttering to their advisors behind their hands. A corner of Lingvi's mouth lifted into a smirk causing anger to boil in the pit of my stomach. Obviously, he assumed Jan was there to speak for me – but he was wrong.

"I speak for myself, Jarl Lingvi," I announced. "And I will fight to remain Jarl of Aros and Roskilde despite the displeasure it causes you or anyone else in these lands."

The jarls jaws dropped, and hisses and shouts erupted from the crowd. I rolled my lips together, concealing the smile that wanted to spread across my face, their shock humoured me. They thought they had won, they thought they had forced me to submit to them, but they were wrong. I was not a dog to be ordered around.

A boom rattled through the air as my men collectively raised their shields. No swords were drawn yet, but the sound of my army readying themselves for attack bolstered me, they supported my decision. They supported *me*.

"Insolent woman!" Jarl Lingvi hissed. "You disrespectful shrew! You must learn your place!"

"I know exactly where my place is, Jarl Lingvi!" I roared over the heckles from my foes in the crowd. "I am a Dane! Despite the Anglo-Saxon blood coursing through my veins, I am a Dane! As a Dane, I kneel to no one – not man nor god – nor do I flee like a dog with its tail tucked between its legs! I stand tall, I fight, and I take orders from no one! I refuse your offer, Jarl Lingvi, I will *not* remarry, I will *not* relinquish my jarldoms and title, *and* I reject your mercy. I am Jarl of Aros and Roskilde, and any man who wants my title will have to take it from me in battle!"

But for the rustle of the wind through the barren trees it was deathly silent in the þing place. I refused to glance at Jan, to spy his reaction, he had his answer to his proposal now …

Lingvi glared at me, his eyes popping from his skull, that vein throbbing on his brow, his face scarlet with fury. I matched his glare with my own, unwavering and unafraid. I curled my fingers around the hilt of *Úlfsblóð*, ready for whatever would transpire.

"You are asking for war, Aveline Birgersdóttir." Lingvi seethed.

"And we are ready for it." I growled. "I am what's right for my people, and I am willing to bet my life to prove it. If you wish for me to step down from my position, you will have to fight me, Lingvi. Raise the holly rods – I will defeat you right here!"

"Stupid hag! As much as you deserve to be beaten like a thrall, I cannot fight you, it's shameful for a man to strike a woman!" Lingvi snarled. "Unlike *you*, I follow the laws of these lands!"

ASHES REMAIN

"If you cannot bite, Jarl Lingvi, then do not show your teeth!" I jeered. "If you aren't willing to fight me for my title then who is?"

I surveyed each of the nine jarls and their advisors in turn, some stared at me with disgust, others seemed ... impressed. Eyes wide, their sight never left me. Regardless of their feelings towards me, not one man stood up to challenge me. Rather than please me, however, I was angered. I had travelled all this way to answer this summons, harvesting had been interrupted and possibly threatened by the absence of myself and my four-hundred-man strong retinue, and for what? For nothing?

"You all had so much to say, yet none of you are willing to challenge me?" I snapped. "Not one of you is brave enough to face me?"

"We are not stupid enough to break the law, nor dishonourable enough to strike a woman!" The Jarl of Kaupmannahǫfn spat.

"Then how will you take my jarldom from me? You seriously expected me to just give it up immediately? Fools! How dare you insult me so!" I roared. "If no man will challenge me, then I have succeeded in my claim!"

"If she wishes to be treated like a man, then I will humour her."

I whipped around to face my challenger.

A young man had stepped forward, perhaps between eighteen and twenty years of age from the looks of him. He seemed familiar, but I couldn't quite put my finger on why. His slender frame was dressed in simple plain clothing, his ebony hair was sleek and long, like a cloak about his broad shoulders. A short beard grew on his face, his mustachio hairs trimmed neatly above his thin pale lips, which were curled in disgust. He looked at me with utter hatred, his cold blue eyes locked on me.

Who was this stranger who despised me so? Despite some hint of familiarity, I didn't know him. He did not live in Aros or Roskilde, that much was for sure. There was a slight lilt in how he talked, perhaps he was a half-Dane or from somewhere else in the Norse lands? Whoever he was, wherever he was from, I didn't understand how a stranger could loathe me as much as he seemed to. Maybe he was just as appalled by my claim as Lingvi was?

"Should I be granted permission by the jarls here today, I challenge Aveline Birgersdóttir to battle." The young man said. "If I win, I demand her jarldoms as my prize."

"Who are you?" Jarl Borgulf asked, staring at the dark-haired contender.

"Háken Tarbenson."

I shuddered violently, as though suddenly doused with icy water. *Tarbenson?* No ... Was he – could he be?

"Not only do I challenge Aveline Birgersdóttir for her jarldoms, but I also have a score to settle with the kin of Vidar Alvarsson. His sons are mere children and he has no living male relatives but for those children, so I cannot take vengeance from them until they are men. Considering his widow wishes to be treated like a man, I demand to take my rightful vengeance from her." Háken Tarbenson said.

"Fighting a woman is *niðingsverk*!" Jarl Borgulf chided.

"She demands to be treated like a man, she demands to hold jarldoms like a man – she is an insolent lawbreaker. I am willing to look beyond her sex and treat her as she wishes to be treated – and, by doing so, teach her the lesson she refuses to acknowledge."

"She is a woman–"

"She is lawbreaker! Her sex should not warrant special treatment nor protect her from her misdoings!" Háken Tarbenson argued.

"Enough! Both of you." Lingvi interrupted. "You say you have a score to settle with the kin of Vidar Alvarsson, state your case."

"Vidar Alvarsson slew my father two years before he overthrew Jarl Erhardt Ketilsson of Aros. Aveline Birgersdóttir seduced my father, and Vidar Alvarsson killed him in a plot against Jarl Erhardt so they could seize Aros for themselves."

"Your father raped me – Vidar killed him for his despicable act!" I hissed.

"Lies! Lies spouted from a whore! You shared Vidar Alvarsson's bed while you were married to Erhardt and my father caught you! You and Vidar killed my father so he wouldn't out your secrets! You would've been killed for your betrayal to Erhardt had my father not being slaughtered by Vidar Alvarsson!" He snarled.

"I will fight you, Háken Tarbenson! I will defeat you and silence your poisonous tongue!" I shouted.

ASHES REMAIN

"Silence – both of you!" The Jarl of Kaupmannahǫfn shouted, standing up from his chair. "Usually I would agree with Jarl Borgulf, that fighting a woman is shameful *níðingsverk*, but since you are so determined to prove yourself equal to a man, I will grant you your chance to be treated like one. All who agree, say *já*."

Three of the jarls raised their hands and boomed '*já*'. Jarl Lingvi took a moment, all eyes upon him, before nodding in agreement.

"All opposed say *nei*."

The four final jarls, including Jarl Borgulf, raised their hands and shouted '*nei*'.

"Five to four, majority wins." Lingvi said.

"If you give the woman an inch, she'll take an ell!" The Jarl of Vorbasse argued. "She is a woman! She cannot fight in a duel of honour, just as she cannot be a jarl!"

"It doesn't matter how the woman wishes to be treated, she is still a woman! This man is a *níðingr* for challenging a woman to a dual! You of all people cannot condone this!" Jarl Borgulf snapped.

"Majority wins." Lingvi repeated firmly. "Aveline Birgersdóttir and Háken Tarbenson *will* fight. The holly rods will be arranged in three days–"

"I will not wait three days!" Tarbenson yelled. "I have waited many years to get my revenge for my father's death. I have been robbed of the chance to slay Vidar Alvarsson and I will not wait any longer to seize my rightful revenge from his kin!"

"I will fight Tarbenson here and now." I said, looking at each of the nine jarls in turn. "Tarben the Beardless was a *níðingr*, he was a snake and a woman-beater. He raped me, he struck me on multiple occasions, and he deserved to be slain by Vidar. I will not have his son sully my name and the memory of my late husband by accusing us of such lies."

"Tarbenson seeks vengeance for the death of his father and also challenges Birgersdóttir for her jarldoms. They will settle this quarrel in a *hólmganga*." The Jarl of Kaupmannahǫfn said, holding his hand up at Tarbenson before he could bark at me again. The jarl turned to the others. "Are we in agreement?"

"*Já*." The eight jarls said – the four disgruntled jarls not hiding their repugnance at the arrangement.

"We're ignoring all other tradition and laws, why not this one, too?" The Jarl of Vorbasse grumbled.

"Rather than the traditional three to seven days, you both have three hours to gather your shields and shield bearers, to ready yourselves and your weapons." Jarl Borgulf said gruffly. "The holly rods will be raised, the *hólmgöngustaðir* will be readied."

The Lawspeaker took a step forward and cleared his throat.

"Háken Tarbenson accuses Aveline Birgersdóttir of plotting, disloyalty and unfaithfulness to her first husband, leading to the death of Tarben the Beardless, Háken Tarbenson's father." The Lawspeaker said, his deep voice resonating throughout the þing place. "He challenges her for the jarldoms of Aros and Roskilde.

"As Tarbenson has accused Birgersdóttir, so Tarbenson is the challenger. If his blood spills first, Tarbenson will receive no compensation for his father's death, instead he will be forced to pay Birgersdóttir a *hólmlausn* of three marks and will be outlawed from Aros and Roskilde for failing to succeed in his claim for the jarldoms.

"If Birgersdóttir's blood spills first, as the insulted party she will be forced to pay Tarbenson a *hólmlausn* of three marks of silver for the death of Tarbenson's father and will forfeit her jarldoms and title to Tarbenson."

Three marks of silver was an outrageous price to pay for Tarben's death! Really, it didn't matter – I didn't intend on losing to Háken so I wouldn't need to pay such an extortionate amount. From the looks of him, I doubted that Háken even had that much money to even give me when he lost ... Being outlawed would be punishment enough for the young man, but if I didn't accept the *hólmlausn* from him, I would shame him further.

"You are allowed three shields and two swords each, and a man each to hold your shields for you. The moment blood spills onto the cloak, the fighting will end." The Lawspeaker continued. "Should Birgersdóttir not arrive for the *hólmganga*, but Tarbenson does, then Birgersdóttir will be branded a *níðingr* and will forfeit her jarldoms and pay Tarbenson the compensation for his father's death.

"Should Tarbenson not arrive for the *hólmganga*, but Birgersdóttir does, then Tarbenson will be branded a *níðingr* and outlawed from the Danish lands entirely. Far worse is a man too cowardly to maintain an insult he has hurled than a one too cowardly to defend against it.

"I reiterate, there will be *no death*. The battle ends the moment blood touches the cloak. Tarbenson," the Lawspeaker turned his steely gaze to Háken. "Regardless of the *hólmganga*, if you kill Birgersdóttir, a Danish woman, you will be outlawed from the Danish lands. You are being appeased with this dual, but killing a woman is a despicable act and you *will* be punished accordingly.

"Do you agree to the terms, Birgersdóttir, Tarbenson?"

"*Já!*" We barked in unison.

"Then it is settled—"

"I volunteer to fight in Jarl Aveline's place!" Jan shouted.

I glared at him, shocked and insulted by his outburst.

"Jarl Aveline is clearly at a size disadvantage to Tarbenson. As someone of similar build to him, I volunteer to fight in Jarl Aveline's stead." Jan continued, avoiding eye contact with me.

"Do you accept, Aveline?" The Lawspeaker asked.

"*Nei*, I reject Jötunnson's offer." I growled. "I am fully capable of defending my honour on my own."

"You have your answer." The Lawspeaker said to Jan. "In three hours, we will return here. Tarbenson, Birgersdóttir, be ready."

***

"HOW DARE YOU embarrass me like that?" I snarled at Jan in the confines of my tent.

"He is almost as big as I am!" Jan retorted. "It's far from an even match – I was trying to help you! You have the right to volunteer a capable warrior to fight on your behalf if you are clearly outclassed."

"*Outclassed?* You think *he* outclasses *me?* Ha!" I spat. "I was summoned here because so many believe I am *outclassed* and unfit for my position, and I am here to prove them wrong. How am I meant to do that if *you* fight this battle for me? By offering to fight Tarbenson, you belittled me in front of all the jarls and their men! You embarrassed me – you insulted me! How could you do that?!"

"I did not mean—"

"To Hel with what you did or didn't mean! You didn't *think*, Jan. You doubted me in front of everyone, you spoke over me as though I wasn't a jarl – damn it, Jan, you contradicted my claim! You might've just sewn doubt in every warrior here today. Will they fight for me now they know my closest friend doesn't think I could take a man in single combat? Damn the gods, you could've just ruined everything!"

"Aveline, I–"

"*Nei!*" I roared. "I thought I made myself abundantly clear, *I do not need you to speak for me*! If I thought I needed you, I would've accepted your ridiculous marriage proposal! But I didn't accept it, did I? Because I can and *will* fight my own battles!"

Jan was stung, his face filled with shame from my comment. A tiny part of me pitied him, regretted saying those hurtful words almost as soon as they'd fallen from my lips, but I was so insulted and angered by Jan's action that I easily smothered my remorse.

"You're right, I didn't think, but I didn't mean to contradict you." Jan said. "I just want to protect you."

"Instead you have put me in harm's way!" I hissed. "I was going to ask for you to be my shield barer, but now I can't do that because you doubted me!"

The hurt on Jan's face brought tears to my eyes. I knew he was sincere, I knew he didn't mean to cause trouble for me, but his panic and determination to fulfil Vidar's promise had possibly destroyed all worth I might've had in my claim.

"Fetch Domnall, I wish for him to be my shield barer."

Jan opened his mouth to argue but said nothing. He gazed at me pleadingly for a moment before striding out of my tent. I rubbed my eyes with the heels of my hands, forbidding my tears to fall. Jan's broken expression pained me, but his betrayal and the insult he had unwittingly cast had struck a sadness in me so deep, I didn't know if I would ever be able to forgive him.

Domnall arrived alone.

"Will you be my shield barer?" I asked.

"*Já*, of course Jarl." Domnall replied gently.

"Let's ready ourselves, then." I said, pausing briefly to clear my throat. "We don't have long before the *hólmganga* begins."

ASHES REMAIN
CHAPTER ELEVEN

IT HAD BEEN a little over twelve years ago when I saw Háken Tarbenson last. He was just a boy of seven then. He had come with his parents and siblings to attend a party Erhardt hosted to celebrate the child I carried – Young Birger, the child Erhardt thought he'd conceived with me.

Háken had been meek and well-mannered. I liked him and his younger siblings very much – but of course I had, aged between seven and two, they were innocent.

Inga, Tarben's wife and the mother of his four children, had been kindly to me during the brief time we spent together. I never knew why – perhaps she knew her husband terrorised me when he could as he did to most women he met. Maybe she pitied me for that? Or maybe she recognised I was trapped in a cold, loveless marriage and empathised with me.

Tarben had been a monster.

The thought of Tarben brought bile surging up my throat. Inga had been too good for him but was caught in his clutches by the binds of marriage. She did what Tarben ordered and overlooked his misdoings by necessity not choice. She couldn't divorce him if she'd wanted to, he would've killed her if she tried.

Tarben admitted his shameless acts without a care in the world for them, he bragged about beating his wife despite striking a Danish woman being an unlawful and shameful act. But Tarben didn't care. He dominated all women in his life – at least the ones he knew he could get away with mistreating. He was cruel and merciless, deriving depraved satisfaction from torturing women.

Erhardt ignored Tarben's wrongdoings for he admired Tarben's cunning and intelligence. Tarben was Erhardt's righthand man, the only man he trusted in Aros. Tarben was as wicked as Erhardt, if not more depraved, and had no qualms with breaking the laws if Erhardt asked him to.

"Tarben is a wolf and a fox! He is a scavenger that feasts on my father's scraps – whether it be women or glory – and he longs to be jarl." Agnes, one of Erhardt's daughters, had explained to me. "My father is old, but still very strong, he could defeat Tarben in a battle, even now. But when he dies, Tarben will slaughter my father's bloodline – my aunt, my sisters, my children, all of us! – and then he will be jarl.

"Tarben is a threat ... My father is a dangerous man, but you need to wrap him around your little finger and use him to take down Tarben. Otherwise, Tarben will take down you."

Thankfully, we never had to see what Tarben was truly capable of for Vidar had killed Tarben perhaps two years after that night, when he caught Tarben raping me.

My body shuddered violently, I could smell the stench of shit and mud when Tarben shoved me on the ground of a sheep shed and shoved my skirts up over my hips. I could still feel those agonising thrusts, his cackling laughter filling my ears as he fantasised aloud about the punishments Erhardt would exact on me when Tarben told him of my transgressions ...

I could still feel Tarben's hot blood splash over me when Vidar slit his throat, Tarben's cock still inside me, before he toppled to the ground, dead.

As much as I hated to admit it, Háken Tarbenson was somewhat warranted in his claim, Vidar and I *had* been conducting an affair together while I was married to Erhardt. Had Erhardt found out, he was legally allowed to kill us for it. And Vidar *had* killed Háken's father after he had caught us laying together, but Vidar hadn't killed Tarben to keep him quiet, he killed him for raping me.

Two years after he'd killed Tarben, Vidar finally got his chance to kill Erhardt. After killing him, Vidar had bragged about our affair to the townspeople of Roskilde to shame Erhardt. Vidar had bragged about getting me with child twice during my marriage to Erhardt, and the people of Roskilde laughed. I went unpunished and Vidar was celebrated for his slyness. The people of Roskilde had suffered under Erhardt's control and celebrated his defeat. Our sneakiness was admired as cleverness, our trickery as cunning.

I didn't feel guilty for either of their deaths nor Vidar and my deceit, I never had, and I never would. Erhardt had forced me to marry him, had beaten and shamed me throughout our marriage, had raped me so many times. Erhardt deserved to die, as had Tarben. Both men had been despicable fiends, rapists and woman-beaters. They deserved to die, and I was glad that Vidar had the pleasure of killing them.

I never knew what happened to Tarben's family after his death. I never saw Inga or their children again. I could only assume that they left Aros after Tarben was killed.

I had hoped she'd found a decent man to marry and he had taken her far from Aros. I had hoped without Tarben in the picture she and her children would have a second chance at life. Inga and I had never been friends, we had only spent time together once and offered a few friendly words at feasts or in passing at the marketplace, but that was all. Regardless I wanted the best for her.

Now, seeing Háken, seeing the loathing in his eyes the moment his sight rested on me, seeing how very like his father he was ... I wasn't sure life had been kind to them after all.

"Are you ready, Jarl?" Domnall asked. "It's almost time."

"*Já*, I'm ready." I replied, tucking away my whetstone into a pouch on the table and slipping my sword in the sheath hanging from the thick leather belt buckled around my waist. "Are you?"

"I am." Domnall nodded.

***

I APPROACHED THE *hólmgöngustaðir*, two short swords sheathed at my hips and a shield slung over my back, with fiery-haired Domnall towering at my side carrying two more shields for me. I'd changed out of my beautiful blood-red gown into a simple woollen dress instead, and my loose curls were now plaited tight to my head and tied high in a bun. I was ready to fight.

The outfit I wore now was much more conducive for a fight, the underdress was made of stout linen and the blue woollen dress on top of it was thick, both items offering me some protection from Háken's blades. The gorgeous billowing skirts of my elegant gown and the underdress beneath it would've hindered my movements. The skirts of the dresses I'd changed into were loose enough to offer me a wide step without flowing enough to trip me.

Háken had the upper hand by wearing trousers. As much as I'd have liked to do the same, I couldn't break yet another law by wearing men's clothing. Not that it mattered for I only ever battled in layers of gowns and dresses – I would not be impeded by them.

Beneath my dresses I wore thick woollen leggings for warmth as well as protection, and on my feet were well-worn goatskin boots, the soles rough, the chance of me slipping greatly lessened compared to the smooth, shining leather boots I'd worn earlier. My jewellery was removed, only my wedding ring on my finger and Vidar's wedding ring tucked beneath my dress remained.

Háken Tarbenson stood waiting for me with his shield-barer, the nine jarls all assembled as though they'd never left. A wry smile twisted Háken's lips as he watched me, his arms crossed over his chest. I scowled back, eager to wipe that damned look off his face.

He hadn't changed his clothing, he was still in his brown linen trousers and thick woollen tunic. I could spy the hems of a couple of undershirts layered beneath the tunic. He hadn't a helmet, and I hadn't thought to bring mine here. But for the layers of thick clothing, our only defences would be our shields. At least the match was even there, I supposed.

I turned my sight to the *hólmgöngustaðir*, impressed by how quickly it had been readied. A cloak five *ells* square had been laid down on the ground, the loops in the corners of the cloak staked down with thick pegs. Three sets of foot-wide furrows were dug around the cloak and *höslur* posts were set in the outer four corners, ropes tied between them. This is where Háken and I would fight.

From the expressions aimed at me from the crowd, the odds were not in my favour. A *hólmganga* featuring a woman fighter was unheard of and quite obviously disapproved of, yet every man here marvelled at me. Breaking laws or not, they were impressed.

Háken and I slipped under the ropes and entered the *hólmgöngustaðir*. The raucous cawing of ravens overhead caught my attention. I rolled my lips, watching the two birds soaring overhead. The Allfather was watching.

Borgulf and Lingvi stepped forward from among the jarls, who had all risen from their chairs and taken prime spot at one side of the *hólmgöngustaðir*, their advisors craning their necks unashamedly to get the clearest view of Háken and me from over their jarls' shoulders.

As the Lawspeaker entered the *hólmgöngustaðir* and the noise of conversation in the crowd immediately silenced. First the Lawspeaker turned to Háken and asked for his blades. He held the swords in turn against his forearm, measuring them to make sure they were an ell long, then he turned to me and did the same. He nodded, handed back my second sword and turned to the crowd. He raised his arms and announced the rules.

"Each contestant is allowed two swords, both one ell long." The Lawspeaker announced. "They are also allowed three shields and a shield barer. When the shields are destroyed, they must defend themselves with their weapons thereafter.

"Aveline Birgersdóttir, as the challenged party, will have the first blow. The moment blood flows onto the cloak, the fighting will cease and the one whose blood touched the cloak first will be deemed the loser and will pay the *hólmlausn* to the other.

"If either contestant steps outside the *höslur* with one foot then it will be called 'he yields ground' and is the mark of a *níðingr*. If he steps outside with both feet, then 'he flees' and he will be branded a *níðingr* and will be the defeated. Fighting will cease and he who flees will be defeated and pay the *hólmlausn* to the other.

"The *hólmganga* should *not* end in death but should that happen the survivor will be granted the defeated man's every belonging and the slain man's kin are forbidden from seeking compensation.

"Do you agree, Háken Tarbenson, Aveline Birgersdóttir?"

"*Já.*" Háken and I replied.

"The *hólmganga* will *not* end in death." The Lawspeaker reiterated firmly, glaring at Háken and me in turn.

We both nodded, glancing at each other.

"Then let the *hólmganga* commence." The Lawspeaker said.

Háken and I brought our shields in front of ourselves, our swords ready. I tightened my grip on the bone hilt of my weapon and squeezed the handle of my shield, the leather digging into my damp palm.

A cawing sounded behind Háken. I briefly glanced over his shoulder and saw a raven in the distance. It was the one with the blind eye, in my gut I knew it was. Blood would spill today, that ebony bird proved it.

I turned to Háken. We paced around the cloak, our eyes locked. Háken was tall, as large as his father had been. His height was not uncommon, most Norsemen and Danes towered over me – they were naturally bigger than Anglo-Saxons. Háken's height intimidated me, but I knew how I would beat him.

Vidar taught me that I would be outsized by the majority of my enemies whether they were monks or warriors, Danes or Franks, it didn't matter, I had to expect to always be smaller. I had to depend on my speed and my small stature to dodge out of my enemy's way, and act quickly with every strike.

That lesson had stuck with me throughout my life – that was how I survived the siege of Paris and all the battles that led to it, that's how I survived the raid in the Wendish lands. I'd never beaten Vidar in a fight, but I lasted long in our battles. With every defeat I learned a lesson and with every lesson my skill increased.

I swung my short sword with as much might as I could, slamming it down upon Háken's shield. Immediately the wood cracked – it would shatter with a few more hard hits. The crowd roared, excited and astounded by my powerful strike. Even Háken's brows rose to the top of his head as he gaped at his shield.

I smirked.

Háken swung his sword, bringing it down hard, but I spun out the way. He stumbled forward but managed to keep on his feet. If he couldn't land a blow on my shield, I would outlast him, I would have a better chance to win. Everyone knew the best way to win a *hólmganga* was to destroy your opponent's shields as quickly as possible – they would lose their best defence.

Just as Háken turned to face me, I struck his shield then leapt backwards, lifting my own shield in front of me. It was not nearly as powerful a blow as my first had been, but that was fine. I didn't want to use all my strength so early in the battle anyway.

Back and forth we swung at each other, iron slamming against wood, shields ramming shields, the iron bosses clanging against each other, accompanied by the raucous noise of the entertained crowd. With every heavy swing of Háken's sword I whirled out the way, dipping and twisting as though I was dancing.

ASHES REMAIN

Háken was young and inexperienced, his movements were clumsy, it was obvious he hadn't seen much battle or had a teacher train him to wield a weapon. I had the advantage, Vidar had been the greatest swordsman and warrior I knew and had taught me meticulously well. Háken had height on me, but I was a better with a sword. So far, I'd dodged every swing he'd aimed at me.

Blow after blow, splinters sprayed until at last Háken's shield was shattered. Grunting, he tossed the remains out of the *hólmgöngustaðir* and caught the new shield his barer tossed to him. Immediately, Háken charged, baring down on me with his sword.

He wasn't aiming at my shield.

I threw myself to the floor and rolled out the way, but I wasn't quick enough, his blade nicked my arm. Thankfully, it was a shallow scratch and no blood touched the cloak, though I could feel it trickle down my arm beneath my sleeve.

I caught the back of his leg with the tip of my blade before scarpering to my feet. His blood didn't spill! It soaked into his trousers and the strips of fabric wrapped around his shins.

Háken snarled, stumbling as he moved to face me. I scowled at him from behind my shield, sweat streaming from every pore on my body. He charged me again – I caught his blade with my shield and the wood turned to kindling from the power of his blow. He ducked behind his shield, avoiding the spray of wood from my broken shield and the sharp edge of my blade as I swung at him.

I threw the remains of my shield aside and Domnall tossed me my second one. I caught it, hurriedly arranging it as Háken swung. Domnall roared at him, accusing him of cheating for not waiting on me to be ready, but the battle didn't pause. I slipped out of Háken's way and slashed at him again, our swords clanging together, the blow reverberating up my arm.

Grinding my teeth, I pushed against Háken's sword with mine and used the force to propel myself backwards. I ducked behind my shield, my aching arms struggling to keep it held up as Háken battered it like he was using a hammer not a sword.

I couldn't take much more, my body was exhausted, my arms were heavy. He was pulverising my shield, each blow shuddering through me. My eyes darted around – the crowds stared at us with a mixture of amusement and shock. And there – there was Galinn, a smile spread across his pointed face. My enemies were taking pleasure in my defeat ... I couldn't let Háken win.

Just as Háken raised his sword, I threw myself across the cloak. Panting, sweat poured from my brow and caught in my lashes. I didn't have a chance to wipe my eyes before Háken brought his sword down on me again. I rolled away just in time, had I been a second slower, he would've drove his sword through my chest.

I hadn't been able to tell who the mass of warriors were cheering for before, but I knew at that moment it wasn't Háken.

"He's trying to kill her!" Jan roared over the bellowing crowds.

"This battle will *not* end in death, Tarbenson!" Jarl Borgulf boomed.

Háken ignored them all, slashing and swinging at me, keeping me pinned to the ground. Háken slammed his blade against my shield, smashing it to pieces. Jan threw my final shield and hit Háken on the back of his head. Háken spun around snarling like a bear, I took advantage of the distraction and scarpered to my feet.

Háken stood as close to the edge of the cloak as he could, hurling threats at Jan who answered with his own equally vulgar insults. Jan, his alabaster face turned ruddy with anger, drew his sword and pointed it at Háken. Háken seemed to have completely forgotten me, so caught up in his quarrel with Jan.

I glanced at my shield. I wanted it, but I knew my heavy arms couldn't hold it up any longer. I swiped the sweat from my eyes with the sleeve of my filthy gown and drew my second sword. Ready as I could ever be, my feet rooted to the ground and knees bent slightly, I pointed both weapons at Háken. I couldn't attack while his back was turned, that was shameful and underhanded.

"Háken! Face me, coward!" I yelled over the din of the crowd.

Háken turned to me, his face contorted in rage. Icy fingers drummed over my flesh, but I didn't shy away. Bellowing, Háken charged at me like a bull, I dodged, parrying his blade with one of mine while slashing at his wrist with the other. He dropped his sword and paid no attention to the gash in his arm. He swivelled round and rammed me with his shield, sending me flying.

I dropped my weapons! Háken stood over me, laughing between each panting breath. He held his shield over his head with both hands and, with an almighty roar–

ASHES REMAIN

I kicked Háken in the groin as hard as I could before he could smash me with his shield. Háken dropped his shield, doubled over, howling in pain. Leaping to my feet, I grabbed his shield and slammed the rounded iron edge into his face.

As Háken collapsed to the ground clutching his nose, I threw down his shield and snatched up my blades. I turned to him, pointing both short swords at him and–

"It's over!" The Lawspeaker bellowed.

Blood poured from Háken's nose and cascaded onto the cloak. I won! His blood touched the cloak first!

"Aveline Birgersdóttir is the victor! Háken Tarbenson has lost in his claim against her. He will pay Birgersdóttir a *hólmlausn* of three marks, he will receive no compensation and he is outlawed from the towns of Aros and Roskilde."

"*Nei*!" Háken thundered.

"Aveline! Watch out!" Jan shouted.

I turned around in time to see Háken swing at me – he'd drawn his second sword! I tried to jump out the way, but I was too tired, too slow – Háken had caught me off guard. The edge of his blade caught my side, cutting through my leather belt and the layered fabrics of my clothing, slicing through my skin. I felt the blade whack my rib, sending awful tremors quaking through my body.

Háken raised his sword again, both hands clasped the hilt.

He lunged.

Shrieking in pain, with every ounce of strength left in my body, I parried his sword with one of mine, slashed his belly with my other. I cut through his tunics and slit his stomach – the wound wasn't deep enough to injure him badly, his thick clothing had protected him. It was enough to hinder him, to hurt him.

Sure enough, Háken staggered back, touching his stomach with one hand. He stared at the blood covering his hand, raised his sword clumsily and stumbled toward me. I batted his blade away and slashed him once more, the tip of my sword drawing a deep gash across his face.

Háken fell, dropped his weapon and clutched his face, his wails ragged and thick with blood. Jan, the Lawspeaker, Jarl Lingvi and a few warriors ripped down the ropes between the posts of the *hólmgöngustaðir*. Jarl Lingvi threw himself between Háken and me, towering over my foe, his own sword drawn and pointed at Háken, poking into the soft flesh beneath his throat.

"You lost, Tarbenson!" Jarl Lingvi bellowed. "*It is over!*"

Háken groaned and gurgled in reply, choking on the blood streaming into his mouth from his sliced cheek.

"Accept your loss with dignity!" Jarl Borgulf spat. "Do not strike your opponent when they are unaware, that is a coward's act!"

Háken didn't reply.

"I know of your father, Tarben the Beardless." Jarl Lingvi growled darkly. "He liked to kill people dishonourably as well – that's why he was outlawed from Norway. Looks as though you inherited his *níðingr* trait."

Háken forced himself to his feet, his body shuddering, his gored cheek flapping with each strained breath. The tip of Jarl Lingvi's blade was pressed into Háken's chest, if Háken moved to hurt Lingvi in vengeance for the insult, Lingvi would kill him. Háken must've realised for he did nothing but clench his fists and scowl, sweat and blood pouring from his trembling figure.

"I *cannot* and *will not* tolerate cowards." Lingvi seethed. "Not only are you outlawed from Aros and Roskilde, but you are outlawed from the Danish lands as well! Striking your opponent from behind *after* the combat has ended is despicable. You disgust me! Leave. If you're still here by nightfall, you *will* be killed!"

Háken glared at Lingvi for a few tense moments before staggering out of the *hólmgöngustaðir*. His shield barer followed after him and they dashed toward the tents. Clutching my bloody side, I watched the men disappear from sight.

I'd defeated my challenger. Now I had to fight for my title.

I dropped my hand from my side and stood tall, my head raised. I couldn't stop the sweat from pouring nor could stop the pain wrenching through my body, but I could stand brave and proud, if only for a little while.

"Well, have I proven myself?" I demanded.

"We will reconvene in three days with a decision." Jarl Lingvi replied gruffly.

"The morning after tomorrow I will be leaving this place." I spat. "My people have given up more than enough time for this damned trial. We must go home and finish the harvest. Should the people of Aros and Roskilde lack food over the coming winter, it will be on *your* heads!"

"You will stay for as long as we–" The Jarl of Kaupmannahǫfn started, but Jarl Borgulf interrupted him.

"Tomorrow at noon we will meet here with our decision." He said, glancing at the other jarls who all nodded in return – except, that is, for Jarl Lingvi and the Jarl of Kaupmannahǫfn. "Seven to two – the majority wins. At noon you will have your answer."

GWENDOLINE SK TERRY
CHAPTER TWELVE

I STAGGERED THROUGH the tents, my head held high despite my wheezing breaths and the pain tearing through me. Blood streamed down my body beneath my clothes. Men congratulated me as I passed, clapping me on the shoulder or briefly clasping my arm, not noticing the severity of my wound. I thanked them without pausing, I needed my wounds tended to, but I couldn't show weakness in front of the warriors.

As I stumbled through the crowds, my children flocked to me.

"*Móðir*, you won!" Sander exclaimed. "You did it!"

"*Þakka fyrir*, my love." I mumbled.

"You're hurt! *Móðir*—"

"I need to see Brynja." I interrupted Young Birger, clutching his arm for a moment. "Make sure she's ready for me, please."

Without another word, Young Birger sprinted ahead of us. Brynja came to Odense intent to sell her salves and bundles of medicinal herbs, luckily for me. She was the greatest healer in Aros and at that moment I needed her desperately.

Æsa panicked, noticing the bloody patch on my dress. I hushed her immediately and feigned nonchalance with a forced smile.

"I'll be fine, I just need Brynja to bandage me. I'll be alright." I said as casually as I could – which wasn't very much at all.

Silent, Sander, Æsa and Einar followed me to Brynja's tent. Brynja and Young Birger were waiting in front of it. I grabbed the older woman's shoulder to steady myself.

"You've some work ahead of you, I'm afraid."

"I'm sure I do." Brynja replied flatly, holding the tent flap open.

"Children, go to Borghildr's tent." I called. "This might take a while. I'll send for you once my wound has been seen to."

"*Já, móðir.*" Young Birger said, before Sander could protest.

Young Birger whisked his younger siblings away, shutting the tent flaps behind them. Hidden from view in the woollen-walled confines of the tent, I swayed on my feet as Brynja unbuckled my broken belt and tossed it onto my bed. It was almost completely severed by Háken's slash. She peeled my clothing from me, examining my wounds and the bruises forming over my body. I clung to her, my body wavering and head spinning.

"I need to sit." I murmured.

Brynja eased me down onto her bed. She pulled a rag from a chest and pressed it against my wound to staunch the bleeding. With one hand, she arranged the bed sheet over me modestly, covering all but the wound on my side and my lower legs. I clasped the sheet over my breasts with one hand, dropping the other above my head so Brynja could see my side clearly.

A variety of chests filled the room and a fire burned in the centre, a pot simmering above it. The tent smelled like her longhouse. The curative herbs filling the chests permeated with an overwhelming scent of sharp and sweet.

Brynja took a bucket to the fire and scooped some of the water simmering above the flames. The bucket was already partially filled with water, I could hear it sloshing when she moved.

She returned to my side, rinsed the bloody rag in the water, rang out the excess then dabbed at my wounds. I couldn't stop myself flinching from the pain shooting through me as she worked. I closed my eyes and tried to concentrate on steadying my breathing, but it was no use, the pain was too intense.

"I was so proud of you, watching you fight." Brynja said. "The other jarls have no reason to keep your jarldom from you now, you have undoubtedly proven your worth. If they try, your men will kill them. They were already proud of their jarl and your actions in the *hólmganga* have impressed them even more so."

"*Þakka fyrir*," I mumbled through gritted teeth.

Brynja took a fresh strip of fabric from the chest and pressed it over the wound on my side. I held it while she shuffled through her chests, pulling out jars, more linen strips and a bite-stick made of leather. I listened to her bustle about the room. I heard the brief scrape of iron being set on stone and swallowed hard.

I'd never had a wound so extensive it needed cauterising before. I'd seen it done both on the battlefield and after terrible accidents in Aros. I couldn't forget the hiss and sizzle of flesh being seared, my nostrils filling with the stench of burned skin. I'd seen even the bravest warrior passed out from the pain.

"Aveline?"

"Jan?" Too exhausted to lift my head, I groaned his name to acknowledge him.

"I saw the children on my way here – they said you're hurt?"

"*Já*," I replied.

Jan approached me, I could hear his footsteps. I half-opened my eyes to look at him. He stood at the foot of my bed, concern etched across his face as he glanced between the bloodied linen at my side and the wound on my leg that Brynja was bandaging. Lights bloomed in my vision, surrounding him in blinding bursts of swirling shapes, a dull ache buzzing in my head.

"You have a horde of warriors outside waiting to congratulate you. They're complaining about waiting for the jarls' decision, but they have faith that you've won your trial." Jan said, assumedly to lift my spirits – and it did.

"I'll celebrate with them later." I said, my cheeks warming with pleasure despite the pain growing in my head.

"They would like that," Jan said. "I would too."

"I need my side sorted first. That bastard got me good."

"Jan, you're in my light." Brynja interrupted.

Jan moved to the top of the bed. I closed my eyes again, the glow of the lamps aggravating my head.

"My skull feels like it's split in two!" I moaned.

Suddenly a wet rag was laid on my brow. Cool droplets trickled down my face and into my hair. I peeked up to see Jan kneeling beside the bed, wiping my face with the rag. The cold water alleviated some of my discomfort, but still my head throbbed.

"I'm here." Jan murmured. "I have you."

I reached for his free hand and he tangled his fingers with mine, holding my hand to his chest. I could feel his heart racing through his tunic. Outwardly Jan looked relaxed, but his heart told a different story. I must've been quite the sight to scare him.

Finished with my leg, Brynja turned her gaze to the wound on my ribs, her brow furrowed. I winced, pain jolting through me every time she touched it.

ASHES REMAIN

"I need to seal your wound up now." Brynja said, holding up the bite-stick. "You must bite down on this, Jarl – it will hurt."

"Will it hurt as much as a sword to the side?" I joked.

"Perhaps worse." Brynja frowned. "I've had many a warrior come to me laughing with an arrow through his shoulder or a knife wound splitting his flesh, then they scream and wail like children when I cauterise their wounds."

"Don't mock me if I cry." I said wearily.

"I wouldn't dream of such a thing, Jarl." Brynja winked.

"*I* might mock you." Jan grinned.

"Only a little, *já*?"

"Of course!" Jan winked.

Brynja placed the bite-stick into my mouth and I bit down hard. Jan flipped the rag over so the cold side laid on my brow. He slipped his other arm under my neck and I squeezed his hands, drawing comfort from his touch and bravery from his presence.

Brynja left my side for just a moment, returning with the glowing iron she'd been heating in the flames of the fire. Nausea surged up my throat at the sight of it. I closed my eyes and steeled myself. My every muscle was tense and I grinded my teeth into the wooden rod, my breath held in my chest.

"Are you ready, Jarl?" Brynja asked.

"Uh-huh."

I growled and hissed, trying hard not to screech or flail as Brynja pressed the iron to my wound. I squeezed Jan's hands with all my might, my body trembling, tears streaming down my cheeks. Brynja remarked on how lucky I was – had it not been for my thick clothing and leather belt, this would've been fatal.

"His blade glanced off your ribs rather than cut between them." Brynja marvelled. "There's no way this was just dumb luck, the god's gave you their blessings, that's for certain!"

It felt as though I'd been struck by lightning. My whole body burned and nausea swelled in my stomach. I squeezed my eyes shut, trying to focus on the sweat and tears streaming down my face instead of the pain that threatened to rip me in half.

A small gasp escaped my lips, surprised by the warm kiss of an oak bark compress Brynja applied to my wound before she slathered it with a foul salve of honey, crushed snails, fenugreek, grease and flaxseed.

Jan helped me sit up so Brynja could wrap bandages around me. The old woman deftly enveloped my ribs with the long linen strips, knotting them tightly. She washed her hands in a bucket before ladling a scoop of steaming liquid from the pot simmering over the fire into a cup.

"Drink this, it will ease the pain." Brynja urged.

She trickled the revolting tasting brew in my mouth. Coughing and spluttering, I managed to drink it all. Settled back in the bed, Brynja tucked me under a fresh clean sheet. Jan dabbed my brow with a cold rag while I let my eyelids flutter closed.

I felt Jan shift beside me, the bed creaked as he moved away.

"Stay with me." I murmured, blindly reaching for him.

"I won't leave you." Jan whispered, closing his hand over mine. "I'm here, I'm just getting a clean rag."

"Stay with me …" I mumbled, before passing out.

***

I DIDN'T KNOW how much time went by when I woke to pain tearing through me. Brynja plied me with brews and medicines and gradually the pain dulled enough for me to dress. I demanded clean clothes and Jan appeased me, rushing to my tent and returning with a thick grey underdress, charcoal coloured leggings, socks and a woollen gown hemmed with violet bands.

Jan and Brynja wiped down my body and dressed me. In my fevered state, I let out a breathy chuckle at the blush on Jan's alabaster face at the sight of my naked body. Jan offered me a half-smile and continued helping Brynja despite his embarrassment.

"The man who walks in on me when I'm bathing is bashful when he's dressing me?" I mocked between each panting breath.

"I'm uncomfortable because I don't *dress* women, I *undress* them." Jan replied, winking at me. "I'm not skilled at this."

"You can leave if it's too much for you."

"*Nei*, I'll do it." Jan replied, his face glowing redder. "My Jarl has asked for my assistance and she will have it."

I grinned.

ASHES REMAIN

Brynja snickered at us both but didn't make any remark.

Fully dressed, they laid me back down and the healer returned to the fire, making me yet another brew. Jan knelt by my bedside, engulfing my hand in his. He brushed his lips against my knuckles. Embers sprung to life in my stomach. I cleared my throat, trying to ignore the warmth rising to my cheeks.

"Are you going to be alright?" Jan asked in a low tone.

"*Já*, I think so." I smiled.

"Aveline, I – I'm sorry for what happened earlier. For insulting you, for risking everything. I didn't think, I was stupid and–"

"Don't think of it anymore – I'm not."

"I request your permission to hunt down Tarbenson and kill him. I want to make amends for my foolishness and make sure he doesn't return to bother you again."

"You have my permission," I mumbled. "Kill the outlaw."

"I want to assemble a small contingent to hunt him down." Jan said. "It's nightfall, he's free game."

"Take whoever you need."

"*Þakka fyrir*, my Jarl. Will you be okay while I'm gone?"

"I'm in good hands. If anything happens, I can defend myself."

"You're the strongest person I know."

Jan kiss my forehead then left.

"Your brew, Jarl." Brynja said as she approached me, offering me the bitter drink.

***

THE MOON WAS high by the time I left the tent. I couldn't stand being there any longer. The stench of my burned flesh filled the woollen walls, mingling with the odours of the herbs, making me sick. With a cup of sweet mead in hand, I approached the fires, drifting unnoticed along the edge of the drunken rabble. I settled on a stool beside a small fire and nursed my drink.

Though I enjoyed the happiness of the men around me, I wasn't ready to make conversation with anyone. Fighting Háken had been an immense task for me, though I won, I couldn't help wondering how well I would've done had Jan not distracted him.

Jan ...

GWENDOLINE SK TERRY

I didn't think I could completely forgive him for speaking out regardless of what I'd told him, but I was glad to have him by my side. His presence while Brynja saw to my wound gave me the power to endure the procedure without screaming, though the pain was more intense than anything I'd suffered before. And his embrace afterwards ...

Jan and I were always comfortable with each other, we'd hugged and danced together many times, but he'd never kissed me before. That small action comforted me more than anything else could, but what was this odd fluttering inside me when I thought of him?

I was surprised by how disappointed I was when I emerged from Brynja's tent and didn't see him. I hadn't seen Ebbe or Domnall either – they must've gone with Jan to hunt Háken – but I didn't feel as dismayed by their absences as I was with Jan's.

I shook my head and took a deep draught of mead. I studied the crowds illuminated by the fires burning in braziers throughout the camp. I watched men play their games, listened to the chatter, smiled at the children playing in the dark, fighting with sticks like they were swords.

I needed to see my children, they had been so worried ...

"A beautiful woman shouldn't be sitting alone at night." Jarl Borgulf said, appearing beside me with a horn of ale in his hand.

I was immediately agitated by his presence. Borgulf seemed oblivious to my prickled reaction to his presence. I didn't speak a word to him, I just sipped my mead and stared into the flames.

"I need a change of scenery. I'm sick of staring at those jarls all the time, I'd much rather sit with you." Borgulf continued, squatting down beside me. "You fought well today, Aveline. I didn't think you had it in you, but you did it! Jötunnson was right, you were far outclassed by Tarbenson, but you defeated him all the same. Very impressive."

"I was not *outclassed*, I was *outsized*." I muttered. "Tarbenson was *outclassed*, I'm a far better warrior than him, I've had more training, more experience. He obviously has none."

"He still managed to get you, though, didn't he?" Borgulf remarked with a wink. "How's your side anyway?"

"Better now." I replied sourly – and I did feel better, the brews and medicines Brynja plied me with had taken the heat away from my pain. "If Háken hadn't caught me unaware, I would've come out of that battle unscathed."

"The *níðingr* is getting his comeuppance now, isn't he? I saw your little team disappear after him earlier. They should be back soon enough, you wounded Tarbenson quite badly."

"He should be easy for my *little team* to kill, then."

"Indeed, he should."

Silence settled over us. After a short while, I forced myself to my feet, ready to take my leave of Borgulf.

"The decision has been made, by the way."

I stared at him, easing myself back down on the stool. Borgulf chuckled.

"There's no need to stay if you don't want to." Borgulf teased. "You will have to wait until noon tomorrow for the results ... Jarl Aveline."

"*Jarl* Aveline?"

Excitement exploded through me like a boiling pot overflowing. I couldn't stop a grin from spreading across my face nor laughter spilling from my lips. It didn't matter how much I disliked Borgulf for at that moment he was the barer of the greatest news.

"By Odin's beard, I slipped up!" Borgulf gasped, feigning horror. "Never mind, you can pretend to be surprised tomorrow when they officially announce it, can't you?"

"I can indeed." I beamed.

I was jarl – undisputed and victorious!

"I commend you on your loyal followers, Jarl Aveline." Borgulf continued. "I've never heard of a woman rising to such a high rank. You must be quite something to inspire so many. But of course you are, I've admired you since the day I met you. I'd be honoured to call you my wife one day."

"*Þakka fyrir* for your kind words, but I said all I mean to say on the subject of marriage this afternoon." I replied firmly.

"I understand." Jarl Borgulf paused to take a draught of his ale. "You've just been confirmed jarl, I doubt you want to be demoted to jarlkona so quickly. Besides, I suppose things might be said if I married the widow of my sister's former husband."

I let his joke hang between us, snubbing the jest with my silence. Again, Borgulf brought up Vidar's previous marriage. Again, he reminded me that there were things about Vidar that I wouldn't hear from his lips – things I'd have to rely on hearsay to discover.

Borgulf stood up. At first I thought he was leaving, but he returned with a small log, spindly branches and dried leaves protruding from it.

The fire spat embers and ash into the air as Borgulf tossed the log onto it. I shuffled back, covering the top of my cup with my hand so none of the ashes would land in my mead. Temporarily smothered by the new log, the flames quickly devoured it, creeping over the wood and consuming it, the flames growing taller, the leaves smouldering away.

I brought my cup to my lips and drained the contents. I breathed in deeply and turned to Borgulf. He smiled brightly at me, the glow of the flames dancing on his features, playing in his pale eyes.

"What's her name?" I asked quietly.

"Whose?"

"Your sister's ... Vidar never told me."

"Her name was Svanlaug." Borgulf raised his brows. "I'm surprised Vidar didn't tell you about her."

"I didn't spend my marriage fretting about my husband's past." I replied stoutly. "He loved me, I loved him, that was all that mattered."

"No truer words have been said." Borgulf said kindly.

"Would – would *you* tell me about her?" I asked meekly.

"Why the sudden interest now when you didn't care before?"

Borgulf's question made my cheeks turn red.

"Now Vidar's dead, I ... I don't like that there are parts of his life I don't know." I admitted, staring into my empty cup. "And ... As stupid as it sounds, when people who knew him fondly speak of him, it brings him back to life ... If only for a little while."

Borgulf reached over and squeezed my hand briefly, sympathetically.

"Well then," Borgulf said softly. "Let's bring him back to life for a while. You should know I didn't spend much time with him. I was a child when he married my sister, I was in awe of his reputation and proud he was my kin through marriage, but he and I weren't friends. Most of what I know about him personally was what I heard from my sister and from the occasional visits over the years they were married.

"I can tell you about his and Svanlaug's life together, if you'd like to demystify that portion, but know it's all from Svanlaug's perspective, what she shared with us."

"It's better than knowing nothing at all." I smiled weakly.

"In that case, where shall I begin?" He paused thoughtfully and took another gulp of ale. "Well, as I told you before, Svanlaug and Vidar married for duty, nothing more. There was no love shared between them at any point, I believe. They tried, I know that much. They attempted to form some sort of bond with each other, but it never grew into love. It was a sort of companionship, but it didn't last, Svanlaug and Vidar could not fit together no matter how they compromised to make things work.

"For my father and Alvar the First One it was a perfect match. Svanlaug was the only daughter of our father's and Vidar was the only living son of Alvar's. Alvar and my father were both seeking to make allies further afield in the Danish lands, so marrying Svanlaug and Vidar was ideal. Both Vidar and Svanlaug were dutiful children and agreed to the union.

"Sadly, that was all that was ideal. They hadn't met more than three days before their wedding and they were too young to know what love was or what it meant to be married. As time went by they got used to each other, Vidar was good to her and she was a good wife for him but love just wouldn't blossom between them.

"*Móðir* filled Svanlaug's head with all these silly solutions, convincing Svanlaug all she needed to do was have a baby for love to grow between them. *Móðir* thought children would bring them together. Our parents had married similarly, they were strangers when they wed and by the time she birthed Svanlaug, they were madly in love. *Móðir* was sure that if Svanlaug gave Vidar a child, he would be happy, and they would fall in love.

"But it was not meant to be. Svanlaug was barren. They tried for a decade to make their marriage work and produce children, but the strain was too much. Had they stayed together longer, I'm sure the alliance between Roskilde and Lund would've suffered. It was better for them to separate – politically *and* emotionally."

"What happened to Svanlaug after they divorced?"

"She remarried and raised a large family with her new husband."

"I thought you said she was barren?"

"She was. Her second husband, Ormarr, was much older than her. His previous wife died birthing their youngest child. He needed a new wife – a mother for his baby. That's where Svanlaug flourished. She raised his baby with the help of a nursemaid. She loved his older children and raised the lot as though they were her own. Ormarr was pleased to have a young, pretty wife regardless that she was barren. He doted on her and loved her for how she loved his children, and I think a great part of her loved him, if only for giving her those children."

"Why do you speak of Svanlaug in past tense?" I grunted, shifting in my seat – Brynja's brew was wearing off.

"Svanlaug died two years ago." Borgulf said. He shook his head at the surprise on my face. "*Nei*, it was expected. She was old, she'd seen almost forty winters. She developed a cough that worsened with the cold and was exacerbated by smoke, she struggled for every rasping breath she took. When she passed, we were ... We were relieved. She didn't suffer anymore."

"May she rest easy in Helgafjell." I said softly.

"*Þakka fyrir*, Aveline." Borgulf smiled. "She lived a happy life. I'm glad to hear that Vidar did as well. He found a woman he loved who gave him the children he wanted and he died an honourable death. He is with the Allfather, now, I'm sure of it."

"*Já* ..."

I hadn't realised my hands were trembling until I noticed my mead cup shaking in the corner of my eye. Inconspicuously I dropped the cup on the ground and entwined my fingers together, my gaze locked on the dancing flames in front of me.

"I didn't see Vidar more than a handful of times immediately after the divorce, but I know he would've been proud to see you today. You were *drengr* unlike any I've ever seen."

I stared at him, my cheeks burning, I'd never been so flattered before. Being called *drengr* by the Norse people was a huge compliment, the best one could ever receive. Being *drengr* meant you possessed bravery, reckless valour, magnanimity and the strength to do what is right despite any danger.

"*Þakka fyrir*, Borgulf. Truly."

ASHES REMAIN

"Don't thank me for telling the truth. You were remarkable!"

"It's a shame Jarl Lingvi doesn't have half the opinion of me that you have." I smiled.

"Oh, but he does!"

"*What?*"

"Lingvi is an insufferable bastard, I'll admit, but he isn't all bad. Lingvi is a fiend for rules, he's zealously against lawbreaking, oath breaking, that sort of thing. He thought you were a shameless villain for flaunting your disregard for the law."

"*Já*, I recall him saying that once or twice." I said facetiously, receiving a grin and snicker from Borgulf.

"I couldn't believe he allowed you to fight – I think you must've driven him temporarily insane for him to agree to such a thing. The Nornir know he will never do that again." Borgulf said. "But you impressed him today. The moment the nine of us assembled in private, he was the first to demand you keep your jarldom."

"You're lying to me, Borgulf."

"Why would I lie and give *him* the glory?"

"True." I grinned. "So – did you vote against me? You've not exactly been *for* me keeping my jarldoms."

"It was a unanimous decision between the nine of us." Borgulf said. "But you're right, I wasn't *for* it. I still believe a woman is meant to be jarlkona not jarl, but you deserve your position."

"I appreciate your honesty."

Whether it was the time I was spending with him or hearing the jarls' decision I didn't know, but I was feeling more comfortable with Borgulf. He was a brazen, silver-tongued fox to be sure, and uncompromisingly forthright with his opinions. At first I'd found him too bold and threatening, but I found myself warming to him.

"Aveline …" Jarl Borgulf sounded reluctant to continue. He swallowed a mouthful of ale before turning to me, his brows furrowed and mouth turned down in a frown. "I want you to know there are terms to your keeping your jarldoms. I can't tell you them now – you must wait until tomorrow to hear them – but there *are* terms. If you wish to retain your title, you should accept them."

Terms? Like I'd been doused in icy water, coldness seeped through my body. The bastards … I'd earned my position yet still these nine jarls sought to control me and my jarldoms.

"I'm *not* remarrying." I replied sternly.

"No one is asking you to – unless you've changed your mind and want to wed *me*?" Borgulf winked. "But seriously, I urge you to accept the terms otherwise you will *not* get to keep your title."

"I'd rather die than roll over like a dog."

"You don't have to *roll over*, just abide by a few rules." Borgulf reasoned, but I could tell by his expression he knew he was fighting a losing battle. "You impressed them a great deal, but you *are* still breaking the law by claiming a man's position. There have to be terms to keep this somewhat *proper* in the eyes of the law."

"I'm willing to do whatever it takes to retain my title, Borgulf." I growled. "Abiding by your summons was a way of handling this situation peaceably. I *will* keep my jarldoms no matter what."

I was making a threat not a statement. Borgulf nodded slowly, understanding my meaning perfectly. Stars glinted in his eyes – it wasn't amusement sparkling in his blues ... It was pride.

"*Já.*" Borgulf grinned. "Which is exactly why you're *drengr*."

"Then you realise I'll not be told what to do by you or the others? You can't put terms to my rule, only *I* can do that."

"Aveline, I know how you feel, but I don't want to see this turn to bloodshed. I vow before all the gods, I will not make my men fight yours – but the others will."

"Would you fight beside me if that came to pass?" I asked icily, knowing full well what his answer would be.

"It wouldn't help you if I did. Their forces vastly outnumber yours and mine put together."

There it was – a non-answer. He passed over my question as smoothly as butter on bread. It was a smart reply, really. He would doom himself if he sided with me.

"You're a wise woman, Aveline. Consider the risks! They *will* kill you if you fight them, and they'll kill you with ease considering the state you're in. The terms are not dreadful – you may even find them agreeable. But you *must* accept them no matter what."

***

MY PRESENCE BY the fire was finally realised by my men. I was whisked into conversation after conversation about the *hólmganga* and the wound Háken gave me. No one realised how terrible it was until my children dashed to Borghildr and told her of it. Jan had confirmed the children's words after he left my tent.

I laughed and claimed my children and Jan were exaggerating. I rolled my eyes at Young Birger who sat yawning across the fire from me, a sleepy grin lifting the corners of his lips. My denial did nothing but spur my men on, they sang my praises, repeating what Borgulf said earlier – that I was *drengr*. My cheeks were rosy with pleasure, but I tried not to be smug or prideful.

"Nothing can kill a man if his time hasn't come and nothing can save one doomed to die." I shrugged. "One should always bare a wound well and fight as long as they can. I know all of you would do the same."

My nonchalant manner seemed to impress them more, my compliment feeding their drink-enhanced egos. After my men had thoroughly flattered me, regaling my victory in dramatic, saga-like narrative, Domnall and Ebbe explained Háken's death in epic detail to the cheer and applause of my men.

I drank another cup of mead before announcing my leave and staggered to my tent using *Úlfsblóð* as a cane. The mead did well to ease my pains, but not as well as Brynja's brews. I craved a yarrow induced slumber. The effects of my previous brew and the deluge of medications were wearing off.

My body ached and my limbs and muscles were stiff, worsened by the cold night air. Winter would be here soon, I could feel it. I made a note of visiting Herra before we left, I wanted to buy provisions in case the harvest suffered in our absence …

I left the fireside alone and stumbled through the labyrinth of tents. Snores drifted from some, the moans and fleshy thumps of couples making love sounded from others.

A pang struck my heart. Maybe I was addled by mead more than I realised, but hearing the couples be intimate reminded me how thoroughly alone I was and how much I craved companionship. I shook my head fiercely before my thoughts could go any further. By the gods, I needed to sleep.

The glow of an oil lamp was visible through the woollen walls of my tent as I neared it. I passed through the tent flap and found Jan laying Einar down in his bed, my youngest child fast asleep. Æsa and Sander were snoring softly beneath their furs, their brows damp with perspiration despite the chill in the air.

"I found Einar asleep in Ebbe's tent. Sander and Æsa were tired too, so I brought them back here." Jan said.

"Þakka fyrir," I smiled.

Jan delicately pulled a fur over Einar while I took the flaxen bag of herbs and an empty cup from the top of a chest near my bed and slipped outside. A few paces from my tent, an iron pot full of water hung from a tripod over a dying fire.

I crouched beside the fire, the bag of herbs and cup beside me, and gently blew on the meagre flames, my head swimming with each deep breath. As the flames grew, I pushed some sticks from the edge of the fire into the centre, coaxing it back to life. Jan appeared soon after with his arms full of firewood and kindling

He fed the twigs and logs to the flames until tongues of fire licked the base of the pot. When the water came to a boil, bubbling and steaming, Jan filled my cup. He sprinkled a few hefty pinches of the herbs into the boiling liquid before giving it to me.

"Borgulf said that the jarls have agreed to let me keep my jarldom." I announced quietly, staring at the herbs steeping in my cup.

"They would be stupid not to." Jan smiled. "You fought as well as any man I have met, you deserve to remain jarl."

"Þakka fyrir."

"Aveline ... I don't want you to think that I doubted you when I asked you to marry me." Jan said. "I–"

"You were trying to help." I interrupted. "I know. You were trying to fulfil your promise to Vidar. Like I said before, it's in the past. I don't wish to speak of it any longer."

"If that's what you want." He seemed to want to speak of it more, to defend himself further, but I just wanted to let it be.

"It is."

"Here, I have something for you." Jan said brightly.

He shuffled through a large pouch hanging from his belt. I peered through the darkness and watched him pull out something long, dark and glossy.

"Háken's hair?" I gasped, shoving my cup in his hands so I could take the thick bundle of ebony hair.

ASHES REMAIN

I stared at the hair, ran my fingers through it, my fingertips catching on the snares and tangles near the tips of the lengths. Háken's hair hadn't been combed after our battle. In life, his tresses had been cut bluntly, neatly. The ponytail of hair I held varied in length, some locks were six inches long, others twelve, some longer than that. Háken's hair had been hacked off and bound with a leather thong after being sheared from his head.

"He's dead. I killed him myself, he's raven food now."

"Domnall and Ebbe said ..." I murmured. "I want to hear it from you, now. Tell me everything."

"It wasn't hard, we'd scouted his *byrðingr* earlier on. There were four others of similar age to him and a boy perhaps five years younger." Jan said. "Maybe they were all hoping to make a name for themselves by backing Háken, I don't know. They were young and inexperienced, killed quickly and easily."

"The boy ... Did he – did he look like Háken?" I whispered.

"He had long black hair, but for that, I don't know." Jan shrugged. "I didn't pay much attention."

There were five years between Háken and his youngest sibling, a brother. Maybe that boy was him? A memory flashed before my eyes, the little boy fast asleep in my arms at Erhardt's feast, drool dribbling down his chin ...

My heart broke for the boys I had known, but I had to think of the fate of my own family. With both the sons of Tarben dead there wasn't much of a chance for more vengeance being sought against me and my children.

I held Háken's locks against my chest.

"*Þakka fyrir*, Jan."

CHAPTER THIRTEEN

THIS WOULD BE the last time I would stand before the jarls. Thick grey clouds smothered the sun and biting winds whipped through my chestnut curls and stung my face. I drew my fur cloak tighter about me. I was eager for the jarls' announcement, but I feared the weather was an omen. Were these terms Borgulf spoke of as agreeable as he suggested?

"Aveline Birgersdóttir of Aros, step forward. We have come to a decision." Jarl Lingvi's voice resonated across the glade.

I did as he bade, standing before him with perhaps only an ells space between us. I tried to be still, the weight of *Úlfsblóð* sheathed at my hip threatening to drag me down. I had to act honourably, I couldn't show pain or weakness. I met Lingvi's steely gaze with my own, my lips pursed, jaw clenched and brows knitted. Borgulf was sitting behind Lingvi, a beaming smile radiating from his face.

"You fought Háken regardless that he was stronger and bigger than you. You had the chance for a man to fight for you, someone equally matched to Háken, but you fought him yourself. You didn't back down from the fight." Jarl Lingvi said stonily. "You faced Háken eagerly, without an ounce of fear. You were willing to risk your life to maintain your honour and the honour of your people. That was *drengskapr*."

It was difficult to hold back my smile.

"We have decided a new law, should a woman not have a living male relative or one not old enough to speak for her then she has the right to speak for herself and settle her own case at the þing until her living male relative reached his sixteenth winter and is old enough to speak on her behalf." Jarl Lingvi glanced at the Lawspeaker who nodded.

The people cheered, none as enthusiastically as the women in the crowd. It warmed my heart to witness their happiness. They would not be trapped as voiceless widows, suffering without a man to speak on their behalf. The ability for women to represent themselves (though limited until her son is reaches his sixteenth winter) was a step toward equality for all women and a way for them to safeguard the legacy of their families.

"*Þakka fyrir*," I said. "The women of Denmark will appreciate this beyond measure, Jarl. I am excited to announce this news to the people of Aros and Roskilde, and all the settlements between."

"We also have made a decision on your claim to the jarldoms of Aros and Roskilde." Jarl Lingvi continued.

I straightened my stance, tilting my chin up. I slowly exhaled a deep breath through my nostrils, steadying myself to hear these terms Borgulf warned me of.

"Aveline Birgersdóttir, we have decided to allow you to keep your jarldoms." Jarl Lingvi said. "How–"

Before he could finish, he was interrupted by an almighty roar from my men. I glanced over my shoulder at them and realised there were several others applauding the jarls' decision – men who were not from any of the settlements or towns under my rule. The nine jarls' men! Not all of them, granted, but a large enough number to surprise and excite me.

"*However*," Lingvi boomed over the din. "Just as a woman can speak for herself if she has no living male kin or male kin old enough to speak on her behalf, so will you lead only until your sons come of age then you *will* relinquish the jarldoms to them."

"You will be a placeholder until your sons see their sixteenth winters." The Jarl of Kaupmannahǫfn said. "If you defy this ruling, we will oust you and your kin from Aros and Roskilde by force."

If I didn't agree to their terms they would kill not just me but my children as well. I turned to Borgulf, scowling. He lifted his brows and nodded slowly, wordlessly imploring me to accept the term.

Anger mounted inside me. Preserving my sons' rights to my jarldoms was exactly what I wanted, but inside me a child was screaming *I don't need your permission!* at the jarls. I bit my tongue and turned to Jarl Mats, who smiled kindly at me.

"Throughout your time here, we interviewed your men and each of them have given quite the compelling argument in your favour. They all support you – and their word has helped us make our decision." Jarl Mats said.

"Your men made their decision and they have been heard. You are allowed to keep your jarldom for now." The Jarl of Vorbasse said darkly. "If Roskilde and Aros fall during your rule, you will be proof a woman *cannot* and *should not* hold a man's position."

"The law will remain that a woman cannot hold a man's position, you are simply a placeholder until your sons are old enough to lead. This is your offer, Aveline Birgersdóttir. If you do not accept, you and your kin will be punished for lawbreaking this very day." The Jarl of Kaupmannahǫfn said.

"This is a reasonable offer, you'd be a fool to reject it. Allowing you to act as a placeholder has made you possibly the most powerful woman in Denmark." Jarl Borgulf said.

"Except that I am beholden to you nine."

"Better to be beholden to us than enslaved for lawbreaking."

"You *should* be grateful. You have no right to inherit any of your late husband's assets or wealth, they are meant only for your sons. We should strip you of your position and wealth, and subject you to thraldom or even execute you as punishment for your offenses." Jarl Porsi Hard-Bone growled.

"But you fought for your jarldom, you spilt blood for it." Jarl Mats said firmly. "We have decided you are worthy enough to keep it. This is victory for you, Birgersdóttir."

"*If* you accept the condition." Kaupmannahǫfn reaffirmed.

"I accept." I announced at last, glaring at each of the jarls in turn.

The Lawspeaker stepped over, holding out a golden band. Jewels were inlaid along the outside of the band and runes were carved on the inside. Ullr's oath ring. Lingvi took it from the Lawspeaker and offered it to me. I gripped it with both hands so tightly the jewels dug painfully into my palms.

"On Ullr's ring, I vow to protect my people. I vow to lead my warriors to victory, to crush our enemies beneath our blades. I vow to expand Aros and Roskilde into thriving trading towns, bringing great riches to my people. I vow to rule generously and bravely, until my sons come of age when I will gladly relinquish the jarldoms – their birth rights – to them."

Lingvi grunted as he accepted the golden band from me. Behind him, I caught a glimpse of Borgulf, his eyes locked on me. His smile grew into another beaming grin as he rose to his feet.

ASHES REMAIN

"Congratulations Jarl Aveline Birgersdóttir of Aros and Roskilde!" Borgulf exclaimed.

"Congratulations, *Jarl* Aveline." Lingvi mumbled. "Don't mess this up."

***

I COLLAPSED ONTO my bed, every part of my body throbbing. After the assembly concluded, we spent the rest of the day eating, drinking and celebrating. It had been a long day, but a successful one. I was the legitimate (if temporary) jarl of Aros and Roskilde. I'd earned my place, I'd proven myself, I was victorious.

I glanced at my children, all four of them fast asleep beneath their furs and blankets. They would continue to live their privileged lives, their inheritance and futures secured. Over the course of the evening I'd even arranged a marriage for Young Birger and attained many prospects for Sander.

Young Birger, red-cheeked and wide-eyed, was pleased with his betrothal to Signý, daughter of Jarl Askold of Ribe. I couldn't have dreamed for such a prestigious match for my eldest son, and I was glad he was excited by it, too.

Sander was too young to arrange a marriage for just yet. That didn't stop Mats, Jarl of Alabu, a trading post in the north of Jutland, imploring Sander to consider his daughter, Fenja, as a future prospect.

I giggled, remembering Sander's reaction. At first he was adamant he would not marry, he was going to travel the world, conquer enemies, seize riches – then he laid his eyes upon the golden haired Fenja, with her rosy cheeks and deep brown eyes. He stopped midsentence, gawping at the blushing girl.

"*She* wants to wait six years to marry *me*?" Sander had asked.

"The arrangement has not been finalised, Jarl Mats and I are merely entertaining the possibility. She might accept a different suitor between now and your sixteenth winter."

"I hope not." Sander replied, making Fenja giggle.

"Be aware, she's three years older than you and already receiving suitors. It might not happen." I pointed out.

"She *will* be my wife." Sander said firmly, and that was that.

With Young Birger set to marry the daughter of Ribe's jarl, the future of Aros and Roskilde – and the futures of my eldest two sons – was assured. Though Young Birger would have to wait a few years until he could marry Signý, their betrothal gave Aros and Roskilde a powerful ally. Ribe was a wealthy town with a large army, an alliance with the town was tremendously valuable.

I kicked off my boots and stripped down to my underdress, wincing with every movement from the pain in my side. Too tired to put anything away, I tossed my clothing on the floor and slipped beneath my blankets. Enjoying the warmth and the softness of the furs, I was glad to be off my feet. My side ached, but the yarrow brew I'd drank before crawling into bed was already taking effect.

A sleepy smile drifted over my face. I did it, I'd proven my worth to the nine prestigious jarls. All of them had doubted me, but I had swayed them. I had earned their respect.

I couldn't help but laugh at the irony of my ascension. It was incredible how far I'd come – had it happened to anyone else, I wouldn't believe them. Two decades ago, I was an Anglo-Saxon child terrified of the monsters who had slain my family, destroyed my village and kidnapped me. Now I was a Danish jarl who ruled two Danish towns and so many of Danish settlements.

Vidar would be pleased with the matches I'd made for our sons, I was sure of it. He would be proud that I defeated Háken. Vidar's diplomatic abilities were vastly superior to mine, but he would've been impressed that I'd swayed the nine jarls to my favour. I could imagine him laughing at how infuriated I'd made Lingvi ... I knew, had Vidar been here to see it, he would be proud of me, impressed to see how far I had come in the seven months I'd been widowed.

I was proud of myself, too, but I wished I'd never had to go through any of this. I wished I'd never been widowed, I wished Vidar was still here, the rightful Jarl of Aros and Roskilde, my husband, my love. I wished none of this had happened.

I stared at the empty half of my bed and wept.

***

THE CLOUDS HAD parted, allowing a glimpse of cold sunlight to gleam on the fjord and the vessels bobbing upon it. I was glad to be off my horse. The mare plodded gently, but I winced the whole ride, my body aching from the motion. I tried to distract myself by talking to Borgulf who escorted us to the docks.

"So, Jarl Aveline, what do you plan on doing now?" Borgulf asked as the last of the belongings was loaded onto Wind-Rider.

"I have four years before Roskilde becomes Young Birger's and seven until Aros belongs to Sander. The towns are thriving, but I want to make them booming trading posts – with people from all over the world travelling through. I want to make sure my sons inheritances will be immense."

"And after that?"

"Perhaps I'll travel the world." I said airily, imagining the city of Constantinople that Herra Kaupmaðr spoke about.

"You don't see a new husband in your future? More children?"

"Do you not have a wife, Jarl? No concubines?" I asked exasperatedly.

"Oh, I have many *beautiful* concubines, but unfortunately my wife divorced me shortly after the end of last winter."

"Oh? Why did she do that?"

"Because I didn't share her bed."

"Doesn't the law state a woman can only divorce her husband if he hasn't shared her bed for *three years*?" I couldn't help but grin.

"That is correct."

"Sounds to me as though you spent too much time with your concubines." I snickered.

"You know, I think you might be right."

***

I KNELT BY the edge of the fjord washing the sacrificial goat blood off my hands until I couldn't take the water's biting chill any longer. I dried my hands on my skirts as I walked up the dock. Safely aboard Storm-Serpent, I gazed at the shore, spotting Borgulf on his mare. He waved to me, I lifted my hand and smiled.

"Are we ready, Jarl?" Ebbe asked.

"*Já*, let's go home."

CHAPTER FOURTEEN

Late Spring, 889

I STOOD IN front of the great monument Jan gifted me years ago, reading the inscription over and over. Raindrops trickled like tears down the great monolith, slipping in the smooth grooves of the runes. The brightly coloured paint had faded, I made a mental note to repaint it when the weather warmed up.

It had been exactly three years since Vidar had died. I swallowed hard and rested my brow against the cold wet stone, my eyes shut tight. I pictured Vidar in my mind, smirking and chuckling mischievously as he had so often done. Sometimes I could see him vividly, as though he was there before me – I could *hear* him, could *smell* him. If I reached out, I might even touch him …

A sigh slipped through my lips and my eyes flittered open. It was bizarre to realise Vidar had been gone for *three years*. It was even stranger to watch my children grow up without their father. Some days were good, others dreadful, but gradually they were getting used to this 'new normal' without him.

It confused me at first – it was hard to believe we could be happy without him, that we could smile in Vidar's permanent absence. Vidar's death had shattered me, shattered our children, yet all around us people continued doing what they always did, as though the world hadn't ended.

But, it hadn't – not for them. *Our* world had ended, and I was bitter – I was furious! – that Aros carried on. Day turned into night and night into day, just as it always had. It felt wrong, like everything should stop, should mourn, should feel as utterly helpless and broken as we did. The birds shouldn't sing, the waves shouldn't roll, Vidar was dead – why did people carry on like tomorrow mattered?

It took time to realise that we *had* to carry on like the rest of Aros. It was strange that 'normal' meant living without Vidar, but slowly we managed to live again. It took time, but we began to look forward to tomorrow again. Despite how much we missed him, as time went by we found ourselves grieving less, crying less. Despite how much we yearned for him, our grief *had* lessened.

Occasionally I was caught in moments of suffocating sadness and I would weep inconsolably. I found myself in moments like those grieving not just for Vidar but for our daughter Alffinna and for Birger, my adoptive father. I even found myself crying for Beric, my only living brother from my Anglo-Saxon family. He was the reason for Vidar's death, he was a man I loathed and missed all at once. Though he was alive, far away in the Kingdom of the East Angles, I grieved for Beric as though he was dead.

My fingertips lingered on Vidar's name for a moment longer before I turned away and picked up my shield. With *Úlfsblóð* sheathed at my hip I headed to the shore. The clouds from the evening's rainfall were dispersing, the moon was high and bright, offering me clear white light to see by.

I scurried through the darkness with a woollen cloak about my shoulders, inhaling the fresh tangy scent of the sloshing waves just beyond the marketplace. Upon the damp shore, I threw down my cloak, unsheathed *Úlfsblóð* and began my sword training.

***

"WHAT ARE YOU doing here, Aveline?"

"I could ask you the same thing."

Wiping sweat from my brow with the sleeve of my dress, I turned and greeted Jan with a smile.

"I couldn't sleep." Jan said.

Jan looked exhausted, his eyes were bloodshot, and his long tawny hair was tousled and loose. His clothing was rumpled, perhaps from tossing and turning in bed. Apparently, he had been too fatigued to even do up the toggles of his boots or put on socks. At least he'd remembered to buckle his sword belt around his waist before he left his home.

Jan must have noticed me eyeing him for a sleepy smile lifted a corner of his mouth and he rubbed the back of his head self-consciously.

"You should carry your shield with you at all times." I scolded.

"If someone attacked me right now, I would welcome it." Jan yawned. "Death might be the only way I'll get some sleep."

I snickered at him as he crossed his arms behind his head.

"What's on your mind, Jan? You're not dressed properly, you forgot your shield. I have no problem protecting you since I have *my* shield," I said pointedly, a small smile playing on my lips. "But I'd like to know what has you so absentminded."

"If we're going to talk about it, let's find somewhere to sit. I'm too exhausted to stand."

I sheathed my sword and picked up my cloak, and together we traipsed up the beach to a grassy patch not far from the marketplace. Jan unbuckled his sword belt, his sword sheathed in the scabbard, and tossed it to the ground before dropping down beside it. He laid back, stretched his long legs out in front of himself and crossed his arms beneath his head.

I laid my cloak neatly on the grass and sat on it, my legs crossed beneath my skirts and my sword and shield set neatly beside me. I watched Jan for a moment wondering what thoughts were drifting through his mind. But for his bloodshot eyes and the lines etched on his face by exhaustion, he looked almost serene.

"What's going on, Jan?" I asked softly.

Jan drew his thick brows together and frowned, deepening the lines on his brow. Jan was blessed to have the stamina, strength and appearance of a man a decade his junior, but in that moment, he looked aged beyond his years.

At less than a handful of years away from his fortieth year, Jan was a grand old age for a man. A lot of men would have died in battle or to disease by their fortieth year, Jan always seemed like he would live forever. Seeing the flash of old age appear, no matter how temporarily, across his face reminded me he was mortal despite his youthful appearance and impressive longevity.

"I can never sleep around this time of year." Jan admitted.

I made a soft noise of acknowledgement and dropped my gaze to the empty space between us. I couldn't sleep this time of year either. Spring used to be a time of rejoice, a time of freshness and hope. Now it was an annual reminder of Vidar's death.

"I think perhaps I need to find a woman ... Maybe cuddling up to a warm body will help me sleep? Else she might find an enjoyable way of exhausting me." Jan winked, flashing me a mischievous grin.

I laughed. The aged look that had flickered across his face was gone, replaced by his usual roguish expression.

"It's worth a try." I grinned. "Why haven't you found one yet?"

"I'm looking, I just haven't found the right one." Jan shrugged.

"Surely any will do for now. You can find the *right one* later."

"I'll keep that in mind." Jan snickered. "What about you?"

"I'm not sure if cuddling up with a woman will help me sleep."

"That is a mental image I wasn't expecting, but I appreciate it. Maybe envisioning you with a woman would help *me* sleep. It would make for some pleasant dreams, that's for certain – ouch!"

Jan yelped when I slapped him. I rolled my eyes as he dramatically rubbed his chest, (I hadn't hit him *that* hard), and we giggled together again.

"In all honestly, I'm jealous of you, Jan. I'd love to go and take a man – any man – and bring him to bed with me."

"The nights are lonely," Jan said empathetically.

"Lonely and cold." I murmured.

"There is nothing warmer than a lover's embrace."

"How skaldic of you." I grinned. "Even if I did find a man, how could I be sure he wasn't just trying to marry me to take my jarldoms from me? Not to mention, it's not like I can just share a man's bed and be done with. What if I got pregnant? If the bastard was a boy, he could make a claim against my sons inheritances."

"He'd be your son, too."

"What – who?"

"The bastard."

"Aros and Roskilde belong to Young Birger and Sander." I said firmly. "If one of them dies without an heir then Einar will inherit their jarldom. If my sons have no sons then only after all three of my sons are dead will the jarldoms go to my daughter's sons."

"I understand, Aveline, I do. I pity you, you have all this to think about when all you want is a good fuck and a cuddle." Jan sighed dramatically. "I can see why you're jealous of me."

I laughed loudly, before flopping down beside him.

"Before, I was actually asking why you're out here again."

"The same reason as you." I replied, shifting beside him. "Move up, would you? My sword and shield are in the way."

"You could move *them*." Jan retorted but shuffled over anyway.

In silence I laid down beside him, staring at the sky. Jan nudged me with his elbows as he moved his arms from behind his head and rested them over his chest, his fingers tangled together.

"I miss him." I murmured.

"Me too." Jan breathed.

Silence settled over us and my thoughts drifted to my children. Each of them handled their father's death in such different ways.

Young Birger did not speak of Vidar, he merely nodded and smiled graciously when people compared him favourably to his father. Stoic as ever, Young Birger missed his father greatly, but would not put into words just how much Vidar's passing affected him. I worried most about Young Birger, he had been closest to Vidar, the one compared to Vidar the most often.

Upon his shoulders Young Birger took Vidar's mantle as the man of the house, strong for all who needed him, his heartache a pain he suffered in silence. No matter how much I tried to urge him to open to me, he refused. He would bare his burden alone.

Sander was the opposite. He spoke of Vidar as often as he could. He was so proud of his father, he wanted to emulate him, to live up to the reputation Vidar left behind. Sander listened avidly to tales of Vidar's life, past battles Vidar had fought, raids and expeditions. Sander's thirst for knowledge about Vidar seemed unquenchable. Each of Sander's dreams were ambitious and grand, and he pledged to make all of them a reality, in the name of his father. Sander wanted to make Vidar proud.

Æsa asked questions about Vidar and shared memories of him when they struck her. I looked at her now, nine years of age, saddened that Vidar was not around to see the young lady she was becoming. Within the next handful of years, she would be old enough to marry, old enough to have children. Vidar would never meet those grandchildren, a fate most men were cursed with.

Einar ... Einar broke my heart for he didn't remember his father at all. Over the first year after Vidar's death, Einar asked where his father was, why his father would not return home to us. He missed Vidar terribly and didn't understand what death meant. As time passed, most of his memories of Vidar disappeared and he stopped asking questions. I tried to keep Vidar alive in his mind, but everything Einar now knew about Vidar was gleamed from me or others. Vidar had been dead for almost half of Einar's life.

Einar was closer to Jan now, more than he had ever been before. Vidar's death caused an emptiness inside Einar, I think, and Einar filled that emptiness with Jan. He found a father figure in Jan, and Jan accepted him with open arms.

I was glad Einar bonded with Jan, but I hated it too. I wished Einar never had to, I wished he had his real father, not this replacement figure Jan had become. I tried to be both mother and father for my children, but it wasn't the same. Einar wanted Jan and I reluctantly conceded.

Our grief did not disappear completely and I doubted it ever would, but slowly things were getting easier.

***

AFTER A WHILE, I rolled onto my side, propping my head up with one hand. Jan's eyes were closed. I watched his chest rise and fall as he breathed, his face betraying no emotion. I knew he was awake, I'd camped beside him on enough expeditions to recognise when he was asleep and when he wasn't. When he slept, Jan's snores were soft but audible. I'd never witnessed him sleep silently.

"Jan ... What if I *had* accepted your proposal at the þing?" I asked. "Would you really have married me?"

"What made you think about *that*?" Jan scoffed, his brows shooting up his forehead in surprise.

"I was just thinking about everything that's happened these last few years." I confessed, a little embarrassed for asking.

Jan must've noticed for his tone softened.

"I'd do anything for you and the children, you know that."

"You would *marry* me, but you won't look for a woman to share your bed with?" I said, partially in jest, partially out of curiosity.

"It's different, Aveline."

"How?"

"I'm not ready for that."

"But you were ready to *marry* me?"

"I would do anything to help you save your jarldom and the boys' inheritances. If that meant marrying you, I would do so eagerly." Jan said, finally opening his eyes.

I met his gaze as I lowered my arm and rested my head on it. I rolled my lips together and scrutinised him silently.

"You're ridiculous." I said at last.

Jan laughed.

"When a man tells a woman, he'd do anything for her, being called *ridiculous* isn't the answer he expects to hear."

"How about *stupid*, then?" I asked.

"Why *stupid*?" Jan grinned.

"You won't take a woman to bed for your own happiness, but you'd marry me for – for *what*?"

"Duty, friendship. You're my jarl and my closest friend. I must help you no matter what, it's the honourable thing to do."

"You'd marry me to help me because you're my friend, yet you realise us marrying would've *destroyed* our friendship?"

"Keeping your jarldom was important to you." Jan replied nonchalantly.

"*You're* important to me!" I exclaimed. "I know we argue, I know I've said some horrible things to you in the past, but you're my closest friend! We've been through so much together over the years. I didn't need to risk our friendship to keep my jarldom. I wanted to keep both – and I did."

Jan rolled onto his side and pulled me into his arms, encasing my body in his. I gasped when he pulled me against him, surprised by his sudden embrace, but relaxed as I held him, melting against his body, the steady drum of his heartbeat filling my ears.

"By the gods, I'm thankful I have you in my life." Jan murmured.

"I'm glad I have you, too."

Like we were carved from stone, we held each other in silence, motionless but for our chests rising and falling as we breathed. A fluttering began in my stomach as an indescribable warmth filled me. Overwhelmed by the feeling, I squeezed my eyes closed, my heart hammering in my chest.

The first time Vidar and I had held each other was beneath the stars. We had been lying on a linen sheet in the garden behind Roskilde hall. We were talking and, after a poignant part of our conversation, Vidar pulled me against him. I'd been surprised, but I'd enjoyed being in his arms. That was that night I realised I had romantic feelings for Vidar.

"Are you alright?" Jan asked. "You're breathing quickly."

A strange feeling was unravelling inside me. A knot was lodged in my throat and my heart wouldn't stop racing. I gripped Jan's tunic tightly, trying to steady my trembling hands.

This feeling … It was the feeling I'd been craving since Vidar's death. I felt safe – comfortable – happy … And that terrified me.

"I'm okay." I lied.

I glanced up and found Jan looking down on me, his rose-coloured lips parted slightly. My breath caught in my throat – our lips were dangerously close. I forced my gaze from Jan's mouth to his eyes, an indiscernible emotion exuding from his sapphire stare.

"Aveline?"

Jan's breath danced on my lips as he whispered my name. By the gods, I shouldn't have been that close to him! I felt guilty, I felt wrong, but both those feelings were smothered by the fire growing inside me, setting aflame to every fibre of my being.

Jan touched my jaw with his fingertips, my eyelids flickered shut and our lips met in the lightest of kisses. He pulled away first, and my eyes snapped open. My heart raced as I recognised my fear, my confusion and my lust mirrored in his eyes.

"If marrying would've destroyed our friendship, what will *this* do to it?" Jan whispered.

"I don't know." I breathed.

GWENDOLINE SK TERRY
CHAPTER FIFTEEN

JAN AND I searched each other's faces for answers but neither of us had any. I parted my lips, wanting to say something to Jan – anything! – but words failed me. Jan tilted his face a little closer, and my gaze fell to his mouth, those full rose lips, sweet and soft, pouted in offer of another tender kiss.

What *would* this do to our friendship? I tried to focus on what was at risk if we continued down this path but those thoughts were fleeting. I couldn't stop myself. I brought my mouth to his, all thoughts washed away with each lingering kiss. Slowly, we shifted, tangling our bodies together, and my guilt and confusion were drowned out by desire.

Jan grazed my bottom lip with the tip of his tongue, silently beseeching me to let him taste me. I parted my lips and greeted his tongue with mine, savouring the delicacy of his touch and the sweetness of his mouth.

My body tingled as Jan's hand slid down my body and pulled me closer against him. His hand travelled lower still. A gasp escaped my lips as he cupped my buttock, squeezing it through the layers of my skirts. He lessened his grip at my sharp intake of breath, but I kissed him deeper, wordlessly begging him not to stop, and he didn't. Consumed by lust, I kissed him passionately, moving past the delicacy of before, and Jan answered just as fervently.

An instinctual almost animalistic need to copulate overwhelmed me. Years of loneliness hastened my actions, urging me to ignore all possible consequences of what Jan and I were about to do. I slid my hands over his body, thrilled by the hardness of the muscles beneath his clothing.

I shuffled his tunic up over his stomach when Jan broke our kiss. He sat up, yanked the garment off and tossed it into the darkness. His tousled hair flowed over his shoulders, a lock hanging over his face. He tucked it behind his ear, his sapphire eyes locked on me.

ASHES REMAIN

Time stood still.

I let my eyes travel over him, drinking in the vastness of his muscles, the tautness of his stomach, the broadness of his chest and the dark silken curls scattered there. The black tattoos etched across his body stark against his alabaster skin, which almost seemed to glow in the moonlight. Jan's trousers were tight around his powerful thighs and the hard ridge of his masculinity between them. Jan possessed the magnificence of a body honed by battle, that I had known since the day I'd met him – but now he was *offering* it to me.

That longing, that animalistic desire consumed me. I straddled him, his arousal pulsating between my legs, straining against the fabric of his clothes. The fair hairs over my body stood on end as I glided my hands over his powerful arms, in awe of the softness of his tattooed skin and the hardness of the muscle beneath.

Jan closed his hands around my waist, gripping me tightly. I stroked his bearded jaw and ran my fingers through his long tawny hair, soft as silk against my palms as I slipped it over his shoulders. Our lips touched, timid for just a moment before our tongues met and continued their eager dance.

Jan bunched my skirts over my hips. I could feel his hesitance to break our kiss yet again, but he did, swiftly pulling my dress over my head and tossing it to the ground beside us. The breeze wafted over my naked body, cool and exhilarating. My eyelids closed, I enjoyed the night air dancing on my naked flesh for a few moments, rolling my shoulders back, a sigh tumbling from my lips.

Slowly I opened my eyes and caught Jan staring at me. A blush burned my cheeks. Jan had stolen brief glances of my nakedness over the years, but nothing like this. The reverence in his gaze as his eyes travelled over me caused a virginal shyness to overcome me. I closed my eyes and turned away, goosebumps prickling my skin as he glided his hands over me.

Jan touched my jaw. My lips parted readily for his kiss and my body ignited the moment our mouths met. I trembled as he left a trail of kisses over my neck and collarbones before burying his head between my breasts and kissing the soft flesh there.

I held Jan's head against me, my fingers tangled in his hair. My breasts responded to his lips and tongue as he tormented them with masterful talent. The deep pulls of his mouth on my breasts sparked a tingling between my legs, a nagging ache for more.

I kissed the top of his head, the scent of lye soap and lavender oil from his hair filling my nostrils, moans rolling in my throat. His cock pressed insistently against me, enticing, inviting.

Jan shifted. He released my nipples and wrapped his arms around me, bringing his lips to mine once more. I pulled away from him this time and he stared at me confused. With both hands on his chest, I pushed him down and he silently acquiesced.

I knelt between his legs, dragging my fingertips over his chest and stomach to the soft flesh of his abdomen. He twitched and I smiled, he was ticklish there. I undid the drawstring of his trousers, glancing up at him as I did so. He watched me eagerly and lifted his buttocks off the ground for me to pull his trousers off.

Jan's erection was a delicious, intimidating sight. I reached out my trembling fingers and stroked it from the head to the root, Jan's pleasure-filled gasp meeting my ears. I closed my hand around the base of his cock and circled the head with my tongue. The delicate flesh was soft and smooth.

Jan's body shuddered as I took his cock into my mouth. His throaty groans grew steadily louder with each sucking pull of my mouth. He rested his hand on the back of my head, urging me to take him deeper and I gladly complied. My head didn't bob between his legs for too long before he tilted his pelvis away from me and gently pushed me off. If I continued much longer, Jan's euphoria would fill my mouth.

He pulled me onto his lap again, his cock slick with my saliva, sliding against me. Jan held my waist with both hands, and I gripped his forearms. A delicious pain rippled through me as I eased myself onto Jan's cock, my insides spreading to accommodate his size. I hadn't realised I'd been holding my breath until I gasped when his cock was completely inside me.

Our eyes locked. I rode him slowly until my ache turned into pleasure. Our bodies parted and joined in a natural rhythm, pleasure growing in my core with every stroke.

As my pleasure mounted, my movements quickened. Jan's fingertips dug into the flesh of my hips, as my momentum grew Jan seemed to take control of me, driving me down on his cock.

ASHES REMAIN

Euphoria boiled in the pit of my stomach, surging through me like wildfire. I lost all control of myself, crying out as ecstasy erupted through me, thundering from deep in my core to the tips of my extremities. With more force than before, Jan drove me down on his cock. I clutched him, crying out, until at last, with an almighty roar, Jan's body shuddered in his own release.

Jan fell back onto the grass, and, breathless, I collapsed on top of him, involuntarily jerking as his cock pulsated inside me. Jan's hands fell to the ground, immobilised by his climax, he couldn't do anything but try to catch his breath.

We laid there in silence, the swells of orgasm fading. I listened as his heartbeat slowed to a normal pace and he wrapped his arms around me. Jan pressed a kiss to the top of my head and I slid off him, pulling away from his embrace.

We dressed in silence, our backs turned to each other. Our desires quenched, now we were left with the repercussions of our actions. What were we meant to do? What should we say? By giving in to lust, we changed our friendship forever. This was worse than anything a platonic marriage could've done.

"I need to go home." I muttered, fastening my woollen cloak over my shoulder and picking up my shield.

We trudged up to the marketplace in silence. His seed was cold and wet on my thighs, an uncomfortable effect adding to the shock of what had occurred. We weaved through a few streets, past animal pens and homes, sheets and clothes pegged on washing lines to dry during the day now forgotten and wavering in the gentle wind like ghosts in the night. Finally we reached the place where we would part company, but rather than turn as he was meant to, Jan continued at my side.

"Shouldn't you go that way?" I asked, stopping.

"I thought I'd walk you back to the hall."

"I can go by myself."

"Are you sure? It's not safe to walk alone at night."

"I'm armed." I offered him an awkward smile. "If anything, I should walk *you* home."

Jan snickered uneasily. Even my joke was not enough to alleviate the nervousness between us.

"If that's what you want, I'll leave you here." Jan said.

We faced each other uncomfortably. Should I kiss him goodnight? Should I hug him? Should I just walk away? I didn't know what to do and by the look on his face neither did Jan. Thankfully he came to a solution quicker than I did, he took a step forward and pressed a kiss to my brow. Before he could pull away, I rested my hand on his chest. He paused. I stood on my tiptoes and we kissed.

"*Góða nótt*," I whispered.

"*Góða nótt*," Jan replied, wide-eyed with surprise.

I could feel his eyes follow me as I walked to the hall alone.

***

THAT NIGHT I couldn't sleep for an entirely different reason than usual. In my mind, I replayed what happened – the first kiss and the lovemaking it led to. I was so confused by the feelings awoken inside me.

I thought back to the kiss Jan had pressed to my brow at the þing. I couldn't deny the feelings that brewed inside me the moment his lips touched my skin nor could I deny the happiness that filled me when he returned from hunting Háken. I hadn't understood what those feelings were then, but now …

Was it really any surprise that I was forming feelings for Jan when he and I had bonded so strongly through grief? I owed him more than I could ever repay him. Even though we bickered and fought, Jan was there for me always during the last three years. He was my confidante, my refuge … Just as Vidar had been.

I woke the next morning not knowing when I'd fallen asleep. The children were in the main room, I could hear them playing and chatting. Slowly I brought my hand to my mouth, touching my lips with my fingertips, wondering if it had all been real or just a vivid dream. The dull ache between my legs and the dried-up mess on my thighs conveyed the truth.

"Jarl?" Rowena's voice was quiet – mindful in case I was still asleep, probably.

"*Góðan morgin*." I replied softly.

"Breakfast is ready." She smiled.

"*Þakka fyrir*. Would you draw me a bath while I eat?"

ASHES REMAIN

"Of course." Rowena replied, leaving the room.

I slipped my legs over the side of my bed. What was to happen now? Would I have to act as though I wasn't tormented over the fact I'd made love to my late husband's closest friend – *my* closest friend? What if I saw Jan today? Would he kiss me? What would my children say if they saw? Would they be angry?

What if Jan *didn't* kiss me? What if he pretended like nothing happened – did I want that? Did I want to continue as before? Last night could be passed off as a lack of judgement, an accident that wouldn't happen again, that should never have happened to begin with, but one our loneliness compelled us into.

I sighed and stumbled out of the bedroom in my underdress. Since Vidar's death I wanted Jan's company and comfort. Last night I wanted someone to hold me, to kiss me, to love me. Last night I wanted Jan … What did I want now?

"*Góðan morgin, móðir.*" Young Birger said as I entered the room.

"*Mumie!*" Æsa beamed.

"You slept *forever*." Einar remarked as I took a seat beside him.

"I needed the sleep." I smiled, nudging him with my shoulder.

"Did you sleep well?" Sander asked.

"Well enough," I replied, rubbing my eyes with the heels of my hands. "Don't worry my loves, I just had a long night."

Melisende brought me a basin of hot water, a bowl of steaming porridge and a plate of strong-smelling cheese and chewy dried fruit. I scrubbed my face and hands with soap before eating silently, listening to my children chatter.

Young Birger and Sander were going to the shipyard today, after which they would go fishing with Domnall and Yngvi. Both boys loved fishing and would do anything to spend time on the ships.

Young Birger was a craftsman and a talented one at that. He loved woodworking whether it was mending and maintaining the ships or carving bows and toys or even cups and plates.

Sander loved the rush of fishing, the boat bobbing on the waves, the thrill of tossing the net overboard and hauling it back bursting with fish. An empty net didn't disappoint him for they would have to row further out to sea where the excitement and danger was heightened. There were all kinds of creatures out there, whales flopping on the water and dolphins or seals to spear.

GWENDOLINE SK TERRY

The boys gobbled up their breakfast and set off. The winter after next, Young Birger would be sixteen and old enough to marry. We kept in close contact with Jarl Askold of Ribe over the past three years, he had even come to Aros with his family and a large retinue to celebrate *Jól* with us this past winter.

In a few weeks, we would be travelling to Ribe to formally arrange Young Birger and Signý's wedding. In his past visit, Jarl Askold said he wanted them to marry sooner rather than later – we'd waited three years already. He asked if I'd object to marrying them the winter Young Birger turned sixteen rather than waiting until the autumn after as was traditional. He let me consider it and when we visited Ribe I would bring my answer for him.

I asked Young Birger whether the lack of tradition and the haste of marrying in the wrong season bothered him, but he didn't mind. He'd met with Signý six times over the past three years, spending a few weeks with her each time, and they were thoroughly smitten with each other. He agreed to the winter wedding.

In little over a year, my eldest son would be married and living with his young wife in Roskilde Hall. Young Birger would be jarl, leader of his own army and town, head of his own household. I knew he was ready, I looked forward to watching him succeed, but my heart was heavy knowing I wouldn't see him every day anymore. My hall would be so empty without him.

Sander himself still had little over three years left until he would marry. Jarl Mats visited us last summer, the first time in the three years since he'd offered Sander his daughter, Fenja. She was fifteen and possessed a more womanly figure than when we first met her. Sander was three years younger than her, but already a head taller than her – he'd inherited his father's height. Sander was besotted by Fenja and determined to make her his wife.

Mats seemed to want Sander to wed his daughter – a wise decision for the Jarl of Alabu as it gave his small northern trading post two powerful allies between Aros and Roskilde – however, he didn't seem as eager to marry his daughter to Sander as Askold of Ribe was to marry Signý to Young Birger. Over the feast one night during his visit, Jarl Mats announced that Fenja had multiple suitors desperately vying for her lovely hand.

ASHES REMAIN

"A woman as beautiful as her is bound to have admirers." Sander had remarked. "In a few years she will be my wife and they will still be competing for her then."

"And what if I agree to marry her to one of these suitors instead of you?" Jarl Mats had asked, smirking at my son.

"She won't wed any of them." Sander said coolly.

"Don't make threats you are too young to defend." Mats replied.

"I'm not threatening anyone, Jarl, I'm just stating a fact: Fenja *will* be my wife." Sander said calmly.

Fenja flushed red with delight at Sander's boldness. Every jaw in the hall was dropped including mine. Sander kept his steely gaze with Mats, who glared at him for a moment before bursting out in a fit of laughter.

"Don't lose your confidence, boy." Mats said, wiping his eyes. "Only courageous men are fit to marry my daughters. Should Fenja have you, I believe you'll make a decent husband for her."

"I will be the *best* husband for her – if she'll have me." Sander said glancing her.

A dazzling beam shone from her pink face as she nodded, meeting Sander's gaze briefly before staring at her lap. Mats surveyed them both over his wine before changing the conversation to something else.

Sander's boldness impressed me, but in the past that boldness caused him trouble. I was intrigued to see how his life would turn out, there was much glory to be had in his future, but equal amounts of danger as well.

I turned to Æsa who was having her sleek white-blonde hair combed by Melisende. I still had time before I'd have to start looking for a husband for her. She was ten, she could begin her menses at any moment, but I prayed they would begin as late as possible. Young Birger would leave for Roskilde soon enough and I didn't want to marry Æsa off and watch her leave too.

Einar finished his porridge and set his bowl and spoon on the table with a clatter. He jumped down and seized the wooden sword Young Birger had made for him, before dashing out to the garden. The wooden blade was dented badly and covered in nicks from Einar playing with it constantly.

Einar was seven. There were still three years until he was a man. I worried I coddled him too much since he was my youngest child, so I tried to make a conscious effort not to treat him differently to his siblings. I didn't want to hinder him and set him up for failure in life. He needed to fight, to be brave and adventurous.

When I had Young Birger and Sander shadow me as I conducted my duties as jarl, I brought Einar along too, expecting the young boy to keep up with his older siblings. He might not become Jarl of Aros or Roskilde, but with effort and ambition he might seize his own jarldom when he was a man.

A horrible realisation flood through me. If I continued to sleep with Jan, there was a chance Einar wouldn't be my final child ...

"I'll be back in a moment." I said to Æsa and Melisende, before whisking off to the sleeping area.

I rushed to a chest in the far corner of the room. I hadn't opened it in three years. My thralls regularly wiped it down, but the hinges and lock were stiff. Inside were Vidar's clothes and some of his belongings I hadn't shared with the children. Resting on top of some neatly folded tunics was a medium sized flaxen bag.

I grabbed the bag and sat on the edge of the bed, untying the cord. Inside was a variety of dried herbs, angelica root, pennyroyal and mugwort leaves and a smaller bag tied shut with twine. Dried wild carrot seeds rustled inside the bag as I shifted on the bed.

I hadn't wanted to bear another child after Alffinna and I didn't want to now. After birthing Alffinna, I started eating a spoonful of the seeds once a day for fourteen days after my menses to prevent pregnancy.

If I ran out of the seeds or they lost their potency, I would drink a hot brew of angelica, pennyroyal and mugwort for five days after my menses instead. If my menses didn't arrive when they were supposed to, the drink would expel anything inside my womb, but I was careful not to consume that brew too often for the consequences could be fatal.

I poured some of the carrot seeds into my mouth and chewed them quickly. They were dry as dust and terribly bitter. Hopefully, they still worked – they were three years old, so I had my doubts.

CHAPTER SIXTEEN

AFTER BREAKFAST, I bathed, washing the remnants of last night from my body. After dressing and combing my hair, I played with Einar and Æsa until I found a moment to leave the hall to visit Brynja. I wanted to purchase a fresh supply of wild carrot seeds and herbs for the decoction to avoid pregnancy.

My walk was slow. In my mind I recited excuses as to why I needed the herbs, nervous to admit I'd laid with a man. What if Brynja asked who I was taking to my bed? What if she asked if I intended to marry the man?

I shook my head. I was the jarl and a widow, I could take whoever I wanted to my bed. I was getting older and wanted to be cautious. I knew many women my age who had got with child and I had seen many of them die during the birth.

I rapped on Brynja's door before pushing it open. Her three daughters were there, tying bundles of herbs and hanging them from the beams and rafters to dry, sealing packets filled with seeds or dried herbs, grinding dried plants into powders. Marta lifted her head and smiled at me before turning back to the customer she was seeing to. The customer, Heimlaug Daðadóttir, turned to me.

"*Góðan aptan*, my dear Jarl." Heimlaug greeted me happily, her voice hoarse and breathing raspy.

"Heimlaug, you sound unwell!" I said, concerned by the sickly state of the elderly woman – her aged face was ashen and haggard.

"It's this damn cough," Heimlaug explained. "Everything from the weather to the fire irritates it. Luckily Brynja has a brew that alleviates it, if just for a while."

"I'm glad to hear that, but I wish you weren't suffering." I frowned sympathetically.

"You and I both," Heimlaug chuckled.

Quickly her laughter turned to raucous coughing. Nefja finished hanging a bundle and rushed to the kitchen.

"You should be resting." Marta scolded gently. "Was there no one else who could fetch the herbs for you?"

"Jan offered, but I wanted to get out of the house. There's only so much time I can spend in bed before I go utterly mad." Heimlaug smiled.

My heart leapt at the mention of Jan's name. When Jan moved to Aros after Thóra left him, he needed a place to live. Heimlaug accepted him into her home under the condition he helped run her farm. Her only child, a son, was killed in the East Angles many years before and her husband died just months before Jan arrived. It was an agreement that suited them both and Jan had lived with her ever since.

Nefja returned with a steaming cup, the strong, fresh scent of mint drifting from it. Heimlaug accepted the brew gratefully and the conversation thankfully changed to children and home, the weather and crops, sickness and health.

Brynja's home was quieter now her four granddaughters, aged between thirteen and fifteen, had been married and gone to live with their respective husbands. Of her seven grandchildren, only Brynja's three grandsons remained in her home, the youngest of whom would see his fifth winter this year. All three boys were at the shipyard with their fathers, Marta and Nefja's husbands.

Brynja's husband died long ago – I'd never met the man. Nor had I met their only son, Hraði. He lived far away in a settlement called Reykjarvík in Ísland.

All three of Brynja's daughters lived and worked with her as healers. When each of the daughters had married, their husbands moved into Brynja's longhouse. A rather untraditional occurrence, usually men would take their wives into their homes. Each woman was determined to stay in Brynja's longhouse to work as healers and if the men wanted to marry them, they had to live there, too, otherwise they would have to find another wife.

Luckily for them, all three of the husbands had agreed. Only two of the husbands, both shipbuilders, lived there now. Káta had lost her husband over three years ago. He died fighting in Francia during our failed siege of Paris months before Vidar died.

I felt for Káta, she had two daughters with her husband and now both were gone. I once asked why her girls hadn't remained at home to practice the craft of healing too, but Káta said that they weren't interested and left it at that. I wondered privately how she could live without her children *and* husband, but I wouldn't ask.

"What may I do for you, Jarl? I've kept you here talking rather than seeing to your needs." Nefja said apologetically.

"Not a problem at all." I smiled. "I was hoping to see Brynja."

"She's in the garden, I'll fetch her for you."

"*Nei*, it's alright," I replied, holding a hand up as she started toward the door. "I'll go to her."

"Are you sure?" Nefja asked.

"*Já*, it's fine." I said. "*Góðan aptan* to you all."

Each woman bid me farewell as I left. I meandered through the garden, admiring the bright young plants and the well-established bushes with their fresh buds and leaves. Brynja's vast garden was beautiful. Glorious scents teemed throughout, some sharp others sweet, a breath-taking blend that overwhelmed the senses. I found Brynja planting seeds in a bed across from her chicken pen. She beamed when she saw me, sitting back on her legs.

"Jarl! What a pleasure it is to see you." Brynja exclaimed.

"I'm happy to see you, too." I grinned, helping the old woman to her feet.

"Most come to me when they're sick, I hope your family is well."

"We're fine," I said, rolling my lips together. I'd have to explain myself sooner than expected. "I'm here for a different matter."

"I'll help wherever I can. Would you like to sit?"

"Please." I nodded.

We wandered to the quiet seating area in the centre of her garden, surrounded by her beautiful flower beds and plants. Bees skittered from flower to flower, collecting pollen and drinking the sweet nectar inside each newly blossomed flower.

"I want to purchase some wild carrot seeds," I said finally.

"Ah," Brynja's brows lifted with surprise. "Anything else, Jarl?"

"*Já*, I'd like to purchase the ingredients to *that* decoction."

"The one that prevents pregnancy?"

"*Já*, I had some leftover from when Vidar was alive, but – but I'm not sure if they will work now." I stuttered, twisting my rings around my finger. "It's been a few years …"

"I'll gather you fresh supplies." Brynja smiled warmly, taking my hand in her knobbly one, her fingers stained from planting, the pungent scent of soil drifting from them. "I'm pleased to hear you're opening your heart to love again."

Love? I spent a single night with Jan and the shock was rattling me to the core. I hadn't thought I was taking a step towards *love* at all. The very idea made me shudder.

"Something like that." I replied carefully.

"Let's get you sorted out then." Brynja offered, rising to her feet.

We made our way to the longhouse. Heimlaug was gone by the time we got there and Brynja's daughters were busy with chores. I sipped a cup of mead Marta gave me as Brynja bustled about gathering what I needed.

Brynja put the herbs in a flaxen bag and gave it to me before walking me outside. The moment the door closed behind us, she gripped my elbow and gazed at me with her watery blue eyes.

"Jarl, let me impart some advice to you, from one widow to another." Brynja said. "If you've met a man who makes you as happy as Vidar did, don't turn him away."

"It's too soon to know if he can make me *that* happy yet." I replied weakly.

"The heart heals at its own pace, but it *does* heal."

"I know …" I said, rolling my lips together. "It sounds ridiculous, but I feel – I feel like I'm betraying him."

Brynja shook her head and squeezed my elbow tighter.

"Don't let the ghosts of the past hinder your happiness. You're *not* betraying the dead by moving forward."

I nodded, each shallow breath I inhaled shuddering in my chest.

"Welcome love into your life, sweet woman, welcome happiness." Brynja said, stroking my cheek with her calloused hand. "Vidar would want you to be happy."

I clutched the bag of herbs to my chest.

"*Þakka fyrir*, Brynja." I smiled.

***

I PAUSED AT the hall door and took a deep breath. As I walked home I was lost in my thoughts, Brynja's words resounding in my

ASHES REMAIN

mind. I was standing at the edge of a precipice of romance, of truly moving forward from Vidar's death, and Brynja was cheering me on. All I had to do was jump, but insecurity and guilt rooted me to the spot. The only person who I could talk to about this was Jan, but the very idea made my heart race.

I sighed again before pulling the hall door open. To my surprise, I found Ebbe and Borghildr with their brood, Domnall, Guðrin and their son Yngvi, Hallmundr, Lars and Einarr all at the table with my children eating cold slices of meat and a wild greens.

"I forgot you all were coming over tonight!" I exclaimed. "By the gods, I'm late for a meal in my own home!"

"We forgive you, Jarl." Hallmundr grinned.

"We only just arrived ourselves." Borghildr said warmly.

"Never mind, you're here now." Guðrin smiled.

"Welcome home, Jarl."

My heart leapt to my throat. Jan was standing in the kitchen doorway holding Einar upside down under his arm. A smile lifted one corner of Jan's mouth, and a light blush coloured his cheeks when our eyes met. Einar wriggled in his grasp, giggling, his face pink from being upside down, his clothes filthy from playing outside. Jan set him down on his feet and he wobbled for a minute.

"Are you alright there, Einar?" Jan laughed.

"*Já*," Einar grinned.

My youngest son stumbled, grabbing hold of Jan to keep himself up as his sight steadied and dizziness passed. Einar's long mane of curls was wildly dishevelled, springing from his head in a frizzy blond mess. He giggled as he settled at the table beside Sander, who ruffled Einar's hair and laughed.

"I didn't see you there." I murmured as Jan neared me.

"It's alright," Jan smiled. "You see me now."

"*Já*, I do."

We stared at each other briefly, that smile playing on Jan's lips. My cheeks flushed, I cleared my throat and sat at the table between Guðrin and Borghildr, avoiding Jan's gaze. My friends stared at me, their eyes narrowed, and brows furrowed – by their expressions, they must've noticed I was behaving oddly.

Jan took a spot opposite me, far better at hiding his nerves than me. Unless he *wasn't* nervous. Perhaps he *was* going to pretend like last night didn't happen … That was probably for the best, yet my heart sank.

***

THE EVENING WAS long. I played Hnefatafl with Hallmundr, Ebbe and Domnall, gossiped with Guðrin and Borghildr, played with the children and belly laughed at Einarr's and Lars' hilarious musical composition.

Einarr played a fine tune on his lyre while Lars accompanied it with an improvised song about romance. He sang out of tune – our late friend Finnvarðr had been the best singer out of the three – but Lars' lack of talent didn't matter. His love song grew more crude and funnier until the musician doubled up with laughter at Lars' vulgar verses, unable to play any longer.

I avoided interacting with Jan as much as I could over the evening, but that seemed to arouse Guðrin and Borghildr's suspicions even more. Quietly they asked if Jan and I had argued, but I shook my head and refused to divulge anything. I wasn't ready to share what had happened least of all in front of my children and all my friends.

Finally, everyone began filtering back to their homes until only Jan, Domnall, Guðrin and Yngvi remained. Sander and Young Birger were chatting with Yngvi, all three boys' eyelids drooping with sleep, but all were too stubborn to call an end to the night.

Æsa had gone to bed hours ago and Einar was slumped in a chair beside Jan, snoring softly. The poor child had tried to keep up with his older brothers, but he just couldn't make it.

"I'll take him to bed." I said, avoiding Jan's gaze as I approached.

I scooped Einar up before Jan could reply and scuttled to the sleeping area. I settled Einar in his bed and pulled a blanket over him. I paused in the doorway and admired my youngest child. Chiselled features were emerging, his soft baby looks were fading.

Soon Einar would be old enough to fight, to marry, to lead, to go on adventures. Soon all my children would be grown. One day I would become a grandmother … I smiled. I hoped I would live long enough to meet my grandchildren – that would be the ultimate blessing the damned gods could bestow upon me.

ASHES REMAIN

I turned around and almost bumped straight into Jan.

"I'm sorry, I wasn't looking." I mumbled, avoiding his gaze.

"It was my fault, I shouldn't have been so close," Jan said. "It's getting late and I wanted to talk to you in private for a moment."

"Okay." I said, breath held in my chest.

"Will you be at the shore tonight?"

"I might, I'm not sure yet." I replied, a hot blush burning over my cheeks. "You?"

"The same," Jan said. "I'm not sure whether I'll sleep well with all the questions whirling around my head."

"I fear I'll have the same issue."

I finally looked up at him. Jan's eyes were bloodshot and bags hung beneath them – it looked as though he hadn't slept at all last night, either. I breathed in sharply, realising how close we were. I rolled my lips and crossed my arms, stepping back.

"Perhaps we should meet and try to work out some answers." Jan suggested, rubbing the back of his neck with one hand.

"When will you be there?"

"An hour?" Jan suggested.

"I'll see you there."

Jan lingered for a moment seeming to notice how close we were, as I was painfully aware. His lips parted, but he said nothing. I lowered my head before hurrying over to Guðrin. She was standing by the door with Domnall, Yngvi, Sander and Young Birger. She eyed me suspiciously before embracing me.

"Everything alright?" She whispered into my ear.

"*Já*," I muttered. "I promise, it's fine."

Jan approached just as Guðrin and I released each other.

"Another wonderful night, Jarl." Jan said.

"If you don't want it to end, you're welcome for an ale at my place." Domnall grinned, his cheeks reddened by alcohol.

"By the look on Guðrin's face, I think we may need to do that another night." Jan smirked.

"I'm an old woman now, I need my rest." Guðrin smiled though she narrowed her eyes a little at Jan.

"Then bed it is, my love." The fiery-haired Domnall crooned, wrapping his arms around his wife's shoulders and pecking her on the cheek. "Nothing is worth passing up a chance to curl up under the furs with you."

Guðrin blushed and bid farewell as they left. Yngvi rolled his eyes behind his parents and grunted goodbye to Young Birger and Sander, red-faced with embarrassment at his parents' romance. Jan glanced at me briefly before leaving with them.

***

THE HOUR DRAGGED by as I waited to meet Jan. Thankfully Young Birger and Sander went to bed right after our friends left, and now all four of my children were sound asleep. As Rowena helped me with my cloak, I let her and Melisende know I'd return in a little while and gave them permission to go to bed and to tidy the hall in the morning. With *Úlfsblóð* sheathed at my hip and my shield in hand, I crept into the night.

I spotted Jan's dark silhouette on the grassy patch near the shore the moment I entered the marketplace. As I neared, I noticed his sword and shield on the ground beside him.

"You brought your shield this time." I commented.

"One should carry their shield with them at all times." Jan winked, greeting me with a dazzling grin.

I returned his smile with a small one of my own, my heart racing. I sat down a healthy distance from him, setting my shield and sword beside me. Awkwardness hung in the air, heavy and tense, each of us waiting for the other to start the topic we knew we needed to discuss. Though bold in battle, neither of us had the courage to face whatever the other had to say.

"Let's go for a walk?" Jan suggested.

I scarpered to my feet, sheathed *Úlfsblóð* and picked up my shield. Jan did the same, carrying his shield on his right rather than his left. As we walked beside each other, our fingers brushed, but neither of us seized the opportunity to hold hands. I wondered if that was why he held his shield in his other hand, but he never reached for my fingers.

We walked silently for what felt like an age, until finally, Jan mustered up the courage to speak.

"What happens now?" Jan asked, his voice low but audible.

ASHES REMAIN

"I don't know." I mumbled, avoiding his gaze.

"Do we ignore it? Should we pretend like it never happened?"

The questions that whirled in my brain all night and day cascaded from his mouth just as they had flooded my mind. I'd hoped speaking about what happened would clarify everything, but instead it increased my uncertainty. If neither of us knew what to do or where to go from here, how could we fix this?

"I don't know if I can pretend like it never happened." Jan said.

I looked up at him, my brow furrowed.

"I don't want to pretend, Jan." I admitted. "There's no point lying to ourselves – *it happened*. We can't change that."

"Do you regret it?" Jan asked.

"Do you?" I replied, shocked by his bluntness.

"*Nei*," Jan replied, finally reaching for my hand. "*Nei*, I don't."

His large hand engulfed mine in the gentlest grasp. It was warm, soft, steady.

"I don't regret it either."

"I'm glad," Jan smiled.

He looked not just happy, but relieved as well. In a way, I felt the same. I was comforted to know he felt similarly, but that didn't mean we'd agree on the same solution. In fact, this complicated matters more. Had we both regretted laying together, we would never do it again. Now we had to decide whether we wanted to continue whatever this was or leave what happened in the past.

"What do we do now?"

Jan didn't answer. He stopped and dropped his shield on the ground. He took a step towards me, leaning forward slowly, offering me a chance to react. As his fingertips touched my jaw, I rested my hand on his chest and rose to my tiptoes.

We kissed gently, softly, our lips lingering together. Jan closed his arms around me, bringing my body against his. I gripped the handle of my shield, squeezing the leather against my palm. Our mouths parted just enough for our tongues to glance between kisses, each timid touch fanning embers deep inside me to life.

"I want you." Jan admitted, resting his brow against mine.

"It this worth risking our friendship?"

"It could be – it could turn into something *incredible*!"

"I don't know if we should ..."

"Why not?"

A frown tugged at Jan's lips and his eyes were wide beneath his thick knitted brows. I cupped his face, stroking his cheek with my thumb, his expression relaxing under my touch. His clenched jaw slackened and lips parted. It took all my strength not to kiss him.

"You know about the lives I owe the Allfather – you know I have two left." I fretted. "The people closest to me are the ones that die."

"My life is at risk whether we lay together or not."

Jan was right, by just being my friend, there was a possibility the Allfather would take his life.

"I should send you away to keep you safe." I mused.

"I'll come back no matter how far you send me." Jan grinned.

I shifted, my body melting against his as he kissed me, all thought leaving my mind by the taste, touch and smell of him.

The leather handle of my shield slipped from my fingers and the *thud* as the round wooden shield hit the ground startled me back to reality. I was too distracted – if Jan held me much longer, if he kissed me again, we would end up making love.

I stepped back and crossed my arms over my chest.

"Jan, it won't just complicate our friendship – it's not just the lives for the Allfather – what of Vidar? What would *he* say if we continued this?" Questions fell from my lips in a rambling mess.

Jan released a deep sigh and stroked my upper arms as though he was trying to warm me up. His eyes searched my face, his lips turned down in the smallest of frowns. He tilted his head, a few flyaway strands dancing over his face.

"Vidar wouldn't be pleased." I pressed.

"Why would he be? You were his wife, of course he wouldn't want anyone to have you but him." Jan said, offering me a half-smile. "I'd like to think Vidar would want you to be happy – he'd want *both of us* to be happy."

Brynja said the same thing ...

"Why do people assume that your loved one would want you to be happy after they die?" I demanded.

"What?" Jan asked, visibly taken back by my question. "If your places were reversed, wouldn't you want Vidar to find happiness after your death?"

ASHES REMAIN

"*Nei!*" I snapped, blushing furiously. "I'd want him to be happy, of course, but would I want him to take another woman to bed? Would I want him to kiss another? Would I want him to marry someone else? *Nei*, I wouldn't! If that makes me selfish then so be it! I don't want to imagine Vidar with anyone else, I want him to be with *me*!"

"But he isn't."

The moment those three softly spoken words reached my ears, I burst into tears. Jan pulled me against him, hugging me as every ounce of guilt and grief poured out of me. I wept uncontrollably, snot and tears streaming down my face. I buried my head in Jan's tunic, unable to hold back my sorrow.

"How am I meant to be a loyal wife to him when he's dead?" I spluttered between sobs.

"You can't." Jan replied, pressing a kiss to the top of my head.

"How can you do that? How can you keep kissing me?" I scowled, pulling away from him. "Don't you mourn Vidar? Don't you miss him? Don't you feel guilty for betraying him?"

"How did *I* betray *him*?" Jan barked, glaring at me. "Did I die and leave him? *Nei*! He's with the Allfather drinking and fighting without the worry of disease or death or loss! *He* left *me* – *he* left *us*! He spends the afterlife in glory while we're left in Midgard trying to find some measly ounce of happiness in his absence!"

My tears halted immediately at Jan's outburst. I staggered back, nausea rising from the pit of my stomach. I hadn't realised how angry Jan was – how much grief he still suffered.

"I miss Vidar with every part of me – he was my *bróðir*." Jan's voice was deep and trembling. "But if he didn't want me to be with his wife then he shouldn't have died! He can come from Valhalla right now and take you from me or kill me, or both – I don't care! If Vidar didn't want any of this to happen, he shouldn't have died!"

My heart lurched, I could hardly breathe. Jan roared in anger and stormed off. Twenty paces away he stopped, flung his shield to down, ripped his sword from his sheath and threw that down, too. He dropped to the ground and rubbed his face between his hands.

Jan sat there like a statue, hugging his long legs against his chest as he stared out at the fjord spread before him, the waves sloshing gently on the shore, dark as the night sky and twinkling just as brightly. I finally let go of the breath held in my chest and approached Jan, my footsteps small and timid. I stopped beside him, clinging to my shield with both hands.

"If Vidar was here, none of this would've happened." Jan said just loud enough for me to hear. "Our relationship would be simple. We'd be friends, everything would be normal, easy, just as it was. But Vidar's not here no matter how much we wish he was."

I placed my shield down, drew *Úlfsblóð* and set it on top. I sat down, tucking my legs beside me, and twisted my wedding rings around my finger.

"I miss him ... I miss my father, my mother ... I miss my brother, Jafnhárr. I miss my children, I miss Unnr, I miss Finnvarðr and all my friends who died in battle over the years. Damn it, I miss Alvar and Freydis, too. Not a day goes by where I don't think of every person I've lost."

Jan turned to me then, his face reddened by emotion. His anger was declining, but a darkness surrounded him so thick and heavy I could feel it. My own heart dropped in my chest and, with a shudder, goosebumps rippled over my body.

"I can't lose myself to misery otherwise I'll fall apart. You can't either, Aveline." Jan said. "If you cling to your loss it will destroy you, at some point, you *must* let go. Whether we like it or not, the Nornir decided when they were meant to die and we can't change any of it – we can't bring them back. That doesn't mean we should forget them. We'll never be able to do that."

I gave him a small nod.

"Vidar kept me strong, helped me through the grief of all those I've lost in the past. When he died there was nothing left in this world for me – except you. These last three years you've given me comfort and love. There are never any expectations with you, I didn't have to be *Jötunnson* or *Jan the Handsome*. There's an ease in your presence, I'm always comfortable with you. If you hadn't let me be with you and the children every day since Vidar died, I don't know what would've happened ..."

I rested my hand on his.

"We needed you." I said earnestly. "You helped us through the hardest tragedy we have and will ever suffer."

Jan brought my hand to his lips and kissed the back of it gently.

ASHES REMAIN

"That's why I don't regret what we did." Jan said. "I don't want to deny myself the happiness I feel with you. When Vidar was alive I didn't spend my life wondering if he approved of what I was doing and I won't start now he's dead.

"The only opinion I want is *yours*, Aveline. Our friendship has already changed now. We'll never be able to go back to how it was. There are many reasons *not* to be together, but just as many to pursue this. I want *you*, Aveline, I want to be with you. If you don't want me I won't try to persuade you to be with me. I'll still be your friend, I'll still be your right-hand in battle and politics, I'll follow you always. I *will* keep the promise I made to Vidar and do everything within my power to protect you and the children, but I do that not just for him, but for you and the children as well.

"You don't need to have a reason for your decision, just tell me what you want and I'll obey."

Silently, I moved to kneel beside him, resting one hand on his shoulder and touching his jaw with the other. Jan wrapped his arms around me and accepted the tender kiss I placed on his lips.

"I'll *always* wonder what Vidar would do or say. I'll think of him with everything I do and I will never stop loving him or missing him." I whispered, losing myself in Jan's sapphire eyes. "But I want you at my side through everything, Jan. I don't know what's happening between us but I don't want it to stop."

Our lips met again, this time unyielding and bold. Jan brought me onto his lap and quickly we disrobed each other. He laid my naked body on the ground, caressed and kissed me, wanting and without fear. I ran my hands over his fair flesh and gasped against his lips as he entered me.

By the fjord in the waning night, Jan and I made love without guilt, wholly and completely together. We had made our decision and we accepted the consequences, whatever they might be.

CHAPTER SEVENTEEN

WEST FRANCIA
Late Summer, 890

STEEL CLANGED AGAINST steel as *Úlfsblóð* was met by the Frankish soldier's sword. A growl rolled in my throat as I bore all my weight into my weapon. We were close, close enough for me to watch sweat trickle down his brow. The Frank's yellow teeth gleamed from beneath his mask of blood, the blood of *my* warriors. Inch by inch, he pushed my blade away, he was stronger than me.

A smile crept over my face before I hocked a wad of phlegm into his eye. He yelped and flinched, distracted long enough for me to draw the seax from my belt and thrust it into his neck. His skin snapped easily, blood spurting from the small wound. I yanked the small blade free, the wound oozing yet more blood.

Gargling and gasping, the Frank dropped his sword and crumpled to the ground clutching his neck, body twitching. I didn't have time to waste watching him die. I sheathed my seax and swiped my shield from the ground.

In front of me, Young Birger was fighting two Franks on his own. He deflected one's sword with his shield, but just as quickly, the other Frank brought his blade upon him. Young Birger knocked it away with his sword. Stuck between the two, Young Birger was struggling. His arms trembled as he tried to shove back the enemies' weapons, he was weakening quickly. The Frank on the left swung his sword back, ready to strike.

Before he had a chance, I lunged, slamming my blade into the Frank's side, slicing through his armour and flesh with ease. Blood spewed from him in a crimson shower as he dropped to the ground like a felled tree.

Young Birger threw his shield at the surviving Frank, hitting him in the stomach. The Frank tumbled to his knees, his breath knocked out of him. With an almighty roar Young Birger plunged his sword between the Frank's shoulders, killing him instantly.

"Well done, my love!" I beamed, panting from exhaustion.

ASHES REMAIN
"*Þakka fyrir, móðir.*" Young Birger grinned.
"Come on, there's not many left."
Together we charged into the fray, cutting down the Franks.

***

WHAT REMAINED OF the Frankish army fled hours ago. The sun was descending, but there were still a few hours left until nightfall. As Young Birger, Sander and I roamed the monastery dormitory searching through chests for hidden valuables, the rest of my men were looting the main rooms and church. Bangs reverberated through the building and echoed off the high stone walls as our fellow Danes hacked apart a huge gilt crucifix.

"Find anything?" I asked Sander.

"*Nei*, nothing." Sander frowned.

"I'm sure we'll find something on their bodies." Young Birger said, ever the optimist. "They wouldn't have wasted time hiding things in here, they were too busy fleeing."

"Let's check outside, then." I smiled. "I'm sure the riders should be back soon."

Together, my sons and I left the dormitory. At noon, the battle ended, I sent a large team of riders to chase down the few surviving Frankish soldiers and any monks who managed to escape. Hours had passed since then, if the riders hadn't already returned, they would be back soon enough.

My sons and I strode through the monastery doors, stepping over corpses of monks and Franks. The riders had arrived, all of them in the process of dismounting their steeds, talking and laughing, admiring the pile of treasures building up outside the entrance. We approached Jan who had headed the team.

"You're back." I smiled as he slid elegantly off his horse.

"No need to worry, Jarl, I could never stay far from you for too long." Jan grinned, wrapping his arm around my shoulder.

"Don't touch me, you reek." I wrinkled my nose and shoved him away.

"*That* is the grand odour of victory, I'll have you know, Jarl." Jan beamed. "We left no survivors and got quite the hoard."

Domnall rode up beside us, a shining metal helmet upon his head. It was dented and covered in blood, but grand enough still.

"Very manly, Domnall. It suits you well."

"With your permission, I'd like to keep it." Domnall said, smiling at my compliment.

"It's yours."

"*Þakka fyrir*, Jarl." Domnall grinned. "It took some effort to get it – I chopped the bastard's head clean off. Dinged the helmet up a bit when it went rolling down the hill, but I've never seen a helm as beautiful as this."

"You did well, Domnall. When it's cleaned up, I'm sure it will be most handsome." I said kindly before glancing up at Jan. "Did you have any luck?"

"Not like him, unfortunately, but enough crucifixes and jewellery for us to make a small fortune." Jan said.

"Add them to the pile." I said, tilting my head towards the monastery. "Now you lot are back I want to start loading the ships. I have men digging a grave, before we leave, we'll bury the dead."

"How many did we lose in all?" Jan asked.

"More than I'd like." I frowned, releasing him. "Fifteen so far, but the battlefield is still being searched."

"They're with Odin now." Hallmundr said, glancing upwards.

"We'll raise a horn to them when we're home." I said. "For now, we must focus on loading the plunder and burying the dead."

"*Já*, Jarl."

***

THE FRANKS DID not attack again that day, thankfully. It was late into the evening by the time our dead were appropriately buried. Men were laid in neat rows, their weapons and the belongings carefully arranged beside them.

Every shovel of earth heaped upon them sent a pang through my heart. By the time the grave was finished, I was exhausted not just physically but mentally as well, as were all the survivors. We ate our evening meal quietly and settled beneath the stars mourning our fallen comrades. The knowledge that they were in a better place did not quell the pain of their deaths.

ASHES REMAIN

We would return home to Aros at first light. Upon our return, we would be greeted by the eager faces of my warriors' families. I imagined the beaming grins as women embraced their men and children danced about their father's feet, excited to hear the stories of the expedition and see the goodies their man brought home.

Then there would be the others ... Their smiles would drop, their faces would grow pale, their bodies would tremble as they realised their warrior had not returned and never would.

Mothers would admonish their children for whimpering while squeezing them tight to their shuddering breasts as they try to hold back their own sadness. It was honourable to die in battle ... Despite that, tears would inevitably fall. Honourable or not, death always made tears flow.

I would console the weeping widows and crying children with the epic tale of their loved ones' deaths, that they were admirable and brave. Eventually, with teary smiles upon their faces, the families would return to their homes and mourn in private. I hated that part of expeditions. We had been lucky – the first few expeditions I had led, we hadn't lost a single man. Our luck had run out and now we had lost plenty. Plenty of men who willingly laid down their lives for glory and gold at my command ...

I could not offer my dead warriors much now. I could not bring their bodies back to Aros and bury them in their homeland, and I could give nothing more than trinkets and kind words to the family that survived them, but at least I could give them a grave and proper funeral rites. They could rest easy in Ásgarðr that way.

Did Vidar rest in Ásgarðr? Without a grave was his spirit restless? Was he unable to pass on to the afterlife because we hadn't followed the funeral rites? By the gods, I hoped not. By the gods I hoped Vidar was at peace.

***

AROS, DENMARK

EVERY YEAR AFTER crops were planted, I would lead my men on raid after raid, compiling quite the hoard of treasures in my hall. The wealth of my people had grown considerably and the widows of the fallen warriors were compensated generously. Every year, we returned at the end of summer, in time for harvest.

Though my people were content with their treasures, I wasn't satisfied. Our plunder was lessening, we had found more abandoned monasteries than bountiful ones. We would have to find somewhere else to raid – further in land, possibly, or maybe somewhere completely different entirely.

I stepped out of the hall and breathed in the balmy night air. My people were feasting merrily and though I was enjoying the evening and the happiness of my people, I was restless already. We had returned from a long summer raiding Frisia and Francia and, as usual, though I was glad to be home, I was already eager for the next expedition and disappointed we had to wait until spring before we could set off again.

In the corner of my eye, I spotted the great monument Jan had gifted me. It had been over four years since Vidar had died. I had been Jarl of Aros and Roskilde for over four years …

Time had gone by quickly. The moment I returned to Aros from the þing, I immersed myself in my duties as jarl and busied myself with chores and food preparation. When I wasn't raiding or handling town obligations, I carded and spun wool, wove sails for the ships and made clothes for my family. I tended my flock of sheep and continued to teach my children their hunting and combat lessons with Jan's welcomed assistance.

Young Birger, Sander and Æsa were proficient in writing and reading runes and Einar was doing marvellously learning them. All four children were fluent in speaking Ænglisc so I had Melisende teach us the language of the Franks, picking up where Caterine left off years ago.

The children and I had almost mastered three languages now. We could even speak a bit of Latin, the language of the church. We couldn't write in any of the languages we spoke but for the Norse tongue. I considered kidnapping a monk on the next raid and forcing him to teach us how to speak, read and write Latin. He might be able to teach us to read and write Frankish and Ænglisc too …

"Jarl, are you okay?" Jan asked, closing the doors behind himself.

"Just enjoying the night." I smiled.

ASHES REMAIN

Jan draped his arms over my shoulders and pulled me against him. My body melted against his, and my eyelids fluttered shut.

On top of my duties as mother, woman and jarl, I made time to be with Jan. A year had passed since the night Jan and I first laid together. Sometimes in solitary moments I wrestled with my emotions, still unsure whether sharing my bed with Jan was right or a betrayal of Vidar's memory, but the moment I was in his presence, I was soothed. Being with Jan granted me a sort of peace, a welcomed end to my loneliness.

Besides enjoying Jan physically, he listened to me and advised me on political matters, fought alongside me during expeditions and raids, hunted, fished and played with my children. We bickered and argued, but we ended our quarrels with a kiss. He was not just my lover, but also my dearest friend.

Birger Bloody Sword would laugh to see me now. Not only was I the mother of four wonderful children, a formidable warrior, and the Jarl of Aros *and* Roskilde, but now I was Jan's woman.

A small smile played on my lips. Birger had wanted me to marry Jan so badly. He thought Jan was a wonderful match for me. Jan was handsome and strong with a great reputation as a warrior. Jan's father, Jarluf, was one of Birger's dearest friends – to have his daughter marry Jarluf's son would've made him so happy. Now here I was, curled up in Jan's arms ...

Of course, Birger was shocked and overjoyed about my betrothal to Vidar. He never considered Vidar as a suitor for me despite his friendship with Alvar the First One. Vidar was the jarl's son and I was an Anglo-Saxon by blood. Birger loved me as though I was his own blood daughter, but neither of us were oblivious to the simple facts of rank and station in society. I wasn't worthy to marry Vidar. And yet, I did ...

"Another great expedition, another great celebration." Jan beamed. "Can you believe there were men who doubted you?"

"I fear they might if we keep coming across empty monasteries."

"Monks are fleeing because of the reputation of the fearsome Jarl of Aros and Roskilde." Jan winked.

"I wish they wouldn't, I want their treasures."

"Stop being so intimidating then they'll stop running."

I rolled my eyes.

"You're flattering me."

"I'm complimenting your success." Jan claimed.

I turned in his arms, grinning. Jan kissed my brow.

"You've bathed, I see." I noted.

"Do I smell more to your liking now?"

"You do."

"Maybe we could go somewhere else and celebrate your success alone, just the two of us?"

"Ah! So *that's* why you're flattering me so much."

"*Nei*, I'm complimenting you because you deserve it. I want to bed you because we *both* deserve it. I don't think we had a single moment alone together this summer." Jan's sapphire eyes sparkling with innocence – but I knew better.

I smirked at the devil as he brought his mouth closer to mine. At first he kissed me softly, sweetly. I parted my lips, meeting Jan's tongue with mine. The very taste of him made my body tingle.

"You've convinced me, Jan Jötunnson. Take me to your bed."

"*Já*, whatever you want, my Jarl."

***

WE RACED THROUGH the darkness. Last we saw Heimlaug, she was eating with a few other elderly women in the hall. We would have the farmhouse to ourselves for a while, free to enjoy each other unrestricted. We hadn't even reached the door before Jan engulfed me in his embrace and pulled me into a kiss. I giggled against his lips, urging him to wait until we were inside.

We tumbled through the door tearing off each other's clothes, a fire in the pit offering us light to see by. We blundered through the room, knocking furniture as we passed. I turned in Jan's arms, trying to see where we were going without breaking anything else. He nuzzled my neck, nibbled my collarbone, drew his tongue over the edge of my ear.

"Heimlaug's here!" I whispered, freezing in the doorway of the sleeping area.

Jan stopped and glanced at Heimlaug. She was lying in her bed beneath a fur, fast asleep from the looks of it. The way Jan stopped, rooted to the spot, his breath held, sent shivers up my spine. Something was wrong.

"She's not coughing." Jan murmured.

Jan released me and rushed to Heimlaug's side. I watched him, the fair hairs over my body standing on end, icy coldness rushing over me. Jan knelt beside Heimlaug's bed, carefully pulled back the furs and rested his hand on her chest.

Jan swallowed audibly and turned to me.

"Aveline, Heimlaug's dead!"

***

I STARED AT the mound of earth in the burial grounds, the latest grave in the heart of Aros. Dear Heimlaug fought her sickness for so long, but she had lost that battle. I breathed in deeply, the bitter scent of dirt covering her corpse filling the air.

Her grave was dug the night before. Rather than thralls digging the grave as was commonplace, Jan chose to dig it himself – his last chance to show Heimlaug how much he appreciated her. I watched him, Hallmundr, Domnall and Young Birger sweat beneath the sun, filthy with dirt, their sticky hands slipping down the handles of their shovels, until at last Heimlaug's grave was set.

I marched behind Heimlaug as her body was carried to its final resting place, and sombrely observed the *goði* as he conducted her funeral. I watched Jan and a few others close to the kinless woman lay items around her, before Jan, Young Birger and the *goði*'s sons buried her with soil.

Hours had gone by since then. No one was standing by Heimlaug's grave now but Rowena and me. Jan stayed with us for a while after all the others left. Ruddy faced with sadness and exhaustion, Jan returned to his and Heimlaug's home some time ago to clean up and change into fresh clothing.

"I'm going to visit Jan." I said to Rowena in Ænglisc. "Please start cooking. I'll be home in a little while."

"Do you need anything before I go?" Rowena asked in our native tongue.

"I'm fine," I shook my head.

Rowena returned to the hall while I made my way toward Jan's home. I weaved through farms, greeted by the grunt of pigs, nicker of horses and bleat of sheep and goats, pausing once or twice to scratch an eager snout. Heimlaug's farm wasn't far, but I wanted Jan to have all the solitary time he needed to reflect on Heimlaug's passing.

When I reached the farm I found Jan alone, dressed only in a pair of indigo trousers, his hair wet and hanging down his back in a slick sheet. He hadn't heard me open the door. I leaned against the doorframe watching him slouch in his chair, tilting it back on two legs, his foot hooked around the table so he wouldn't fall. One of his hands was curled around the arm of the chair, the other held a chalice of drink – ale from the smell of it.

Between gulps, Jan hummed the sombre dirge Einarr and the other musicians played during Heimlaug's funeral. A beautiful song, deep and resonating, complemented by Einarr's low throaty vocals and the heart-wrenching lament of a young female singer.

"I didn't realise you could hold a note so wonderfully."

Jan looked up at me and smiled. I stepped into the room and shut the door behind myself. Jan beckoned me to him with a pat on his leg. I set *Úlfsblóð* on the table before crossing the room and curling up in Jan's arms, resting my head on his shoulder. The heady odour of ale oozed from him, mingled with the strong scent of lye soap on his skin. Jan wasn't yet drunk, but if he continued much longer he'd lose his wits completely.

"The house is so empty without her." Jan mumbled.

"I always thought Birger's farmhouse was cramped and tiny. When he left for war, it was suddenly so big and hollow." I commented quietly, pressing a kiss to his neck.

"How could you stand it?" Jan asked, squeezing me briefly.

"I lived elsewhere," I replied cryptically – I had stayed the nights at Alvar the First One's hall. "When Birger came back his company filled the place again, even when he was sick ... I miss that house."

"Elda and her husband have been taking care of it." Jan said, kissing my brow.

"And filled it with many children. I never thought that little place could fit so many people." I chuckled.

ASHES REMAIN

Jan drained the rest of his ale. I took the silver chalice from him and turned it in my hands, admiring the carvings in the metal and the gems encrusted in it.

"Einar gave you this years ago."

"It's my favourite cup."

I put the chalice on the table before settling back in Jan's lap. He folded his arms around me, his heart thumping steadily against my ear. Jan breathed heavily with drink, sighing occasionally. I could practically hear thoughts whirling around his mind.

"It's odd, losing a mother for the second time."

"Mmm." I mumbled, thinking of Birger.

My father's death when I was nine years old had devastated me. Birger's hadn't hurt any less despite the fact we didn't share blood. Losing a father twice ... There were no words to describe the pain.

"Is there anything I can do for you?"

"Another ale wouldn't hurt." Jan said.

I slipped off his lap and took his chalice to the kitchen. I refilled it with ale and poured some mead into a cup for myself. Before returning to Jan, I took a sip, allowing the cold, crisp flavour to dance on my tongue before swallowing.

"It's odd, inheriting all this from Heimlaug considering I wasn't her kin." Jan said as I handed him his cup.

"You might not have shared blood, but you *were* family. You did so much for her, you deserve to inherit from her." I said, sitting in the chair beside him. "Like you said, she was a second mother to you and you were a second son to her. You deserve it, Jan."

Jan took a deep draught from his chalice.

"Here, come to me." He beckoned with a tilt of his head.

I rose from my seat, took Jan's drink from him and set it on the tabletop with mine. Jan closed his large hands around my narrow waist and pulled me onto his lap. He wrapped me in his arms and kissed me. Our tongues met tenderly, tasting softly.

"I love you, Aveline." Jan whispered.

My eyes shot open.

"What?"

"I love you." Jan said, delicately stroking some stray hairs from my face. "I don't remember being as happy as I have been with you this past year ... Marry me, Aveline."

I stroked his face, admiring the sincerity of his expression, the hopefulness in his eyes. I kissed him, his lips so soft and sweet.

"*Nei*," I whispered.

"Why not? We've been happy, haven't we?" Jan asked, running his fingers over my side, his brows knitted and a frown tugging at the corners of his mouth.

"You're only asking because you're afraid to live here alone."

"I'm not afraid of anything, let alone *that*." Jan argued.

"Prove it." I grinned.

"Aveline, I'm not playing." Jan said. "I want you to be my wife."

"I know, but now isn't the time, Jan." I said gently. "Think about things carefully – if we married, you'd have to move into the hall and then what would you do with Heimlaug's farm? Get rid of it? Let it rot? Sell or rent it? Heimlaug *just* died. You can't turn your life upside down so quickly. Give yourself time, Jan. Let yourself mourn for Heimlaug then we'll talk about this again."

Jan nodded reluctantly.

Relief washed over me. I'd pacified him, but for how long? I'd been happy with Jan the past year, too, but I couldn't marry him. When I told Jarl Lingvi I never intended to remarry I meant it. I would *never* relinquish my jarldoms or my position as jarl to any man. I knew I could trust him – other than my children, I couldn't trust anyone as much as I could Jan – but I wouldn't risk my sons' birth rights for *anyone*, not even Jan.

I glanced down at Jan's hand as he gently touched my stomach.

"Considering how often we enjoy each other, I'm surprised I haven't got you with child yet." He commented softly. "If you carried my child in your belly, would you marry me then?"

"Oh, Jan, I–" I realised I'd never told him of the wild carrot seeds and brews from the healer. "Brynja gives me medicines that prevent pregnancy – I-I'm sorry I didn't tell you."

"Oh – *nei*, it's fine." Jan said, pulling his hand away and staring at me as though I was a ghost. "*Nei*, of course. I – I didn't realise there were herbs that did that."

"*Já* – I'm sorry, Jan. I'm just not ready–"

"*Nei*, it's fine, I understand."

"Jan–"

ASHES REMAIN

"Aveline, it's alright, really." He kissed the top of my head. "Anyway, there's some things I need to do around here, and I'm sure you are probably needed back at the hall by now."

"You want me to leave?" I asked sadly.

"I'll see you tonight." Jan replied firmly.

I slipped off his lap and took a few steps back. Jan stood up, folding his arms over his chest.

"Are you angry with me?"

"I'm just surprised you're going to such extents to avoid having a child with me." Jan replied softly.

"It's not you, Jan. I just – I'm not ready to have another child."

"When you are, tell me."

I rolled my lips together and nodded. I made my way to the door, glancing frequently over my shoulder. Jan was standing with his back to me, running a hand through his long tawny hair. On the funeral day of his second mother, I'd rejected his proposal and admitted I didn't want to bear his children.

CHAPTER EIGHTEEN

Winter, 890

DESPITE THE HEAVY snowfall the marketplace was bustling. The heavy clanking of the blacksmith hammering on hot metal, the call of vendors selling fabrics and food, the chatter and bargaining of customers and merchants thundered through the place. A few merchants were moored by the docks unloading their wares on the outskirts of the marketplace, their calls and yells barely audible over the noise.

Askold and his huge retinue were allowed passage through the gates and were gathering in and around the marketplace, many of their number on horseback.

"Are you ready?" I asked Young Birger.

"I am." He smiled.

This was Young Birger's sixteenth winter. He was finally old enough to marry Signý and inherit the jarldom of Roskilde. As was tradition, the wedding would be hosted in Aros, Young Birger's home. After the wedding, Askold and I would accompany Younger Birger and Signý to Roskilde to present the newlyweds as Jarl and Jarlkona of Roskilde.

I'd been looking forward to this day yet dreading it, too. My son was a man, ready to rule and take on the world. I'd never been prouder of him, but I would miss him terribly.

"In three days you'll be a married man." Jan beamed.

"*Já*," Young Birger nodded with a smile.

Though he seemed outwardly calm and collected, his minute sentences betrayed his nerves. I opened my arms to my son and embraced him for a moment.

"I love you, Birger." I said. "Your *faðir* would be proud of the man you've become – I know I am."

"*Þakka*." Young Birger kissed the top of my head. "I love you, too, *móðir*."

ASHES REMAIN

We approached our guests, welcoming Signý, Jarl Askold and his wife, Bersa, their younger sons and their retinue of forty men. Along with his retinue, Askold brought the widow of his late brother and her children, and his elderly mother. Their horses were stabled while we made our way to the hall.

The wedding would take place in three days, giving Young Birger and Signý a chance to spend time together before their oaths, under the eagle-eyed view of Askold. He was determined his daughter's maidenhead would be preserved until her wedding night and not a moment sooner.

Signý was a kind girl, and very beautiful. With long brown hair that fell from her head in delicate waves, forest green eyes and pale skin that flushed pink when Young Birger complimented her or even smiled in her direction. She was the same age as Young Birger, but unlike him Signý was innocent and naïve.

I remembered myself at her age, just as naïve yet not half as trusting as Signý. I supposed watching your family get slaughtered had a way of forcing one to grow up and view the world in a suspicious light. I had been *Danethrall* back then, distrusted and hated by Danes and thralls alike. How things had changed ...

Luckily for Signý, she was the beloved daughter of the current jarl, niece of the previous jarl and granddaughter to the jarl before that. She was raised with love, respect and wealth, sheltered from the dangers of life.

She was a sweet thing and would undoubtedly be a good wife to my eldest son. When we weren't feasting, she sat dutifully with her mother, aunt, grandmother and nieces. She spoke with Young Birger surrounded by witnesses, never alone, to maintain her virtuous reputation. Bersa, Signý's mother, suggested Young Birger show them around Aros, and so the group joined the young lovers for a stroll about town.

Signý's mother, aunt and grandmother were taken with Young Birger the moment they first met him years ago. Handsome, strong and intelligent, they declared him to be the perfect match for sweet Signý. Now he was sixteen they were even more resolute in their opinions, fawning over my son like he was a fine silk.

At evening time, we held a small feast made up of tender cuts of meat, rich stews, top quality alcohol and sweet fruits. The breads were freshly baked, crusty on the outside and delightfully fluffy on the inside. Wine was poured endlessly, without care of the expense or luxury of such a drink.

On the second night, Askold's men amused themselves with my friends, playing games and fighting both in the main room of my hall and outside of it.

Hallmundr and Askold were engaged in a drinking contest, each guzzling mead from the longest horns we owned. Young Birger was sitting with Signý at the main table while my younger children were running about with the other children in attendance.

Though a glorious fire roared in the central firepit, I was chilled to the bones. I left my spot at the main table after eating my fill, hoping to warm myself to no avail despite huddling as close to the fire as possible. Guðrin was sitting with me, drinking wine and watching the happy chaos unfold around us.

Amongst the crowd, I spotted Jan with Einar on his shoulders, dashing about the hall like a fool. I grinned, I loved to watch him play with my children. Jan would make a great father one day …

"You seem distracted." Guðrin mentioned.

"The wedding is the day after tomorrow." I smiled, tugging my fur cloak closer about me.

"It will be wonderful, I'm sure."

"*Já*, it will be." I nodded.

"Time has gone so quickly, I can't believe he's already old enough to marry." Guðrin said.

"What of Yngvi? Why haven't you found a wife for him yet?"

"It's not for lack of trying." Guðrin grumbled. "He has his eye on one girl, but she's entertaining other suitors. He stupidly only has eyes for her and is holding out for her to choose him."

"Has Domnall spoken to her father? What does he have to say?"

"Her father would be proud to have Yngvi as his son-in-law, but she's his only daughter so he's letting her pick her husband." Guðrin rolled her eyes. "Honestly, she is a spoiled little thing! When I was a girl you married whoever your father chose for your first husband and picked who you wanted for your second."

"Isn't Domnall your first husband?" I asked with a grin.

"Luckily for Domnall I happened to agree with my father's choice." Guðrin winked.

ASHES REMAIN

I giggled and took a mouthful of wine, the tart berry flavour dancing on my tongue.

"What about you? Have you considered marrying again?"

I almost spat out my drink.

"You're very subtle. I do wish you'd be more forward with your questions, you'll never get your point across otherwise." I said sarcastically, dabbing my mouth with the hem of my sleeve.

"Domnall tells me that all the time," Guðrin grinned. "But really, Aveline. You've been with Jan for over a year now, when do you intend on marrying him?"

"Have you ever considered I might be happy keeping things how they are?"

"Not for a moment."

Before we could say more, Jan stumbled towards us, Einar on his shoulders and Askold's two youngest sons hanging on his legs.

"I've been viciously attacked!" Jan gasped, grabbing my shoulders. "Help me, Jarl!"

We burst into laughter, as did more than a few women nearby.

"You'll have to defend yourself! Honour be damned – I dare not attack such a mighty foe!" I replied, hiding behind my cup.

"Don't believe him, *móðir*, Jan lies! He's a vicious *jötunn* and we're brave warriors taking him down!" Einar exclaimed to the cheers of his friends.

"In that case, is there any way I can help you, brave warriors?"

"Betrayer!" Jan cried, feigning shock. "*They* are the ones who lie! I want nothing more than to drink mead in peace!"

"I don't think so, Jan Jötunnson. Are you telling me I'm supposed to believe *you* over the word of my handsome, brave, noble son?" I grinned.

"We win, *jötunn*! We'll defeat you!" Einar and his friends cried out, gripping Jan's clothes and shaking them.

"Oh *nei*, my plan didn't work!" Jan yelped. "I think I'm going to fall! I'm overpowered by the might of these three young warriors!"

Jan staggered across the room to a platform covered in furs and dramatically tumbled down onto it. The three littles ones squealed with delight, beating on Jan with their fists. Jan held Askold's youngest child up in the air, his large hand spanning the boy's entire stomach, while Einar and his other friend tried to save him, but Jan knocked them back gently with his free arm.

Almost every female in the hall gawped at Jan, drooling over how sweet he was with the children. Dressed in bright blue and covered head to toe in fur, gold and jewels, Askold's wife, Bersa, approached us, smiling, her gaze locked on Jan.

"His wife is a lucky woman." Bersa swooned.

"He's unmarried." I replied.

"I'm surprised to hear that. I expected a man as handsome and wonderful as him to be married. I will have to introduce him to my dear sister-in-law." Bersa winked. "It's about time she found a new husband. He'd be perfect."

Bersa scurried after Jan before another word was uttered.

I watched Bersa approach Jan. She said a few words to the boys, that smile fixed to her face. Immediately the three darted off, eager to do whatever Bersa told them. Bersa pointed to the main table and seemed to urge him to join her there. Jan did as she bade. I doubted he had any idea of the matchmaking she had planned.

My stomach tightened as jealousy seeped through me. I rolled my lips and shook my head, trying to stop myself acting so repugnant – jealousy was not an admirable trait, yet I couldn't help scowling as the scene unfolded before me. It took every ounce of strength inside me not to leap up and claim Jan as my own rather than allow Bersa to introduce him to her sister-in-law.

"What was that?" Guðrin demanded

"What?" I barked, snapping out of my thoughts.

"Why did you tell her Jan's not married?" Guðrin said.

"Well, he isn't."

"Aveline, he's *yours*. Why would you let Bersa introduce *your man* to her unmarried sister-in-law?"

"Guðrin, *nei*."

"I'm just trying to understand why you would invite a woman into your lover's bed." She pressed.

"Of course I don't want Bersa introducing her sister-in-law to Jan! But I–" I stopped myself.

"What Aveline? Why would you do something stupid like that?"

"Because Jan wants a wife and I don't want to marry him!"

ASHES REMAIN

Guðrin gawped at me. I swallowed hard and breathed deeply, trying to calm the anger boiling inside me. From Guðrin's point of view, what I had done was ridiculous, but she didn't understand. I couldn't take my temper out on her when I truly wasn't mad with her – I was angry at myself.

"Jan wants a wife and a family of his own and he deserves that – he deserves happiness. There are so many women out there who want to be his wife and have his babies and he *should* meet them." I explained miserably. "I care for him, but I know I will never be the woman he deserves. He should be free to find someone else who wants what he wants. I'm not that woman ... I'm – I can't marry again – I don't want to have another child ..."

"What if he proposed to you? You might change your mind."

"He already has, and I declined him. If I marry Jan, I won't be jarl anymore. If he and I have a child together, that child will get Aros, not Sander. I won't let anyone take Aros from him."

"Aveline–"

"*Nei*, Guðrin – I want Sander and Young Birger to inherit their birth rights. Young Birger will have his in just a few days and I will *not* remarry and rob Sander of his own."

"And after Sander takes on Aros?"

"I'll be too old by then. If Jan is to have a family, he needs to do it now." I frowned, watching Jan laugh with Bersa and her sister-in-law. "It kills me to see him over there with them, but what if she's the one to make him happy? What if she wants what he wants? He *should* meet her."

CHAPTER NINETEEN

YOUNG BIRGER'S WEDDING was beautiful. Signý dressed in maroon and silver, adorned with jewels and furs, a divine wedding crown upon the gentle waves of her brown tresses. Her lips were reddened with berry juice, but there was no doubt in my mind the blush upon her cheeks was natural.

Young Birger dressed in his finest clothes. Upon layers of undershirts, he wore a forest green tunic embroidered at the hems and neckline in silver. He wore dark straight-legged trousers and new polished leather boots on his feet. Upon his fingers and wrists he wore gold and silver armbands and rings, and around his neck he wore one of Vidar's pendants.

The wedding was held outside. The couple wore thick bearskin cloaks pinned closed with large golden brooches over their shoulders. My heart swelled with pride by their magnificence, together they exuded splendour and grace. I had never seen such a beautiful, charming couple – they were made for each other.

After the ceremony and traditions were observed, their celebratory feast was in full swing. In a few hours Signý and Young Birger would be led to the sleeping room by firelight to consummate their union. Until then, music played, people danced and laughed, and many games were played. My townspeople revelled with Askold's retinue, children ran around squealing and giggling. It was hard not to be joyful at such a wonderful occasion.

I sparred with my men and Askold's outside. Over the heads of the crowd, Jan and I hurled bones from the meal at Hallmundr and Lars who whipped them back at us just as sharply. I gambled on dice, winning sometimes, losing others, enjoying myself no matter the outcome. I danced with Guðrin, Borghildr and my children. I even danced with Lars, but Jan put an end to that quickly. Mead gave Lars too much confidence for Jan's liking, he extracted me from his arms and whisked me away from him.

ASHES REMAIN

"I need fresh air – and another drink!" I panted, staggering to the nearest table and swiping a mead abandoned upon it.

"I'll go with you." Jan grinned.

We drained our cups, set them on the table and left. As we stumbled outside, I caught Bersa's sister-in-law glaring at us. I took satisfaction at the sight of her but scolded myself for being petty.

Jan was a charmer, he spoke comfortably with everyone, man or woman, and Signý's aunt had become hopelessly infatuated with him during their introduction, as most women did. From what I saw from across the room two nights previous – and over the days since – Jan humoured her with chatter, compliments and jests, but firmly declined her physical advances to her dismay. Now she knew why. Though I knew my behaviour was childish, I was pleased by her chagrin.

Jan and I gulped the chilly night air the moment the hall doors shut behind us. Both of us were sweaty from dancing and playing. We wandered away from the hall, out of earshot of the people drinking and talking outside.

"It's so much nicer out here," I sighed, tugging at the neckline of my gown. "It's so hot in the hall!"

Jan slipped his arms around my waist from behind me and pulled me against him.

"Let's go somewhere else for a while."

"Oh *ja*? Where?" I purred as Jan slipped my hair from my neck and nipped the tender flesh with his teeth.

"It'd be much cooler and quieter at my house." Jan murmured.

I turned around in his arms, grinning, my body tingling. We kissed, our tongues clashing hungrily. Jan's hands roamed my body, squeezing my waist, my hips, my buttocks and my breasts through my layers of clothing.

"I've wanted you since the moment I set eyes on you this morning. You looked so beautiful in your red gown." Jan said.

"Are you insinuating I don't look beautiful in anything else?"

"Don't tease me woman." Jan growled.

"I can't help it, it's so fun." I giggled.

Jan kissed me again, harder, wanting. I reached between his legs and ran my hand over his hard cock through the fabric of his trousers. He groaned, deep and husky, his hands travelling my body more fervently than before.

"We won't be gone long." Jan mumbled.

"I can't leave my son's wedding feast to share my lover's bed."

The more Jan kissed and groped me, the more temptation increased. Breathless, I pried myself from him despite the lust coursing through me. Suddenly cold from the absence of his body enveloping mine, I regretted extracting myself from Jan's embrace.

"If you keep this up you're only going to rile yourself up further." I said. "No matter how much I'd like to, I can't leave. You *must* wait until later."

"Alright, but it'll be difficult." Jan winked.

"Let's walk *that* off." I grinned, eyeing the bulge in his trousers.

Jan closed his hand around mine and we ambled towards the hall. Rather than going inside, we walked the edge of it to the sheep pen behind.

"I've been thinking." Jan announced abruptly.

"Don't do that too often, it might become a habit." I teased.

"Don't you want to know what I've been thinking about?"

"*Já*, do tell."

"I've been thinking about *us*," Jan said. "We've been together for two years now, and I've enjoyed every moment of it."

"It's been a year and a half."

"It will be two years in spring – just a few months away."

"Not that you're counting."

"Not at all." Jan winked.

"Regardless of how long it's been, I've enjoyed it, too."

"I'm glad to hear that." Jan beamed, kissing my hand softly. "Bersa introduced me to her sister-in-law the other night – offering her to me as a romantic prospect, I believe. The woman was bold with her touch and honeyed words, there was nothing else the introduction could be for."

"What did you think of her?" I asked stiffly.

"I told her my heart belonged with you."

"You told her that? Really?" My jaw dropped.

"Of course. She said that until we were betrothed, I was free to take on other lovers or even a wife if I wanted, without fear of law or being disloyal, and she's right." Jan said. "We both could."

ASHES REMAIN

I bristled at his words. Biting my bottom lip, I raised my brows at Jan, my heart hammering in my chest.

"I don't want any other woman, Aveline – and I don't want there to be a chance another man might take you from me."

"No one will take me, Jan." I smiled with relief.

"I want to marry you, Aveline." Jan said.

"I already told you *nei*."

"And I proved to you I can live alone – I've done that for a while now." Jan winked. "Marry me, Aveline. Sailing and raiding with you, fighting alongside you, sharing my bed with you ... There's no other woman out there like you, and none that make me feel how I do when I'm with you."

"I'm thankful for every moment I'm with you." I sighed. "But I can't marry you."

"Why? We're happy together – you want to be with me, I want to be with you – it only makes sense for us to marry."

"Jan, stop! We've had a lovely evening, don't ruin it!"

"*I'm* ruining it? Aveline, I've confessed my love to you and proposed and *you've* rejected me – yet *I'm* ruining the evening?"

"Jan, I care about you–"

"But you don't love me?"

"But I don't want to marry you!"

We stopped, our eyes locked, both of us rooted to the spot. My breath stuck in my chest, I rolled my lips, my heart dropping as I watched disappointment spread over Jan's face.

"Jan – I care about you deeply, but what I said at the þing still stands. I *don't* want to remarry. I won't relinquish my jarldoms to you, and I don't want to bear you a son and have Sander lose his jarldom! I'm sorry – I care for you, but I *can't* marry you."

"You won't marry me because of your jarldom?" Jan breathed.

"I'm sorry." I hung my head.

"Then I won't ask you again."

Jan turned on his heel and left.

***

I DIDN'T SEE Jan for the rest of the night. I assumed he must've gone back to his home. It was hard for me to smile for the rest of the night, so concerned about him. I slumped in my highbacked chair on the platform, Vidar's empty one beside me. Lost in my thoughts, the merriment of my people was nothing more than a noise in the background of my mind.

Slowly my hall emptied. My townspeople and friends returned to their homes. Askold's men slept where they fell, some slumped in chairs others curled up on platforms amongst furs alongside Askold and his family. Guðrin, Borghildr, their families, and my closest friends bade me goodnight hours ago.

Melisende, Rowena and Askold's thralls stumbled about tidying, carrying armfuls of cups, tankards and horns to the kitchen, plates and bowls covered with grease and dried juices from meats and stews. After gathering the dirty dishes into the kitchen, they scraped the plates and gathered the leftovers from them in a large bowl to feed the neighbouring farm's pigs in the morning.

"Go to bed all of you, this can wait until morning."

The thralls thanked me profusely and curled up on the floor of the kitchen by the fire to sleep.

I was the only person left awake to see the morning light creep in through the smokeholes. I rubbed my face with both hands and sighed audibly. My limbs were heavy, my movement slow, but still my mind would not let me rest.

I ruminated over Jan and my conversation. Jan had taken my refusal to his proposal well in the past – of course, I hadn't snapped at him then as I had last night. I was honest, painfully so, of course it wasn't taken well. Who would be pleased with their heartfelt feelings being rejected so harshly? Jan was important to me, I couldn't have made it this far without him, but I couldn't give up what I'd worked so hard for.

A deep sigh fell from my lips.

Would I consider marrying him after Sander was old enough to inherit Aros? I wouldn't be jarl anymore and I had already lost my right to speak at the þing now Young Birger was old enough to speak on my behalf. Despite this, I didn't think I could marry Jan even when that time came.

I cared for Jan, but did I love him? We'd been together for nearly two years and I couldn't answer that question. Jan held a special place in my heart, that fact was undeniable, but every time he confessed his love to me, I couldn't respond in kind. I knew I had feelings for him — strong, irrefutable, passionate feelings — but I couldn't utter those three measly words to him.

Perhaps this argument happened for a good reason. What I said to Guðrin still stood — Jan deserved more than a bed mate or lover, he deserved a woman who reciprocated his feelings, who wanted what he wanted. Jan was worthy of love, romantic, loyal, unbreakable love. I could offer him only so much, not half as much as he deserved. My children, my duties and my jarldom would always come before him.

Jan deserved so much more than me.

Had I wasted the past two years of Jan's life? I refused to believe that. Jan and I needed each other, no one else could've helped us as we helped each other. We healed together, we comforted each other, we were each other's sanctuaries, diverting our attentions from the strains of life and the hollowness inside us. We were a shred of happiness in each other's lives while fickle gods toyed with our fates. It was only a matter of time before we fell into bed with each other, sharing an intimacy we'd both long been without.

I was using Jan for my own happiness while disregarding his. I wanted Jan by my side, I wanted to be with him, but I refused to give him what he truly wanted, a wife and family of his own.

I knew the risk of embarking on a relationship with Jan, that he might fall in love with me, want to marry and start a family. I ignored that, too preoccupied with my own needs. I'd already lived his dream — I'd married the love of my life and birthed five amazing children with him. Now Vidar was dead and I didn't want to ever feel that way again. There were other things that took precedence now.

I worked hard to keep my jarldom, I fought and spilt blood to keep it — the ugly scars over my body were testament to that. I'd worked hard to prove myself equal to all the men who challenged me, who thought less of me because I didn't have a cock between my legs. I'd proved myself, I'd solidified my children's positions in the world, I didn't let Vidar's legacy fade away.

Marrying Jan would ruin everything.

I laid my hand on my stomach. Over the last two years, Jan had got me with child three times, but thankfully Brynja's brew had expelled the unborn babies from my womb while they were too small to survive outside of my body. Each time was worse than the last and now there seemed to be a permanently dull ache in my womb, a reminder of the dangers of being intimate with Jan.

Though I didn't want to hurt Jan – the disappointment on his face last night had been heart wrenching – I couldn't imagine how upset he would be if he found out I'd got rid of his unborn children. All I could offer Jan was heartache and disappointment. It was better if we ended our relationship. It was better if Jan stopped loving me.

A few men from Askold's retinue stirred awake. They bade me a slurred morning greeting, rubbing their bleary eyes with their fists. Some rolled over and went back to sleep, while others stumbled outside in the pale morning sun, their footfalls crunching in the snow, off to find a place to take a piss most likely.

Melisende and Rowena woke from the bang of the hall doors swinging shut. They woke Askold's team of thralls and set them to the gargantuan task of cleaning the hall and readying breakfast.

At first the children were surprised by Jan's absence. Usually he was at the hall for morning meal, Melisende even set a place at the table for him. The hours went by and he didn't arrive. I didn't share with them the reason, only said that he was too busy.

Noon came and went. By evening time I realised how badly I must've hurt Jan. At night-time I climbed into my bed alone, my bed seeming much larger and emptier than normal.

"*Mumie?*"

"I didn't know you were still awake." I smiled as Einar crawled into my bed.

We nestled under the furs, my youngest son curled up in my arms. The moment Einar was settled, he launched into a detailed explanation of his day. Every now and again I shushed him as he grew louder and more animated. His curls were tangled and knotted from a busy day playing.

"Why didn't Jan come here today?" Einar asked.

"He was busy, my love." I replied softly.

"Will he visit tomorrow?"

"Maybe, we'll have to see." I murmured. "Now shush sweet boy, it's time to sleep. I'm exhausted and so are you."

ASHES REMAIN

"*Nei*, I'm not." Einar argued, but his yawn betrayed him.

"Maybe we'll see Jan tomorrow, but for now we must sleep."

Einar didn't protest anymore, and thankfully he didn't speak of Jan anymore. He settled beside me and with one last yawn, he closed his eyes. I watched the rise and fall of his little chest with each gentle breath. I wanted to see Jan just as much as he did, hoping beyond hope I hadn't ruined everything.

***

WE DIDN'T SEE Jan the following day, nor the day after that. On the fourth day after our fight, Jan found Young Birger and Sander while they were helping load the ships in the harbour. According to my sons I'd been speaking with Askold at the time, overseeing the loading of Storm-Serpent, and Jan thought it best to have them relay a message to me rather than interrupt.

His message was short, it was with his deepest regret that he couldn't accompany us to Roskilde. He gave no reason but apologised profusely to Younger Birger. He gave his best to him – from what my eldest son had said, they'd had a touching, heartfelt goodbye.

I was furious, enraged that Jan decided not to accompany Young Birger on such a lifechanging journey. It didn't matter how heartfelt their farewell had been, nothing should've got in the way of such a significant event.

Hallmundr was moving to Roskilde to watch over my son and aid him with whatever he needed. Yngvi, Domnall and Guðrin's son and Young Birger's closest friend, was also settling in Roskilde with him. It appalled me that Jan decided to not attend such a significant event, to settle our friends and my son into their new home. Rather than hunt Jan down and demand an explanation, I let it be. I had to focus on my son and my new daughter-in-law.

If Jan didn't want to come then so be it, it was his loss. The next morning we boarded the longships and began our voyage to Roskilde to present Younger Birger and Signý as Jarl and Jarlkona of Roskilde and settle the newlywed couple into their new hall.

It had been almost two weeks since then. We returned to Aros five days ago. Askold and his retinue returned to Ribe soon after, eager to go back to their home.

The hall was quiet, Young Birger's absence formed a deep hole in the place. The children were not used to being without their eldest sibling. No more was he sitting beside the fire carving toys or weapons for them, no more was he there to play or hunt with them. The three still had each other for which they were glad, but they pined for their eldest brother.

"Jan! You're back!" Einar exclaimed, dashing across the hall.

I glanced over my shoulder. I had been working at my warp-weighted loom all morning. Jan stepped into the hall, pulling his hood off as he strode towards me. Three people stepped into the hall from behind him, wrapped in cloaks and hoods.

"Sorry I've been gone for so long." Jan said, catching Einar and returning his embrace just as tightly.

"Where have you been?" I asked, stepping away from my loom, my arms crossed over my chest.

Jan set Einar down and stepped aside to reveal his companions. The woman removed her hood, revealing her long black hair. Her luscious locks were streaked with grey, the silver hairs startlingly bright against the ebony spill cascading to her waist.

My jaw dropped as she tucked one of those long silken locks behind her ear, revealing the puffy and dark skin over her left eye, a bruise that was subsiding. It was the size of a man's fist …

Briefly she met my stare with her light blue gaze. Her thin pink lips parted as though she intended to say something, but she didn't. She closed her mouth and stared at the ground.

"Thóra?" I gasped. "Is that you?"

"It's good to see you again." Thóra replied, though her stiff tone implied the opposite.

"Aveline, you haven't formally met our son." Jan said, gripping the other figure by the shoulder. "This is Thórvar."

The boy nodded his head, his ebony hair hanging about his face. He avoided my gaze, a bloom of pink upon his cheeks. Sander, Æsa and Einar stared at me. We never told them Jan had a son. When Jan spoke about him, it was when he was alone with me.

ASHES REMAIN

The children had quickly and easily accepted the change of Jan's position in my life, adoring him just as deeply as before. I had expected jealousy and resentment, but instead they welcomed him into our family. Now he stood before them with a strange woman at his side, his arm around the shoulder of a boy he claimed to be his son.

They might accept his son, but what would they do when they found out this woman standing before us was Jan's wife? Damn it all, what would *I* do now she was here?

Years ago, Jan had been so angry at Thóra, still heartbroken that she abandoned him and took away their son. He hadn't known how he would react if she ever returned. I'd suggested he might be relieved to know she and their son were alive – it seemed I was right. Rather than being happy for Jan, though, I was furious.

"And who is this?" I nodded to the third figure huddled behind them, cloaked in wool rather than fur like Thóra and Thórvar.

"Their thrall, Valens." Jan explained.

"Valens, go to the kitchen and get warm. Rowena, get mead for everyone, Melisende, food for our guests. Afterward, see to their thrall." I said as calmly as I could muster.

The thrall, Valens, turned to Thóra for permission. She nodded to him and he strode across the room to the kitchen as I bade. I turned to Thóra, Jan and Thórvar, eyeing them severely.

"Sit. There is a lot we must discuss."

CHAPTER TWENTY

I HOVERED AROUND the edge of the room, too tense to sit. Thóra was sitting close to Jan at the table, a handful of dried fruit set on a plate in front of her. She brought a piece to her dried lips and nibbled at it delicately.

When I met Thóra a decade ago, she possessed a figure even the goddess Freyja would envy – she was buxom and curved in all the right places. She had lost an enormous amount of weight over the since then. Her skinny frame was hidden beneath layers of sumptuous, albeit filthy, clothing. Her deep blue linen dress was bunched around the belt revealing the narrowness of her waist.

Despite her severe weight loss, Thóra was as beautiful as ever. The paleness of her flesh juxtaposed with the darkness of her tresses like ink on ivory. The creases of age and streaks of grey hair did nothing to take away from her loveliness.

Thórvar was a statue beside his mother. He'd seen ten winters now and was already taller than her – he'd inherited Jan's height. He was broad, not as skinny as his mother, but just as wrecked by the life he'd endured alongside her. The frown on his face and his permanently knitted brows suggested he was far older than his age.

A soft sigh slipped from my lips. Whatever had happened to them, it hadn't been kind – yet they wore such expensive clothing. They'd both removed their cloaks revealing their lavish apparel. Their garments were filthy, but they were expensive, nonetheless. Both wore blue, a colour only the wealthy could afford.

Golden embroidery hemmed Thórvar's pale blue tunic and dark blue trousers. Puttees, strips of fabric, were wound around his shins to keep him warm, and upon his feet were fine leather boots. Gold bands and chains jangled around his wrists and neck and sheathed at his hip was a sword. Only the affluent owned swords.

Thóra's gown was indigo in colour, patterns embroidered over it with golden thread. From the neckline and hems, I could spy

ASHES REMAIN

multiple layers of linen underdresses and her thick leather boots were hemmed with fur. She jingled with jewellery like her son.

Were they wealthy? Who had given Thóra the bruise on her face? If she could afford such elegant clothing and jewellery, why was she so malnourished?

Sander, Æsa and Einar were sitting beside the fire staring at Jan, Thóra and Thórvar. They kept their distance, obviously unnerved by the situation. I moved to stand beside them, resting my hand on Einar's shoulder to comfort him. He glanced up at me, curling his hand around mine, but he didn't say a word.

"What are you doing here, Thóra?" I asked.

I kept my voice as level as I could though rage bubbled inside me like water simmering in a pot, threatening to boil over. She was the woman who broke Jan's heart, who stole away his child when she abandoned Jan. She was the one who hurt Jan worse than any weapon could. Regardless of the state she and her son were in, I couldn't scrape together much sympathy for her.

"The night of Young Birger's wedding, I returned to my home and found Thóra and Thórvar on my doorstep with their thrall." Jan explained. "They were panicked, Thóra was weeping, her right eye was swollen so much she couldn't see from it."

"She's been living in your house for almost three weeks and you decide to tell me *now*?" I demanded. "Why didn't you come to me the moment you found her?"

"It was Young Birger's wedding night." Jan replied sharply. "I didn't want to interrupt you when you were celebrating with him."

"There were five days before we set off to Roskilde—"

"And I waited until now so that you could enjoy the time remaining with your son until he left." Jan growled.

"Do *not* interrupt me." I scowled, my voice trembling.

"My apologies, Jarl." Jan replied just as tersely. "I thought I was doing right by you."

"Enough. I will not bicker with you like a child." I spat.

I turned to Thóra and glared at her. She shrank in her chair, eyeing the tabletop nervously. I watched her shift, clutching Jan's leg beneath the table. He lowered his hand from the table, assumedly resting it upon hers. Nausea surged up my throat at the sight of them, knowing Jan was holding her hand, comforting her because of me. I swallowed hard.

"Who hit you?"

Jan opened his mouth, but I held up my hand to silence him.

"I'm speaking to *her*."

Jan closed his mouth. Thóra glanced between Jan and me. Realising Jan wasn't going to defy me and speak on her behalf, she sat up in her chair and finally met my gaze.

"M-my husband did." Thóra admitted timidly.

"Your *husband?*"

"*J-já.*" She stammered.

I stormed to the platform where Vidar and my highbacked chairs were situated and threw myself into mine. I gripped the arms of my chair so tightly, my knuckles turned white.

"Thóra, I'm confused." I said quietly, scowling at her still. "What in Hel's name happened to you all those years ago? What has brought you to my hall? Tell me *everything*."

"Everything?" Thóra repeated, her watery eyes wide.

"*Everything.*" I confirmed with one slow nod.

"I-it started before I came to Roskilde." Thóra said, clearing her throat. "A-as you know, I was born and raised in Heiðabýr. One day I went to the marketplace and met a man named Torfi Axelsson. He was from Túnsberg and had come to Heiðabýr with his foster father, a merchant, selling pretty things made of ivory and whale bone. We spoke for a while a-and he claimed he'd fallen in love with me and wanted me for his w-wife.

"At first he seemed sweet, but there was something about him that set me on edge ... He was polite and well mannered, but in my gut I knew there was something not right about him.

"I went home a-and told my family. My father gathered information about Torfi and sure enough, my suspicions were true. My father found him out to be a vicious man! Rumour had it, he'd beaten his first wife to death when she was w-with child. My father refused his proposal on my behalf and threatened to kill him if he came near me again. Torfi wasn't put off though, he swore he'd have me no matter what it took ...

"Thankfully, Torfi left with his foster father a few days after my father sent him away. Before my father and brother set off to the

ASHES REMAIN

Anglo-Saxon lands, my father arranged f-for me to move to Roskilde and live with his sister, to keep me safe while they were gone. Her husband and sons were going to fight with the Great Army, but they decided I would be safer hidden away in Roskilde alone with my aunt than I would be in Heiðabýr.

"I-I *was* safe for a while. A year passed and I met Jan. As you know, we married, I left my aunt's home for Jan's, w-we had Thórvar. We were happy, we were safe, but when Jan went to raid, my aunt came to me with news that Torfi knew I was in Roskilde and was coming for me."

"How did she come upon such information?"

"She overheard one of the merchants at the marketplace telling his customer that he didn't have the item the customer wanted in stock, but his associate would be coming to Roskilde in a few days. His associate was my husband's foster father."

"You both *assumed* he found you? You didn't actually *know*?" I raised a brow at her.

"I *know* because that's what Torfi said when he found me on his and his foster father's way to Roskilde." Thóra replied, losing her nervous stutter.

I clenched my jaw, trying to calm myself down.

"Why didn't you talk to Jakob or Burwenna rather than flee?"

Jan's younger brother, Jakob, and his wife, my dear friend Burwenna, lived with Jan and Thóra in Roskilde. The longhouse was built by Jan and Jakob's great-grandfather, it was the home they were been raised in. When the brothers each married their wives, their families lived together in the building.

"I didn't have time. I had to leave – I couldn't risk Jan being killed. Torfi was cruel and vicious, I knew that he wouldn't give up until he found me, so I fled. I couldn't risk waiting for Jan to return." Thóra replied, glancing between Jan and me.

"How did this man become your husband?"

"Torfi came upon me after I left Roskilde. His foster father helped him find me. Once they forced me and Thórvar into the ship, they returned to Túnsberg and Torfi forced me to marry him, threatening to kill Thórvar if I didn't."

At this, Thórvar glanced at his mother, alarmed. As swiftly as he'd turned to her, his gaze returned to his lap. Had he not known any of this? Or was he ashamed his mother had married such an awful man to save his life? I rolled my lips together, making mental note of his reaction.

"At first he was kindly, but he changed. He started beating me for any perceived slight – he made me avert my eyes when men visited him then beat me if he thought I'd looked at them. Eventually he made me hide when he hosted guests …" Tears slipped down Thóra's face.

I watched her carefully, watched her eyes dart over the tabletop as she revealed her secrets, her body shaking as memory engulfed her. Thórvar watched his mother, too. He bit his lip and shifted in his chair, wringing his fingers on the tabletop before drawing them into his lap. He did not reach for his mother to comfort her.

"Why did you take Thórvar with you?" I asked. "Surely it would've been safer for him if you'd left him in Roskilde."

"Aveline!" Jan barked. "Thóra–"

"Thóra is here in my hall assumedly asking for sanctuary." I interrupted, speaking over him. "I *will* know all the details of what has happened before I make a decision."

"You can't possibly turn her away after all she'd been through?"

"She is asking for my protection. If this Torfi – her *husband* – comes looking for her here, he is a risk to the safety of not just *her*, but my people as well. I will know *every* detail."

Jan and my eyes were locked, but Jan said nothing more.

"Why did you take Thórvar with you? Why didn't you leave him in Roskilde with your aunt or Jakob and Burwenna?"

I couldn't leave my son in case Torfi found him. I didn't want anyone else to get hurt. I hoped if there was no sign of Thórvar and me, Torfi would leave everyone else alone."

"Torfi found you both anyway."

"Aveline! That's enough!" Jan boomed, standing so quickly his chair flew out behind him.

I flinched at Jan's sudden action and the clatter of the chair. I refused to meet his gaze, my glare locked on Thóra.

"H-he hurt me almost every day, but he never laid a finger on Thórvar." Thóra said meekly.

"How did you escape?" I asked, ignoring her statement.

"Aveline!" Jan barked.

ASHES REMAIN

"*How did you escape?*"

"Torfi went to battle with a town far north of his home. The moment he left, Thórvar, my thrall and I stole a *byrðingr* and rowed to Roskilde. I spoke to Jakob and he said Jan moved to Aros. He brought me here, to Jan's home. I've been with Jan ever since."

"You've received no news of your husband?"

"I don't know if he's still at war or not ..." Thóra's voice trembled. "All I know is I need to be as far from him as possible. He's a dangerous man – if you send me back, he'll kill me!"

Beneath her furrowed brow, her bright blue eyes pleaded for mercy. She held herself, clinging to the tattered sleeves of her ruined gown. The fear exuding from her was palpable. Thórvar took one of his mother's hands and Jan moved to stand behind her, gripping her shoulders protectively.

My heart plummeted into my stomach. Whether I liked it or not, this was how it was meant to be. Thóra needed help, she needed mercy and kindness. She needed to stay here in Aros ... With Jan.

"I won't send you back, Thóra." I finally declared.

Jan thanked me softly and I acknowledged him with a small nod.

"They're your responsibility." I said to Jan. "Let them stay with you or find them their own home. Should Torfi come searching for them, he will be killed."

"*Já*, Jarl." Jan said.

"Thóra, you have my permission to stay in Aros. If you hear news of your husband, you must come to me – you will *not* flee. We will end this once and for all."

"*Þakka fyrir*, Jarl! How can I ever repay you?" Thóra beamed.

"Go. We're done here."

Thóra turned to Jan, brimming with delight. She leapt up from her chair and hugged him. My stomach twisted into knots at the sight of them – Jan's eyelids fluttered closed briefly as he held her. I swallowed hard, unable to look away. Jan must've felt me staring, he glanced at Thóra and took a step back, ending their embrace.

"Melisende, send Valens in and retrieve our guests' cloaks, they're leaving." I struggled to get my words passed the lump in my throat.

"Jan, don't go yet!" Einar shouted, dashing across the room.

"I'll come again soon, I promise." Jan said, ruffling Einar's hair.

"I didn't think you'd come back." Einar frowned.

"I'll *always* return." Jan reassured him. "I won't leave you, Einar."

My eyes travelled from the endearing sight of Jan comforting Einar to Thóra who was watching the pair with slight yet visible confusion. It seemed Jan hadn't told her of his relationship with me and my children.

"Jan will visit again as soon as he is able, my love." I said to Einar. "Let him be for now, he must settle his—"

I stopped, unable to refer to Thóra as Jan's family, yet she and Thórvar were obviously far more than just Jan's guests.

"I'll see you soon," Jan said. "I promise."

Einar nodded and reluctantly stepped back from Jan. Sander, a scowl upon his face, took hold of Einar's shoulders and pulled his younger brother to him.

"I will see *all of you* soon." Jan said to Sander.

Sander turned his back on Jan and took his brother outside with an offer to play. He scowled over his shoulder at Jan as the two hurried out of the room. Æsa glanced between her brothers and Jan nervously before hurrying after Sander and Einar without uttering a single word to Jan.

"They're upset with me." Jan commented quietly.

"They're strong." I said stiffly. "Take Thóra and Thórvar back to your home. You must decide what's to happen now."

"*Já*, Jarl." Jan said, gazing at the kitchen door where the children had disappeared through.

With their cloaks around their shoulders and Valens behind them, they made for the hall doors. I didn't want to see Jan leave. I didn't want him to leave me for Thóra …

I sighed.

Jan needed to be with his son. After eight years apart, they needed as much time together as they could get. They were strangers and it was time for them to learn about each other. His son was more important, as he should be – just as my children were most important to me.

I caught Thóra glance over her shoulder. Our eyes met and a small smile crossed her face as she reached for Jan's hand, tangling her fingers with his. My stomach writhed, anger rushing through my veins. Her smile deepened – was she *smirking* at me?

ASHES REMAIN

"Jan, before you leave–" I called as he took a step through the doors. "Send Einarr, Lars, Ebbe and Domnall to me immediately."

"Is there anything I can help with?"

"I plan to send them to Roskilde to give a message to Young Birger. I want him to be aware of the situation in case Torfi shows up there." I said – not that I owed him an explanation for anything.

"I'll go." Jan said. "I–"

"*Nei* – you must stay here with your son. Send the men to me."

Jan nodded. He gave me a final glance before shutting the hall doors behind Thóra, Thórvar, Valens and himself.

I stared at the doors. Had I imagined Thóra's smirk? I must have. I was furious for all the hurt she had caused Jan and I was upset that she'd returned – my feelings were twisting her smile into something more malicious than it actually was. I wanted a reason to hate the woman – the woman who was replacing me …

Jan deserved happiness. I would never be the woman he deserved, yet my heart ached for him as he left me, as I realised whatever it was we'd had for the last two years was at an end. The man who had comforted me, who made me happy and saved me from the darkest time of my life, was gone.

I sprang up from my chair and rushed toward the hall doors. I pulled one open and stared out, watching Jan, Thóra, Thórvar and Valens' silhouettes disappear. A raucous cawing pierced the sky above me. I looked up to find a raven perched upon the rooftop of a nearby building.

"You're late." I muttered, glaring at the bird. "I already know."

I slammed the door shut on the raven.

I slammed the door shut on Jan.

CHAPTER TWENTY-ONE

Late Winter, 891

THE TWELVE DAYS of *Jól* ended a few weeks ago. It was a wonderful celebration, the *Jól* log was burned, lots of mead was drank, boar, goats and horses were sacrificed. Runes and decorations still hung from trees, though the bits of food that were tied with string and hung on the branches had long since been eaten by birds, cats and the few creatures awake during the winter season. Spring was drawing closer, but snow still fell in abundance.

The small crew of men I sent to Roskilde returned within a week of setting sail. Sander went with them. Despite the fact he had only seen thirteen winters, I gave Sander authority over the crew. It was his first time captaining a ship and was only a short voyage, but I thought it a great moment to test his skill.

From what the men said, Sander did well, mastering the icy waves with bravery and an intelligence far beyond his years. Though the men – far more seasoned than Sander – offered advice when needed, the moments Sander needed help were minimal.

When it came to his lessons, Sander didn't pay attention to much except for fishing, hunting, fighting and sailing. The crew who sailed under his command had praised him sincerely – with more time and experience under his belt, I knew he'd achieve his dream of travelling the world.

Upon their return, Sander told me that Young Birger hadn't heard of anyone named Torfi Axelsson. They interviewed the merchants, but none had heard of him either. Young Birger met with Thóra's aunt, but she claimed she hadn't been visited by the man. Young Birger gathered all of his townspeople together and warned them of Torfi Axelsson. If he ever approached them, they were to bring him to Young Birger's hall immediately.

Thóra and Thórvar had lived in Aros for seven weeks now including the three weeks they'd been here without my knowledge. I didn't know how well they had settled in, but from the few brief conversations I had with Jan it seemed like they were doing well – Thóra more-so than Thórvar, but Jan didn't go into detail.

Jan visited periodically since Thóra and Thórvar's arrival, keeping his promise to Einar. The children had grown accustomed to Jan's daily presence over the last few years, his occasional visits now were not enough for them. They resented him, Thóra and Thórvar, though Æsa and Einar were not half as bitter as Sander.

My youngest two children enjoyed Jan's company when he was around, but Sander didn't – in his mind, Jan betrayed them, abandoned them for Thórvar, and he couldn't forgive Jan for that. On the rare days Jan came to visit, Sander immediately left the hall, sometimes with excuses, other times he stormed out in silence.

Countless times I explained to Sander he was being too harsh, of course Jan should spend as much time as he could with his son, but Sander didn't care. In my stubborn son's perspective, Sander and his siblings had been in Jan's life far longer than Thórvar, thus Sander believed they deserved more of Jan's attention than they were currently receiving.

"I understand you're upset, you miss Jan, but his son was taken from him for *eight years*." I repeated for what felt like the hundredth time over the past few weeks. "Imagine yourself in Thórvar's place. How would you feel if you met your father for the first time in eight years and he preferred to spend time with three children of no relation to him, rather than getting to know you?"

"Jan should've thought of that before he started spending every day with us then." Sander argued.

"You think he *expected* his son to appear after a decade missing?"

"I – I don't know!" Sander barked, scowling at me. "It doesn't matter – this isn't fair!"

"*Nei*, none of this is fair!" I snapped back. "It isn't fair on Jan, it isn't fair on Thórvar, and it isn't fair on you or your siblings. But this is the life the Nornir have crafted for us and we must make the best of it – we *cannot* change it."

"I don't care about the Nornir, Jan can't just abandon us!"

"He didn't–"

"He did!"

"That's enough!" I bellowed, my patience worn out. "You will see your fourteenth winter this year, Sander Vidarsson. You must stop acting like a child and behave like a man! If you are so displeased by this situation, think of what you can do to deal with it *honourably*. If you want to spend time with Jan, talk to him! Don't bellyache about it here, do something about it! I'm tired of arguing with you – you're not listening to me so you must handle this yourself – like a *man*, not a child."

Sander's face was red with fury, I'd insulted his pride. He whipped his cloak around his shoulders and stomped outside, the hall doors slamming in their frame behind him.

I rubbed my face between my hands. I was too hard on Sander, but he needed to stop. We'd had this conversation countless times over the weeks, but Sander wouldn't sympathise with Jan and Thórvar. I understood his pain, but it didn't counter the fact Jan needed to be with his son.

I stared at the doors. I wanted to be with *my son*, too, but I couldn't run after him. In just three years, Sander would be old enough to marry. He needed to learn to fix his problems by himself, without his mother doing it for him. The truth was, I *couldn't* fix this for him. I, too, was resentful that Jan had left us. I couldn't get over the jealousy I felt every time I imagined what Jan and Thóra were doing together.

Did they hold each other at night? Did he share her bed? Did he kiss her? There was an obvious intimacy between them, she was always clutching his hand or clinging onto his arm … I knew Sander's pain – I, too, had been replaced.

Jan and I wanted different things yet every time I saw him with Thóra, part of me regretted declining his proposals and ridding my body of his children. Perhaps if I'd given Jan what he wanted, he wouldn't have been so quick to return to his long-lost wife …

I thought I could let him go, let him be with a woman who deserved him, but seeing Jan with Thóra broke my heart.

***

"JAN!" EINAR BEAMED. "We set some traps last night! We were hoping you'd check them with us."

"I'd enjoy that." Jan smiled. "Let me speak with your *móðir* then we will check them. Get Æsa and Sander, I won't be long."

ASHES REMAIN

"Sander's not here. He and *móðir* argued earlier and he left."

"Oh?" Jan remarked. "Well, maybe we'll see him while we're out. Fetch your sister and we'll see to your traps."

"If she doesn't want to go, let her be." I called from my loom.

"*Já, móðir.*" Einar nodded before rushing to the sleeping area.

Æsa was still in bed. For the past week she'd been complaining of body aches, constant tiredness and trouble sleeping. I'd sent Melisende off that morning to purchase a brew to ease Æsa's symptoms. I worried in case she'd caught a sickness, but there was the possibility she was beginning her menses. She'd just seen her eleventh winter, I'd hoped she'd have another year at least before she became a woman, but I feared there were only days.

"Your drink, Jarl." Rowena said in Ænglisc, handing me a cup of apples boiled in honey water.

I smiled, set down my weaving tools and sat at the table, sipping the hot brew. Bits of chopped apple bobbed in the boiling honey water, the steam fragrant and soothing as it drifted from my cup.

"You and Sander argued?" Jan asked, taking a seat opposite me.

"We've been arguing a lot as of late." I admitted.

"What about?"

"This and that," I replied softly, staring into my cup.

"Aveline, you can talk to me about it, you know that."

"*Já*, I know ... It's fine, really."

Jan stared at me, brows raised, lips turned down in a small frown.

"Would you like a drink?" I asked, hoping he'd let the topic be.

"When we get back, I would. It smells delicious."

"It is." I smiled, offering him my cup.

He smiled, accepted the cup and took a mouthful.

"I would *definitely* like some when I get back." Jan said.

I giggled, accepting the cup from him.

"I've missed that." Jan said, laying his hand palm-up on the tabletop between us.

"Missed what?" I asked, gazing at his hand.

"Hearing you laugh. It's been so long." Jan replied.

I reached out and timidly brushed my fingertips over his. Lightning shot through my skin the moment I touched him. Jan closed his hand around mine, warm and tight.

"I've missed *this*, too." I murmured, gazing at our hands.

"I'm sorry I haven't been here much lately."

"It's fine." I lied, pulling my hand from his and curling it around my cup, stiffening at the thought of Jan and Thóra together.

"I hate how much has changed." Jan said, drawing his hand onto his lap. "I miss you, I miss–"

"Æsa isn't coming." Einar said as he entered the room. "She's grumpy today."

"She's not feeling well." I said, watching my son sling his cloak about his shoulders.

"What's wrong with her?" Jan asked.

"I think she's becoming a woman." I replied.

"*Already?*"

I answered with a nod.

"You'll be looking for a husband for her soon, then?"

"Birger waited until I was fifteen – three years after my menses began – and I plan to do the same for Æsa."

"You'll have men asking about her soon enough."

"And they can wait until I'm ready to marry off my only living daughter." I said, firmly ending the discussion.

"I agree. Come then, Einar, it's just you and me." Jan stood and turned to me once more. "I'll see you later?"

"I'll be here."

Jan nodded before he and my youngest son left, a grin spread across Einar's face. My heart swelled at the sight of them though I knew things weren't as they used to be. They never would be.

"*Móðir!*" Æsa shouted, her voice shrill. "Come quickly!"

I rushed to the sleeping area, finding my daughter standing by her bed staring at the linens. On the back of her night dress was a red stain and upon the bed sheet the same.

"Welcome to womanhood, my love." I smiled, resting my hands on her shoulders and pressing a kiss to her head.

***

WHILE JAN AND Einar were out, Æsa bathed, her sheets and clothes were washed and I'd repeatedly promised her that I had no plans to marry her off yet. She had caught snippets of Jan and my conversation and feared I planned to find her a husband

ASHES REMAIN

immediately. Somewhat consoled, she spent much of her day stomping about miserably or curled up in furs by the fire.

Jan stayed with us the whole day, much to my surprise. He and Einar returned a few hours after they left with the six rabbits they'd found in the traps. Melisende and Rowena set to work skinning and preparing the animals for stew. As they cooked, Jan and Einar sparred with their swords, I weaved at my loom, the stone weights clacking as I worked, and Æsa sat beside me spinning wool.

"I'm tired of this, I want to visit Borgunna." Æsa grumbled, tossing her wool and tools into the basket beside the loom.

"I want to go!" Einar piped up, wiping sweat from his brow.

"Be back for evening meal."

"*Já, móðir.*" They replied in unison.

They readied themselves and left, hoods pulled over their faces. Daylight was waning fast, the cold draught rushing in from the hall doors behind my children indicated another freezing night was coming. I wondered where Sander was. Jan and Einar hadn't seen him while they were checking the traps. I would wait until nightfall, if Sander didn't return by then, I would search for him.

"Shouldn't you be leaving soon?" I asked without looking at Jan.

"Are you trying to get rid of me, Jarl?"

I could hear Jan's grin. I turned to find him leaning against the table watching me. He tilted his head to the side, his tawny hair loose like a cloak falling about his shoulders.

"What are you smirking at?" I asked, blushing.

"I'm not *smirking*, I'm smiling. I like watching you weave."

"Oh *já?*"

"You're so graceful when you work, you're quite a pleasure to behold." Jan said. "Your movements are so delicate yet precise."

"What are you trying to accomplish by flattering me?"

My feet seemed to have a mind of their own. Drawn to him, I stepped closer, my arms folded over my chest, a smile curling the corners of my mouth. I stopped opposite Jan. He opened his arms to me, but I refused to step closer despite how much I wanted to.

"Why won't you come to me?" Jan pouted.

"Ah! *That's* why you were complimenting me."

"You *are* a pleasure to behold. But if you would be so inclined to let me embrace you, I wouldn't say *nei*." Jan said with a wink.

"I don't think your *wife* would be pleased if I let you enjoy me."

My words hung in the air. I hadn't meant to say them out loud, but they spilled from my lips the moment they formed in my mind. Jan crossed his arms, his playful expression disappearing.

"*Wife?*"

"*Já*, your wife." I muttered, my face burning red.

"Aveline – Thóra *isn't* my wife." Jan said firmly.

"You seemed close with her when you presented her to me."

"She was scared," Jan said, his gaze on me was severe – like I was a child being scolded. "And you were cruel to her."

"I'm sorry I hurt your wife's feelings, Jan, but I stand by what I said. She's bringing danger to Aros. I needed to hear her side of the story before I allowed her to stay here."

"*Her side of the story*? You're insinuating there might be something more than what she has claimed."

"I'm not insinuating anything, I'm stating the facts. I do not know this woman, nor do I have any reason to trust her."

"Why *shouldn't* you trust her?"

"Why *should* you? This woman abandoned you, took your child away, then returned a decade later with some outlandish story about a violent stalker." I rolled my eyes.

"And what's so outlandish about that? I was raiding, I wasn't there to protect her. She had no other choice but to flee–"

"She *married* the man!"

"Otherwise he would've killed Thórvar!"

"When you were searching for her, you asked the townspeople if they'd seen her, *já*? Did any of them mention another man was searching for her?"

"*Nei.*"

"Why was that? If this man was searching for her, someone would've told you that you weren't the first one to ask about her."

"Unless they assumed he was part of my search party." Jan reasoned almost condescendingly.

"Well, what of her aunt?" I barked. "Why didn't *she* tell any of you about Thóra and Torfi?"

"Maybe Thóra made her vow to say nothing?"

"Why would she keep her silence when Thóra went missing?"

"Because she made a vow!"

ASHES REMAIN

"This whole situation is suspicious!" I snapped.

"Aveline, you're making a fool of yourself – you're searching for any excuse to distrust Thóra."

"You're the fool for believing every word she's spouted!"

I was surprised by how well Jan managed to remain composed while I lost every ounce of my patience.

"Aveline, tell me the truth." Jan said. "Why are you angry?"

"That is the truth!" I barked. "She suddenly appeared after all these years with some ridiculous story and you welcome her into your home without question! You don't know her anymore yet you're trusting her! You're holding her and coddling her!"

"You're jealous." A smirk lifted the corner of his mouth, increasing my fury tenfold.

"*I'm not jealous.*" I snarled. "Of all the things I've been through in my life, you really think I'd debase myself by being jealous over a man? I just don't understand why you're bending over backwards for a woman who didn't care about you one bit when she left you."

"She didn't *want* to leave! She left because she felt she had to for her safety – my safety – the safety of our son!"

"She's lying!"

"What would she gain from lying about *that*?"

"I don't know!" I shouted. "I just – I don't trust her!"

"You're just being jealous and petty because I'm spending more time with her rather than *you*!" Jan's patience was finally worn thin.

"You're right, Jan!" I snapped, hammering my fists on the table. "I'm petty and jealous because she returned and now I'm *nothing*! She returned and I don't matter anymore! I just have to accept the fact you're living with another woman!"

I glared at Jan, tears brimming in my eyes. The truth was out – I *was* jealous and petty – but did I not have a right to be? Did that even matter? Jan ran his hands exasperatedly through his hair. He crossed his arms, nostrils flaring. He glared at me in bristled silence, but gradually his expression softened.

"Over the two years we've been together, you've given me a host of excuses to not further our relationship beyond being lovers." Jan said softly. "Thóra returns and what – you've changed your mind? Do you want to marry me now? Do you love me?"

"Jan, I–"

"Aveline, if you love me, tell me."

I couldn't speak. I wanted so much to tell him yes – but I couldn't. I gazed pleadingly at him, wanting this whole conversation to end, wishing this all never happened. Jan shook his head slowly, his frown deepening.

"You haven't changed your mind at all ... Don't think I haven't noticed your silence when I tell you I love you – you're silent even now ..." Jan groaned with frustration. "By the gods, Aveline, why are we continuing this? Whatever in Hel's name *this* is."

"Because I–"

A glimmer of hope flashed in Jan's eyes. I dropped my head, cursing myself inside my mind. It didn't matter how much I wanted to open up to Jan, I just couldn't do it.

"Aveline, I love you – I love *you*!" He emphasised each of those three words, his eyes locked unblinking on mine. "I want to be with *you*, I'm not going to be unfaithful or disloyal to you. You might not reciprocate my feelings, but that doesn't change mine.

"I know Thóra living with me is hardly ideal, but I have to let her stay with me while I get to know Thórvar. He doesn't trust me. He barely speaks to me! He refuses to spend time with me unless Thóra begs him to! I *have* to get to know my son, Aveline."

"And you should! If I was in your shoes, I'd move mountains to get to know my son. I truly understand that Thórvar comes before everything – I just don't trust Thóra."

"Thóra left *me*, not you. If I can forgive her, why can't you?"

"I just can't ..."

Jan closed the distance between us. He cupped my jaw in one hand and held my hip with his other. With gentle pressure, he lifted my face to his. I closed my eyes, avoiding his gaze, but I couldn't ignore the warmth of his touch tingling on my flesh nor the emotions roiling inside me.

Jan's mouth neared mine, his breath danced on my face. Delicately he kissed me. I relished the softness of his lips, savoured the taste of him as our tongues glanced against each other.

"Stop," I breathed, breaking our kiss despite every fibre of my being screaming for more.

"Why?" Jan whispered.

"If Thóra realises we're together, she'll use Thórvar against you." I replied miserably.

Jan stopped kissing me then.

"You think she'd stoop as low as that?"

"Maybe, *já*. And I don't believe she told us the real reason she left." My heart lurched in my chest as Jan stepped back from me. "Think about it! None of it makes sense – she's hiding something!"

"Again with all this!" Jan groaned.

"She's tricking you! She's not as innocent and sweet as you think she is." I argued. "What do you think she'll do if we continue to make love when she wants you for her own? She wants you back and she'll do anything to keep you!"

"Aveline–"

"She took your son away once, I've no doubt she'd do it again."

"By the gods, you've changed so much over the years, Aveline." Jan murmured. "You used to take mercy on the downtrodden, you befriended thralls! Now look at you ... What made you *so* cold?"

Jan's words hit me like a battering ram.

"I trusted Theodric Holt – I trusted my brother – and they betrayed me." I whispered, choking back tears. "They killed Vidar because of me – because of my naivety ... I can't make that mistake again."

"This is different, Aveline! You're not risking any lives – you're *saving* Thóra and Thórvar's by letting them stay here." Jan pressed. "Open your heart, Aveline. If you chose to be cold and distrusting, you're choosing to be miserable for the rest of your days."

Jan rested his brow against mine, still holding me tight against him. Rather than comfort me, I fell apart in Jan's arms. Tears streamed down my cheeks and my body quaked.

"I don't want things to change between us." Jan murmured.

"They already have." I mumbled.

"How do we fix this, Aveline?"

"I don't know ..."

***

I FOUND SANDER on Storm-Serpent. He was leaning on the bow watching the icy waves roll. The sky glittered with stars, the moon a curved sliver in the sky like a shining white bow. I crossed the gangplank and made my way to him. Without speaking, I leaned against the bow beside him. The ship rocked gently and water lapped the hull. With the chill breeze wafting over me I felt almost tranquil – almost. If only my heart wasn't so heavy.

After my conversation with Jan, the urge to gather my men and row somewhere, anywhere, was strong. I wanted to sail away and leave Aros and Thóra behind. The seas would be treacherous in this season, I had to wait until late spring before we could raid again. Hopefully raiding would quench my impulse to run away ...

I was ashamed for losing my temper with Sander that morning when I behaved the same way with Jan. How could I reprimand him for not managing his emotions when I couldn't control mine?

"Why would the Nornir give me two fathers then take them both away?" Sander murmured.

His words were barely louder than a whisper yet they struck me like a hammer. I knew he was close with Jan, but I hadn't realised Sander regarded him as a father. Jan had filled the empty space Vidar's death had wrought, but I didn't realise Sander looked up to Jan as a *parent* ...

"I've asked that many times, too." I replied softly, thinking of my blood and adoptive fathers. "Jan isn't gone though, he's still alive, he's still here."

"Is it better that he's still alive?" Sander asked. "*Faðir* is dead, I understand why I'll never see him again. Jan's still here ... That – that feels worse somehow."

Jan said the same thing about losing his wives before Thóra returned. He said although the death of his first wife, Unnr, hurt him beyond measure, not knowing whether Thóra and Thórvar were alive or not was worse. Jan consoled himself that Unnr's death was fate, nothing could bring her back. He was able to work through his grief – the same way Sander consoled himself over his father's death. With Thóra and Thórvar there was no consolation, nothing that could keep him from questioning why they left, where they'd gone or whether they were even alive.

Sander knew his father couldn't return to him. He didn't understand why Jan wouldn't.

"Jan *does* want you." My voice was thick with emotion.

ASHES REMAIN

"I don't care what Jan wants." Sander spat, sniffing loudly.

"What do *you* want, my love?"

"If *faðir* hadn't died none of this would've happened." Sander rubbed his nose with his sleeve. "There would've been no need for Jan to take his place then leave the moment Thórvar returned. He's parading about with Thórvar like we don't matter anymore!"

"Jan did not take your *faðir*'s place." I said so severely Sander turned to gawp at me. "Jan is special to us, he was when your *faðir* was alive and he has been since your *faðir* died, but he didn't *replace* him. No man could do that so don't even insinuate that Jan did."

Sander nodded meekly, his pale eyes round as coins.

"Don't forget your *faðir*, Sander Vidarsson." I scolded, glowering at the young man. "Don't try to replace him or blame him for what's happening now. Jan didn't replace his son with you, and you will *not* replace your *faðir* with him. You can love Jan and he can love you, but he will *not* replace your *faðir* and it's wrong of you to try to replace his son."

Tears slid down my cheeks. I rolled my lips, biting my bottom one between my teeth, glaring at Sander. My expression softened swiftly when I noticed him chewing his bottom lip, his eyes glistening with unshed tears.

"I miss *faðir* so much." A tear slipped down Sander's face, but he quickly wiped it away with the heel of his hand.

"Me too." I replied, refusing to wipe away my tears.

"How does this not bother you?" Sander demanded, sniffing hard. "Thóra took Jan from you, why aren't you angry?"

I sighed deeply, my heart skipping a beat at Sander's words.

"I *am* angry, Sander, but if your *faðir* returned tomorrow, I would leave Jan in a heartbeat." I admitted. "I'm hurt, I miss Jan, but if I was in his position, I'd leave him for your *faðir* immediately."

Sander stared at me, his mouth agape. Slowly he turned back to the waves, silent, visibly processing my words.

"What of you, Sander? If your *faðir* returned tomorrow, would you choose him or Jan?"

"*Faðir*." Sander said without a moment of hesitation.

He dropped his head, seemingly ashamed of his confession.

"It doesn't mean we care about Jan any less." I said gently. "We can empathise with Jan and his situation. It hurts, but Thórvar's return is something Jan has dreamed of for *so* long. We need to put our feelings aside, as hard as that is, and be happy for him. His happiness is important, *nei?*"

"It is." Sander mumbled reluctantly.

"I've no doubt if our positions were reversed, Jan would be happy for us. We *must* be happy for him." I rested my hand on Sander's shoulder. "This is hard for Thórvar, too. He doesn't trust Jan – he doesn't know him ... He could do with a friend, someone to talk to who isn't his *móðir*."

"How do you know Thórvar doesn't trust Jan?"

"Because Jan told me. Jan was at the hall all day today. He wanted to spend time with you and your siblings."

"Is he still there?" Anxiousness was audible in Sander's voice.

"He left a little while before I came looking for you." My heart dropped as I watched Sander's shoulders slump. "Which reminds me, I have an apology to make to you."

"What?" Sander glanced at me, his brows lifted in surprise.

"I'm sorry I snapped at you this morning. I'm a hypocrite."

"How are you a hypocrite?"

"I yelled at Jan for abandoning us today ... I'm sorry, my love."

"It's alright, *móðir*."

"*Nei*, it's not. I shouldn't have been so hard on you and I should've composed myself better with Jan ..." I shook my head. "He wants to do better by us. Maybe we can do the same – make the best of this situation by getting to know his son?"

"And Thóra?"

"One step at a time, my love."

Sander snickered and turned back to the grey waters.

"I'm going home. Do you want to come with me?" I asked.

"I'm going to stay here for a bit longer."

"Come back when you're ready – stay warm."

Sander made a small hum of acknowledgement. I kissed his shoulder lightly before making my way down Storm-Serpent. I strode up the shore a short way before gazing back at my son, his silhouette barely visible in the darkness. Though Sander hadn't said anything, I knew he wanted to disappear as badly as I did.

I was tired of Aros. I was tired of the memories, the rules, the people. I had to settle other's disputes and issues while I couldn't find a solution to my own. If I could assemble a crew and go anywhere, free from the confines of the hall, the expectations and duties – if I was free to see the world ... That's what I wanted.

For the first time in my life, I was looking forward to Sander turning sixteen and receiving his jarldom. I would gain my freedom, but Sander ... My poor son already craved freedom and his rule had not yet begun.

CHAPTER TWENTY-TWO

Spring, 891

THE SNOW HAD finally melted away and a lukewarm sun shone in the sky. It was birthing season and women across Aros were busy with new-born foals, kids, lambs, piglets, chicks, goslings, calves and more. Some births were smooth, others difficult. Women watched their livestock like hawks in case they needed to aid their animals. Six lambs were born in my flock, and I had twenty or so pregnant ewes due in the coming weeks.

It was also time to assess the damage the winter had wrought on my fleet. Ships needed to be mended, sails aired and repaired, rotten planks replaced. The stench of boiling tar drifted on the salty air and the pounding of hammers echoed over the waters. Men carried sacks of animal hair and moss over the shore, to be shoved between the planks with tar to waterproof the ships.

Sander reached out to Thórvar as I'd suggested. Thórvar looked up to my son from what Jan said, finding it easier to speak with someone closer in age to him. Thórvar was only a year older than Einar, but whatever his life had been like previous to Aros had matured him immensely. Thórvar seemed intellectually matched with Sander even though my son was two years older than him.

The more time Sander spent with Thórvar meant he had more time with Jan. I missed Jan – he and I still didn't spend as much time together as we used to, and we hadn't shared a bed in months – but knowing my son was happy made my spirits soar.

Privately I was pleased Sander didn't have much to say about Thóra. He viewed the woman as a homewrecker, despising her for what she'd done to our family. He may have befriended Thórvar, but he had no intention of finding common ground with Thóra. I didn't push him to either, for I felt the same way.

Sea-Serpent was set on timbers on the shore. Men climbed all over her, replacing planks and renewing her waterproofing. Sander and Einar were working at the harbour with the men as were most boys their ages. There were a few clusters of women bringing food and drink to their men, as I was doing. Over my arm I carried a basket filled with hunks of cheese and a loaf of bread wrapped in kerchiefs for my sons.

A group of women stood by Storm-Serpent, chatting together while watching the men finish what they were doing. The men washed their hands and faces in the fjord waters before approaching their women, eager for the break.

Happily, I strode towards my sons. Seeing my fleet repaired meant only one thing – soon my ships would be ready to sail. Fields were being tilled and readied for seed – once all the planting was done, we'd be able to raid again. I'd already started planning where we'd travel to. It was just a matter of time before I could escape the confines of Aros and seize freedom upon the waves.

"Jarl, I didn't expect you to be here."

I mustered the sincerest smile I could and turned to greet Thóra. I hadn't noticed her in the group of women when I approached Storm-Serpent, but there was no mistaking her voice. To my surprise, she wore a *hustrulinet*, hiding her ebony tresses away as a respectable married woman should. She must've noticed my gaze, for she lightly touched the white fabric, a smug grin on her face.

"You still wear *that*?" I asked curtly.

"Of course, I am a married woman after all."

"You don't owe Torfi anything." I cocked a brow at the woman.

"I'm not wearing it for *him*, I'm wearing it for Jan."

"For *Jan*?" My jaw dropped.

"Of course," Thóra said haughtily. "We're reunited at last. We have a farm, our son – we're a family again."

"Speaking of sons, I must find mine. *Góðan dag*." I turned my back on her and started off towards Sander and Einar.

"Jan told me about Vidar and Alvar the First One. You have my condolences, Jarl." Thóra called after me, her words halting me.

Slowly, I turned to face her, my brows knitted and lips pursed. She approached me, leaving her flock of companions.

"I didn't know them personally, but I do know they were great men. They're with the Allfather now." She said politely.

I rolled my lips together, surveying her dubiously. I doubted there was any sincerity in Thóra's words despite the comfort that phrase was supposed to provide. Regardless, I'd heard that phrase so often over the years, it had lost all meaning.

"You've taken a lover, perhaps?" Thóra continued.

The audacity of the woman! Speaking to me so casually – like we were friends! I wanted to slap her for her boldness, but from the corner of my eye I spotted Jan. He beamed at us and waved. He probably thought I was trying to befriend Thóra after avoiding her since she'd moved to Aros. I rolled my eyes – I didn't care to settle my issues with her at all.

"From your expression I assume your lover is not yours anymore." Thóra said, innocence like a mask fixed to her face. "Loneliness is terrible, isn't it? I'm sure you'll find happiness again – just as I am happy to be with *my husband* again."

The emphasis she used when she said 'my husband' made my blood boil. I should've controlled myself, I should've just smiled and walked off, but I didn't. Since she'd come to Aros, I found my temper was shorter than normal – and at that moment, I snapped.

"You divorced Jan, remember?" I spat. "Your only legal husband is the man you're hiding from."

"Neither of us announced our divorce in three places, he's still legally my husband." Thóra replied haughtily.

"You married another." I growled through gritted teeth.

"That marriage wasn't binding since I was still Jan's wife." Thóra said, sticking her nose into the air. "All that matters is Jan and I are reunited – our family is whole again."

Thóra's expression softened. I followed her gaze: Jan had Sander, Einar and Thórvar with him. Sander and Thórvar were holding a plank between them. While Sander hammered his end into the ship, Thórvar held the plank steady. A few paces from them, Jan was sawing a plank while Einar held it still.

Jan looked happier than ever. Surrounded by the boys, he was the epitome of a father working hard alongside his sons. This was what Jan wanted all his life.

"I love watching Jan and Thórvar." Thóra sighed dreamily. "Thórvar has had trouble coming here. Torfi made me raise Thórvar as his son. When we escaped, I told Thórvar the truth – quite a lot for one as young as him to understand. He's doing well, though. Jan is a patient, loving father – so very different to Torfi."

ASHES REMAIN

"You *really* couldn't find a way of returning to Jan over the eight years you were in Túnsberg?" I cocked a brow at her.

"*Nei*, I couldn't." Thóra said stiffly. "It doesn't matter now, of course. It's all over – *nothing* will make me leave my family again."

"You may want to speak to your *husband* about that." I scoffed.

"What do you mean by that?" Thóra spat, scowling at me.

"Jan is very dear to me and my family – he's been my righthand man since my husband died." I said. "We speak of everything together, even *you*."

"And what has he said about me?"

"You should ask him yourself." I smirked, satisfied by her displeasure. "As for my lover, you'll have to ask him when he *next* intends to propose to me."

Thóra's fury radiated from her.

"*Next* intends?"

"He's proposed a couple of times now." I replied nonchalantly. "Should he ask me again, I think I might accept this time."

"Don't raise your hopes, Jarl." Thóra's voice was low enough that only I could hear her. "Jan doesn't need you or your family anymore. He's happier with *us*. You should've married him before I came here – you won't have that chance ever again."

"I wouldn't say that." I replied coolly.

I tried to remain as unconcerned as possible even though my stomach twisted into knots at her words. Truth be told, I *had* worried that Jan didn't want or need us anymore now his long-lost wife and son had returned, but I refused to let Thóra know my fear or give her the pleasure of riling me up.

"You need to leave Jan alone. Leave our family to our peace!"

"I am Jarl. Every person who lives in Aros answers to me, including you and your son." I matched the darkness of her scowl with my own. "I take orders from no one, especially not *you*. I will respect whatever decision *Jan* makes – if he comes to my bed, I will have him. If he wants to be with you, he has my best wishes."

"You will hear it from his mouth and no other?"

"*Only* from him."

"Very well." Thóra snarled. "Have no doubt, he *will* choose me."

"We'll see." I shrugged.

"If you truly love Jan, you wouldn't try to ruin his family."

I rose to my full height, staring down my nose at the woman, my lip curled. She had some fucking nerve to speak to me like this. Were there anyone close enough to hear us talk, I could punish her for her impudence.

"What has you so insecure, Thóra? Last time I saw you, you quaked before me like a terrified mouse. Now you're taunting me and ordering me about. Is this bravery or desperation? Or have you simply forgot your place? Were you lying when you arrived here? Maybe you weren't as afraid as you were acting?"

We glared at each other, both of us visibly seething with rage.

Thóra straightened her *hustrulinet*.

"Speaking of families," Thóra said, recovering her calm demeanour and steady voice. "Jan told me all about Vidar's death – you see, we speak about everything, too. Vidar was killed by an escaped thrall in a riot started by *your* brother, *nei*?"

My nostrils flared as I held back from striking the awful woman. The fact my brother's actions led to my husband's death was a shame that hung over me constantly. The heinous little viper must've tricked Jan into telling her. What was she trying to do with that information – disparage me to Jan? Dishonour me?

"Jan said he avenged Vidar and slayed his killer, but what of your brother?" Thóra said, touching her chin with her fingertip in feigned confusion. "Jan didn't say whether you sought vengeance against your brother for starting the riot in the first place."

"I will not kill my brother." I growled. "That vengeance is for my children to take, not me."

"Didn't your brother disown you?" Thóra pressed. "From what I heard your brother wanted you *and* your family dead. Why would you defend the man who wanted to kill your children?"

"When my sons are older, they will have his blood. As they say, revenge is best served cold." I muttered, coiling my fingers around the hilt of *Úlfsblóð*.

"I'm surprised at you, Jarl." Thóra wrinkled her nose. "Anyone with a shred of honour would seek to punish *all* those who wronged their family. You should've killed every man involved in that riot! The fact your brother began it all warranted him even greater punishment – and instead, you let him go. A good wife and a noble warrior would *never* have done that."

ASHES REMAIN

I squeezed the hilt of my sword – I wanted to run the bitch through. How dare she insult and scold me! Did she believe she was immune to my wrath because she'd birthed Jan's damned child? How fucking wrong she was.

I turned to Jan. If only she was speaking louder! She was a coward, purposely speaking low so no one would hear, provoking me to attack her in front of Jan. How sorry she'd be if I did attack her – she wouldn't survive. If witness heard what she said, I'd be justified in my actions ...

I had to stop. I couldn't kill or maim the woman, but I couldn't let her continue to dishonour me either.

"Watch your words, Thóra Arnsteinsdóttir," I warned. "Rather than scold me for my choices, why don't we discuss the feud between my family and yours?"

"What?" Thóra barked, narrowing her eyes.

"When was the last time you spoke to Thorn?" My voice trembled with danger.

"Maybe decade ago, why?" Thóra's tone lost all confidence.

"I'm surprised Jan didn't tell you." I said quietly. "Thorn came to Aros years ago and accused Jan of murdering you. He challenged Jan to a *hólmganga* – and lost. The dishonourable swine was sore for losing and tried to kill the woman he'd mistaken for Jan's lover. She wasn't – she was my thrall and a dear friend – and she was holding my daughter."

Thóra's pretty blue eyes bulged from their sockets, the blood drained from her face. She has no idea any of this had happened.

"Thorn attacked them, wanting to kill the child, too, for he had mistaken my child for yours. He wanted to destroy every link to Jan – *including* your baby."

"You're lying!" Thóra whispered, reaching for her thrall.

Valens dutifully stood beside his mistress, holding her shoulders tight, trying to steady her.

"Have no fear, Thóra." I soothed. "Vidar killed your brother and every man who came to Aros supporting him – as a noble warrior should. *But–*"

I paused to let my words to chill Thóra to the bone. From how tightly she gripped her thrall, how the shaking of her body worsened, I knew she was terrified. Any number of male relatives of hers could've been there supporting her brother – and all of them were now dead.

I dropped my soothing tone and stepped closer, so close she stumbled back against her thrall. Trapped between us, I brought my face to hers.

"If I'm to kill every relative of the men who wrong me, think of your brother – and look at your son." I whispered.

"You won't do that – you wouldn't kill Jan's only child!" Panic lit up her pale blue eyes.

"Would you like to take that risk?" I replied softly. "Your brother wronged me, Thóra. Shall I destroy his *entire* family line? Like a noble warrior would?"

"You wouldn't!"

"Jan wonders why I don't trust you, Thóra. Ever since Thorn arrived in Aros accusing Jan of murdering you, I've been most perplexed. What made Thorn think Jan had murdered you? What an odd accusation. You're hiding something, Thóra, and I *will* find out what it is."

Valens shifted in front of Thóra, glaring at me, his dark eyes smouldering with hatred.

"Next time you insult me, I *will* have your tongue." I vowed.

Without bidding farewell to Thórvar or Jan, Thóra scurried off, clutching Valens' arm. I smirked as they fled, but my promise was true. She was right, she did have a sliver of immunity to my wrath – which is why I would take her tongue rather than kill her.

***

I COULDN'T STOP thinking about Thóra all afternoon. That woman brought out such a darkness in me – just looking at her made my blood boil. Her words, her threats, her brother Thorn, her outlandish story, the information she'd gleaned about me ...

My heart lurched in my chest. Thóra had been living in Túnsberg, Norway, for the past eight years. She had long black hair and blue eyes ... Tarben the Beardless was a Norwegian who also had long black hair and blue eyes. Were Thóra and Tarben related in some way? If they were, had Inga escaped to Norway and found shelter there with Thóra?

ASHES REMAIN

Thóra's family lived in Heiðabýr and had no link to Norway that I knew of. That didn't stop my suspicions though – there were a lot of secrets Thóra was keeping, I was sure of it. There was so much I didn't know about her.

I didn't remember meeting Thóra in Roskilde when she first moved there, I'd only met her at my wedding to Vidar. Then again, sometimes I would stay in the hall beside Vidar when he held town meetings, other times I didn't. Maybe I hadn't been there when she'd come seeking permission from Vidar to live in Roskilde. I wouldn't know for certain now ...

Thóra said she'd met Jan soon after she'd moved to Roskilde. Tarben had been dead for a while by that point, but no one had sought vengeance for his death until Háken Tarbenson challenged me at the þing. Vidar killed Tarben, I killed Háken, Jan had possibly killed Inga's youngest son as well, then Thóra arrived and was gathering information about me ...

It was a stretch – perhaps too coincidental to be legitimate – but I couldn't shrug my suspicions. Maybe Thóra hadn't been in an abusive marriage at all, perhaps she'd come to Aros to spy on me on behalf of Tarben's widow, gleaming information before attacking us to avenge the sons of Tarben?

By nightfall, I decided I had to do something. Where did Torfi Axelsson fit in to all this? Maybe he *was* Thóra's husband. Maybe he would be the one to rally an army and attack Aros to avenge Tarben's sons? The boys who could possibly be Thóra's kin, therefore his through marriage.

I surveyed my men. Domnall, Einarr, Lars, Ebbe and Sander were standing before me, excitement sparkling in their eyes. Herra Kaupmaðr, bundled in silks, stroked his wiry yellow beard with intrigue, pondering over the plan I'd shared with them.

As I allowed Herra a few moments to think over what I'd asked of him, Jan stepped through the hall doors with Thóra behind him. Noticing the group I'd gathered, Jan's face screwed up in confusion – I knew what he was thinking, why hadn't I called on him? I usually called on him first.

Truth be told, I didn't feel comfortable telling Jan my suspicions for the same reason I hadn't told my men. I trusted Jan with my life, but I doubted he'd see reason in my theory – I'm sure he still thought I was suspect of her out of jealousy. Based on one town name, her hair and eye colour, I was branding Thóra a spy and a traitor. It was quite a venture, but I wouldn't be able to put my theory aside without first checking to see if I was right.

Not just because I didn't want them to think I was a jealous madwoman, I couldn't tell my men my suspicions and order them not to tell Jan. They would assume I didn't trust Jan, thus possibly not trust him themselves. Jan was my right hand-man, he was guilty only of being the ex-husband of the woman I suspected to be a traitor – he was not a traitor himself.

Through all my secrets, I had a plan, one I was sure would work.

"Do I have your agreement?" I asked, eyeing the merchant.

"As I stated before, this is not something I usually do," Herra said finally – the silence waiting for his decision had been torture. "But for you, Jarl Aveline, *já*. Anything for you."

"*Þakka fyrir*, Herra!" I beamed. "You are the key to the success of this plan! Of course you will be compensated for your part in all this upon your return."

"You are most generous, Jarl." Herra said with a deep bow.

"As all of you will." I said to my men and son. "This is a daring feat, but I have faith you will succeed. You will set sail at first light – you should make it to Roskilde just before nightfall. Make sure the team Young Birger sends with you is small. Too many men will arouse suspicion."

"What's all this?" Jan asked, his arms crossed over his chest.

"There has been no word of Torfi Axelsson anywhere so I'm sending a party out to Túnsberg." I replied.

"W-why?" Thóra yelped, her eyes wide and face suddenly pale.

"I've told you many times that I will end this." I said, leaning back in my high-backed chair, my hands clasped on my lap. "The knowledge that Torfi might appear here looms over us constantly. Rather than wait for an attack, I'm going to hunt him down."

"But why send them to Túnsberg?" Thóra gasped.

"You said that's where he is from, correct?" I asked, answered by her small nod. "Then it is the best place to find him, is it not?"

"*J-já*, Jarl, but won't it be dangerous for your men to go to Torfi's town and kill him there? *They* might be killed instead!" Thóra stammered. "Torfi has supporters – lots of them!"

ASHES REMAIN

"It's a risk we're willing to take to assure the safety of Aros," I said. "And your safety, too, of course." I added offhandedly.

"I want to go." Jan said from behind them.

"*Nei*, Jan. Should Torfi arrive here while the party are away, Thóra will need you at her side." I said, nausea rising in my throat as those words fell from my lips.

"*Þakka fyrir*, Jarl." Thóra's voice was faint.

"Go," I said to Herra and my men. "Ready yourselves. I want you all in Túnsberg as soon as possible."

My men nodded and strode out of my hall, but for Sander who dashed to the sleeping area. The men greeted Jan or clapped him on the back as they passed him, no time to spare and fill him in on the details. It was long passed evening meal and they needed to prepare their belongings and go to sleep quickly, ready for first light when they would set sail.

"Jarl, I appreciate what you're doing, but I fear your plan might draw Torfi to me. If he finds out I am here, he might evade your men and find me." Thóra said, wringing her hands together.

"We are prepared." I said dismissively.

"He is strong – five men might not be enough to slay him."

"My men know what they're doing."

"Let me at least send Valens with you – he could help lead you to Torfi?" Thóra offered, her voice shaking.

"How helpful of you." I said dryly.

"Are you alright?" Jan asked, touching Thóra's arm.

"*J-já*," She swallowed hard. "I – I must tell Valens to be here tomorrow. I-I'll see you at home."

"*Já* – of course, *góða nótt*." Jan called as she scurried away.

"Skittish isn't she?" I remarked.

"You're hunting down a man she's terrified of." Jan said, turning to me. "Is it really a surprise?"

"If you're just going to bicker with me then leave. I don't have time to waste on this again."

"I didn't come here to bicker." Jan said just as snippily. "And I didn't expect to see all the men here. Why didn't you call for me?"

"I figured I could explain it to you after they'd left. You need to stay here to protect Thóra, after all." I replied, rolling my lips together briefly. "Why did you both come here anyway?"

"I missed you." Jan said simply. "Thóra said you had a pleasant chat together at the harbour today, so she wanted to come, too."

"She lied to you then because it wasn't pleasant at all."

"Oh?" Jan lifted his brows. "Dare I ask what you spoke about?"

"*You*, of course." I cocked an eyebrow at him. "I want to talk about it. Of all the things I've done in my life, bickering over a man is embarrassing."

"How honourable of you." Jan smirked. "I'm sorry speaking about me is embarrassing for you."

"Don't tease," I scolded. "I've had a long day."

"Is there anything I can do for you?"

"Sit and drink with me?" I suggested.

"I think I can do that." Jan said, settling down on the platform in front of me.

"Rowena," I called as I slipped off my highbacked chair and sat on the edge of the platform beside Jan. "Fetch us some mead, please. Then you and Melisende can go to bed."

"*Já*, Jarl." Rowena said.

Jan rested his hand on my thigh and squeezed it briefly. I turned to him and smiled – just the weight of his hand on my leg warmed me through. I leaned my head against him and he wrapped an arm around me.

"I missed you too." I murmured, answered by a kiss pressed to the top of my head.

It didn't take long for Rowena to return with our drinks. She and Melisende disappeared into the kitchen, leaving Jan and me alone, just as I'd instructed.

"Well, we're sitting together," Jan said, holding his cup out.

"Now we drink." I smiled, tapping my cup against his. "*Skål!*"

CHAPTER TWENTY-THREE

ROWENA COAXED ME awake. I opened my bleary eyes, my mind fuddled by the amount of mead I'd consumed over the course of the night. I rubbed my eyes and peered up at the smokehole, it was still dark. I'd slept for less than a handful of hours and felt all the worse for it. My stomach churned and a headache brewed – how I wanted to go back to sleep!

"It's almost daybreak, Jarl." Rowena whispered in Ænglisc.

"Thank you, Rowena." I murmured in our native tongue. "Please get me a brew – mint or fennel. I feel awful."

"Of course, Jarl. Should I fetch one for Jan as well?"

"For Jan?"

She nodded and glanced behind me. A warm smile touched my lips at the sight of him. As rotten as I felt, seeing him there filled me with happiness Sound asleep, Jan was naked and laying on his stomach, his face barely visible beneath the wild tangles of his hair, his round, firm buttocks a startling white in the darkness. The events of last night flooded through my mind.

"For Jan as well, yes." I replied softly, watching a few of his tawny hairs waver on his breath.

Rowena nodded and left the room. I rolled onto my side and watched Jan sleep by the light of the small fire burning across the room, happy to have him beside me. Carefully, I tucked his hair away from his face and snickered at the drool glistening by the corner of his mouth. I dragged my fingertips over his back and buttocks, watching goosebumps spring up on his skin.

It had been many months since I'd woken up with Jan beside me – far too long. Seeing him there, feeling the warmth emanating from his body, filled my heart with pleasure. I wondered what Thóra would say if she knew ...

A tiny part of me felt guilty – who knew what Thóra would do if she found out Jan and I were sharing a bed again. Would she take Thórvar away? I wouldn't put it passed her at all. I didn't want Jan to lose his son again, lest of all because of me.

A larger part of me didn't care. At some point over our drunken night together, Jan and I forgot about everyone and everything, wanting only to please ourselves, Thóra be damned. If Jan wasn't afraid of what Thóra might do, why was I?

Because Jan trusts her too much.

I shook my head and sighed deeply, burying my head in my pillow. Had I truly become this? I was the first female jarl in all the Danish lands, I'd conquered villages and towns, I headed one of the largest armies in Denmark, I'd defeated every man in single combat who'd ever challenged me, and I'd been reduced to fighting over a man. I *was* ridiculous.

I groaned. I needed to stop. If anything, I didn't want to spoil this moment with thoughts of *her*. I didn't have enough time to relish this moment, anyway – I had to get ready to see my men off.

Beside me, Jan stirred, not fully roused from sleep yet. My heart softened as I watched him. Jan was a fearsome warrior, I'd seen the bloodlust gleam in his eyes on the battlefield, I'd seen him kill men with no remorse, yet he was so endearing as he woke up. The way he rubbed his face into the pillow to get rid of the drool from his mouth, the little noises and sounds he made as he stretched – it was sweet. *He* was sweet.

"*Góðan morgin.*" Jan said, peering at me from behind his tresses.

"Did you sleep well?" I smiled.

"Not particularly – *someone* kept me up all night." Jan smirked.

"Poor you." I grinned.

Jan rolled onto his side and pulled me against his chest. A soft noise of satisfaction rolled in my throat as he held me – his body was so deliciously warm.

"Poor me indeed." Jan murmured, bringing his lips to mine.

Both of our breath stank of mead, the flavour stale on our tongues, but neither of us cared in the slightest. I nestled deeper in his embrace, listening to his heart beating in his chest, a soothing drum against my ear. By Freyja's cloak, how I missed this!

"I've sorely needed a night like that." Jan said contently. "I never thought I'd share your bed again – I didn't think you wanted me anymore."

ASHES REMAIN

"Of course I want you! I never stopped wanting you, I just shouldn't for your sake." I replied.

"I appreciate your concern but let me worry about myself." Jan said, kissing the top of my head. "Your heart is in the right place, but I'm a grown man, I can handle what's thrown at me."

"I'll always worry about you, Jan – telling me not to is pointless." I said matter-of-factly, tugging the sheet over my shoulder. "I care about you too much not to worry."

"I care about you, too." Jan replied softly.

Our eyes locked. His lips parted, I swallowed hard. He reached out for my cheek, as gentle as a breeze he touched me. My eyes fluttered closed. Our lips met softly, sweetly, as timid and tender as the first kiss we'd ever shared.

"Your drinks, Jarl." Rowena said as she entered with two steaming brews in her hands, the fresh scent permeating the room.

Against everything I wanted, pulled away from Jan. I sat up in bed, tucking the sheet beneath my arms to conceal my breasts. I thanked Rowena as she handed me my cup. She went to Jan's side of the bed and waited patiently for him to sit up. For a moment he stayed there gazing at me before finally sitting up and acknowledging my thrall.

"Morning meal will be ready soon," Rowena said in the Norse tongue for Jan's benefit. "Shall I wake Sander?"

"*Nei*, I'll wake him once I'm dressed, *pakka fyrir*, Rowena."

"*Já*, Jarl." Rowena nodded and left the room.

I held my cup against my bottom lip, feeling the heat seep through the polished wood. Just breathing in the hot minty steam abated my nausea. Rowena had made our beverages strong to combat our mead-induced ailments and it was working.

"Will this happen again?" Jan asked.

"I want it to."

"Me too."

Jan held his hand out to me. I stared at it, momentarily in awe. Worn and calloused, these hands had rowed ships through storms, had felled trees with axes, had built homes and ships, had hauled nets bursting with fish to feed my townspeople, had sewn fields with seed and reaped bountiful harvests.

These hands had gripped the hilt of swords and thrust them through his foes' chests, thrown spears at soldiers, had strangled enemies to death. These hands had delicately supported my children's heads when they were new-born, had held me tightly, had pleasured me. These hands were capable of destruction and creation, of harming and tenderness, of pain and comfort.

I laid my hand in Jan's. He brought it to his lips and kissed my knuckles. This moment was so perfect – at least, it would've been if my mind wasn't consumed by other thoughts. I turned my gaze to my cup, watching the finely chopped mint floating in the scolding honey water.

"She claims you're her husband. She told me you're a family again." I murmured.

"I am *not* her husband or lover," Jan said firmly, squeezing my hand. "She and I are *not* family. She's the mother of my son, nothing more. I protect her because she *needs* protecting, not because she's my wife. I'm yours, Aveline, only yours."

"Truly?"

"For as long as you'll have me, *já*."

"Jan, I want to give you the things you want – I just need time. Marriage, children – I can't give you them now, but one day I will. Just don't leave me for that woman. Wait a little longer, please."

A loud yawn from across the room indicated Sander was waking.

"I'll wait for as long as you need me too, Aveline." Jan whispered. "Just tell me when you're ready."

***

CURIOUSLY THÓRA DIDN'T see off her thrall. I knew the moment she volunteered him that he was not there to help us hunt down Torfi Axelsson. Thankfully, my men arrived earlier than intended, breaking their fast in the hall with Sander, Jan and me.

In a quiet moment with Sander and Domnall, I warned them to keep a careful eye on the thrall. Though I hadn't been open about my suspicions, I made them vow to watch him, to never leave him alone for even a moment, and to not ask me why. When I was ready to explain my reasons, I would, until then I asked for their trust. They agreed immediately, indisputably loyal.

Valens arrived after my men finished eating. I gave him a sack of dried fruits, cheese and nuts to eat on the ship and walked him to the harbour with my men. I tried initiating conversation with the thrall to no avail. I asked him why Thóra hadn't escorted him to the ship, and he simply replied, "I'm just a thrall.".

Herra Kaupmaðr met us at the shore, wrapped in silks and furs. Two of his men were standing with him, holding ropes tied around the necks of three goats. The rest of Herra's crew was in position on his *knarr*, his goods organised on the cargo ship neatly.

"*Góðan morgin*, Jarl Aveline, you're as radiant as ever." Herra greeted me with a deep bow.

"You lie," I smiled.

"I do not!" Herra exclaimed.

I knew how awful I looked, Sander had noticed the puffy bags beneath my eyes immediately and made no effort to conceal his surprise at them. I would drink enough to feel merry, but hardly ever to the point of drunkenness. Every time I did get intoxicated, I felt terrible the day after – which was the very reason I avoided getting inebriated in the first place.

Thankfully, the porridge settled my stomach, but at the back of my head an ache still resided and my mouth was awfully dry. I needed water and I needed sleep. Once I'd seen everyone off, I would return to my bed.

"I see you and your crew are ready."

"We are, Jarl. And your men?" Herra asked.

"They are ready, too." I nodded.

"Then it's time to embark." Herra beamed. "Will you aid me in the ceremony?"

"Of course."

I bid farewell to my men and as they boarded the ship, Herra and I sacrificed the goats to the gods. Jan was standing nearby, his arms crossed, staring at the ship with a furrowed brow and pursed lips. I knew he wanted to go with them, but I couldn't let him.

The ceremony complete and the men safely aboard, Jan and I watched the ship set off for Roskilde. By the time the first few rays of daylight sliced through the fading night, Herra's ship was already a shadowed silhouette in the distance.

"Do you want to go back to bed?" I asked, lacing my fingers in Jan's.

"I'd like to, but without Valens there, I need to make sure Thóra is al–" Jan stopped abruptly.

Unfortunately, he was too late to stop himself.

"You need to be there." I said softly, pulling my hand away from him. "I understand."

"Aveline–"

"It's fine, really." I shrugged away from Jan as he tried to reach for me. "Go to them."

"Aveline–"

"Jan!" I took a breath to calm myself. "Please, Jan. Just go."

ASHES REMAIN
CHAPTER TWENTY-FOUR

Summer, 891

IT WAS LATE at night when Sander and my men returned. Sander woke me, whispering my name, a big shining grin spread across his face. I squealed at the sight of him and hugged him tight, ecstatic to see him after so many months. Somehow Æsa and Einar managed to sleep through my elated cry. Though Sander had been away for so long, I didn't want to wake my two youngest children at such a late hour. They'd have to be surprised and find Sander home with us in the morning.

"What news do you have for me, my heart?" I asked, unwilling to release him from my embrace – I'd missed him terribly. "How are Young Birger and Signý? How was Túnsberg?"

"I'll tell you about Túnsberg out there, *móðir*. The men are waiting." Sander said, peeling himself from my arms. "Young Birger and Signý are well – they were going to send a messenger, but then we arrived. I decided to bring their message myself."

"A message?"

"*Já, móðir*," Sander's delight lit up his face, even in the darkness. "Signý bore Young Birger a son just days before we arrived."

"A son? Young Birger's a *faðir*?" I spluttered.

"*Já!* Young Birger named him Ísarr. You'll love him, *móðir*, he has Signý's hair, but he has *faðir*'s eyes!" Sander grinned.

A pang struck my heart and tears welled in my eyes.

"I can't wait to meet him." I beamed. "I want to set sail as soon as possible – before winter comes."

"I told Young Birger you would." Sander laughed. "First, the news from Túnsberg–"

"*Já, já*, go wait with your men, I'll be with you in a moment."

Sander nodded and strode out of the room. I rubbed my eyes with the heels of my hands and took a few steadying breaths before I yanked the gown I'd worn the day before over my nightdress and slipped on my boots.

Young Birger was a father – Signý had given him a son! My heart overflowed with love for my son, his wife and their baby. As I buckled my sword belt around my waist, I couldn't stop imagining what my newborn grandson looked like.

I paused in the entryway to the main room. I had to focus, I had to find out what had happened in Túnsberg. I took a breath and swept into the main room, smiling at the warriors that filled my hall, keen to hear the news they had brought me.

"Sander just announced the birth of Jarl Birger's firstborn son." I grinned as I entered the hall. "Ísarr Birgersson – my *sonarsonr*."

"Congratulation, *Amma*." Domnall grinned, wrapping an arm around my shoulder and hugging me briefly. "He's handsome and strong, even at just a few days old."

"Of course he is, he's Birger's son after all." I glowed as I strode to my high-backed chair on the platform. "Before we get carried away with Birger's good news, I'd like to know how Túnsberg went. Rowena, Melisende, food and drink for the men, please."

Sander, Herra, Domnall, Einarr and Ebbe regaled their journey to me as they sipped ale and chomped on the food my thralls set out before them at tables in front of my platform. It had taken far longer than I'd predicted for them to return, but they had returned safely and with interesting news indeed.

The news of my firstborn grandchild temporarily placed to the back of my mind, I paced on the platform, my heart racing. For the very first time, I was eager to speak with Thóra.

The hall door finally creaked open. Rowena led Lars into the hall, Jan close behind him. Hiding behind Jan's mighty frame was Thóra, paler than ever. Her eyes darted about the room, presumably searching for Valens.

I'd ordered the thrall to remain in the kitchen under the guard of two of Herra's burley crewmen. I didn't want Thóra and Valens to speak together until I had a chance to interrogate her first.

Jan led Thóra to me. To my disdain, she clung to his arm. I surveyed her from the platform, holding a cup of wine in my hands. Lars leaned closer to Einarr, whispering behind his hand, both of them eyeing the woman. All six men stared at her. They might not have shared my loathing, but they were all puzzled by what they'd discovered.

ASHES REMAIN

Jan and Thóra stopped before me. I loomed over Thóra on the platform. Jan seemed to sense the tension in the air, noticed how hard the men and I stared at Thóra. He opened his mouth to speak, but I began before he could say anything.

"I have a lot of questions, Thóra," I said calmly. "And you will *not* leave this hall until you have answered every one of them."

Thóra gulped audibly and nodded slowly.

"It's been no secret that I've not trusted you since you came to Aros." I said. "Between the single private conversation we've shared and the dubious reason you gave for your return, things just haven't added up about you.

"I sent my men to Túnsberg to not just hunt down your husband and end the threat he poses, but to find more information about you. For Jan's sake – and *yours* – I was hoping to be proven wrong. I was hoping I'd find evidence that corroborated your claims, but alas, I was proven right. You *cannot* be trusted."

Thóra swallowed hard. Jan turned to her, his brow furrowed. She avoided his gaze, staring at her feet.

"My men posed as merchants working for Herra Kaupmaðr. Under the mantle of Herra Kaupmaðr's exceptional reputation, they were trustworthy and unimposing. First they travelled to Roskilde to gather a few of Jarl Birger's warriors. Jarl Birger has an interest in all this, you see, since Roskilde was your last known whereabout, you have put his town at risk from attack.

"Remind me, Thóra, your husband's name *is* Torfi Axelsson, correct?"

Thóra gazed pleadingly at Jan. He tilted his head towards me, signalling for her to answer. I was almost ashamed of how pleased I was by Jan's reaction – at last, he was suspicious of her.

"*Já*, J-jarl – it is." Thóra replied, her voice trembling.

"And you lived with him in Túnsberg, correct?"

She gave the smallest nod, barely a twitch of her head.

"Then imagine my men's surprise when they went to Túnsberg and found not even a single man by the name of Torfi Axelsson."

The hall was deathly silent. I sat down on my highbacked chair and sipped my wine, allowing a few more moments of silence. Jan slowly withdrew his arm from Thóra's grip. Her eyes darted between Jan and me – she was caught in her lie and she knew it.

"Herra and my men questioned the merchants who were very willing to speak with them, but none of them had heard of a merchant with a foster-son named Torfi Axelsson. They questioned the townspeople and found a few men by name of Axelsson, but not one of them claimed a relative named Torfi. Why is this, Thóra?"

Thóra made a few indecipherable noises, but sure enough, she could come up with nothing. She reached for Jan, but he shrugged away, refusing her touch.

"Answer her." Jan muttered at Thóra.

"Maybe they lied – your men are foreigners, possible enemies to them." Thóra suggested, wringing her fingers. "They shunned me for being a Dane at first."

"Oh really?" I asked dryly. "Were you close to the Jarl of Túnsberg, Thóra? Apparently Jarl Kveldúlfr knew you well and had only positive things to say about you."

Thóra whimpered, uttering not a single decipherable word.

"This whole situation gets curiouser and curiouser, Thóra. Out of the entire town of Túnsberg, only the Jarl knew Torfi Axelsson. Not only that, but he had fantastic news – apparently he knew of the abhorrent treatment you endured at your husband's fist and killed him for his shameful actions."

I made note of each twitch of Thóra's knitted brows, the quiver of her bottom lip, the widening of her eyes and deepening of her frown. Surely the news of Torfi's death should've pleased her, given her even an ounce of relief? Her anxiety had not abated – indeed it had worsened. I decided to press further.

"Jarl Kveldúlfr is pleased to know you're safe here in Aros."

That was it. Her jaw dropped, her face completely drained of colour and her trembling worsened. Rather than gain pleasure from her reaction, my heart plummeted in my chest. There was fear in her eyes, legitimate soul-shaking terror. I hadn't just caught her in her lie, I had found the real reason she had left Túnsberg.

"Thóra?" I asked softly. "Torfi Axelsson isn't real, is he?"

With the slightest of movements, Thóra shook her head.

"What is your relationship with the Jarl of Túnsberg?"

Tears spilled down her ashen cheeks. She opened her mouth, but no words came out – she couldn't speak even if she wanted to, her emotions were too great. I realised at that moment the gravity of the situation – she'd made up this fictional Torfi as a cover for the man she was truly afraid of – a man who now knew exactly where she was hiding. A man with power, money, a vast army and fleet.

By the gods what had I done …

"Everyone, leave." I said quietly.

Nobody moved.

"Leave!" I bellowed.

Thóra whipped around and lunged toward the door.

"Not you, Thóra! You stay."

At my order she stopped and reluctantly returned to her spot in front of the platform, gulping for air and clutching her chest, tears and snot glistening on her face. My men glanced over their shoulders at the quaking woman and their fearsome jarl before exiting as I'd commanded.

Sander stepped towards the sleeping area but stopped in the doorframe. Bathed in shadow, he was hardly visible, there he stayed, watching.

Jan held the iron ring pull and let the others pass him. He was the last man in the hall, but rather than go out into the night with the others, he stayed. He shut the door and turned to face me. His jaw was set hard, his brow furrowed. He was prepared to receive my wrath, prepared to argue with me, but I didn't order him out.

I rose from my chair and set my wine cup beside it.

"Thóra," I said gently, crouching on the edge of the platform. "Kveldúlfr was the one who struck you."

I knew it to be true, it wasn't a question. Thóra wiped her face on her sleeve. Her bottom lip quivered with sadness, but loathing oozed from her glare.

"Please, Thóra. Tell me everything." I asked. "Let me help you."

"Why in Midgard should I believe you?" Thóra hissed.

"Things are different, Thóra–"

"How?" She spat.

"It was one thing when you were hiding from a man – it's something entirely different when you're hiding from a jarl."

Thóra's hands curled to fists at her sides, trembling and white. She was obviously holding back her urge to strike me. I rolled my lips together, pitying the woman. I needed her to tell me what

Kveldúlfr had done to her – I needed to hear the words from her mouth so I could act upon them.

"Despite our personal issues, Thóra, I *am* your jarl now." I said softly. "It's my duty to protect all of the residents of Aros. You are a resident here. Whether I like you or not, I *will* defend you from your enemies. I *will* protect you from the Jarl of Túnsberg. Tell me everything, and I will raise my army and slaughter the entire town of Túnsberg to protect you, if that's what it takes."

"I will *never* need your help, you home-wrecking bitch!"

Thóra spat on the ground in front of me, turned on her heel and left, slamming the door behind her. Ignoring the glob of spit at my feet, I slowly picked up my wine and stepped towards my high-backed chair. I didn't understand – why wasn't Thóra seizing her chance to have my army kill the Jarl of Túnsberg?

"Jarl Kveldúlfr is pleased to know you're safe here in Aros."

Why was I so stupid? Of course she didn't – how could she trust me to do that? I had told Jarl Kveldúlfr where she was now! I had put her at risk!

With a roar, I threw my cup across the room. Wine splashed over the tables and the cup slammed against the wall, rattling the shields hanging upon it.

"What have I done?" I groaned, dropping onto my chair, rubbing my face with both my hands.

"Aveline?" Jan finally stepped forward.

I glanced up at him, I had forgotten he was still here.

"What do you know about the Jarl of Túnsberg?" I asked.

"Not much. Roskilde fought alongside his father, Halvard Sturluson, during the attack on Britain over twenty years ago. He was a good man, an honourable man. He had many sons, but I only met maybe three of them during the campaign." Jan replied.

"Was Kveldúlfr one of them?"

"I don't know which of his sons earned that byname."

Realisation washed over me.

"Valens! Come to me!" I shouted out.

Valens appeared from the kitchen, Herra's burley men standing behind him, their large arms crossed over their broad chests. The thrall scowled at me, his hands balled into fists at his sides. He'd heard everything and was apparently just as angry with me for putting Thóra at risk.

"Tell me about Jarl Kveldúlfr." I ordered.

The thrall was silent. I soared from the platform, whipped my dagger from its sheath and pressed it against his throat. The thrall leapt out of his skin, not expecting my sudden movement or the cold metal of my blade against his neck.

"Tell me about him or I'll cut out your tongue and give you a reason to be mute!" I growled.

"Jarl Kveldúlfr is more terrifying than you could ever be!" The thrall replied, though his quivering voice betrayed his fear. "She escaped him, but now you've thrown her to the wolves! No one can defeat Kveldúlfr let alone a *woman*!"

Consumed by fury, my mistake thrown in my face by a thrall, my hand twitched, nicking the thralls neck. He squeezed his eyes shut and swallowed hard, wincing at the sharp pain of my blade slicing lightly through his skin. A trickle of blood ran down the blade. I staggered backwards and dropped my knife to the ground.

"Jan, take Valens home and stay with Thóra – she needs you to guard her." I said softly. "You two – send Herra to me. I'm in need of his assistance again."

***

I SPENT THE night hanging off Herra's every word. He had a wealth of knowledge about Jarl Kveldúlfr – because of everything he knew, Herra didn't do business in Túnsberg. Jarl Kveldúlfr's reputation presented him as a dishonourable monster, the type of man Herra was not inclined to transact with. Despite the fact Herra had no problem taking thralls and beating them into submission, Kveldúlfr was the kind of monster that made Herra seem an angel in comparison.

Jarl Halvard Sturluson, a respectable, but somewhat rash jarl of the Norwegian town of Túnsberg, had a slew of sons. His youngest was Kveldúlfr – 'Night Wolf'. No one seemed to know how he'd earned the byname, perhaps it was some affectionate moniker bestowed on him by his parents, no one knew. He was Kveldúlfr, that was all.

As Kveldúlfr grew older it became apparent that he was not Halvard's son, but Halvard's brother's. When Kveldúlfr was sixteen years old, his resemblance to his uncle was uncanny and Halvard couldn't deny the rumours anymore. Kveldúlfr was not his son. Halvard killed his brother and banished his wife and Kveldúlfr from Túnsberg.

At the time, Kveldúlfr was betrothed to the daughter of another Norwegian jarl, but their troth ended when he was outlawed. Soon into their banishment, Kveldúlfr's mother died. Over the years he was outlawed, Kveldúlfr struggled, and his heart hardened.

In 865, Kveldúlfr joined the Great Army to fight in Britain, most probably to earn a new reputation. He succeeded, earning a favourable name for himself as a capable warrior. Word had it he fought like a *berserkr*, ruthlessly slaying all enemies in his path.

Kveldúlfr fought in Britain for a decade, seizing riches and glory beyond measure. During that time, each one of Jarl Halvard's sons were killed, some in Britain, others in battles or raids in Norway.

With no heirs left to inherit his jarldom, the aging Halvard had no choice but to call upon Kveldúlfr. He had heard of Kveldúlfr's accomplishments and strengths and decided to revoke Kveldúlfr's outlaw status, adopt him and make him his heir, much to Kveldúlfr's delight. Not just that, but Halvard quickly arranged a marriage for Kveldúlfr to the Jarl of Kaupangr's only daughter, a gorgeous woman with hair like spun gold.

Kveldúlfr quickly got his wife with child, but that was where his downfall began. Perhaps it was his time roaming the craggy Norwegian wilderness or the decade of constant killing in Britain, but Kveldúlfr did not take well to being cooped up in Halvard's hall like a caged wolf, even with the most beautiful woman in Norway as his wife.

"As time went by, Kveldúlfr became bitter. He had an erratic, unforgiving temper, and not a soul in the whole of Midgard was safe from it. His wife, you see, was the product of the Jarl of Kaupangr and a concubine." Herra explained softly, his eyes bloodshot with sleepiness. "Kveldúlfr was the heir to Túnsberg, and he was forced to marry a bastard rather than a legitimate daughter. She was accepted by her father, but Kveldúlfr still saw her as a bastard, not worthy of a man of his standing.

ASHES REMAIN

"One day Kveldúlfr's terrible temper got the best of him – in a drunken rage, Kveldúlfr beat his pregnant wife to death, killing both her and their unborn child."

Word of her murder got around fast and Túnsberg and Kaupangr soon went to war. Túnsberg defeated Kaupangr with ease. After getting away with killing his wife without repercussion, Kveldúlfr developed a habit for beating women – both his concubines and thralls. He became just as infamous for his woman-beating as he was for his battle skill, if not more so.

"There was more to it than just beating them." Herra said, his voice harsh, his face contorted with disgust. "He'd torture them – he'd tie them up and molest them in all sorts of foul ways. Rumour has it he'd tied one woman to his bed, inserted a glass drinking vessel inside her, bound her legs together so the vessel wouldn't come out, then beat her until the glass shattered inside her body."

"Oh, god!" I gasped, covering my mouth, vomit rising inside my throat.

"After the glass shattered, he made her – *nei*, I can't go on, Jarl Aveline." Herra said, his face pale. "He did so much to her that death was a blessing – when he finally killed her, at least."

"How did the fiend get so many women if *this* was his reputation?"

"I imagine he preyed on his thralls – what could they do, but obey?" Herra shrugged. "He could do what he liked to those women, they have no rights. He'd send his hunting dogs to find the ones who tried to flee. If they hadn't torn the women apart by the time he found them, he'd torture them and kill them himself.

"As for the Norse women, not all of his women were Norwegian, some were Swedes, others were Danes and Lappir. The women from places far from Túnsberg couldn't know of his reputation and by the time they did, it was already too late."

Maybe he'd disguised himself, too? Maybe Thóra's story about Torfi Axelsson was actually about Jarl Kveldúlfr? Maybe that was the name he'd introduced himself as. He'd travelled to Heiðabýr under that guise, searching for a woman in the Danish lands since no father in Norway would marry his daughter to such a fiend.

After hearing all about Kveldúlfr from Herra, I understood why Thóra didn't want us to know about her link to the jarl. He was a rich and powerful man, and a violent, terrifying monster who seemed to be immune to the law.

A merchant's son was not much of a threat against Aros, but a jarl who commanded an army? By hunting down the man who had beaten her I had not only put Thóra and Thórvar in danger, but the entire city of Aros as well.

I was a terrible leader. Consumed by jealousy and hatred, furious at Thóra for trying to seduce my lover, I'd put all my townspeople at risk. By keeping Kveldúlfr's identity secret, Thóra was protecting Aros. She wanted to hide here – and marrying Jan would guarantee someone to protect her against the jarl in case he did somehow track her here.

Even if Kveldúlfr didn't find her, Thora needed a husband for survival – a man to financially support her and her child. Obviously, she set her sights on Jan – they shared a child and she already knew Jan was a skilled warrior and seaman. She came to Aros looking for him and found him wealthier than when they were married. Jan would be the perfect husband and I ruined it.

"You've given me so many answers, but now I have to decide what to do with them." I slumped back in my chair.

"My apologies, Jarl." Herra said sympathetically. "Might I help?"

"*Nei, þakka fyrir*, though, Herra, truly." I said. "I'm indebted to you for all you've done for me. Let me give you the coin I promised then you may go back to your ship and rest."

"Keep your money, Jarl. Being of service to you was reward enough." Herra said, bowing deeply as he rose from his chair.

I gawped at him.

"But Herra – why?"

"I insulted you many years ago – I hope I've earned your forgiveness now. Perhaps we can call each other friends again?"

"*Já – já*, Herra, of course." I spluttered.

"*Góðan morgin*, my Jarl." Herra chuckled. "Should you need me again, I'll be here."

***

THROUGHOUT JAN AND my relationship, I never wanted to acknowledge how selfish I was. I never appreciated Jan, I wanted him for his company, for his loyalty, for his comfort. I wanted him to fill the empty space in my bed and in my heart, the space Vidar had left, but not completely.

I was never willing to take Jan as my husband or give him any children. I knew Jan deserved a woman who wanted what he wanted, which was why I had him introduced to Bersa's widowed sister-in-law. Even then, I knew Jan would turn the woman down.

When Thóra appeared, I should have let her have him. I may have stopped sharing his bed at first, but it turned into a competition and I refused to let Thóra win, I refused to let Thóra have her husband back. It was at that moment I knew I didn't want Jan to find happiness with another, I wanted him for myself.

Thanks to that selfishness, I'd put Aros in danger.

Over five years ago, when my ship rowed away from the bloodsoaked shores of Gipeswic, I vowed to myself to never be naïve again, for my naivety led to Vidar's death. I failed that – I broke the oath I made to myself and now, due to my petty jealousy, every townsperson of Aros was in danger.

I had convinced myself Thóra was some conniving liar who wanted only to steal my lover from me. In the end, she lied to protect herself and her son, she lied to protect Jan and she lied to protect Aros. From everything Herra told me, I knew it was only a matter of time until Kveldúlfr appeared in Aros in search of Thóra, and he would do whatever it took to get her.

It was time for me to do right by Aros. I would spend as much of my wealth as I needed to fortify the town and protect my townspeople. When Kveldúlfr arrived I would defeat him and I hoped for as little casualties as possible.

As for Thóra, there was no way I could ever make up for my mistakes to her. There was only one thing I could do …

"Aveline." Jan said coldly, entering the hall behind Melisende.

Melisende scurried to the kitchen. It was late, Rowena was already asleep. Before I sent Melisende to get Jan, I ordered her to go straight to bed and leave Jan and me alone. The children had been asleep for hours, I knew Jan and I wouldn't be interrupted.

I hadn't managed to rest since Sander and my men had returned. I'd gone over a full day without sleep, kept awake by the nagging voice in my head reminding me of my failures. I hoped by settling what I could with Thóra I might finally be able to sleep, but knowing what I was about to do, I doubted that very much.

Shame welled inside me the moment I saw Jan. I turned my gaze downwards, unable to meet Jan's searching eyes. With a few wide strides, Jan was beside me, but he didn't reach out to touch me or take my hand ... He was just as disappointed in me as I was.

"I've made a lot of bad decisions lately." I said softly.

Jan said nothing. He sat down on a chair beside me and rested one of his hands on the table. I wanted to reach out for it, wanted the comfort of Jan's touch, but I stopped myself. I didn't deserve it – I didn't deserve comfort and I certainly didn't deserve Jan.

"I hated Thóra the moment she came here." I admitted quietly. "I knew you deserved better than me, but I couldn't let you go. I was so scared she'd take you away from me ..."

"Aveline–"

"*Nei*, Jan. Let me finish." I said, forcing my words passed the lump in my throat. "I've put her and Thórvar in danger – she needs you by her. S-she deserves you, Jan. She wants what you want, she's already given you a child and I'm sure she'll give you more. I – I didn't want to trust her because I knew she was lying. I only wish I'd known she was lying to protect us ... And I ... I lied to you, Jan, but only to protect myself."

"What are you talking about?"

I took a deep breath, tears spilling down my cheeks. By the gods, I didn't want to do this! But I had to – for Jan.

"Jan – the seeds I chew to avoid getting with child – they aren't guaranteed to work." I whispered. "But Brynja has other things, brews that expel the unborn child from a woman's womb. They're dangerous if consumed too often, but they work."

"Why are you telling me this, Aveline?"

Confusion and anger laced Jan's words. I glanced at him and found his sapphire eyes glaring at me beneath his tightly knitted brow. The frown that twisted his lips made me wish I'd never said anything but I couldn't hide the truth from him anymore.

I hated Thóra for lying, but I was no better.

No ... I was worse.

"Over the two years we've been sharing a bed, w-we conceived three children together. I used Brynja's brew to get rid of them ...

ASHES REMAIN

T-they're buried in the grounds, near the monument beneath large flat stones. I–I'm sorry, Jan."

Jan stood up, flinging his chair out from beneath him. I yelped as he grabbed my shoulders and pulled me to my feet.

"You killed my children – you got rid of *our* unborn children? Why in Hel's name would you do that?" Jan shook me as he hissed at me. "Of all people, how could *you* do this to me?"

"I'm sorry!" I wept. "I – I couldn't give you a child until after Sander became jarl!"

Jan's nails dug into my arms, his grip like a vice. I tried to jerk my arms free, but I couldn't, he was too strong. My heart raced – never in my wildest nightmares had I thought Jan would hurt me. Caught in his grasp and unable to break free, I was a doll in his hands – if he wanted to harm me, he could.

"I haven't trusted anyone completely, but for Vidar!" Jan seethed. "Until *you*, Aveline! I confided *everything* in you! You know my past, you know I want a family more than anything, yet you got rid of my children? You took my chance at fatherhood from me! You killed *our* babies!"

"I know!" I wailed. "I'm sorry!"

"You words mean *nothing*!" Jan snarled.

"Jan – please! I'm sorry I hurt you, but I told you I couldn't give you a child until after Sander became jarl!"

"You think that excuses you from what you've done?" Jan roared. "Damn it, Aveline! Don't share a bed with a man if you're afraid to conceive a child!"

"You know it's not that easy!"

"*Nei*, it's far easier to kill my children than keep your legs shut!"

I quailed beneath his fearsome stare, trembling in his grasp. Finally, Jan released me. I crumpled to the ground. Through tear-stricken eyes, I watched Jan tear across the hall, kicking or shoving furniture out of his way as he made for the door. He yanked the door open by the ring pull but stopped suddenly.

"I never thought you'd hurt me just to meet your own ends." Jan spat. "You are not the woman you once were, Aveline."

The door slammed shut behind him.

I couldn't breathe. It was like an invisible force gripped my throat. I scratched at my chest and neck as I sucked in each gasping breath. I knew I'd hurt Jan, but I never imagined this – never thought he'd grab me or hurt me – never thought I'd see such dark, bitter loathing in his eyes.

All at once, a raucous cry ripped from my throat. Overcome by anguish, I lost control. I beat my fists against the packed-dirt floor, wailing and howling, tears pouring in an endless cascade. Melisende and Rowena fell to their knees beside me and wrapped me in their arms. They held me, offered me soothing words in panicked tones, but their voices were muffled by the noise of my heart hammering in my ears.

I did it – I admitted my secret to Jan, a secret that hurt him, a secret I should never have kept from him to begin with. Incensed and horrified by my confession, he left me. I had successfully driven him away. Now he would stay with Thóra, a woman who loved him, a woman who would do right by him and give him the life he wanted.

I wouldn't stand in Jan's way anymore.

CHAPTER TWENTY-FIVE

Late Summer, 891

BLOOD GUSHED FROM Sander's nose as he fell to the ground. Galinn Johansson dived on top of him, grabbed the front of his tunic, fist drawn back, ready to drive another brutal blow into my son's face. Sander whipped his arms up just in time. He visibly grinded his teeth, hissing and groaning at every mighty hit Galinn landed on his forearms, Sander's own hands balled into fists.

Galinn was tiring, but so was Sander. My son endured every blow, his arms shuddering violently. Panting and grunting, Galinn hammered Sander with an unrelenting wave of punches.

My heart raced – every moment Galinn raised his fist was a chance for Sander to strike him – but why didn't Sander take it?! Why did he wait still? There – there was another opening! Why wasn't Sander trying to hit Galinn?

By the gods, the urge to kill had never boiled in my blood as hotly as that moment. It didn't matter how much I wanted to, I couldn't jump into Sander's fight and rescue him. I would insult his honour – Sander had to win this on his own. I ignored the screaming of my mind's voice. My sight focussed on the battle, I silently willed Sander to win.

There was no way Sander could last much longer yet still he waited despite the opportunities to fight back! Damn it, why wouldn't he strike Galinn?!

Galinn landed yet another blow!

Sander waited.

Galinn struck him again!

Sander roared in pain.

Galinn raised his fist–

Sander grabbed the neck of Galinn's tunic, yanked his surprised enemy closer and smashed his head into Galinn's face. Galinn toppled off Sander, clutching his face, groaning and writhing. While his opponent was dazed, Sander scarpered to his feet.

Galinn tried to stand up, but he was too slow, too exhausted, his arms gave way as he tried to push himself up from the ground.

Sander took his chance – he kicked Galinn as hard as he could. Galinn's nose crunched audibly – he crumpled to the ground, unconscious. Sander, red faced with fury, had won – but he wasn't finished yet. He kicked Galinn in the face again, another crack rattling through the air.

"Sander! Stop!" I screeched as Sander kicked Galinn a third time.

At my yell, Sander whipped around. My heart stopped in my chest – doused in his enemy's blood and his own, Sander glared at me, his face contorted fiercely with an expression I'd never seen on him before. My blood ran cold, I knew that expression – at that moment Sander didn't look like himself, he looked like Vidar.

Blood mingled with sweat dripped down his face and neck. He panted heavily and his fists quaked at his sides. He was exhausted, beaten and bruised, his body trembled not just from pain and fatigue, but from adrenalin as well. And there in his ice-blue eyes was a terrifying glint – bloodlust.

I stared at my second-born son and my own body shook – it was as though Vidar's ghost stood before me! Ósk, Galinn's mother, shoved through the crowds, knocking me as she passed. I tore my gaze from Sander and watched Ósk drop to her knees beside her son. She screamed for Brynja, screamed for Brynja's daughters, screamed for help. A handful of women rushed to her side including Sibba, Galinn's young wife, and Thóra.

At the sight of the tears streaming down their cheeks, I felt a prick of sympathy for Ósk and Sibba, but I hardened myself to their sadness. If the boys meant to solve their argument with their fists then that was how it would be.

"It's over, Sander," Jan said, appearing from the crowd. "Go back to the hall. It's done."

Jan's voice was low and steady. Did he not notice the haunting resemblance between Sander and Vidar? How was Jan not unnerved? Sander spat a bloody gob of saliva on the ground. They glowered at one another until at last my son relented. He stormed to the hall, the crowd separating to allow him passage.

The moment Sander was out of sight, Jan strode to Galinn's side. I followed slowly, pausing a few paces away from them. I needed

ASHES REMAIN

to know what the two had fought over. Fights between boys and young men were common – as long as they didn't injure each other too badly, they were left to sort their squabble out between themselves.

This was different. Galinn and Sander wanted each other's blood and no one stepped in – it wasn't a spat, but a battle of honour – one that Sander won, thank the gods.

Jan ordered the women to stop flapping about the wounded young man like panicked hens and knelt beside him, examining Galinn's wounds himself. I peered passed Jan and wrinkled my nose in disgust. Galinn's face was grotesque, his flesh was red with blood and blackened by bruises. Just slits of white were visibly between his swollen lids, his eyes rolled to the back of his head in his unconscious state. Galinn's face had doubled in size and his nose was a pulpy mess.

"Sibba, go to Brynja's longhouse and tell her to be ready for Galinn. I'll carry him there." Jan said to Ósk and Sibba.

"What happened?" I asked, my voice low and steady.

Ósk and Sibba glowered at me, tears dripping down their cheeks. Sibba, her mouth pinched and eyes puffy, dashed to Brynja's as Jan bade. Ósk opened her mouth to speak, but words failed her. She turned to her son, gripping his hand with her shaking fingers.

And there was Thóra.

She rose to her feet pointing at me with her index finger, her other hand curled into a fist.

"Your son attacked mine!" Thóra hissed. "If it hadn't been for Galinn, who knows what would've happened to Thórvar?"

"*What?*"

"Your son is a menace! He attacked Thórvar and Galinn bravely stepped in!" Thóra snapped. "Had it not been for him who knows what state Thórvar would be in?"

"Of course, you're worried about Thórvar rather than the one bleeding before us." I sneered. "Where is Thórvar? He's old enough to fight his own battles yet I don't see him anywhere."

"That's enough!" Jan snapped. "Thóra, go back to the farm!"

"What of her?" Thóra barked.

"She's the jarl. She can do what she wants." Jan said bitterly.

"Of course you defend her! You–"

"Don't scold *me*, woman! Go! Now!"

Thóra flinched at Jan's roar and darted off like a dog with its tail between its legs. I turned to Jan, my nostrils flaring with each breath I inhaled. He met my stare for just a moment, his lip curled and brow furrowed. He turned back to Galinn and carefully scooped up his limp body. With Ósk scurrying behind him, Jan marched towards Brynja's longhouse.

I watched him disappear, feeling the heavy stares of my townspeople resting on me, listening to their whispers. I turned my back on them all and followed Sander's path to the hall.

***

"WHAT HAPPENED?" I demanded.

Sander was sitting at the table holding a wet rag to his nose. Scowling at me, he leaned over a bowl of water on the table and spat into it. His phlegm was bloody – he must have broken a tooth or bitten his lip or the inside of his cheek during the fight.

"Don't make me seek answers from Thóra or Ósk, I doubt they'll paint you in a fair light." I warned, sitting beside him.

"Thórvar insulted you." Sander growled. "He said you were a whore and unworthy of being Jarl of Aros – I couldn't let him get away with that, so I punched him."

Sander paused to spit in the bowl again, pinching the bridge of his swollen nose.

"Galinn jumped in, claiming he was defending Thórvar, but the shit-head was just waiting for an opportunity to fight me." Sander continued angrily. "He's hated Young Birger and me for as long as I can remember – he always insulted us and tried to goad us into fights, but none of the damned things he said were enough to warrant us beating him without us looking bad."

"He got his wish in the end," I commented. "He got his fight."

"And the bastard lost." Sander smirked.

"Serves him right for underestimating you."

"I look forward to telling Young Birger when I see him." Sander grinned, though his smile faltered – he missed his brother.

"I'm sure he'll be proud of you." I said, rubbing his shoulder. "You did well out there. I hate to say this but fighting Thórvar and

ASHES REMAIN

Galinn is not beneficial to us right now. Jarl Kveldúlfr of Túnsberg could arrive in Aros any day, if you're too busy fighting over some name-calling, you won't be alert for a possible attack."

"It wasn't just *name-calling*, he insulted your honour!"

"And I appreciate you defending me, but now is not the time." I said firmly. "Revenge is best served cold, my heart. Hard as it may be, ignore insults and slights for now. When we've defeated Kveldúlfr then you can get your revenge on Galinn and Thórvar."

"And if Kveldúlfr never comes?" Sander grumbled.

"You wait. You wait until the perfect opportunity, which won't come while we're living under threat of a larger enemy's attack."

"I won't wait until my *móðir* tells me when." Sander grumbled.

"You *will* wait until your Jarl tells you when." My voice was low and burned with superiority.

Sander's brows shot to the top of his head, staring at me wide-eyed. He needed to remember I wasn't just his mother, but the leader of Aros and everyone in it – including him. His disputes didn't matter compared to my decrees.

Sander spat in his bowl again. He folded his filthy rag in half and tossed it onto the table, scowling at it.

"You looked like your father today." I said softly.

Sander said nothing, but pleasure pinkened his cheeks.

"I've seen your father consumed by battle many times, and today you were the epitome of him." I smiled. "He knew when to stop, when to fight and when to wait. You're different in that regard, Sander. You're curious, excitable and impatient. You *must* learn the right moment to pounce otherwise not only will you lose your prey, but you'll put yourself at risk."

Sander nodded.

"You must also think about what you'll say to Jan." I remarked.

"I didn't hurt Thórvar *that* badly."

"You hurt his pride and his honour. Far worse than a physical wound." I pointed out. "You've injured Jan's pride as well."

"What?" Sander barked.

"His son wasn't man enough to finish the fight he started – he had someone else do it for him." I explained. "It would've been more honourable for Thórvar to get his head kicked in rather than have Galinn fight his battle for him."

"That's between Thórvar and Galinn." Sander replied. "*I* didn't tell Galinn to step in. Anyway, I don't care if Jan's upset – Thórvar shouldn't have insulted you."

"Oh really? Would you say that to Jan? And what about Thóra? You know she despises us – unfortunately, with just cause. Did you consider how she'd react before you beat her son? Do you realise you've worsened the feud between us and her now? Especially after Túnsberg ..."

"She—"

"These people – Galinn, Thórvar, their friends – these are the people whose support you'll need when you become jarl. If you continue to act recklessly, the moment you are announced jarl, you'll be challenged by every damned one of them – *if* you survive long enough to get to that point."

"I'll defeat them all! Just like you defeated all the men who challenged you!"

"Unless you lose all of your supporters by then."

"I defended your *honour*! That isn't a shameful cause for a fight!"

"It is when I've invited an enemy to our door!" I snapped.

The astonishment on Sander's face made my cheeks burn red. I cleared my throat.

"Unfortunately you inherited your thoughtlessness from me." I sighed. "The mistakes I've made effect how you must react to your own problems and for that I'm sorry. If I hadn't sent you to Túnsberg this fight never would've happened."

"I would've fought Galinn eventually." Sander said.

"And you would've beaten him that time, too." I smiled. "For now I advise you to make amends with Jan. You've made solid enemies of Galinn and Thórvar now."

"I'm not upset by that." Sander said pompously.

"Wash your face and change your clothes you insufferable boy."

"*Já, móðir.*" Sander grinned, rising to his feet.

"Sander," I called, he glanced at me over his shoulder. "You have your father's nose now – his had been broken many times by the time I met him."

Sander straightened his stance and puffed out his chest as he strolled to the kitchen. I snickered, but my smile waned when my gaze fell upon the bloody rag on the tabletop.

ASHES REMAIN

Yes, Sander had made two enemies now – that is if Galinn survived. If he didn't … Well, Galinn was not Sander's first kill, he had slayed many in battle, but this would be his first death through dispute, and what a death it would be. Kicking someone to death when he had not yet seen fourteen winters …

I hoped Galinn survived – hoped his wounds looked worse than they were. I couldn't stomach the notion that Sander could kill so brutally at such a young age, especially in my name.

Thórvar …

Thórvar hadn't been wrong, either. I'd whored myself to Jan by sharing his bed outside of marriage, and I'd put Aros in danger because I couldn't contain my petty jealousy. I found myself wondering if Sander knew Thórvar was right. If so, did Sander beat Thórvar and Galinn to defend my honour or to silence them and the shameful truth they threw in his face?

It had been a few weeks since Sander and my men returned from Túnsberg. My warriors waited in anticipation for the day a fleet of Túnsberg ships would appear on our fjord, but that day hadn't yet arrived. I was thankful there was no sign of the jarl, but I didn't lower my guard and neither did a single man in Aros. All were ready for when Kveldúlfr arrived.

Would Kveldúlfr arrive? His reputation insinuated he would if he wanted Thóra badly enough. The fear Thóra exuded at the mention of his name was palpable … Yes, he would come for her, it was just a matter of time. This was a form of torture, something Kveldúlfr apparently revelled in. We were high-strung, constantly on alert – we'd get exhausted and the moment we wavered would be when Kveldúlfr would strike.

My thoughts drifted to Jan.

Today was the first time I'd seen him since I'd admitted my secret to him in the hall. I hadn't expected the venom that dripped from his stare nor the hateful tone with which he spoke about me. But what *did* I expect? My actions were unforgiveable.

Would Sander try to make amends with Jan? The night I'd admitted my secret to Jan, the night he'd shaken me and stormed out of my hall, Melisende and Rowena had rushed to my side. As my wails subsided, Sander sent the thralls to be with Æsa and

Einar, who watched, terrified, from the sleeping area. He then curled up on the ground and held me.

I didn't know how much they'd seen or heard of Jan and my fight, but it must've been enough to change their feelings towards Jan. His name had not been mentioned in the hall since that day, his appearance was not missed nor questioned.

I had no desire to clear things with the children, to let them know Jan's reaction was warranted. I would have to one day, but I was not strong enough to admit more of my failings to them yet.

ASHES REMAIN
CHAPTER TWENTY-SIX

Spring, 892

THE SOUND OF hustle and bustle outside the hall set my heart racing. Aros was busy with preparation. After an excruciatingly long winter it was finally time to raid. The fields were sewn, new life sprang from every corner of Aros – at last, it was time! In the early hours of tomorrow morning, Sander and my trunks would be packed onto Storm-Serpent and we would set sail.

Domnall, Lars, Einarr, Ebbe and Sander were sitting at the table in my hall discussing the pending expedition, while Æsa and Einar snacked on dried fruit and nuts and listened avidly. I was just as excited as the children. How I yearned to escape Aros and all it held. How I longed to be free, if just for a while.

Bang-bang!

The hall doors burst open and slammed against the walls. I lurched in my seat and the men whipped around, grabbing their weapons. I jumped to my feet, furious at whoever in Hel's name thought they could enter my hall like that.

"Who are you?" I demanded as a hulking brute of man and his group of followers entered my hall.

"I am Jarl Kveldúlfr of Túnsberg." The leader of the pack announced, his mouth twisted into a half-smile. "My apologies for scaring you." He added with no sincerity in his tone.

My heart skipped a beat. Immediately the air became suffocating, tense. So, this was Jarl Kveldúlfr ... Broad and swelling with muscle, he was as mighty as rumours portrayed him to be. He was the only man I'd ever met who rivalled Jan in height. A web of pale scars laced over his face, silvery in the glow of the flames dancing on his alabaster flesh.

A shiver ran down my spine when I met Kveldúlfr's gaze. I had been around warriors long enough to recognise the glint of bloodlust alight in his wild cobalt eyes, no matter that we were far from a battlefield.

"Welcome to my home, Jarl Kveldúlfr. What can I do for you?" I asked, my voice level and low.

"I apologise for my interruption, Jarlkona. I'm in search of the Jarl of Aros," Kveldúlfr explained. "Though I'm pleased to be greeted by such a beautiful creature as yourself instead."

I had been waiting for this moment for so long – and Kveldúlfr had no idea who I was.

"You flatter me, Jarl." I said dryly, turning to Rowena briefly. "Fetch mead for our guests while they wait for the Jarl."

Rowena nodded slowly, both she and Melisende equally confused by my order and intimidated by the newcomer. Thankfully, Kveldúlfr didn't seem to notice their confusion, his dark blue stare locked on me, overwhelmingly heavy. Like an instinctual warning of danger, goosebumps prickled all over my skin and the fair hairs over my body stood on end.

"Please, sit," I said to Kveldúlfr, feigning calmness. "While we drink, you can tell me why you're looking for the Jarl."

"I would enjoy that very much." Kveldúlfr said, his sordid gaze travelling over my body shamelessly.

"Children, fetch your *faðir* and let him know he has a guest." I said, locking eyes with Sander.

Sander nodded, a look of fierce determination on his face. He understood what I meant. He knew the threat Kveldúlfr posed. I knew he'd get his younger siblings to safety and rally the men.

"Don't send your children off on my account, Jarlkona. My ships fill the fjord and we had quite the audience when we came here. I'm sure the Jarl knows of our arrival by now." There was no denying the threat veiled in Kveldúlfr's casual tone.

"Hence your remarkable entrance." I cocked a brow at him.

"My apologies, I was excited to get here." He winked.

"It will do no harm to send for my husband. I'd hate for you to wait longer than necessary. Go, children, get your *faðir*."

I was nervous Kveldúlfr would order one of his warriors to stop my children from leaving, but thankfully he didn't. They scurried out, Sander holding his siblings' hands tightly as they left, their cloaks forgotten. If he was telling the truth about his fleet of ships, the numbers Kveldúlfr arrived with suggested he was here for war. I needed to get my children as far away as possible.

ASHES REMAIN

"Please make yourselves comfortable while you wait." I offered.

A few of Kveldúlfr's men sat in my children's empty seats while the others remained standing. There were far more men in the hall than there were chairs, not that it mattered. Like well-trained dogs, Kveldúlfr's men stood still and quiet while their master spoke, waiting keenly for his command.

Acting as the courteous hostess, I stepped aside and offered Kveldúlfr my place at the table. I needed a reason to take my seat on the platform for behind my highbacked chair was my sword. Kveldúlfr rested one hand on the back of the chair then paused. Audaciously, he reached out and brushed a stray curl from my face, his cobalt gaze oozing lust.

Those eyes ... I recognised them. But from where? I had little time to ponder and little care to, incensed by Kveldúlfr's touch. How dare he do something as amorous as touch my hair in public! Especially since he thought I was the Jarl's *wife*. Kveldúlfr was here for a fight and he started it the moment he touched me.

I caught sight of Lars and Einarr. They glared at Kveldúlfr, visibly outraged. Thankfully they remained still. Kveldúlfr was bold and daring – combined with his violent reputation, I wouldn't put it past him to attack me if I so much as brushed his hand away.

"Why aren't you wearing a *hustrulinet*?" Kveldúlfr asked, stoking my hair. "You look like an unmarried maiden like this."

"I wasn't expecting guests." I replied.

"Of course not," Kveldúlfr said, cocking his brow as he glanced at my men seated at the table. "Your husband lets you have your hair down in front of others?"

"Why don't you tell me of your voyage rather than worry about what my husband lets me do?" I replied sharply.

"Quite the brazen one, aren't you?" Kveldúlfr chuckled as he took a step closer to me. "And lovely, too. I admit, I've not heard much about the Jarl of Aros, but what little of him that has reached my shores did not describe how magnificent his wife is."

"What do you think you'll accomplish by flattering me?"

"I meant no insult, Jarlkona. It's difficult for a man to lay his eyes upon the treasure of another and not give in to jealousy." Kveldúlfr said, drawing his hand away from me at last.

"Again, you compliment me. Please, sit, make yourself comfortable while we wait." I said, hoping I didn't sound sarcastic.

I smiled and stepped back, feeling Kveldúlfr's ravenous gaze follow me as I made my way to the main platform. I slid my hand over the edge of Vidar's highbacked chair as I took my place at my own, eyeing my blade behind my chair, exactly where I'd left it.

With one hand rested on the hilt of his sword, Kveldúlfr strolled towards me, a smile lifting one corner of his mouth, his eyes glinting. He was so focussed on me, he didn't seem to notice my men glowering at him, following his every step. That or he wasn't threatened by them. His men outnumbered mine five to one.

"Your husband must be quite the man to have a woman like you as his wife." Kveldúlfr said, stopping in front of me.

"You must be hungry, Jarl, you're drooling." I teased, not breaking eye contact with him as I accepted my cup from Rowena.

"Oh, I am," he winked. "How can I not be when I'm in the presence of someone as exquisite as you?"

I brought my hand to my mouth and touched my lips, concealing my smile. His grin widened, he was pleased with my reaction.

"You are quite the honey-tongued charmer, aren't you, Jarl? Do you flatter your wife like this?"

"*Nei*, she isn't half as beautiful as you."

I took a sip of my wine, surveying him over the rim of the cup. His ebony hair was carelessly tied back, a few long strands loose and framing his handsome face. His skin was pale as porcelain and his scars were bright as silver.

Rowena and Melisandre brought tankards on platters into the room and set them on the table. Kveldúlfr's men accepted the tankards and drank deeply, but the Jarl didn't. He remained before me, one hand on his sword, gawking.

"You've brought a lot of men with you." I commented.

All his warriors were dressed for battle. Some had helmets, others wore a form of armour, mail or padded fabric. All of them were armed with spears, swords or axes.

"I have more waiting outside." Kveldúlfr bragged. "Rumour has it your husband has something of mine. I came to take it back."

"Oh?" I raised my brows in feigned surprise. "And what's that?"

"My wife, Thóra Arnsteinsdóttir."

ASHES REMAIN

"I can assure you, my husband does *not* have your wife."

"Beautiful women tend to be liars, I hope that's not true of you."

"Am I beautiful, Jarl Kveldúlfr?" I asked sweetly, tilting my head.

"I think you're one of the most beautiful women I've ever seen," Kveldúlfr smiled. "Which means I can't trust you."

"I won't try to tell you what you should or shouldn't do, Jarl, but I can assure you, my husband does *not* have your wife."

Kveldúlfr stepped up onto the platform, rested his hands on the arms of my chair and bent down to me, his face inches from mine. My heart raced and my grip tightened around my polished wooden cup, but I tried to remain as outwardly relaxed as possible.

"For your sake, I hope you're telling the truth, Jarlkona. It would sadden me to kill your husband for I do *hate* to see pretty women cry." Kveldúlfr's voice was low and husky.

"Now *you're* the one who is being dishonest. Rumour has it you *do* like to see pretty women cry."

Kveldúlfr grinned, drawing his tongue over his teeth like a wolf licking his chops. He made no attempt to deny what I'd said, in fact his eyes seemed to sparkle brighter.

"Your husband should've been here by now. He isn't a coward is he?"

By Týr, if I could pull my knife from my belt without him noticing, I could stab him in the gut that moment and end the battle before it began … I straightened my posture, closing the space between our lips until only a finger-width of space remained.

"I have a few secrets to tell you, Jarl."

He offered me his ear, visibly amused by the situation. I placed one hand on his shoulder, feeling the solid muscles beneath his tunic. Bent over me like this, if he spotted my hands moving, he'd grab me immediately. Damn it! I had to think of a new plan.

By Týr, I hoped my men were assembling outside the hall …

I brought my lips close to Kveldúlfr's ear. I noticed the hairs on the back of his neck bristle.

"You're going to be waiting a long time for my husband, Jarl Kveldúlfr, adopted son of Halvard Sturluson. My husband died many years ago. It isn't him you seek, but me. *I* am Jarl of Aros."

Kveldúlfr stepped back, eyeing me with disbelief, before bursting into laughter.

"*You* are the jarl?" He howled, his men snickering along with him. "I heard there was a woman-Jarl in the Danish lands, but I didn't realise she was here in Aros!"

I rose to my feet.

"I am Aveline Birgersdóttir, Jarl of Aros and a hundred more settlements, and I do not have your *wife*, Kveldúlfr."

"See? Beautiful women do lie!" Kveldúlfr laughed. "It doesn't matter who is Jarl, I know my wife is here. Give her back to me."

"I didn't lie. My *husband* does not have your wife, and nor do I."

"Enough of the games, *Jarl* Aveline, you're wearing my patience." Kveldúlfr scolded. "Where is Thóra Arnsteinsdóttir?"

"She lives here in Aros under my protection. However, she most certainly is *not* your wife."

"I came here for Thóra and I'll be leaving with her." Kveldúlfr said. "I should warn you, I came not just for her, but for the Jarl of Aros's blood, as well."

"You'll be leaving here with neither."

Kveldúlfr snickered. Even in that quiet laugh there was darkness.

"I'll have Thóra," Kveldúlfr said. "And I have no problem killing you, but there is something *else* you can give me instead."

"It's bold of you to assume I'd choose bedding you over death." I remarked, rolling my eyes. "From your reputation, it might be better if I choose the latter. Whether I'm your concubine or not, my blood would spill sooner or later, *nei*?"

"Dear woman, if you know so much of my reputation, you'd realise I don't care what your opinion is. If I want you, I'll take you." Kveldúlfr said, gripping the back of my neck. "I'm not negotiating with you. Our back-and-forth is tantamount to foreplay, nothing more."

With lightning speed, Kveldúlfr grabbed my hip and pulled me against him. Chairs screeched, kicked out from beneath those sitting upon them. My men drew their weapons. Kveldúlfr's lunged at them—

"*Nei*!" Kveldúlfr barked and immediately his warriors stopped.

"You've trained your dogs well." I smiled.

"*Þakka fyrir*," Kveldúlfr smirked. "I recommend you make yours back down, too. I don't wish to draw blood yet, but if they so much as touch one of my men, I'll have them slaughtered."

ASHES REMAIN

Reluctantly I raised my hand to halt my friends.

"A wise decision, Jarl. I'd like to finish our conversation before my men kill yours."

"They've survived worse odds." I growled.

"Then it will be an exciting battle." Kveldúlfr sneered.

Kveldúlfr's grip on my waist tightened. I gripped the knife hanging from my belt. Kveldúlfr's gaze dropped to my hand for a moment, but he didn't seem threatened at all by the small blade.

"I came here for my wife and *your* blood. I *will* take Thóra back to Túnsberg with me that much is certain. Give her to me or I'll burn Aros to the ground. Make your choice, Jarl. I'll have you – and your blood – regardless of your decision."

As he spoke, Kveldúlfr placed his other hand on my shoulder, slipping his fingers beneath the neck of my gown and drawing them over my skin.

"Thóra left you because you're a murderous *bacraut*." I watched the glimmer of lust in his eyes turn to anger. "Why are you willing to kill for a woman who wants nothing to do with you?"

Kveldúlfr's glare twisted into a vicious smile.

"She's my wife. Would you accept anything less than blood for your spouse?"

"Absolutely not. Of course, I'm honourable enough that I wouldn't lay a hand on my spouse. I suppose that's the difference between us, isn't it? *Honour*." I paused, watching my insult sting him. "If I return her to you, you'll hurt her again."

"How else will I punish her for running away?"

"You're inciting a war just to punish a runaway wife." I sneered. "By the gods, it must've embarrassed you, being outsmarted by a woman! She tricked you and left you and now you're so angry, you're willing to kill to get her back."

Although Kveldúlfr managed to keep that smirk on his face, I could tell I'd hit a nerve. His left brow twitched and his smile had dropped slightly. Rather than a wide toothy grin, it looked as though he was grinding his teeth.

"Jarl Kveldúlfr, I will *not* return the woman."

"Don't be stupid, Jarl. You're willing to lay down the life of every man, woman and child in this town just to protect her?"

"This all would be much easier if I just killed you, wouldn't it?"

Kveldúlfr laughed, releasing me at last.

"I'd like to see you try." He scoffed. "Woman or not, I won't shy from a battle. If it's a fight you want, Jarl Aveline, it's a fight I'll give you."

"How *decent* of you." I rolled my eyes.

At last, his smile vanished.

"When I defeat you I'll take your jarldom and before I kill you I'll take your body."

"I won't lose, Kveldúlfr." I spat.

"I admire your passion, Jarl. I do hope you're as fiery in bed as you are out of it. It's such a shame I'll have to kill you, your death will sadden me greatly."

"At least in death, I'll not have to listen to you prattle on anymore, you woman-beating coward!"

Kveldúlfr cocked his fist back, but I was faster. With all my might, I brought my knee up and slammed it between his legs. Red-faced and gasping, the Norwegian Jarl collapsed to the floor, his hands clutching between his bollocks.

For a split moment I realised the hall door was open and there stood Jan, sword and shield in hand, armed warriors behind him. How long he'd been standing there I didn't know, but I was glad to see him.

"Melisende – Rowena!" I roared, swiping up *Úlfsblóð*.

Immediately, furniture clattered and blades clanged as warriors attacked each other. My thralls dashed to the kitchen and out the door, two Norwegians on their heels. Without a second thought, I darted after them. Ebbe, Einarr, Lars and Domnall faced terrifying odds with Kveldúlfr's men, but with Jan and the reinforcements, I had faith they could take the Norwegians in my hall. I couldn't let my thralls get killed.

I crashed through the kitchen after Kveldúlfr's warriors, following them into the back garden. The warriors had my thralls cornered. Melisende and Rowena held each other weeping and praying, the warriors raised their axes–

Quick-footed and silent as a cat, I hefted my sword high, lunged at the warriors and slammed the blade into the back of one of them. First I heard the crunch of his bone before his agonised howl filled the air and he crumpled to the ground.

ASHES REMAIN

The other warrior spun around and swung his axe at me – I dodged out the way just in time, bringing *Úlfsblóð* up protectively in front of me. His weapon was mediocre compared to mine, but he vastly outsized me.

I swung at him ceaselessly, but he blocked each hit of my sword with the handle of his axe, unperturbed by the force that must've travelled from the axe-shaft and up his arm from the ferocity of my blows.

Dodging, lunging, swinging, cursing, I narrowly missed being struck by his axe multiple times, but at last I managed to knock the weapon from his hands and sink my sword into his gut. He fell down dead beside his companion, their blood mingling in a pool of red that sank into the earth.

"Run to the nearest settlement and send for help!" I ordered Rowena and Melisende. "If you find the children, take them to safety with you!"

"Yes Jarl, of course!" Rowena promised.

My heart broke for my white-faced, terrified thralls, sweat pouring from every inch of their shuddering bodies.

"Go, now! Run!"

Rowena and Melisende climbed over the fence and fled. I hoped they would find safety – as I hoped my children already had. The din of fighting rang out all around. The whole of Aros was submerged in combat. I climbed over the fence and sprinted to the streets where the battle raged.

Give me strength, Allfather!

CHAPTER TWENTY-SEVEN

THE CRUSH OF battle spilled from my hall to the marketplace and harbour. In the midst of the chaos, I didn't know whether we were defeating Kveldúlfr's men or if they were conquering us. I was far from the hall, forced by the swell of battle to the houses near the harbour.

Beneath the grey sky, warriors charged at one another, screams and roars filling the damp air. Weapons clanged and wooden shields shrieked beneath the thudding blows of metal blades. Warriors dripped with sweat and blood, battle lust surging through their veins and numbing their bodies to their wounds.

"Come old woman!" My foe jeered, spittle flying from his lips. "Let me end your suffering before Jarl Kveldúlfr gets you!"

I tightened my grip around the hilt of my sword, my arms quivering as I pressed my blade against his. I tried to root myself to the spot, but the hairy brute shoved a little harder and my feet slipped back a few inches. If we continued this way, he'd win …

"Who are you calling old, you fat *bacrauf*?" I hissed.

In one swift movement, I leapt to the side. He toppled to the ground like a felled tree – as quickly as I'd jumped out from in front of him, I plunged my sword into his back. The scrape of metal against bone rattled up the blade and through my arms, his cries muffled by the hammering of my heart in my ears.

A woman's scream stole my attention – two Norwegians were chasing her. She sprinted down the road, her dress ripped and breasts bared. The bastards must've tried to rape her. Even from this distance I heard their laughter as they pursued her.

I yanked *Úlfsblóð* from my foe and ran after them. They would die before they would rape her, I'd make sure of that.

Bodies were strewn about the streets, Danish men, women and children slaughtered by the Norwegians in cold blood. In the distance, women and children fled, some by foot, others rowing away in fishing boats. Here and there, clusters of warriors were caught in the clutch of battle. I noticed some of my people fighting with farming tools, some quickly killed, others victorious.

At some point I found a shield. I squeezed the leather strap, concealing my torso with the battered wood, my sword raised and ready. I'd lost the Norwegians, but I sprinted onwards, desperate to find them and rescue my townswoman.

Laughter streamed from a house close by. Catching my breath as quietly as I could, I crept around the back of the building and found the door ripped off its hinges and lying on the ground. I hugged the wall and peeked around the doorframe. There inside were the two Norwegians. At their feet was the townswoman – she was naked, still and bloody.

I was too late.

"Argh!"

Someone had grabbed a fistful of my hair from behind!

"There you are, my fierce little Jarl! I was hoping I'd find you!"

Kveldúlfr had crept behind me without making a sound! Where did he come from? I swear there was no one here when I arrived!

"Drop your sword and shield," Kveldúlfr ordered, his sword at my throat.

"You'll have to take them from me!" I snarled.

"Have it your way." Kveldúlfr chuckled.

With lightning speed, Kveldúlfr smashed my head against the wooden wall of the house. A flash of light blinded me and pain tore through my skull – I dropped my sword and shield.

"You talked so bravely in the hall – then I saw you flee the battle. I was so disappointed! I know now you weren't, and that pleases me." Kveldúlfr said as he dragged me inside by my hair.

I groaned and hissed, too dazed to make any intelligible reply. With trembling hands I reached for his wrist and dug my nails into his flesh. The bastard seemed to have skin as thick as hide, he didn't even wince. As he dragged me through the house, I caught glimpses of his men snickering at the sight of us.

"I would've preferred to fight you in front of your people, but this will have to do." Kveldúlfr said, dumping me on the ground. "Get yourself together, Jarl Aveline. It's time for the fight you promised me."

"Are you so afraid of me that you won't fight fair?" I taunted as I stumbled to my feet, my vision steadying. "I must be unarmed and dazed and surrounded by your dogs for you to fight me?"

Slowly I paced the room, attempting to keep as much furniture between the Norwegian and me. My eyes darted about the room. I needed to find a weapon – he would slaughter me if I remained unarmed. I had my utility knife hanging from my belt, but that tiny blade was no use against his damned sword.

"We agreed to a fight – there was no mention of whether it was going to be fair or not." He cackled, slowly pursuing me.

"Only a coward would fight like this. Are you a coward, Kveldúlfr? Do you really want to embarrass yourself in front of your men?" I continued, laying my hands flat on the table between us. "Drop your weapon and we'll fight like equals."

"I couldn't care less about their opinions." Kveldúlfr replied. "But I admit, this might be far more enjoyable using my hands."

Kveldúlfr winked at me as he tossed his shield to one of his men before sheathing his sword. The insinuation behind his words brought bile to my throat. His blue eyes were locked on me, that awful, snarling grin fixed on his wolfish face.

"Here, I'll do you one better–" Kveldúlfr glanced over his shoulder at his men, who had gathered together and blocked the doorway. "No one touch her! She's mine."

"Ever the noble one, aren't you, Kveldúlfr?" I mocked. "You're not as *argr* as I first thought."

"Don't throw insults like that around so freely," Kveldúlfr cautioned, darkness whirling in his eyes. "You better be prepared for the repercussions."

Without warning, I flipped the table, lunged at the nearest item – a basket of weaving tools – and hurled it at Kveldúlfr. He leapt back to avoid the table, but the basket struck him square in the chest, the contents clattering over the floor at his feet.

"Ooh, terrifying!" The Norwegian laughed, rubbing his chest where the basket hit him. "You can do better than that, surely?"

"I'd do better with a sword and shield in my hands."

"Use your initiative, Jarl Aveline." Kveldúlfr chuckled, shoving the chair out from between us. "You must've been at least *slightly* capable in battle to be made jarl."

"Fuck off!" I growled.

I grabbed anything and everything – plates, cups, bowls, jewellery boxes – whatever was within reach – and hurled them at the Norwegian. He continued to taunt me, kept dodging or ducking the things I threw. Some he even let hit him, laughing as the damn things bounced off him and fell to the floor. I tried to keep furniture as a barrier between us, pulling chairs and tables in front of me, but nothing deterred him.

I was running out of objects to block him or throw. I snatched up a stool, the last hard item in reach, and threw it – he dove out of the way, damn it! He kept urging me to do better – his encouragement a mockery that angered me beyond measure.

In the corner of my eye, I spotted the cooking fire. The fire was out, but an iron pot hung above it. It would be heavy enough to knock him out if I managed to strike him in the head with it. Then I'd have to deal with his men ... Maybe I'd have time to snatch up Kveldúlfr's sword?

"You tried, Jarl Aveline, but it looks like it all ends here." Kveldúlfr sighed dramatically. "All this death could've been avoided, but you made your decision to fight. I commend you for that – it's the honourable thing to do. Now it's time for you to–"

I dived at the cooking pot.

I snatched it off the hook –

Kveldúlfr lunged at me –

I swung the pot at Kveldúlfr!

"Argh!"

The pot crashed into Kveldúlfr's chest, sending him flying to the ground, winded and aching. I seized a large stone from the base of the cooking fire and flung it at him, grabbing another and throwing that, too.

"Jarl!" One of his men shouted, drawing his weapon and taking a step towards us.

"*Nei*! She's mine!" Kveldúlfr wheezed.

Clinging to his chest, Kveldúlfr threw himself across the room, taking cover behind the over-turned table. I snatched up the stones, hurling them wildly. They thudded against the table, a few ricocheting towards his men at the door. They dove outside, glancing around the doorframe, visibly longing to attack me.

I ran out of stones – all that was left was the metal tripod the cooking pot had been hanging on. I ripped it from the ground and held the legs outwards, bracing myself for battle.

Kveldúlfr came out from behind his shelter smirking. He must've realised I didn't have any more projectiles to hurl at him. The tripod wasn't much of a weapon – we both knew it. Kveldúlfr was done playing. He ran at me. As he neared, I swung the tripod like a sword. He caught the blow on his forearm, slamming his arm against the tripod and knocking it clear out of my hands. At the same moment, he kicked me in the stomach.

I crumpled to the floor gasping, lights swarming in my eyes, obscuring my vision. Kveldúlfr grabbed the front of my dress and hauled me to my feet. I flailed blindly, landing a few blows, but it wasn't enough. Kveldúlfr punched me again and again.

Cackling, Kveldúlfr dragged me to one of the fur-covered platforms lining the walls. He dropped me down platform with a thud. I tried to get up, but my head swam – I couldn't tell which way was up or down, stunned by his blows.

"You fought well, Jarl Aveline." Kveldúlfr mocked, kneeling over me, one of my legs trapped between his. "Accept your fate, now. You've lost – it's time for me to take my prize."

"I'll kill you!" I hissed.

"You keep saying that, yet here we are." Kveldúlfr laughed.

I writhed beneath him, struggling to get out of his grasp. I clawed at his face and kicked at him, but he overpowered me.

"I like it when you struggle." Kveldúlfr sneered.

He pinned my arms over my head, crossing my wrists and trapping them with one of his massive hands. I couldn't stop from crying out, my wrists crushed beneath his weight. I thrashed beneath him, but it was no use. Kveldúlfr reached down with his other hand and yanked my skirts up over my stomach.

"*Nei*! Stop!" I shrieked.

"I told you I'd have you before I killed you." Kveldúlfr chuckled.

"Help!" I screamed desperately. "Help me! Help!"

"Scream louder, Jarl! No one can hear you!" Kveldúlfr jeered, his wolfish grin spread across his face.

Exposed, fear constricting my heart, I screeched louder, hoping beyond hope that someone would hear me. I caught a glimpse of the naked, bloody body of the townswoman across the way. No one, but I had spotted her running from these fiends – no one had heard her scream – no one had rescued her. By the gods, I prayed I wouldn't share her fate.

Kveldúlfr kicked my thighs apart and managed to kneel between them despite me thrashing my legs. He pressed his lower body against me, grinding his erection against my nakedness, his hard cock straining against the fabric of his trousers.

"*No*! Stop!" I shrieked, panic crushing my heart. "Help me!"

"Help!" Kveldúlfr bellowed over me. "Someone come quickly! The Jarl's being raped!"

Ice filled my veins. I flailed and writhed beneath him. He wouldn't rape me, I wouldn't let him! I screamed until my throat was raw and voice was hoarse, and I continued to scream through the pain, struggling against the Norwegian with all the strength I could muster, tears pouring down my cheeks.

"Help me! By the gods, someone help!"

"Jarl – warriors are coming!" One of Kveldúlfr's men warned.

"Help!" I shrieked harder. "Help me!"

"They can hear her!"

"Why are you waiting? Kill them!" Kveldúlfr thundered.

His men ran out the door, their weapons raised.

"We're going to have to hurry this up, unfortunately." Kveldúlfr said, that damned smirk still on his face!

He released my wrists and unleashed a wave of blows on my face and stomach. My limbs fell limp. I wavered in and out of consciousness as Kveldúlfr beat the shit out of me. My face and body throbbed, I could feel bruises swelling all over my body. Darkness tried to swallow me, but my inner voice commanded me to get up, to get out of Kveldúlfr's grasp.

Kveldúlfr's knuckles brushed against me as he reached down to untie the cord of his trousers. I conjured up the last of my strength, pulled the utility knife from my belt and plunged it into his side.

"Fucking bitch!" Kveldúlfr roared.

Three times I stabbed Kveldúlfr before he lurched backwards, scrabbling for the knife sticking into his side. He yanked the blade out and tossed it across the room. Too weak to stand, I tried to drag myself across the floor to the doorway.

"Get back here!" Kveldúlfr boomed.

Kveldúlfr recovered faster than I expected – he grabbed my ankle and hauled me to him, seething with rage.

"The fun is over!" He snarled, flipping me onto my back.

Kveldúlfr knelt over me and closed his hands around my throat. I clawed at him, desperate for air, but Kveldúlfr held tight, squeezing my neck, crushing my windpipe between his hands. With each second that passed, my strength seeped out of me. Blood pounded in my ears, my hands dropped to my chest.

Kveldúlfr smirked down on me as my vision faded.

"Get off her!"

By Týr's justice, Jan charged into the room just in time! He lunged at Kveldúlfr and tackled him off me. I rolled aside, huddling against the wall, gasping for breath, grasping to consciousness.

Jan and Kveldúlfr were equal in size and strength. Like two brutish giants, they brawled, crashing around the wrecked longhouse, demolishing everything in their path. The sound of them fighting was thunder in my ears. I cowered against the wall, watching them fight through my steadily swelling eyes, two bears tearing each other to shreds.

At some point they tumbled outside. My mind was spinning, but I couldn't stay there. I scrambled around the wreckage and found my knife before I staggered to the doorway.

Praise the gods, my sword and shield were still there! I leaned against the door frame and eased myself down to pick them up. My body shuddered and knees threatened to buckle, but I managed to grab my things and stand up. I glanced around, but Jan and Kveldúlfr were lost in the fray.

***

I STAGGERED THROUGH the corpses, searching for Kveldúlfr's body. As I approached each body, I prayed I'd find Kveldúlfr's corpse not Jan's. The battle dissipated soon after Jan and Kveldúlfr disappeared – Kveldúlfr's men rushed to their ships and sailed away under a blanket of my archers' arrows. Perhaps Kveldúlfr managed to get away from Jan and fled with his fleet?

ASHES REMAIN

After a while of inspecting the broken bodies of the dead, I found myself on the shore. My eyes were swollen almost completely shut, I could only see through narrow slits. Kveldúlfr's ships were dark blotches in the distance. I didn't tear my sight from the horizon even after they vanished completely.

"I lost him."

I hadn't heard Jan approach. I kept my back to him, peering at the waters even though nothing was there.

"I stabbed him in the gut, but he wouldn't stop." I croaked, my horse voice barely louder than a whisper.

"If he's not dead already he'll be dead by morning." Jan meant to give me comfort. "He was bleeding badly. If he didn't die here, he'll die on his ship. We'll find his corpse on our streets or we'll hear of his death in the coming weeks."

I shook my head, my bloody hands balled into fists at my sides. I'd searched the streets and houses thoroughly but hadn't found his corpse. Alive or dead, he was on a ship, I knew it. I wouldn't be able to rest until I had confirmation of his death.

"Where are my children?" My raw throat ached with every word.

"Safe. Borghildr and Guðrin readied their horses the moment Kveldúlfr's ships were on the horizon. They took Borghildr's children, Sander, Æsa and Einar to a nearby settlement."

"What of Thóra and Thórvar? Are they safe?"

All of this – this battle, the deaths and bloodshed – occurred to protect them. All these lives were sacrificed to save them from Kveldúlfr. If the Norwegian had them, my warriors and townspeople suffered and died for nothing.

"They went with Borghildr and Guðrin."

"Thank the gods!" I exhaled, the invisible fist that had clenched my heart since I sent my children from the hall finally released – I could breathe again.

"I sent Domnall and Ebbe to fetch them now the Norwegians are gone." Jan said softly, his boots crunching in the grass as he took a step toward me.

"We need to send out search parties to gather those who fled. All the injured need to be taken to my hall – Brynja and her daughters will have enough room to tend to the wounded there."

"*Já*, Jarl."

My mind raced with things we needed to do. The hall needed to be readied for all the wounded. Beds and tables needed to be prepared, we needed to start boiling buckets of water – we needed bandages and clean rags. Brynja the healer and her three daughters were going to be inundated with injured – I'd need every able-bodied woman available to assist them.

Then there were all the women and children who had dispersed in all directions during the chaos. I needed to send the men with the fewest wounds to find them and bring them home. We needed to gather our dead, and we needed to gather Kveldúlfr's too. We'd had to start a pyre and the goði needed to officiate the mass funeral. We had so much to do.

Among all my thoughts, a pang of pride resonated in my chest. Caught as unaware as we were, Aros had risen from the battle victorious. We won. We fought and we won!

Jan's hand closed over my shoulder. My eyelids fell shut, my skin tingled, and all thoughts vanished from my mind in that moment. I let him turn me, heard his sharp intake of breath. After the beating Kveldúlfr gave me, I was sure I looked as terrible as I felt. Jan cupped my face between both his hands and tenderly stroked my cheeks with his thumbs.

"Look at you, Aveline," Jan's voice trembled. "By the gods, look what he did to you!"

"I'm still here." I mumbled, looking down at my feet, my cheeks burning with embarrassment, I must've looked hideous.

Jan pulled me against him. I rested my head on his chest and took a deep breath, inhaling the musk of his sweat and the metallic tanginess of the blood soaked into his clothes.

Despite the chaos, despite everything that happened and that we still had to do, in that moment I cared for nothing. Tears slid down my cheeks. My body was broken, my town in chaos, but my heart swelled. This was the first embrace we had shared in so long. I missed Jan terribly. By the gods, I didn't want our embrace to end.

"I'm sorry." I whispered, squeezing the bloody fabric of his tunic in my fists.

"You're sorry?" Jan exclaimed. "Look at you! *I'm* sorry, Aveline. I was too late to stop him from hurting you!"

"You were just in time." I smiled.

ASHES REMAIN

Jan touched my jaw, urging me to look up at him. I tilted my face upwards, peering at him through my swollen eyes. Sadness tugged his features, his eyes filling with tears. He brought his mouth to mine, a kiss, deep and filled with yearning.

My swollen lips parted readily, my body ignited by his kiss. A soft moan rolled in Jan's throat as my tongue found his. Pangs of need resounded through my body, leaving me breathless.

"I missed you, Aveline." Jan murmured between kisses. "By the gods, I missed you."

"I missed you, too." I breathed.

I gasped against Jan's lips as our hands raced over each other, touching, grabbing, squeezing. Spasms of pain shot through me – wherever Jan touched me there seemed to be a bruise or wound. I didn't want him to stop – I needed him too much.

Jan rested his brow against mine, panting like me. In my mind, I prayed to every god I could think of, thanking them for returning Jan to me.

"I can't go another day without you." Jan said softly. "When I saw Kveldúlfr strangling you – when I watched your hands fall–"

Jan took a shuddering breath. My heart lurched as a tear drop fell from his eyes onto my cheek and slipped down my face as though I had shed it. I looked up at Jan, meeting his sapphire gaze.

"I can't lose you, Aveline." Jan said. "What you did cut through me worse than any blade could ... I thought I hated you, but I couldn't stop missing you. Being without you and the children – I've never felt so empty. When I saw Kveldúlfr and you – I thought he killed you!"

Jan's voice faltered again. He pulled me against him, crushing me in his desperate embrace. I felt his tears drip onto my hair and clung to him tighter, my own tears falling.

"When your hands fell, I thought you were gone. At that moment all I wanted was to kill Kveldúlfr, after that I didn't care if I lived ... In fact, I think I preferred to die ..." A soft humourless laugh fell from Jan's lips. "Then I heard you gasp for breath, I saw you move – you were alive!

"Things can't go back to how they used to be, but I *need* to be with you. Whether you take me as your lover or friend, I don't care, I just need to be with you. I want to be your righthand man again."

"Oh Jan!" I wept, grinning up at him through my tears. "You'll always be my righthand man."

"I – I still don't know if I'll ever forgive you, but I can't be without you. I *need* you, Aveline."

"I regret it all, Jan. I wish I'd done things differently, I wish–" I swallowed hard, emotion knotted in my throat. "I wish for so many things ... I can't change what I've done, Jan. I want you beside me – I want your friendship. I want your love – but you deserve so much more than me."

"I don't care what I *deserve*, Aveline, *I need you*! No one else, just *you*." Jan exclaimed fiercely.

"I'm yours, Jan." I whispered. "For as long as you'll have me."

Jan's lips crashed against mine.

"I've always loved you." Jan murmured. "I never stopped, and I never will."

ASHES REMAIN
CHAPTER TWENTY-EIGHT

Early Summer, 892

HERRA TRAVELLED TO Túnsberg a week after the battle to gather word on Kveldúlfr. My warriors were still recovering from the assault. I couldn't send one of my ships nor attack Túnsberg so soon. Herra gladly volunteered much to my surprise and relief.

Unfortunately, Herra's ship was spotted before he'd got close to the harbour. He had no choice but to leave, avoiding the wave of arrows that hailed down on his ship from Norwegian archers. They must've seen his vessel in the harbour the day they attacked.

Not all was lost, however. Rumours from travelling merchants over the passing weeks said Kveldúlfr was gravely injured after the battle. Túnsberg had hosted many funerals for warriors who succumbed to their battle wounds. One of the funerals was said to be far grander than the others, worthy *only* for a jarl.

Most of my warriors considered the grand funeral confirmation of Kveldúlfr's death, but I refused to be optimistic. It could have been a trick, Kveldúlfr might want us to think him dead then attack us when our guard was down. I wouldn't rest until I received undisputable proof that he was dead.

Weeks turned into months and there was no retaliation. The seasons changed, winter came and went and soon enough a year went by with no sight of Túnsberg. My townspeople seemed to move on – two years was a long time, especially with all the indicators pointing to Kveldúlfr's death. Life went back to normal, even Thóra seemed more relaxed than ever.

Was I too suspicious? I was loath to be naïve and repeat my mistakes, but if Thóra could relax, maybe I could too? Still ashamed of my actions and the bloodshed it led to, I was too cowardly to face Thóra and Thórvar. I avoided them at all cost, but Jan filled me in about them when I inquired to their welfare.

I would see Thóra tomorrow, though, for that was the day Sander would marry Fenja Matsdóttir and be named Jarl of Aros.

Sander had seen sixteen winters and was now old enough to marry and take on the jarldom. I would stand proudly by his side as everyone in Aros bid their fealty to him and his new wife.

Would Thóra and Thórvar bid their fealty to Sander? Or did Thóra's grudge run deep enough that she would refuse? I doubted two years had changed her feelings towards us … We would find out soon enough. At that moment it didn't matter. I strode down the beach with Sander, Æsa and Einar, examining the ships in the harbour. Young Birger was coming to visit.

"There he is!" Sander exclaimed, pointing at a crowd of people disembarking from the ship.

"Where? Can you see him, *móðir*?" Einar asked, craning his neck to see over the heads in front of us.

"*Já* – there he is! There's Signý and Ísarr!"

"Look how big Ísarr is!" Æsa cooed.

"And Signý is with child again!" I cried out happily, noticing her large protruding stomach.

"Or perhaps Young Birger is just keeping her fat and happy?"

"Shut up, Sander!" Æsa scolded, much to his amusement.

"She looks fit to burst!" Einar gasped, spotting his sister-in-law.

"Einar!" Æsa exclaimed, glaring at her youngest brother.

"Maybe the little one will be born here?" I mused dreamily. "Wouldn't that be wonderful?"

We rushed to the harbour, meeting Young Birger, Signý and Ísarr, on the shore. Hallmundr was among their retinue, striding along behind them. In a weepy, elated reunion, I hugged them all in turn and scooped up my three-year-old grandson. Ísarr laughed and squealed as I sprinkled his face with kisses. I hadn't seen him since autumn! He had grown so much!

"The healer thinks the baby will be due within the next month." Signý explained, rubbing her stomach.

"I can't believe you came here when you're so far along, but I am so happy you did." I smiled warmly.

"I couldn't miss this." Signý beamed.

"Poor Fenja will need all the support she can get when she's given to *him*," Young Birger said, eyes glinting mischievously.

"It's funny you say that – I thought Signý would've come to her senses and divorced you by now." Sander shot back with a grin.

ASHES REMAIN

"Welcome home, Jarl Birger."

I jumped, not realising Jan had arrived. We hadn't seen him since morning meal, he'd been busy on his farm all day. When the horns blazed in the harbour announcing Young Birger's arrival, I sent Rowena to fetch Jan. I hadn't waited for him, too eager to greet my eldest son and his beautiful young family.

"Jan," Young Birger nodded at Jan, his smile replaced with a stoic gaze. "You're taking care of my *móðir?*"

"I'd like to think so, but you'll have to ask her."

"He'll do I suppose." I replied wickedly, winking at Jan.

Young Birger and Jan stared at each other in silence for a few moments, measuring each other up. I was confused – so, it seemed, were my children and companions. Before we could question their frosty reception, Young Birger and Jan lunged at each other, laughing as they crushed one another in their embrace.

"I've missed you." Young Birger grinned.

"And I, you!" Jan chuckled. "By Thor's thunderclap, when I lay my eyes on you it's like I'm looking at Vidar's ghost!"

"And you're the same as I last saw you – if a little more scarred and a lot greyer in the beard." Young Birger smirked.

***

THE DAY PASSED in a blur of merriment. Sander's betrothed, Fenja Matsdóttir, and her family arrived a few hours after Young Birger. Jarl Mats Olafsson of Alabu strutted about my hall, a tankard of mead constantly in hand, heartbroken that his daughter was leaving his home and joining mine.

Jarl Mats interrogated Sander ruthlessly on every subject he could think of, but Sander always came out on top. By the end of the day, both were jolly with drink and laughing together. Despite Jarl Mats' sadness to lose his daughter to marriage, he was glad Sander was the one to wed her.

When they weren't attending to their guests or talking with Jarl Mats, Fenja and Sander spent as much time together as they could. Fenja's mother and brother kept a watchful eye on them, determined the young couple would remain virtuous before their wedding night.

Sander was besotted by his beautiful golden-haired bride-to-be, and she was equally enamoured by him. At three years Sander's senior, Fenja had been proposed to many times and rejected every suitor presented to her, holding out for the day Sander would be old enough to wed.

They waited six years for this day, determined to wed one another – quite a feat for two as young as them. They'd visited each another at least twice a year since they were engaged and sent gifts frequently – especially Fenja. She had gifted Sander a wealth of precious articles over the years. Their day had finally come and nothing would stop them – Fenja would make sure of that.

"So when are *you* going to marry?" Young Birger asked Æsa as he sipped his mead. "You've seen fifteen winters now, you're more than old enough to take a husband."

Æsa scowled at her eldest brother, prickling at his question.

"When I'm ready." She replied stoutly. "Fenja has seen *nineteen* winters and she's only *just* getting married now."

"That's different, she was betrothed for six of those winters."

"If I find a man worth marrying then I'll wait six winters too."

"You're just like your *móðir*," Jan chuckled. "She was a few years older than you are now when she was betrothed to your *faðir*. She rejected every suitor offered to her – she didn't want to get married either."

"What's good for the goose is good for the gander." Æsa said smugly. "If *móðir* could wait to marry then so can I."

"You don't want to be an old maid, do you?" Young Birger cocked his brow at his sister.

"Are you insinuating I was an old maid when I finally got betrothed?" I glared at my eldest child.

"Of course not!" Young Birger's cheeks bloomed red.

Night fell hours ago and many of our guests were asleep on the platforms of the hall, warmed through by the low fire and the balmy night air. Jan, Young Birger, Æsa, Sander, Einar, Fenja and I were the only ones still awake.

Finally alone together, Fenja's family fast asleep, Sander and Fenja disappeared for a walk outside. I didn't mind what they got into together, their wedding was going to happen in just a few hours after all.

ASHES REMAIN

Jan and Young Birger were sitting on the platform where Vidar and my chairs were situated. Einar, Æsa and I were sitting on a table in front of them, picking at a bowl of dried fruit while we spoke together.

Æsa was now teasing her eldest brother, much to our amusement. Every now and again, Einar wickedly injected with a comment or two to fuel his siblings' bickering. I laughed until my gaze settled on the high-backed, ornately carved chairs.

By this time tomorrow, those chairs would belong to Sander and Fenja. I wouldn't be Jarl of Aros anymore, Sander would. Part of me was relieved, the burden of ruling finally lifted from my shoulders. The other part of me was afraid.

I'd been Jarl for eight long years – what would life be like now? What did fate have in store for me? I hadn't been anything, but jarlkona or jarl for the last twenty years, would I return to being a farm girl as I was when I was a girl? The fire of battle blazed in my blood, could I really go back to raising sheep when the taste of killing coursed through my veins?

Æsa yawned loudly.

"As enjoyable as it is to knock Young Birger down a peg, I'm off to bed." She announced.

"I need to find somewhere to sleep, I'm sure Ísarr and Signý have taken up the whole bed." Young Birger said, standing up and stretching.

Young Birger did not speak unkindly, there was a warmth in his words, a hint of pride when he spoke of his wife and son. When he looked upon his wife and son or even said their names, a smile touched his lips and his eyes sparkled. He was happy, truly *happy*.

In the past, Young Birger possessed a sober disposition, quiet and reserved, but always politely cordial. When he cracked dry joke or a witty comment it caught people off-guard. Signý and Ísarr had softened Young Birger, had drawn him out of his usual reticent persona. He was still calm and quiet, but he smiled more, he joked more. Family life suited him well.

I reached out and took Young Birger's hand, my heart welling with love for him, for the wonderful father and husband he had become. Vidar would be so proud of his eldest son – he'd be proud of all our children.

"Come on, Einar, you're going to bed, too." Young Birger said.

"I'm not tired." Einar retorted, though his bloodshot eyes betrayed him.

"You're *going* to bed. Let *móðir* and Jan be alone." Æsa barked.

Einar balked under Æsa's steely glare and nodded reluctantly.

"*Sof þú vel*, my loves." I said, kissing them each on their cheeks before they headed to the sleeping area.

"We've outlasted the lot of them." Jan chuckled.

"We always do." I smiled, watching Jan stretch.

"What do you want to do now?" Jan asked.

"As sweet as Æsa's attempt to give us alone time is, I'm exhausted. I think I'd like to go to bed."

"May I join you?" Jan asked, slipping his arms around my waist.

My eye fluttered closed and I leaned my head against Jan's chest, my hands resting on his strong forearms. He kissed my neck and shoulder, sending shivers rippling through me.

"I'd prefer it if you did." I purred.

Over the two years since Kveldúlfr attacked Aros, Jan and I renewed our relationship. We took each day slowly, careful not to rush, learning to forgive and love each other again. Over the past few months, however, Jan slept every night in my hall, he even had a chest full of belongings beside our – *my* – bed.

When we went to bed together, we'd fall asleep more often than we'd copulate. It was difficult to deny ourselves each other, but we needed to – we couldn't enjoy each other as frequently as we had before. I'd vowed never to drink the tansy brew again.

On the occasion we did give in to the throes of passion, Jan did everything he could to avoid spilling his seed inside me. I was ashamed when he pulled out of me and spilled his seed on my stomach or back – a constant reminder that I'd broken his trust. I understood, though. I deserved his distrust.

"I love you." Jan murmured.

"I love you, too." I smiled.

***

I WOKE ON the morning of Sander and Fenja's wedding curled up in Jan's embrace. My small body cocooned in his large form, heat radiating from his naked torso through the thin fabric of my nightclothes. I stirred in his arms, overwhelmed by desire – the wedding hadn't even begun, but the romance of the occasion already gripped me.

Jan's erection twitched against my buttocks as I shifted against him. He moved the arm I'd been sleeping on, crossing it over my torso so he could cup my breast. His other hand travelled over my thigh and dragged my skirt over my hips, exposing my buttocks to him beneath the blanket.

A soft gasp fell from my lips as Jan leaned over me and nuzzled my neck, his kisses gradually travelling higher. He drew his tongue over the curve of my ear, making me squirm against him, goosebumps prickling my skin. Giggling quietly, I pressed my buttocks against the hard length of his cock, knowing how it strained for freedom against the fabric of his night-trousers.

Jan's knuckles brushed against me as he fiddled with the ties of his breeches. Within moments his cock was free, warm and solid against my skin. He pressed it between my legs slowly.

"Ah ha!" Jan said victoriously as he entered me.

I hid my face in my pillow to smother my giggles at his triumphant exclamation, but I didn't laugh for long – Jan thrust his cock deeper into me. I rolled my lips together, trying to stay silent as he pushed deeper, deeper. I didn't want to wake everyone sleeping in the room around us.

At last, the whole length of Jan's cock was inside me, filling me. He rocked his hips back and forth, fucking me slowly, gently, deliciously, his fingers alternating between teasing my nipples and squeezing my breasts.

"*Amma*! You're awake!" Ísarr exclaimed, running to our bed.

Jan and I froze.

"*Afi*'s awake too! Hurry, *fǫðurbróðir* is getting married!"

"Ísarr!" Signý called from the main room. "What are you doing?"

"*Amma* and *Afi* are awake!" Ísarr called back. "Come! Now!"

"We're getting up now, my heart." I promised, laughing at the seriousness of his expression. "Go now, let us get up."

"*She's* sleeping!" Ísarr exclaimed, pointing accusingly at Æsa.

"Leave her be, I'll wake her once I'm dressed."

"*Föðursystir*! Wake up!" Ísarr ordered.

"Ísarr, come here!" Signý chided as she waddled into the sleeping area and scooped up her son. "Leave everyone be!"

"But *mumie* – they're sleeping!"

"Sorry, Aveline, Jan." Signý offered us an apologetic frown before entering the main room.

"We'll have to finish this later." I chortled, slipping away from Jan and swinging my legs over the side of the bed.

"Did you hear that?"

"What?" I asked, noticing the surprise in Jan's question.

"Ísarr called me *Afi*."

***

FENJA WAS A stunning bride, laden in gold from the wedding crown upon her sleek golden tresses to the embroidery hemming her sumptuous violet dress. Sander's clothes complemented hers exquisitely, dressed in a deep marigold coloured tunic, gold and silver armbands jangling on his wrists, rings gleaming on his fingers. Around his neck, Sander wore one of Vidar's amulets – just as Young Birger had when he married Signý.

Their ceremony went smoothly. Held outside on such a beautifully warm day, it was the perfect wedding. After the traditions were observed and the bridal ale was poured and drank, I raised my horn and announced that I bequeathed my jarldom to Sander, that he and Fenja were now the Jarl and Jarlkona of Aros. Thankfully, Sander was not challenged, the townspeople cheered and applauded the happy couple.

The rest of the day was spent playing games, drinking and celebrating the young couple. Townsfolk approached their new Jarl and Jarlkona, wished their union well and bade their fealty to them. By midnight, almost every townsperson old enough to make the vow had done so – except Galinn, Ósk, Thóra and Thórvar.

"Did Thóra tell you she'd be here?" I asked Jan stiffly.

"Last we spoke she said she would." Jan shrugged. "That was a few days ago. I doubt she'd change her mind – where else does she have to live but here?"

Heiðabýr. I thought, but I didn't say it aloud. Though Jan and I had rekindled our relationship and I had done everything in my power to apologise to Thóra – slaughtering her ex-husband and his army for one – she still loathed me with every fibre of her being. She was a thorn in my side that I just couldn't remove.

I had spoken once to Jan about Thóra's living arrangements, asking him why she didn't try to move to her family's home in Heiðabýr now the threat of her ex-husband was gone. Apparently she told Jan she didn't want to take Thórvar away from him. He had seen fourteen winters now – he was a man, old enough for battle though not old enough to wed – and could choose whether he wanted to live with his mother or father. She knew he'd choose her and she said she couldn't bear doing that to Jan.

I'd rolled my eyes then and I rolled my eyes now as I thought of it. Ever the honourable one that Thóra. I was wrong for what I'd done in the past and I tried to make it up to her, but I quickly realised that wouldn't happen. I could give her the world and she'd still hate me. Thóra wanted Jan, but he chose me. That was *his* decision, not mine. I'd tried giving him to her before, but still he chose me. There was nothing more I could do for her.

"They'll have to wait until tomorrow." Sander said impatiently, overhearing us. "I don't expect Galinn or his mother to give me their fealty anyway. They're probably packing to leave right now."

"Sibba bade her loyalty to you, perhaps her husband is just late?" Jan suggested.

"She was smart to bid her fealty to us. She'd be smarter if she'd divorce that bastard husband of hers."

Sander spoke so coarsely about Galinn, I wondered whether that was due to the drink that pinkened his cheeks. No, Sander was always outspoken – some might even say brash. Sander hated Galinn – he almost killed him a few years back. It took Galinn months to recover, which was a miracle in itself. He wasn't the same since the day Sander beat him, but he was alive.

Though I didn't voice my opinion, I didn't doubt Sander's statement. If they didn't bid their fealty to their new jarl, they'd be forced to leave – or worse. Sander had proven himself once when he was such a young man, now he was bigger, stronger, smarter, I had no doubt he would prove himself again.

"Excited for the consummation, are you?" Jan teased, nudging Sander with his elbow.

Sander grinned at Jan and winked. Soon Sander and Fenja would be led to the sleeping area by firelight to consummate their marriage – the last tradition of the day.

"Perhaps they won't have to wait." I said, nodding at the door.

Thóra and Thórvar crept into the hall and slipped through the throng of merrymakers. Neither of them looked happy, both their lips curled with obvious displeasure.

"Get Fenja," I said to Jan, watching Thóra and Thórvar.

Thóra was giggling with Æsa, Signý and Borgunna at a table nearby. Jan swiftly did as I asked. As the mother and son neared us, I wanted Sander and Fenja ready to receive their fealty.

"Sander," I said, but he'd already stood up.

Sander was watching them, too, his drunken smile replaced with a steely glare. He strode towards the platform, dragging his fingers over Fenja's shoulders as he passed her on his way to Vidar's high-backed chair.

Sander sat on the chair stern-faced and still, his icy eyes following Thóra and Thórvar. His sheathed sword balanced across his lap upon the arms of the grand chair, he rested his hands on his blade. He was the epitome of Vidar.

Fenja sat beside her husband, taking her place in my chair. Regal and magnificent, she sat straight, her chin raised slightly, her lips pursed. By Freyja, they were striking! Despite their youth there was no doubt they were fated to be Jarl and Jarlkona.

"Thóra Arnsteinsdóttir, Thórvar Jansson, welcome." Sander said, his voice booming over the banter and music.

The hall fell silent, all faces turned to my son and his beautiful new wife. Nearby I heard some townspeople whispering to each other – my heart burst with pride at their words.

"They look like Vidar and Aveline!" The old man marvelled.

"Like the day they seized Aros from Erhardt!" The old woman agreed.

The couple stopped speaking the moment Sander began.

"I was saddened you didn't join the festivities." Sander said to Thóra and Thórvar calmly, this severe persona so foreign on him. "I assume you're here to bid us your fealty?"

"*Já*, Jarl Sander." Thóra nodded, visibly intimidated by my son.

ASHES REMAIN

Thórvar said nothing. He looked as though he was trying not to scowl at Sander – and failing miserably.

"Excellent." Sander offered them a small smile. "Approach us."

The pair stopped in front of the platform. Sander loomed over them. Sander towered over Thóra normally, he was tall and broad like Vidar. Thórvar was much taller than Sander, however. Thanks to the added height from the platform, Sander managed to stand a few inches taller than Thórvar for once – something Sander appeared to revel in by the way he eyed Thórvar up and down.

Young Birger appeared beside them, holding a small wooden box. It was dark brown, polished, and ornately carved with images of Týr, the god of law and justice, and Vár, a handmaiden of Frigg, and goddess of oaths, agreements and marriage contracts.

Young Birger gave the box to Sander who removed the lid and passed it back to his brother. Inside the box, upon a bed of silk, was a gilded oath-ring set with precious stones that glittered in the firelight. Sander held the box out to them. Thóra reached out a timid hand and took the armband.

"I, Thóra Arnsteinsdóttir, bid you, Jarl Sander Vidarsson, and your wife, Jarlkona Fenja Matsdóttir, my fealty. I bid you both my loyalty and swear that I will be faithful to you, my Jarl and Jarlkona, for as long as you rule with justice and honour. If I should break this oath, I accept the punishment of death – the only punishment suited for one dishonourable enough to break an oath." Thóra said before placing the oath-ring back in the box.

"*Þakka fyrir.*" Sander said, nodding at Thóra.

He offered the oath-ring to Thórvar.

My heart hammered in my chest. Thórvar stared at the oath-ring, one fist curled around the hilt of the weapon at his hip. He could challenge Sander if he dared, but my son would strike him down.

A sigh of relief fell from my lips as Thórvar reluctantly grabbed the oath-ring. Though I knew in my heart that Sander could slay Thórvar if he wanted to, I'm glad that moment did not come to pass today. Thórvar made the right decision.

"I, Thórvar Jansson, bid you, Jarl Sander Vidarsson, and your wife, Jarlkona Fenja Matsdóttir, my fealty." Thórvar grumbled just audibly enough for me to hear. "I bid you both my loyalty and swear that I will be faithful to you, my Jarl and Jarlkona, for as long as you rule with justice and honour.

"I vow my sword to you, that I will fight before you, that I will wrest glory from the foemen we face. I vow to never forget the goods and wealth I receive from you. I vow I will never flee one footstep from the battlefield, that I will avenge you if you are slain and I will continue to fight until I am slain. If I should break this oath, I accept the punishment of death – the only punishment suited for one dishonourable enough to break an oath."

Thórvar practically threw the oath-ring inside the box. Sander picked it up and held it in the air, his eyes locked on Thórvar's.

"I, Jarl Sander Vidarsson, vow to rule with honour and justice. I vow to bring glory to all of those who have bade their fealty to me. I vow to fight beside you in battle, to cut down our foemen beside you, that we will wrest glory from our enemies *together*. I vow to share all goods and wealth we earn in battle, and vow never to flee one footstep from the battlefield. I vow that under me, should you fall in battle, you will be avenged, and you will be honoured."

Sander placed the oath-ring inside the box then handed the box to Young Birger. All were silent and staring at my second-born son. Jarls didn't usually make oaths when receiving the fealty of their people. They'd make speeches, yes, but they wouldn't take the oath-ring and make vows like Sander just had.

Even Thórvar was surprised, his scowl dropped and his brows knitted in confusion. Sander had made the same vow to his people as they made to him – a smart decision and noble act.

Sander knew exactly what he was doing.

ASHES REMAIN
CHAPTER TWENTY-NINE

I AMBLED AROUND Aros with no destination in mind, lost in my thoughts. After a while I found myself in the marketplace, absentmindedly browsing the wares for sale. Young Birger, Signý and my darling Ísarr returned to Roskilde a few days ago, and Fenja's family returned to their home in Alabu a week after the wedding. The hall was now quiet and empty.

It had only been a month since I stepped down from being Jarl of Aros, but already I'd lost my sense of purpose. I stood by Sander and Fenja while they dove into their new duties as Jarl and Jarlkona, guiding them when they needed me to, but they quickly proved to be more than capable on their own.

Sander had been preparing for this his whole life under Vidar's careful tutelage and my own, and it was apparent that Fenja had been preparing too, assumedly since her betrothal to Sander was confirmed. I was proud to admit they didn't need me, but I was sad to admit that, too.

Of course, I didn't *want* to be with Sander and Fenja at all times. They excelled in their duties and they needed to be seen as the competent jarl and jarlkona that they were – not fledgelings under my wing. They also needed to enjoy their time as newlyweds.

As for Æsa and Einar?

At twelve years old, Einar was eager to prove himself as the man the laws determined him to be. When he didn't accompany Jan at the shipyard or when he wasn't hunting and trapping, Einar was immersed in weapons training and sparring with other boys in Aros. I wouldn't infantilise or emasculate him by making him spend all his free time with his mother, but I missed him terribly. These days Einar spent more time with Jan than he did with me.

Thankfully, I had Æsa. Æsa spent a lot of her time at home with me, weaving, spinning and carding wool as all women were expected to do regardless of societal ranking. Borgunna, my friend

Borghildr's daughter, was usually with us. Both young women were practically attached at the hip since they were babes.

Unfortunately that would change once Borgunna was married. Unlike Æsa, Borgunna was betrothed. The girls giggled and gossiped about her upcoming wedded life constantly. As the wedding day crept closer I realised how much I was failing Æsa by indulging her refusal to marry.

Æsa had seen fifteen winters and began her menses four years ago, at this point she should've been married or at the very least betrothed. She was more than adept at running a household – she had run the hall numerous times while her brothers and I were visiting settlements or raiding, but still I let her revel in the freedom of being unmarried. She was grateful to me for not forcing her to take a husband, but I couldn't shake the feeling I was holding her back.

A deep sigh fell from my lips. Over the next four years, Einar would be immersed in training, fighting, working and raiding, earning experience and a bit of wealth before he would be old enough to take a wife. All four of my children were adults now, they had no need for me.

I had been so caught up in retaining the position as Jarl, I hadn't considered what life would be like after I abdicated both my jarldoms to my sons. I hadn't prepared for my loss of purpose. Responsibility had been lifted from my shoulders and now – now what was left? I hadn't realised how much of my identity was wrapped up in being jarl. Now I wasn't jarl – who was I?

With thralls aplenty to cope with my herd of sheep there wasn't anything for me to do with my livestock but dote on them. I filled my time weaving, carding and spinning wool or preparing and preserving food with my thralls. By the gods, I missed the demand and duty my jarldoms necessitated of me ...

A cool breeze wafted over the marketplace. I closed my eyes and inhaled deeply, enjoying the salty air caressing my face. In a few weeks, Sander would set sail, leading his first expedition as Jarl.

Usually the very mention of an expedition sent electric through my body. Now it did nothing more than weigh heavily on my heart. I wasn't allowed to fight in expeditions or raids anymore. Without the privilege of being jarl or jarlkona I was relegated to the camp with the other women, to cook food, brew healing remedies and tend the wounds of men returned from battle. Even when I was jarlkona I only participated in battles a handful of times because I had Vidar's permission and no one dared tell him he was wrong for letting me fight.

I'd lost my place in the world now. I wasn't a healing woman and my cooking skills were mediocre at best. I could already feel the gnaw of boredom and the itch to fight, how would I be able to contain myself on the raid?

"Perhaps you should remain home with Fenja then?" Sander had suggested delicately. "I'm sure Fenja would love to have your company and help while I'm away."

"*Já, móðir*, I'll need your advice while Sander is away—"

"As sweet as you are, Fenja, I'm not a fool. We both know you're more than capable on your own." I had interrupted sharply.

Fenja and Sander had passed a look between each other, their brows lifted, and lips rolled together. After a few tense moments of silence, I sighed deeply.

"I mean not to insult you, *móðir*—"

"You're right, Sander, perhaps I will remain home. It would be for the best." I had said, rising to my feet.

"If that's your decision, *móðir*, I'll support it." Sander had replied swiftly, relief noticeable in his voice.

Since that conversation Sander would occasionally ask if I was sure about my decision. Of course I wasn't, but he was jarl and I had to remember that. I couldn't cause trouble for him – especially not on such an occasion as this. I refused to embarrass my son.

"*Frú* Aveline, are you alright?"

"*Já, já*, I'm fine." I lied, smiling at Herra.

The Swede's lips turned in a sympathetic frown. He obviously didn't believe me, but I hadn't tried very hard to conceal my melancholy.

"I have a new shipment from *Miklagarðr*. I'd love for you to look through it with me." Herra said, gesturing to a table neatly stacked with lengths of exquisite fabrics.

"*Þakka fyrir*, Herra, I'd enjoy that." I decided after a moment – I was going to refuse, but what else did I have to do after all?

Herra had a wealth of goods for sale, including, but not limited to oil, wine and salt, medicines, wax, ceramics, linens and woven cloth. He also had an impressive selection of silks, perfumes and spices. Those items were rarities and incredibly expensive because of that reason. We sifted through Herra's wares, politely admiring and discussing their scent, flavour or quality depending on what we were examining.

"What about that one?" I asked, catching a glance of a gorgeous silk at the back of Herra's stall.

"You have an eye for the luxurious." Herra beamed as he swiftly fetched the article. "That is one of the finest cloths *Miklagarðr* can offer, it cost me an arm and a leg to purchase it."

I accepted the richly patterned Byzantine silk, embroidered with all kinds of beautiful imagery, meticulously woven animals and people framed by fanciful patterns. Sumptuous in design and so smooth in texture, it felt like water gliding over my hands.

"It's beautiful." I smiled, offering the fabric back to Herra.

"*Nei, Frú*, you have it. When I'm upset or out of sorts, I feel better when surrounded by something beautiful." Herra grinned warmly, closing his hand over mine, the fabric trapped between our palms. "That's why I only employ attractive hirelings!"

I laughed with him, touched by his want to cheer me up.

"It's too much, Herra, you can't possibly gift this to me – it cost you an arm and a leg, after all."

"Luckily for me, I have both a spare arm and leg if I decide to buy more." Herra jested, winking at me. "Take it, *Frú*, it's yours."

"Could I have your time instead?"

"You may have both." Herra glanced over his shoulder at one of his *attractive hirelings* who was in the middle of weighing a bag of salt. "Leifr, take over for me, I'll be back later."

"*Já*, Herra." Leifr nodded.

Herra and I meandered through the marketplace to the harbour. As we ambled beside the fjord, the hum of the market replaced by the gentle wash of the waters, Herra told me the tale of how he got his hands on the lovely cloth he'd gifted me.

We spoke for an age yet Herra didn't try to politely return to his market stand. He indulged me with all his tales and stories, vividly describing whatever I asked him to. He told me of the Varangian trade route, the path he travelled to reach *Miklagarðr*. He told me of all the towns and villages he passed by, of the people and the food, of the great fortressed city itself.

"I hope I've entertained you well enough, *Frú*. *Miklagarðr* is a place I could describe in the most incredible detail, but I still wouldn't be able to accurately portray its true beauty."

"I've been hanging off your every word, Herra. I admit, I'm rather jealous. You've travelled the world more than I could ever dream of doing." I said, clutching the fantastic fabric to my chest.

"The Danes insist on travelling west whereas the Swedes go east." Herra chuckled. "There's a whole world out there to explore than just the Anglo-Saxon or Pictish shores."

"Perhaps one day I'll visit *Miklagarðr* myself." I mused.

I chuckled at the preposterous idea, though excitement brewed inside me at the thought of traveling to the southern country.

"Sometimes I don't know if I'll leave it." Herra said wistfully. "It gets harder every time. The summers are hot and long, the winters cool, but nothing as frigid as here. Even the food is worth killing for! It's a magical place, *Frú* Aveline."

"It certainly sounds so." I sighed yearningly.

"I plan to go there in a month. I'll be spending the rest of the summer there, possibly the winter, too. You're welcome to join me, *Frú*."

"Don't say that Herra, I might very well accept your invitation."

"I would be honoured if you did."

***

I COULDN'T STOP thinking of what it would be like to leave Aros and visit the incredible Shining City. From the fabric I held, the spices I'd tasted and the countless objects I'd purchased from Herra over the years that originated from *Miklagarðr*, I knew Herra wasn't lying when he spoke of the city's magnificence. I yearned to see the place in person, to breathe the air, to touch the stone, to taste the food – to witness it all first-hand!

Most of all, I yearned to be anywhere but Aros.

As much as I wanted to, *could* I do it? Could I leave Aros?

Well ... Why not? I wasn't jarl anymore – I was Aveline Birgersdóttir. Townspeople respectfully referred to me as *Frú* Aveline because I was the mother of two jarls and because I *used* to be jarl – but I wasn't one anymore. I had nothing tying me here, no obligations that forced me to stay. I could leave Aros for good if I wanted, let alone just visit *Miklagarðr* for a few months.

I rolled over and gazed at Jan, his features just about visible in the predawn light that trickled in from the smokehole. Morning was approaching, in just a few hours the hall would be alive with activity and noise.

Timidly I reached out and touched Jan's face with my fingertips, drawing his tousled tawny strands over his shoulder. Jan's lips were parted and I was overwhelmed by the urge to kiss them. I resisted, not wanting to wake him. He looked so peaceful when he slept.

I'd made my decision.

I would miss him.

I couldn't pass up such an opportunity. Jan would leave on the expedition, I would leave for *Miklagarðr*, maybe we would arrive back in Aros at the same time?

A pang rattled my heart, what if Thóra followed Jan and Thórvar on the raid? What if she decided to be one of the camp women? I shook my head. I wouldn't let that nonsense fill my mind. I trusted Jan, he wouldn't take that woman to bed behind my back, try all she might to seduce him, Thóra would fail.

"*Góðan morgin*," Jan murmured next to me.

With a deep yawn, Jan focussed his eyes on me, smiling dreamily.

"You're still half asleep." I remarked, smirking at him.

"If you weren't thinking so loudly maybe I'd have stayed asleep."

I giggled softly.

"I apologise for waking you."

"What were you thinking about?"

"I spoke to Herra yesterday. He said he's going to *Miklagarðr* in a month and he invited me to join him."

"What an opportunity!" Jan marvelled. "I've heard many stories about *Miklagarðr*. How wonderful it will be to see it in person!"

"I'm glad you think so because I've decided to go. I'm not attending the expedition and rather than sit around here, I want to go with him." I said, somehow managing to keep up a calm exterior while my heart ricocheted inside my chest.

"I think you'd be a fool not to." Jan said warmly, kissing my hand again. "I'm rather jealous, I'd love to go with you."

"You don't want to go on Sander's first expedition as jarl?" My jaw dropped and brows shot to the top of my forehead.

"I think Sander will do well whether I'm there or not." Jan said. "I've fought at his side countless times, I know how excellent he is. As much as I enjoy raiding, I'd prefer to go to *Miklagarðr* with you – if Herra has room on his ship for me, of course."

"I'll ask him today." I said, my voice faint with surprise.

"Do you want me there? If not, I'll go on the expedition – I don't want to intrude on your adventure."

"*Nei!* I'd love nothing more than for you to join me!" I gasped. "We'll speak with Sander first thing about it – I'll summon Herra today and let him know I'm going, and that you are, too, and—"

Jan interrupted me with a kiss. I was rambling, planning everything at lightning speed. His kiss froze me, nothing else mattered but the weight of his lips on mine, the prod of his tongue as it searched for entry, the taste of his mouth.

Jan slipped his arm beneath my neck and pulled me against him. We snuggled in silence for a while, the sleeping area brightening as the sun scaled the sky.

"I still find it hard to believe that Sander and Birger are jarls, and both of them married." Jan said. "Birger has a son and another on the way ... Time has gone so quickly."

"Ísarr is so much like Birger was at that age." I smiled, picturing my grandson's sweet plump face. "I wonder if the new baby will be, too? Or if he'll be a troublemaker like Sander."

"You know, Ísarr called me *Afi* all throughout his stay here – in front of Birger and Sander and Æsa – and none of them made him call me 'Jan' instead."

"Why would they? You've been like a *faðir* to them since Vidar died. You more than deserve that title." I said, surprised he hadn't come to that conclusion himself. "You're essentially my husband anyway, it would be strange if Ísarr called you anything, but '*Afi*.'"

I giggled at the huge grin that spread across Jan's face.

"When do I change from *essentially* being your husband, to *actually* being your husband, anyway?" Jan asked mischievously.

"When you ask me to be your wife one last time."

I could feel my cheeks flush, intensified by Jan's wide-eyed stare.

This was it – this was the moment. Jan had patiently waited for me all this time and I planned to give him exactly what he wanted. He deserved so much more than me, but if it was me he wanted, he would have me completely.

"Aveline Birgersdóttir," Jan said slowly, as if he couldn't believe this was happening. "Will you marry me?"

"*Já*, Jan Jötunnson, I will." I beamed. "And if the Nornir will it, I will bare your children."

Jan snatched me up against him and crushed my mouth with his. I laughed against his lips, surprised and amused by his excitement.

"I'll make offerings to them – I'll sacrifice to every god!" Jan gushed.

"I'm an old woman, now, Jan." I cautioned. His reaction was endearing, but my heart dropped in my chest at his hopefulness. "I fear you made a terrible decision waiting all these years for me."

"*Nei*," Jan said firmly. "Waiting for you was *never* a terrible decision."

ASHES REMAIN
CHAPTER THIRTY

CONSTANTINOPLE
Late Summer, 892

BATHED IN SUNLIGHT, the shining city stretched out before us gold and striking against the dazzling blue sky, its reflection dancing on the crystalline waters. The city was built on seven hills surrounded by a moat and multiple sets of parallel, tower-studded walls. It was the most fortified city I'd ever seen. Magnificent and intimidating, it could've homed the gods.

Sunlight blinded me, but I didn't tear my eyes away. I squinted at the domes, colonnades and gilded monuments that dotted the horizon, glaring down on our ship as we neared the city.

Sea walls enclosed two sides of Constantinople, a fantastic marble palace built inside one. It was covered with balconies set with marble statues of beasts and creatures. It even had its own marble quay and private harbour where a frightening statue of a bull and lion stood.

We rowed into port and moored Herra's ship beside one of many docks. In a daze I drifted down the gangplank and followed the paved path, my head spinning.

It had taken so long, but we were finally here the Byzantine city of Constantinople, *Miklagarðr* in the Norse tongue. We'd travelled countless rivers, portages and waterways stretching from the Varangian Sea all the way along the Dnieper River to the Black Sea, following its western coast to this glorious place.

We stopped in several towns along the way here to buy, sell and barter, but moved keenly onwards. Some places and peoples along the way were like us, their gods were similar to ours, but referred to by different names. However, the further south we travelled the more differences emerged.

These people's homes, gods, clothes – even their hair! – were nothing like ours. Swarthy and dark, their words were unintelligible to all, but a few crewmen and Herra, who seemed to speak every language imaginable.

The sun beat down on me as I wandered through a huge archway in the harbour wall that led to a steep stone staircase – the entrance to the dazzling city.

Majestic trees, luscious plants and verdant bushes and shrubs embraced the great stone walls and structures. Foliage spilled over the walls and vines clung to the stone. Wildflowers blossomed everywhere, great bursts of vivid colour amongst the rich emerald, jade and viridian foliage. The air was thick with an almost delicious mixture of sweetness from the blossoms' nectars and the salty tang of the surrounding seas.

I slumped against the archway, the warm stone rough against my back. My eyes fluttered shut and I breathed in deeply, dizzy from the overwhelming sights, sounds and scents.

"Are you alright?" Jan asked, placing a hand on my shoulder.

"*Já*," I replied breathily, beaming up at him with dreamy eyes. "Isn't this phenomenal, Jan? Just look at it all!"

"You haven't seen the best part, yet." Herra chuckled, pausing beside us, his chest puffed out with pride. "This is just the outside, wait until you see what's inside the walls."

***

WE STAYED IN Constantinople for weeks and I doubted we had seen even half of the city, despite the fact we explored it from sunup to sundown. I wished Sander and Young Birger could have been here with us. Every day was an adventure, there were so many things to see and do and such a rich history to learn. My eldest sons would love it here. I was thankful that at least I had Æsa and Einar with me. One day I would accompany Sander and Young Birger here, and little Ísarr, too! One day.

Not even Thóra's presence could ruin the excitement that coursed through me every morning I woke up in Constantinople. We accompanied Herra to sell and trade his wares, and haggle for and purchase goods on his behalf, things for him to take and sell in the Norse lands. When we weren't assisting him, we explored.

When Herra could not accompany us, he allowed a few members of his crew to take his place. Herra's men led us through the city, their chests puffed with pride. They had visited the Byzantine city many times in the past and showed it off to us as though it was theirs. Herra or his crew (whoever was guiding us at the time) orated the fascinating history of the city, explaining the stories of every building and monument.

Monuments loomed over us, positioned along the high spine of the city. Marble columns crowned with statues and crosses filled the city, some wrapped in spiralling bands of sculpture. My jaw dropped at the sight of a column crowned with a gilt statue of a previous emperor, (Emperor Justinian, Herra said), on horseback, towering over everything nearby.

Giant gold and bronze statues of men, some on horses, were erected on stone podiums, so realistic they looked as though they could jump down at any moment. There were fountains and streams pouring down into limpid pools. Golden lions stood guard outside of buildings, spitting jets of water into the streets.

Mosaic and painted walls gleamed under the hot sun, brightly coloured and intricate. Everything about this city was decadent, from the towering walls to the paved courtyards and stone pavilions. It amazed me that something as magnificent as this existed in Midgard. Privately I wondered whether Asgard or heaven were as opulent as Constantinople.

I marvelled at the decadence, but not all was splendid. Beside the palaces and mansions were hovels and shacks. Ragged beggars sat at the feet of golden columns, their skin blistered and filthy.

The juxtaposition of wealth and poverty caught me off guard, the very rich and the extremely poor lived side-by-side, palaces housing wealthy nobles were positioned beside squalid five-story tenement buildings. Fantastic stone mansions boasting paintings, mosaics and luxurious furnishings were situated beside wooden huts or courtyard homes with communal dome ovens.

Rather than impress me, the towering tenement buildings made my skin crawl. So many families were squashed inside those buildings, one on top of the other. I clung to Jan's hand, feeling suffocated as we walked by the buildings. The stench emitted from the tenements was vile. I covered my nose and mouth with my sleeve and walked quickly to escape the foul odour.

Labyrinthine roads, some dirt and some paved, weaved through the houses, shops, taverns, public buildings and churches. In particularly affluent looking areas luscious gardens hid behind waist high stone walls, perfectly manicured and bursting with colour, offering a modicum of breathing room inside the overcrowded city. It was obvious the wealthier one was, the more space he could afford.

The deeper we walked through the city, the more I realised that population density varied between the different neighbourhoods. I was also surprised to note that large areas were given over to public gardens and more than a few large vast tracks of farmland.

Herra showed us the Forum of Constantine at the centre of the city. It was apparently built immediately outside the old city walls of Byzantium and was a central point along the Mese, the main ceremonial road through the city. Colonnaded porches of shops lined the wide road, people buying and selling all manners of items inside those grand stone walls.

The circular forum that was paved with stone had two massive gates to the east and west and was surrounded on the outside by tenement buildings and courtyard homes. The Column of Constantine loomed in the centre of the forum – a tall red column made of porphyry stone, topped with a gilt statue of Constantine.

Herra showed us an arena called the Hippodrome of Constantinople. Herra said it had been built hundreds of years ago for chariot racing, parades and the like, and was said to seat one hundred thousand spectators. It was filled with gold, bronze and copper statues of old gods and emperors, animals and heroes, horses and chariot drivers.

Due to its position on the strait that separated the west from the east, Constantinople was an incredibly prosperous crossway of trade. The city was bursting with gold – coins, jewellery, thread – you name it, *Miklagarðr* had it gilded.

The finest building in the city – in the entire world! – was the Hagia Sophia. The Hagia Sophia, (which meant 'holy wisdom' according to Herra), was a massive rectangular building adorned with dazzling mosaics and superb wall paintings, with a great domed ceiling that rested on four massive arches.

"Does their God live here?" Jan marvelled.

"Not that I have seen in all my visits, but they honour him richly to be sure." Herra laughed.

ASHES REMAIN

"The Anglo-Saxons honour God with great cathedrals and churches, but nothing like this." I gaped.

The Hagia Sophia wasn't the only place of worship in the city, though it was the finest and largest – Herra said it was the largest church in the entire world and I didn't doubt that for a moment.

Churches towered tall and proud, great monuments of these peoples unwavering faith to the Christian God, made of the finest cuts of stone, with domed ceilings, stunning arched windows and marble columns. The chapels were just as lavish as the churches, and monasteries and convents could be found all over the city. Herra said a lot of people would retire to them and spend the rest of their lives helping the poor and sick.

"You see that bridge there?" Herra pointed ahead of us. "That is an *aqueduct*. It was built by the Romans hundreds of years ago – as was much of this city. The aqueduct carries water to hundreds of cisterns – underground chambers – buried beneath the city, to supply to the people here. One of the cisterns is said to be as large as a cathedral. The ceiling of that particular cistern is supported by a forest of hundreds of tall marble columns."

I gawped, hardly understanding the words Herra said. A bridge that carried water and stored it beneath the city in massive chambers ... It was all so strange and incredible!

Herra pointed out schools – places where boys would go to learn the Greek education, things like philosophy and rhetoric – whatever they were. Jan sneered, remarking that the boys must be weak for spending so much time training their minds rather than learning to fight, but privately I was impressed. If learning those things led to such fantastic cities as this, was it really a bad thing?

CHAPTER THIRTY-ONE

Late Autumn, 892

"HEY, AVELINE, CATCH!"

I lurched as Jan tossed an apple at me. Clumsily I caught the fruit, almost dropping it, my cheeks flushing at Jan's laughter. I squeezed the apple's firm green flesh as Jan flicked a coin to the vendor. I hurled the fruit at Jan, he whooped as he caught it, cackling like a child – had he not expected me to throw it at him?

"Let's make this harder, shall we?" Jan winked.

He weaved through the crowds filling the marketplace, a full head taller than everyone at least. He tossed the apple above them – eliciting a few shocked cries, a few chuckles and a few jeers.

"A-ha! Caught it!" I exclaimed, just as surprised as Jan was.

I dashed ahead, throwing the apple back at Jan. I didn't have the privilege of extreme height like Jan, the moment I tossed the fruit, my luck was with the gods whether I hit someone or not.

"Got it!" Jan shouted happily.

"Well done!" I beamed.

"Oh, *móðir*." Æsa sighed, rolling her eyes at our childishness.

She might have been embarrassed, but that didn't stop Æsa from giggling. Einar was thoroughly amused, laughing and cheering along with us. They were sitting at Herra's pavilion, watching Jan and me. Behind them, Thóra hung back like a dark cloud, glaring at us furiously, just like the strangers in range of the fruit.

"You can beat him, *Frú* Aveline!" Herra chortled.

We continued the silly game, lacing through the crowd and darting about the marketplace, slinging the fruit at each other. We hurled the apple harder and further, forcing each other to lunge to catch it, narrowly missing people or unluckily crashing into them. As we became more reckless it was much more difficult to avoid colliding with people or hitting someone with the fruit. Still, Jan and I persisted, both riding the high of adrenalin and fun. I hadn't laughed like this in far too long.

ASHES REMAIN

"Sorry!" Jan called, a group of men cursing him in their tongue as he stumbled into them.

"Watch out!" I warned mischievously.

I hurled the fruit high and hard – too far for Jan to catch. I didn't think he even tried to catch it. I watched the apple zoom through the air before slamming into the back of a man with short black hair and gorgeous silk clothing who was talking with a couple of slave traders. He whipped around, clasping the back of his head, glaring and shouting. The slave traders were equally unamused. The man's coal-black eyes caught mine.

"Sorry!" I called to him.

"Run!" Jan hissed, suddenly beside me, his hands on my waist, pushing me away from the marketplace.

Clinging to each other, we dashed through the crowd and down the street. I caught quizzical stares or disapproving glares aimed at us as we passed.

"Here, let's hide in here!" I suggested, pulling Jan through the doorway of a busy tavern.

Jan and I found a tiny table in the back of the tavern. We snuggled together, giggling as we tried to catch our breath.

Once we'd calmed down, we bought a delicious meal of red wine and *dolma*, meat-stuffed vine leaves, followed by *kopton*, a layered pastry filled with chopped nuts and sweetened with honey, hoping the man at the slaver's platform would be gone with enough time.

I wasn't half as wealthy as even the lowest noble in Constantinople, but I was privileged enough to afford mouth-watering meals and delectable drinks for us all to gorge ourselves on at taverns and inns every night. Occasionally Thóra swallowed her pride and accepted one of the delicious meals, but not often.

I eyed the *kopton* scrupulously, hoping to decipher its recipe by sight alone. It was by far one of the most luscious delicacies I'd tasted in all our time in *Miklagarðr*.

"I hate that our time is nearly done here." I sighed, draining what wine was left in my cup. "I wish we could stay for longer."

"Perhaps we can return here with Herra next time he comes?"

"I hope so. I'll miss this place desperately the moment we leave." I replied, staring at the little flakes of pastry that remained on my plate, glistening with honey.

"There *are* things to look forward to when we return to Aros." Jan said, straightening himself in his chair.

"Oh *já?*" I smiled. "And what's that?"

"Our wedding of course." He said, tossing a grape into his mouth.

"Oh?" I replied, wickedly acting nonchalant. "I don't know … I've changed my mind, Jan. I don't think I want to marry you anymore."

"You'd break my heart like this?" Jan looked as angelic as a cherub, but I knew better than to fall for it.

Dramatically, I paused, pretending to consider his question.

"*Nei*, I suppose I'll still marry you." I said flippantly, shrugging.

"You're a cruel woman, Aveline Birgersdóttir."

"And you love me, Jan Jötunnson, you foolish, *foolish* man."

"I certainly don't love you for your cruelty, but I *do* love you."

Jan cupped my face with one hand and pulled me towards him. Our lips crashed together, filled with yearning and want.

"I don't know if they'll allow us back in *Miklagarðr* if we keep up our current behaviour." I mumbled, breaking our kiss, conscious of the disapproving tuts sounding around us.

"At this moment, I don't think I care."

"Let's return to the inn." I suggested.

"Let's rent a room here?"

"I like the way you think, Jan Jötunnson."

***

I STRETCHED MY arms high above my head, yawning deeply without covering my mouth. I caught Thóra curl her lip and roll her eyes at me. What her issue was with me this time, I didn't know and I didn't care. I paid her no mind, filled with contentment from yet another wonderful night sleep in *Miklagarðr*.

Einar was sitting beside me, tucking into a bowl of fruit and oats. Æsa was beside him, taking small bites of crusty buttered bread. I left Jan asleep in bed, a thin sheet draped over his naked body, the warm morning sun blazing on him from the window in our room.

"*Frú* Aveline, how are you this fine morning?" Herra beamed.

"I have no complaints," I replied happily.

"I fear you might complain about me." Herra said, pouting dramatically.

"Oh? Why would I do that?"

"I must take Jan for a while. I'm meeting with a slave trader in the afternoon and when dealing with this particular one, the more muscle I have, the better." Herra said ominously. Almost immediately, he returned to his original bubbly demeanour. "It shouldn't take long, just a couple of hours at most."

"Would you like me to come with you?"

"Don't take this the wrong way, *Frú*. We know how capable and strong you are, but he doesn't. I fear–"

"It's not a place for a woman." I finished for him. "I understand, Herra."

"It's alright, *móðir*, we can explore the city together again." Æsa said. "I want to buy a gift for Borgunna, would you help me?"

"Of course my love," I replied, resting my hand on hers.

She was pacifying me – just as Sander had about the expedition. Had I truly become this old, useless woman with brittle feelings to the point my children felt the need to mollify me?

***

THE DAY PASSED uneventfully, as all the days did in Constantinople. After eating, Jan, the children and I spent a few hours shopping. We purchased gifts for Æsa and Einar's friends and I found a few more presents for Sander and Fenja, Young Birger, Signý and little Ísarr, as well as a few presents for my unborn grandchild – who, I realised, must've been born by now considering how heavily pregnant Signý was last we saw her.

After shopping, we rested at the inn for a few hours before it was time for Herra's meeting with the slave trader. Rather than wait around, the children and I went out. We strolled down the coast, walked the arena and explored ruins.

My heart dropped to know we only had days left here. We hadn't worried about starving, farming, sacrificing, raiding. Every day had been easy. I missed my children, I missed my grandchild, I missed my friends, but I found myself not missing much else about home.

Sitting on a worn settee beside the large arched window of my room, I watched the few people awake at this hour walking along the street below. A towering figure caught my eye – Jan had returned. He must've felt my gaze for he glanced up. I offered him a smile, which he returned before entering the tavern.

I considered going downstairs and joining him for a meal, but I wasn't hungry. I felt morose and didn't particularly want to go down and have anyone harass me with questions about my mood. I didn't need to worry, however, for Jan came directly upstairs.

"That was *something*," Jan said, shutting the door behind himself.

"Oh?" I patted the space on the settee beside me.

"I've bought and sold slaves before, but that was *different*." Jan continued. "*Everything* about this place is opulent."

"Including buying slaves?"

"Including buying slaves." Jan confirmed, sitting beside me.

His footsteps were heavy and the smell of wine exuded from him like a cloud. Jan wasn't drunk, but he was close enough. His words were slightly slurred and his eyes were heavy.

"You're not giving me many details."

"He held a small feast, a party – we were offered drinks and food and there were women dancing and serving us and they wore see-through dresses!"

"Sounds like you had quite a fun time." I said, raising my brows at him and smothering my smile – Jan looked genuinely perturbed.

"There were other traders, but the one hosting the party … I expected him to be a big monster and he wasn't. He was small and lean, but he was the most powerful man in the room. Everyone abased themselves to him, but us, of course."

Jan pulled me closer to him. I laid down on the settee with my head on his lap. Jan stroked my hair with one hand, the other rested on my stomach, his stare locked on the floor.

"He could speak the Norse tongue fluently." Jan continued. "And he took an instant dislike to me for some reason."

"Perhaps he was jealous of your height and good looks?"

"Most definitely," Jan winked at me. "It's funny … I think I recognised him from somewhere."

"Maybe he's sold slaves in Aros or Roskilde before?" I suggested. "That would explain why he can speak Norse so well."

"Maybe." Jan said, trailing into silence.

Jan leaned over me and kissed my forehead. I shuffled up his lap, sitting on his legs and resting my head on his shoulder. Jan engulfed me with his arms, holding me tight.

"The most peculiar thing were the slave girls ... They all looked like you."

"Like me?" I laughed.

"Maybe I missed you so much I was imagining things." Jan yawned.

"Come to bed, it's late." I pressed, trying to climb off Jan's lap, but he held me tighter.

"There was something about him ... Something dark."

"Thank the gods that was the first and last time you'll meet him."

"Aveline – you need to make me a promise." Jan said, turning me on his lap to face him.

Jan held my face between both his hands, staring into my eyes. My heart raced – I'd never seen him like this before. Had drink addled him more than I realised? I gripped his wrists, but couldn't pull his hands down, he was too strong.

"Aveline, don't you, Æsa and Einar leave the marketplace without me. This town is a labyrinth – if he found you–"

"You needn't worry, we're leaving in a few days."

"Promise me!" Jan barked.

We stared at each other, his face filled with determination, mine filled with fear and shock. How had one meeting with this slave trader rattled someone as mighty and formidable as Jan?

"I promise." I murmured.

With my vow, Jan kissed me, dropping his hands from my face and wrapping me in his arms instead. Jan's behaviour startled me, but I didn't deny his advances. I returned each kiss, caressed his shoulders. He lifted me and carried me to bed, hurriedly untying his breeches and shuffling my skirt over my hips.

Jan was in a rush – he didn't want to make love, he didn't want passion or tenderness. He didn't want my body for the pure enjoyment of the act nor an instinctual need to copulate. Jan sought refuge inside me.

CHAPTER THIRTY-TWO

WITH A HEAVY heart, we said goodbye to *Miklagarðr*. The final two days were a blur. We sold the last of Herra's stock and packed all the wares he intended to sell in the Norse lands – not to mention our own belongings. We were leaving Constantinople with a lot more than we arrived with. Thankfully there was a lot of space on the ship.

We left a few hours after first light, sailing the day and night away, the favourable wind at our back as we headed home. If all continued as well as it was, we might get home a few days earlier than expected. As it was, we would arrive just before winter – this was not usually a recommendable time to sail, but the Norsemen want to make it home in time for *Jól*.

In the early morning, while the majority of the crew and passengers were still asleep, I stood at the stern of the ship, mournfully staring at the horizon. Hidden behind the huge tent erected in the centre of the ship behind the mast and surrounded by neatly stacked casks and trunks, I found a moment of solitude that was so rare upon a ship.

The shining city was gone, nothing in sight, but the sea and the sky and a few merchant ships far in the distance. My heart ached terribly for the beautiful city. I didn't realise how much I actually detested the idea of going back to Aros until that moment.

"*Góðan morgin*, Aveline."

"*Góðan morgin*, Thóra." I replied just as tautly as her.

How did she find me in my secluded spot? I didn't turn to face her, hoping she'd get the hint that I wanted to be alone. She must've been searching for me, but why in Frigg's name did she want to talk to me?

Thóra and I spent much of our time in Constantinople ignoring each other, even when we explored the city together. Of course, we had Herra, his crewmen, Jan and the children to turn to for conversation so we didn't have to speak to each other, thankfully.

ASHES REMAIN

"Did you enjoy *Miklagarðr*?" Thóra asked, standing so close to me, I felt her arm brush against mine.

"*Já*, you?"

"There were one or three things I would change, but other than that, it was a wonderful time, *já*."

I knew exactly what those 'one or three things' were. Instantly filled with fury, I glared at the bitch.

"Why did you even come here?" I demanded.

"You didn't think I'd let you go off to some beautiful city alone with Jan, did you?" Thóra chuckled. "*Nei*, you stupid woman. Anyway, I wasn't going to stay in Aros with Thórvar *and* Jan gone. You may have felt like a special little star for being invited by Herra, but he lets anyone sail with him, as long as they ask nicely."

"Did Jan also tell you that we're getting married?" I blurted, wanting only to upset her.

"Unfortunately he did." Thóra wrinkled her nose. "That's no matter, though."

"You've finally accepted that he chose *me* over you?"

Thóra shrugged indifferently.

"I'll be there to console him."

"Console him?" My brow knitted. "Console him for what?"

"For his loss. Don't worry, Aveline, I'll take care of him."

In one fell swoop, Thóra swung her arm back – what was that metal thing in her hand? Before I could register what was happening, Thóra bashed me in the head with whatever it was.

Staggering backwards, I clutched my head with one hand and the edge of the ship with the other, all breath knocked out of me.

Pain tore through my skull! I couldn't string a single thought together before I felt my feet pulled up from beneath me. I didn't have a chance to scream, so blindsided by her attack. My hair whipped my face and my skirts billowed about me as I plummeted to the waters below.

***

COOL AIR WAFTED over my body, tearing me from a dreamless slumber. I groaned, the more I wakened the more pain I registered throbbing in every muscle of my body. My chest was tight, my throat raw, and my breath came in shallow gasps that seared my lungs. I was alive, that much was certain.

Groggily I opened my eyes, but there was nothing to see – wherever I was, it was black as pitch. With trembling arms, I tried to push myself up from the ground, my fingernails scraping against the cold stone slabs I was lying on. I forced my aching body upwards, wincing at every stab of pain.

As the moments passed, I became more aware of my surroundings and of myself. Wherever I was, it stank of piss, shit and sweat, and it was cold and windowless like a sealed tomb. My clothing was stiff and sodden in places, reeking of seawater. Wherever I was, I hadn't been here long enough for my clothing to dry out completely.

There was something around my neck … Something heavy and cold. I struggled to lift my sore arm and touch whatever it was. I dragged my fingertips over the rough, aged metal. Thick, the width of two fingers, and fastened shut with a heavy ring … It was a thrall's collar.

Ignoring the pain ripping through my muscles, I bolted upright and gripped the collar with both hands. I spun it around, trying to find the latch – I tugged on it, but it wouldn't come off. Nausea surged up my throat and icy fingers stormed down my spine – *had I been taken as a slave?!*

My head was spinning, worsening my queasiness, and my heart raced. Where was Jan? Where were Herra and the others? Where was that bitch, Thóra?

I froze. Voices sounded, speaking a language I couldn't understand, growing louder. Blinding grey light poured into the windowless room as a door opened across the way. I winced, my eyes unaccustomed to the brightness.

Two men were standing there, illuminated from behind, their faces dowsed in shadow. For a few suffocating moments we stared at each other, my eyes narrowed against the glaring light. I couldn't see their eyes, but I could feel their gazes weighing on me like the iron collar around my neck.

I couldn't distinguish their clothes or faces from the shadow, but I did see the whip coiled into a loop and tucked behind one of their belts. Horribly aware of the fact I was unarmed, my fingers searched for *Úlfsblóð*, but there was no sword to be found, not even the scabbard. My blade was still on Storm-Serpent – unless Thóra had tossed it into the sea after me.

Like a rabbit cornered by hungry wolves, I scrambled back, slamming against the rough wall behind me. The crumbling plaster scratched my back and caught my hair. The two men dove at me, barking in their foreign words, snatching at my clothes, my arms, my legs. I kicked and flailed, ripping myself away, snarling and shouting back at them in Norse.

I rolled out of their grasp and threw myself towards the doorway, tripping on my skirts. My leather boots were tight and damp, squeezing my feet and slipping on the stone slabbed floor. I crashed to the ground, scraping my forearms and knees.

One of the men leapt on top of me and slammed my face into the stone, pinning me down. Beneath his crushing weight I rasped for breath, digging my fingers into the dirt around the slabs, trying to claw myself out from beneath him.

All the while, the two men barked at each other like agitated dogs. They must've agreed on something, for the man atop me quickly rolled off. I didn't have time to scarper away before–

Crack! Crack! Crack!

"Argh!" I shrieked.

My vision obscured by a flurry of sparks, I crumpled into a pile, writhing and weeping. Three lashes of the whip! I felt my skin snap as the leather thongs cut through my clothing, slitting open the fabric and slashing my back. Blood streamed from the long skinny rends in my flesh, cascading down my body and soaking my clothes. I rolled onto my side and vomited.

Before I could catch my breath, one of the men flipped me onto my back. The filthy stone floor grated my torn and bloody flesh. While I coughed and cried, one of them tied a rope to the ring of my collar and the other coiled his whip back up.

The one with the whip crouched beside me and tapped my face with the end of the whip's handle as he spoke. I didn't need to know his language to understand what he was saying. His message was clear as day, if I tried to flee or fight, he'd whip me again.

I watched my captors cross the room. In my panic, I didn't realise there were other women huddled together in the shadows, their clothes tattered and hair matted. The men pulled the terrified creatures to their feet and tied ropes to their collars as they had mine. The women didn't fight like I had – they were too afraid.

One of the men led the women out of the room, dragging them behind him like dogs by their ropes. The man with the whip took the rope hanging from my collar and pulled me to my feet, chiding me in his language. He pulled me out of the room, following his companion and the women. Anger simmered in my blood, but I did nothing, excruciatingly aware of the whip at my captor's waist.

***

I STUMBLED BEHIND my captor, tripping on uneven paving slabs. The slavers led us to a wagon – more like a cage on four wheels – harnessed to two mules. A third man was leaning against the cage picking at his nails. As soon as the slaver at the front called to him, the third man sprang up and unlocked the cage door. The women ahead of me were forced to pile into it.

My captor pulled his whip from his waist again, pointing at me with it, then to the wagon, a smirk twisting his lips. *Get on or he'll make me.*

I climbed up the rough wooden planks, scraping my feet on the worn boards. The slaver shut the cage door behind me, grinning as his accomplice locked it with an iron key. The slavers went to the front of the wagon, snapped the reins and yapped at the mules.

Crushed together, the women wept, clinging to each other. Three were adult women, perhaps with families somewhere. The others were young, one was practically a girl. How long had these poor creatures been trapped in that room? Some of them were far filthier than the others, the ripe stench exuding from them suggested they'd been trapped in that horrid place for a while.

The women were from all over the world. The likelihood of them returning to their homes was impossible. Of the eight, four were from the Blálands, three from the Arab lands and two were from Britain. I was the only Danish captive. I listened to the Anglo-Saxons weep in Ænglisc, but I didn't talk to them. I knew what our fates were. There was no point comforting them.

ASHES REMAIN

The slavers took us through steep winding streets where tall, dilapidated buildings towered over us on both sides. The noise and chatter of the city was deafening and the streets stank of piss and shit, concealing the tang of the sea nearby almost entirely. Numerous faces clustered in the windows, curiously watching the slavers take their new wares to the market.

This was a part of Constantinople I hadn't seen during our trip.

Through another narrow, crooked street, under another stone archway, finally the streets opened to a bustling marketplace, one of many in the city. Thankfully here the stench of excretion was overpowered by the smells of the food and drinks for sale at various stands, the fish laid out for customers to examine, the pungent trace of seawater hinted on the breeze.

The marketplace was situated atop a gradual slope, lording over the streets and harbour below. Had the situation been different I could appreciate the view. From behind the iron bars of the cage it was nothing more than the taunt of unobtainable freedom.

We neared the slavers platform. I eyed the posts sunk into the hard ground, out in the open under the blistering sun. Hooks were screwed into the posts awaiting the ropes that hung from our collars. Behind the platform was a canopy with chairs beneath for the slavers to sit on, skins of water leaning against the legs. A crowd formed about the platform, eyeing the wagon.

The wagon stopped, I was first to be dragged out. The slaver pulled me to the posts, whip already in his hand. I didn't fight, I let him lead me. The slaver was as careless as I expected him to be. I gripped the rope, gently at first, so the slaver wouldn't notice. I held my breath, counting every step.

We were only a few paces from the posts. With an almighty pull, I jerked the rope free and lunged towards the crowd. To my dismay, hands clawed and clutched me, forcing me back to the slaver as quickly as I'd escaped. The slaver struck my face with the back of his hand, yelling at me and shaking the whip in my face.

"Eat shit!" I hissed, spitting on him.

The slaver's face contorted with fury, my spittle leaking down his cheek. I'd almost managed to spit in his eye. Without wiping it away, he threw me to the floor.

Crack! Crack!

GWENDOLINE SK TERRY

Wrenching screams ripped from my throat, the agony of the lashes too much to bear. The slaver grabbed my collar and threw me at the nearest post. He dragged me to my feet and tied the rope to the hook, growling at me in his language. As he tied the rope to the hook, I leaned against the post gasping for breath, dipping in and out of consciousness. If I collapsed, I would hang myself. I had to stand, I *had* to stay awake.

With all the captive women lined up and tied to the posts, the slavers sat in their chairs, gulping water from their skins. For hours we were standing beneath the boiling sun with no water or shade, dizzy and dehydrated. Men groped us and jerked us around, examining us roughly, conversing with the slavers as they did so.

Blood dried to my back in crisp, crumbling patches. I leaned from one leg to the other, trying to keep myself up, but my consciousness fluttered. Through hazy eyes I watched the crowd, plans formulating in my mind.

If I could somehow untie the rope from the hook, I could dash between the fishmonger stalls and through the alley on the far left. From there I could navigate the winding streets to the harbour – maybe I could find a ship to hide in …

It seemed like the only solid plan – the crowd thinned behind the fishmonger's stall. It was my only chance … But I was tired. I was *exhausted*. My skin was blistered and cooked beneath the burning sun. I couldn't even stand, how could I run to the alley and escape the slavers?

I had to try. My chance of success was low. The moment the slavers caught me, I would face the whip again … Was it worth it? It didn't matter – first I had to figure out how to undo the rope without being spotted …

A man appeared before me, cupping my jaw in his soft hand. I lurched at first, surprised by his gentle touch. A bright smile shone from his handsome face and a soft laugh slipped from his lips. I shook my head and glared at him. He snickered again and called to the slavers behind me. Immediately one scurried to my side and untied my rope from the hook on the post.

The stranger held my rope tightly. He reached out, I steeled myself to his touch, maintaining as fierce a scowl as I could muster, my cheek twitching from fatigue. Delicately he brushed my hair behind my shoulders, gliding his fingers over my face and down my neck. I grimaced as he touched me, but I didn't move. He dropped my rope, letting it dangle down my front as he stepped behind me, only his fingertips touching me.

I waited.

The seconds passed slowly and excruciating as he studied me, chatting and laughing with the slaver. Why did he release the rope? Did he think I was too weak to escape? That was his mistake. Now was my chance to escape.

I focussed on the light touch of his fingertips as he drew them over my shoulders, waiting for the moment the man would drop his hand. With them both behind me, they couldn't see me coil the rope in my fist, the rough fibres scratching against my palm.

From the tone of their conversation, I could tell the man was bartering with the slaver. The man hummed and hawed, apparently disapproving of the price the slaver wanted for me. He drew his hand away from me as he bickered further with the slaver, waving his hands about as he spoke.

Now – *now!*

I ran.

My sight locked on the fishmonger stall, I dashed towards it. I held the rope, making certain no one could grab it nor would it hit me as I ran. I shoved through the crowds. Some people gasped and stumbled out of my way, others tried to catch me.

Voices bellowed at me from behind. Quickly I put distance between myself and the slavers. I got behind the fishmonger stall, bolted further, my aching feet slipping and sliding on the grass.

"*Argh!*"

Someone tackled me from behind! I toppled down, the wind knocked out of me, the weight of my captor unbearable. I wheezed as we grappled – I writhed in his grip, kicking, flailing. My elbow collided into his chest – he cried out – I tried to scramble up, but I leaned on the rope and jerked my own head into the ground.

The man recovered fast, grabbed my collar and yanked me towards him, strangling me. I tried to shove my fingers beneath the iron collar, but the man wouldn't relent. A fist slammed into my stomach, and again, and again. I doubled up, wheezing, as blow after blow struck me.

Finally my attacker stopped. He squatted, puffing for breath, evidently exhausted from beating me. But for light and darkness, I couldn't see a thing, so blinded by tears. A few more shadows cast over me. Cracks filled the air before the knotted leather strips ripped through my flesh. I screeched and wailed, crumpled on the ground, a defenceless target for the merciless whip.

The voice of the man from earlier reached my ears and my captor stopped lashing me. I forced my eyes open, peering at the men through my tears and the sweat leaking down my face.

The man handed a purse to the slaver.

I was sold.

ASHES REMAIN
CHAPTER THIRTY-THREE

THE SWEET CHIRRUPING of birdsong drifted to my ears, waking me. But for the birdsong and my own raucous breathing, there was no other noise around me. White light glared through my closed eyelids and a blissful warmth danced over my skin.

Sleep held a tight grip on me still, I was too drowsy to open my eyes and my limbs were too heavy to lift. I could move my fingers, though, and I did, stroking them against the soft sheets beneath me. I wasn't lying on a hard stone floor nor the dusty ground of the marketplace, I was in a bed – a warm, cosy bed in a room filled with sweet balmy air and peaceful silence.

A sudden thirst overwhelmed me. I licked my lips, attempting to moisten the rough cracked skin, but there didn't seem to be a drop of saliva in my mouth. I'd been asleep for so long, I was dehydrated. But *where* was I sleeping?

As my senses returned to me so did the memories of my beatings by the slaver's whip, sending shivers down my spine. None of this made sense! I'd gone from the violent clutches of a slave trader to the softness of a feather mattress.

The warm breeze wafted over me, dancing on my skin as softly as a lover's caress. My skin ... I was naked! I shifted in the bed, wincing at every ache, but was somewhat relieved to find a sheet covering my lower body. I needed to find my clothes – I needed to find out where I was – I needed to escape.

"It really is you, isn't it?" A male voice said in the Norse tongue.

I recognised the voice. I forced my eyes open, wincing at the blinding light. The room we were sitting in was painted white, which made the light pouring in from the huge open window that much more dazzling.

In my peripheral vision, I could spy the scenic view of trees, fields and buildings outside the window. I couldn't tear my eyes from the man sitting beneath it, though. Relaxing on a settee covered in plush cushions with a large cup in one hand, the man smiled at me.

He was the man who purchased me from the slaver.

I scowled.

"Where are my clothes?" Each word scratched my sore throat.

"They're in the chest over there." The man said, nodding towards an ornate wooden trunk across the room. "You've been unconscious for a week. It was easier for the thralls to bathe you and redress your wounds if you remained naked. Don't worry, we kept your dignity, only women have been tending to you, and the moment they finished, you were covered by the sheet."

I flinched and cried out – one of my calves sizzled. I glanced down and found a pale woman with long curly chestnut hair dabbing the cuts on my leg, her lips pursed and big brown eyes trained on my wounds. At her feet was a pile of bloodied rags and beside her was a low table. A bowl of steaming water, a neat pile of linen strips and jars of medicines and salves were on the table.

The man chuckled before speaking to his thrall in Greek as he handed her his cup. I listened to her footsteps plod softly on the wooden floor as she left the room, my eyes locked on the stranger.

"You don't recognise me at all, do you?" There was a hint of humour in his voice.

"You purchased me." I croaked.

"Yes – but not *quite* what I meant. I suppose it's to be expected, it's been many years after all." He chuckled softly. "I recognised you the moment I saw you. It was quite the shock – I never thought I'd see you again, let alone *here*!"

I let his words hang in the air. Despite his cheery disposition, the man unnerved me – and not just because he was the one who purchased me from the slaver. It didn't matter that he'd kept me well while I was unconscious, I didn't trust him.

The thrall returned, gave the man the cup and sat down again on the stool beside me. I listened to her open one of her jars before smearing a pungent salve over my wound. I flinched at the biting sting of the concoction and jerked my leg away from her.

I was too vulnerable, lying prone of the bed before the stranger. Despite the agony screaming from every inch of me, I forced myself into a sitting position, watching him.

ASHES REMAIN

The thrall said something to him, but he held up his hand and shook his head. She had a linen strip in her hand – I guessed she wanted to wrap my leg, but I wanted answers before I'd let her continue.

"Who are you?" I spat, beads of sweat dribbling down the side of my face as I pulled the sheet over my breasts.

"Let me get closer so you can see me better."

Without waiting for permission, he moved to sit beside me, so close his knee brushed against mine. The man's eyes, black as coal, twinkled with amusement as I tilted my legs away from him.

Curiosity overwhelmed me. He seemed so sure I knew him … I examined his face, searching my memories for any hint of who he might be. The voice … It was familiar, but was that because I heard him speaking to the slaver?

"I don't know you." I stated finally.

"You do! Look closer." He pressed.

His olive flesh was bright and smooth, his ebony hair was oiled with something sweet smelling and fell in soft waves just below his earlobes. His mustachio and beard were thick, luscious and neatly trimmed.

"Maybe this might help you remember." The man said, holding his hand out to me.

I stared at it, surprised by the lack of calluses. I was so used to the rough palms and fingers of all the men in my life, earned by farming, seafaring, hunting and fighting. Though his hands were soft, his skin was marred by silvery scars and there was a large crescent shape that spanned over his palm …

My heart pounded in my ears. I gawped at him, goosebumps springing up over my flesh. He was right – I did know him!

"Kainan?" I whispered.

That crescent shaped scar was made by one of my old sheep, Audrey. She had been an ornery thing with a habit of biting. I'd warned Kainan of her temper, but he didn't pay attention one day when we were seeing to my flock. He was careless and she took her chance to sink every one of her uneven incisors into his hand.

"The one and only." He grinned.

After all these years – *Kainan*?! Last I saw him was the summer of 872, twenty-two years ago. By the gods, so much had changed!

Yes – I saw it now. Examining his face, I remembered the Kainan from years ago. I recognised his high cheekbones and sharp jaw, but now he was broad and strong, a far cry from the scrawny thrall I had once known. Back then, Kainan's hands were rough and worn from labouring in the fields. Now they were as smooth and silken as a king's, the faint scars faded reminders of his past life.

"Drink some of this, it will calm your nerves." Kainan offered me his cup of wine.

I'm sure I'd turned pale with shock. I took the cup with both hands and brought it to my lips, sipping the dry red, my eyes locked on him.

"What are you doing here?" I asked hoarsely.

"I live here." Kainan explained, extracting the cup from my grasp. "This city was my home before the Varangian's took me to the Danish lands. Don't you remember?"

"The Danes call Constantinople *Miklagarðr* or some such nonsense ..." I breathed, quoting him from a long-forgotten memory.

"That's right." Kainan beamed. "After you and me – er, *went our separate ways* – Vidar sold me to a Danish merchant."

There was something about the way Kainan said Vidar's name – a harshness in his pronunciation, a bitterness. It made my stomach twist into knots and the hair on the back of my neck stand on end.

"I travelled the world at my new owner's side until he came to Constantinople." Kainan continued. "Unfortunately, he was killed after trying to cheat a customer – a Varangian, of course. I managed to escape and settled here as a freeman.

"I had nothing, no home, no family, no money. I stole what I could before the Varangian could stop me and I sold it. With the coin I made, I purchased other goods and profited from them. So on and so forth, I quickly began my own business – and what a lucrative endeavour that was!

"It took a few years and a lot of hard work, but I managed to become quite an affluent merchant. I own a small fleet of ships and employ many hirelings to travel the world to sell my wares and bring back goods for me to sell here.

"I apologise – I'm boasting. Enough about me, what about you, Aveline? How has life treated you?"

ASHES REMAIN

How was life treating me? I was just sold as a thrall!

"W-well enough, until I came to Constantinople, that is." I replied, touching the collar around my neck.

"Ah, yes, *that*. If you'd like, we can speak more of this over some food and wine?" Kainan suggested.

I nodded hesitantly. Kainan stood up and said something to the woman, to which she nodded.

"Let my thrall tend to your wounds. I'll be back in a while with food and wine." Kainan said as he crossed the room. "The lashes on your back need particular attention."

"K-Kainan – the collar!" I called out, wincing as I turned to him.

Unfortunately, he hadn't heard me. He left the room and shut the door behind himself. I slumped in the bed and rubbed my face in my hands, the collar so damn heavy.

After a few moments, the thrall rose stood over me silently. I peeked over my shoulder, uneasy beneath her gaze. We caught each other's eyes, she patted the bed and I complied, lying on my belly again. Without a word, the thrall bandaged my leg, picked up a clean damp rag and dabbed the wounds on my back.

***

SOMETIMES ERRORS AND coincidences cross each other in a mysterious pattern that suddenly resembles a plan. Perhaps the Nornir wove this fate for me so I might finally close the door on my past for good. I wouldn't be long for this world if that was the case, I knew that much. What could I learn here? What wisdom could I gleam from associating with figures from my past?

So far, I learned Thóra could still not be trusted – I'd set my mind to kill the bitch for what she'd done, but what could I learn from Kainan?

Many years ago, when I was a naïve fifteen-year-old girl living in Roskilde, I met Kainan. He was my first love, but I turned my back on him – I chose Vidar over him, a decision I didn't regret and never would in a thousand lifetimes. But Vidar was gone and here I was with Kainan after so many years …

The affection I'd felt for Kainan had long since disappeared. My heart didn't race at the sight of him, it didn't strain with yearning for him ... I remembered once feeling comfortable in his presence and now it was quite the opposite. Being here with him, away from the slavers' platform, my stomach twisted into knots. I was awkward and uneasy in his presence. I couldn't think of a word to say to him, except to thank him for saving me from the slavers.

Those months with him when I was a young woman, when Kainan and I were lovers ... They were all just memories. The decades of time between then and now had dissolved the emotions tied to them. Now he was just a man to whom I was grateful, but I would feel the same towards anyone who rescued me from the slavers. This hero just had a familiar face, that was all.

There had to be a reason I was here – despite my resentment towards them, the Nornir had woven a purpose here for me. Glory? Wisdom? Reconciliation? If I focussed, I would see the threads and follow them to the reason, to the lesson I was meant to learn. If Kainan was to be my teacher, my guide, then so be it.

But ...

What if I wasn't here to learn from Kainan, but the other way around? What if I was a tool to aid Kainan in some mysterious purpose related to his life's tapestry? Obviously, our threads had crossed, we were both meant to be here, in the same building, under the same Mediterranean sky, but for what reason?

Kainan and I had been lovers, now we were strangers. We had met each other in Denmark, a country foreign to both of us. Now we were in his lands, the city he grew up in, the city he was stolen from. He was sold to and suffered at the hands of both Varangians and Danes. Now I was a Dane ... A Dane who had hurt him, who had broken his heart.

Perhaps the Nornir were offering me to him to heal him of his hatred? No. Could I really be naïve enough to think I could heal him of *that*? When I couldn't even convince my own brother to open his heart to me and my Danish children ...

There was something else – something Jan said that nagged at me when I glanced at the thrall tending to my wounds. She looked just like me – the same hair, same heart-shaped face, same pale skin ... Her eyes were darker than mine though. Jan said the slave trader he met owned slaves that looked like me. Was Kainan the man who rattled Jan?

ASHES REMAIN

"Aveline?"

Kainan reappeared, a smile spread across his face, snapping me from my thoughts. I had no proof that Kainan was a slave trader, and I found it hard to believe Jan would be intimidated by him.

"You look nice. White suits you." Kainan commented as he handed me a cup of wine.

It had been a few hours. The thrall had cleaned my wounds and bandaged me up and dressed me in a simple dress. I wanted to wear my own clothes but had no way of communicating that to the thrall who spoke only Greek it seemed.

I accepted the wine politely and brought it to my lips. A gorgeous bouquet of sweetness emanated from the cup. With the first drop that hit my tongue, I could taste every aspect of summer. It was the most exquisite drink I'd ever tasted, and I told Kainan so. I guzzled it down, thirsty beyond measure.

"I'm pleased you like it." Kainan beamed. "I'm pleased you're here, too. Never in my wildest dreams did I think I'd see you again, Aveline. I've thought about you constantly over the years – wondering how your life has been."

"You flatter me." I smiled uncomfortably for I couldn't reciprocate his feelings.

"It fills my heart to see you here now, in my home, away from the damned Danes ... To think, I was a thrall when we met, now I'm a master. I worked all hours of the day, breaking my back for Alvar and his damned family – now I'm lounging on expensive furniture, ordering my own thralls around." He paused to chuckle. "Years ago, you and I were sneaking around together, now we're sitting together openly, sharing wine of all things!"

Another heavy pang struck my heart at the bitterness in his voice when he spoke of Alvar, Freydis and my beloved Vidar. I rolled my dry lips together and tried not to glare at him. He had saved my life, but I didn't know how many more times I could listen to him speak harshly about Vidar and his parents.

"It's strange how things change over the years." I said carefully.

"Do you like the wine? I have casks of it in the cellar. To think, twenty years ago I couldn't imagine I'd be able to say that!"

"I'm happy life has turned out well for you, Kainan."

"And you? Are you happy with your life?"

"I'm happier now I'm not with the slavers." I said pointedly. "I will never be able to thank you enough for saving me."

"I couldn't let you stay there, Aveline." Kainan said, taking my free hand in his and squeezing it briefly. "I would've spent every coin of mine to buy you from them."

"*Þakka fyrir*," I smiled. "I regret I must ask you to do another thing for me even though you've already done so much."

"I'll do anything for you." Kainan said. "Tell me what you want. Silk gowns? A horse? Jewels? Name it and you'll have it. I'm only glad to have you here – if it hadn't been for your friend Thóra, I never would have this chance."

"*What?*"

I was going to ask him to remove my collar and get me passage on a ship headed to the Danish lands, but I stopped in my tracks at the mentioning of Thóra, I froze.

"Thóra – your friend, *já?*" Kainan continued ignoring or not noticing my shock, I couldn't tell which. "I thought I saw you in the marketplace a few weeks ago – you hit me with an apple. I wasn't sure it was you so I approached your friend at the inn."

My jaw dropped. Kainan spoke so calmly, but he held my hand tightly, ignoring my attempts to pull it from his grip.

"I asked if she knew you and she said she did. She did not speak highly of you at all – she claimed you were having an affair with her husband and trying to steal him from her, among other things. I asked what your name was and she told me – *Aveline Birgersdóttir*. 'Daughter of Birger Bloody Sword – from Roskilde?' I asked. She nodded, surprised I knew you – of course, I was equally shocked you were in Constantinople! – But I digress.

"I told her it was her lucky day and offered her a deal. 'You'll remove that thorn from my side?' She said." Kainan chuckled. "I agreed and together we developed a plan."

My body trembled and my stomach churned at his words.

"What did you do, Kainan?" I whispered.

"We planned that you would fall from your ship with a helping push from Thóra. Slave traders would fish you out of the water. I arranged the whole debacle at the slave platform, my purchasing you, everything. I wasn't prepared for you to be so fiery! You're much braver than you used to be."

ASHES REMAIN

Finally, Kainan released my hand. I pulled it away so abruptly, I spilt wine over my lap. Kainan tutted, amusement alight in his eyes.

"It's alright, I have other clothes for you." Kainan said.

"Why would you do this? This makes no sense! Why would you make the scene at the trading platform? Why, Kainan, *why*?"

"I wouldn't have proof I'd purchased you fairly otherwise." He said, nodding at the collar around my neck. "You're mine now."

I threw the cup to the ground and lunged out of the room, slamming the door shut behind me. My body trembled, every muscle screamed in agony. I spotted a set of stairs and stumbled down them, glancing in every doorway I passed for an exit.

The damn house was like a labyrinth! Every door I opened led to another damned room, another dead end. I heard Kainan shouting to his thralls in Greek. I burst through another door, hoping beyond hope that it led to the city streets. Damn it, it was the kitchen! At the back of the room, however, was an open door, a paved street visible beyond it. I ran towards it, my heart racing.

"Urgh!" I cried out, tumbling to the floor.

A thrall was beneath me – I'd run straight into her. In one of her hands was a thick bundle of fresh herbs cut from a plant – in her other hand was a knife. I wrestled it from her grip with ease, scrambled to my feet and took a step towards the door–

Kainan shut it. He stood in front of it, blocking it.

I held the knife in front of me, pointing it directly at Kainan.

"Let me go." I growled, emphasising each word.

"You're not Jarl anymore," Kainan's voice was still unnervingly warm. "*I own you*, you do as *I* say. Now, put the knife down."

How did he know I was a jarl? Had Thóra told him?

It didn't matter, I needed to find another exit – fast.

The thrall got to her feet and shut the door I'd entered through. She stood in front of it, quaking. Could I shove her aside? I could jump out the bedroom window, but would I survive the fall?

I couldn't push past Kainan, my body was so weak he could overpower me easily. There was another door to the right of me – I'd have to be fast to get through it before Kainan could catch me.

I lunged at the door to the right, ripping it open to reveal a flight of stairs leading downwards. Kainan laughed as he strolled after me. With no other way, I ran down the stairs. Perhaps I could find a hiding place and sneak past him ...

It was an earthen cellar. Shrouded in darkness, I hastily felt my way around the room. There were casks and heavy baskets filled with vegetables I guessed from the pungent scent of dirt drifting from them. I tried to slip behind the containers, but they were lined too close together, too heavy to move.

Damn it all, I couldn't see a thing! I was a rabbit in a trap.

The stairs creaked as Kainan stepped down them. The glow of orange light filled the room. I whipped around – he was leaning against the wall, blocking the stairway, an oil lamp in his hand.

"Kainan, let me go!" I demanded, pointing the knife at him.

"Again, with the orders." Kainan rolled his eyes. "In a situation like this you ought to *beg* for me to spare you, not *threaten* me."

Kainan placed the oil lamp on a hook hanging from the wall and moved towards me. He was unarmed, I had a blade. He wasn't much taller than me. I was weak, but I had fought in worse conditions, I had a chance to win – I hoped.

By his third step closer, I lunged at him.

I slashed at Kainan with the knife, but he dodged! I dove at him again – he sidestepped far enough from the stairs that I had a chance to flee. I ran up them, my feet pounding on the wooden steps, but Kainan was close behind.

"Argh!" I cried out as I slammed down onto the stairs.

Something hard had struck the small of my back, hitting a knot of whip wounds. I thudded down a few steps. Kainan gripped my ankles and dragged me down the rest of the stairs. I tried to turn, slashed at him with the knife, but he twisted my leg, pain like lightning shooting through me. He dragged me across the room.

All of a sudden, Kainan released my ankles and stomped on my arm. Yowling, I dropped the knife. Clutching my arm, I glanced around looking for it – it was too late, Kainan had snatched it up.

The moment I staggered to my feet, Kainan booted me in the stomach. White light flashed in front of my eyes, my legs buckled, I collapsed to my knees.

Kainan kicked me again–

I fell to the ground, writhing in agony, all breath knocked out of me, my aching body jerking with every kick. Curled up on the floor whimpering, I vomited, gasping for breath. Pain blazed like fire in my stomach, constant, searing.

Kainan stood over me, grabbed a fistful of my hair and jerked my head upwards. From my tear-filled eyes, I watched my long chestnut curls fall to the ground as Kainan hacked them off with.

"Stop, Kainan! Stop!" I howled.

"You call me 'master' now!" He snarled. "I *own* you, Danethrall!"

Kainan flipped me onto my back. With no energy left to fight, I wept as he ripped the white dress from my body. Finally, he staggered back, glaring at me. I watched him cross the room and pick up an apple. He paused at the foot of the stairs, staring at me, not even a hint of anger visible on his face.

"How ironic – it was an apple striking my back that made me notice you here. It was an apple striking your back that made you stay …" Kainan chuckled softly. "You're a lot fiercer than you used to be … I will change that. Goodnight, Danethrall."

He stomped up the stairs, taking the lamp with him. I heard the cellar door shut and all light disappeared. A key turned in a lock.

I was trapped.

I felt around the floor, furiously gathering my hacked-off tresses, clutching them against my naked chest. I buried my face in my armful of hair and wept, anger pouring from me.

I wasn't here to help Kainan heal. No … Whatever the reason was, whatever the plan, this tapestry laid out for me, I couldn't see it. Perhaps I was simply here to suffer for the amusement of the gods? Just a short while ago I was a jarl, now I was Kainan's thrall. Kainan had taken my clothes, my jewellery, my hair. All that was left on my body was the iron slave collar around my neck.

With help from Thóra, Kainan had taken everything from me, but I would take everything back – and I would take their lives.

***

I DIDN'T REMEMBER falling asleep, but I woke to someone shoving me roughly. Immediately, I crawled away from the figure, hiding my body behind the chopped off lengths of my hair.

"Get up, Danethrall." Kainan commanded. "Come upstairs."

I glared at him, but forced myself to my feet, dropping my tresses to the floor. My muscles were tight and sore, pulsing with pain like lightning was woven beneath my skin. I couldn't stand straight, my stomach swollen from Kainan's brutal kicks, but I did as I was told, wincing with every step.

Kainan was a fool to think just one beating would have me obeying him. I would let him think that if it got me closer to freedom. I knew which door led to the street.

The pungent scent of smoke met my nostrils, a fire was burning in the kitchen, odd considering how warm it was. Just climbing the stairs, the air grew thicker and hotter. In the kitchen, two male thralls were guarding the doors, while two others were standing silently either side of the cellar door. Kainan waited at the top of the stairs, smiling. I stepped into the room and the two nearest thralls slipped down the stairs.

"I have new clothes for you." Kainan said, offering me a neatly folded rough, flaxen cloth. "Put it on."

My lip curled in disgust. The cloth was tattered old material sewn into a pitiful excuse of a dress. I'd met many thralls dressed better than this. Impatient, Kainan snatched the dress from my hands and shoved it over my head, forcing my arms through the holes.

"You should thank me for my kindness." Kainan said, anger smouldering in his words.

"Thank you, Kainan." I spat.

Kainan struck me. I clapped my hand to my face, holding my throbbing cheek.

"Thank you, *who*? What do you call me now, Danethrall?"

I wanted nothing more than to tear him apart.

"I won't ask again." He warned.

Before I could do anything, Kainan slammed me facedown onto the tabletop, pressing his elbow into my spine, pinning me down.

"Thank you, *who*?"

"I'll kill you!" I hissed, blood streaming from my nose.

"And I *will* break you, Danethrall." Kainan growled.

He yelled something to his thralls who lunged at me, grabbing my wrists and ankles, spreading my arms and legs wide. I shrieked and writhed beneath Kainan as the thralls tied my limbs to the table legs with cords.

ASHES REMAIN

Secured to the table, Kainan got off me, lifting the skirt of the slave dress up over my thighs. He crossed the room and grabbed a wooden spoon from one of the pots, returning to me with a smile on his face. He grabbed a tuft of my ruined hair and jerked my head up.

"Bite down on this." Kainan said, shoving the handle of the spoon horizontally in my mouth. "This is going to hurt – terribly."

I flailed on the tabletop, trying hard to pull my arms and legs free, but the more I pulled, the tighter the cords squeezed around my wrists and ankles. From the fireplace I heard the scrape of metal on stone.

Hot pain erupted high on my right calf. My skin hissed as it melted beneath the searing metal, the sickening stench filling the air. The spoon fell from my mouth as I screeched.

He was burning me!

I thrashed and wailed. Never had I felt an agony such as this!

"It's an old tradition, branding slaves." Kainan said, his voice terrifyingly calm. "If you flee, your collar will show you're a slave, and the brand will say who you belong to. You're mine, Danethrall. This brand proves it."

***

KAINAN LEFT ME tied to the table, drifting in and out of consciousness, as his thralls carried containers out of the cellar. My body couldn't take much more – I was too weak, too broken. Frissons of pain surged through my body from my branded calf.

At some point, a thrall slipped into the room and sat behind me. I listened to her setting things down on the table and opening pots, tearing fabric. Without warning, she dabbed at the burn with a cold wet rag – I shrieked at her touch.

"The cleaner the brand heals, the clearer it will be." Kainan said, stroking my scruffy hair as the thrall wound a linen bandage around my calf. "I missed you so much and now here you are, my initials burned into your flesh for the rest of your life ..."

Once the cellar was empty, Kainan unbound me and shoved me down the stairs. The room was empty, not even my hair remained on the dirt floor. The stairs creaked as Kainan climbed up them, the door closing with a thud behind him.

I collapsed in the middle of the room

The rasp of the key turning in the lock echoed in my ears.

I pounded on the floor with my fists and screamed.

ASHES REMAIN
CHAPTER THIRTY-FOUR

FOR FIFTEEN DAYS I was locked in the cellar – or so I guessed. Fifteen times Kainan strode down the stairs, cheerily exclaiming, "Good morning, Danethrall!". Fifteen times he left, shutting me in total darkness with no bed, no blankets and no hope.

Once a day, Kainan brought me a chunk of bread and cheese, and a skin of water. If I didn't leave the empty skin on the bottom step of the stairs for him to collect in the morning, he wouldn't refill it and I'd go without water for a day.

Exhausted and weak from my wounds, I spent most of my time lying on the dirt floor – sometimes I fell asleep, other times I stared listlessly into the darkness. The moment the door opened, I sat up and watched Kainan stride down the stairs with his thrall scurrying behind him carrying a bucket of water and a change of bandages.

The thrall cleaned my wounds, applied medicine and redressed them – Kainan said I was healing well. If I didn't eat my food by the time she finished, Kainan took it from me. I wouldn't eat again until he came down the next morning. Every few days, the thrall would clear the corner I was defecating in, offering me precious extra time to eat the coarse bread and dry cheese.

On the fourteenth day, my wounds were healed enough to remove the bandages. My bruises were fading, the brand and the lash wounds had no sign of infection. I could stumble about the dark cellar for a few days by the time the bandages were removed.

On the fifteenth day, Kainan came down alone. I missed the thrall immediately even though she never uttered a word to me. I was afraid to be alone with Kainan.

"Good morning, Danethrall. Shall we play a game?"

I didn't answer. Kainan hung the oil lamp on the hook by the stairs, bathing the room in orange light. He tossed the water skin at me, his coal-black eyes glinting.

"Come get your food." He said, showing the bowl to me.

Inside was the usual bread and cheese, but today he included two boiled eggs and a handful of berries. My belly growled loudly at the sight of the food, even Kainan heard it, chuckling at the noise. Slowly I rose to my feet, eager for the meagre meal.

"Not like that." Kainan said, holding up a hand, a smile slithering across his face. "Crawl on your hands and knees."

"*Nei*, I am *not* an animal." I spat through gritted teeth.

"You'll do as I say, Danethrall. Get on your hands and knees."

I refused to degrade myself for his amusement. Kainan tutted, shaking his head side to side. He took the empty skin from the bottom step, turned his back on me and left. I didn't eat that day.

***

THE SIXTEENTH DAY arrived. Kainan returned.

"Good morning, Danethrall!" He said. "Are you hungry?"

My stomach ached all through the day and night. I could smell the boiled eggs and dry cheese before I could see them. I eyed the bowl ravenously as Kainan hung the oil lamp of the hook. Today he kept the skin of water tucked under his arm.

"Let's try this again, shall we?" Kainan said. "If you want your meal you will get on your hands and knees and crawl to me."

"*Nei*." I spat.

"So be it." He shrugged.

Kainan turned, took the oil lamp from the hook and left.

I had no food or water that day.

***

I BARELY SURVIVED a third day without food and water. My body weakened significantly, as did my will to fight. My stomach ached constantly, my lips were dry and flaking, I couldn't sleep, my temperature fluctuated drastically from hour to hour. My mouth was dry, my eyes hurt and my head throbbed relentlessly.

On the eighteenth day of my captivity and my fourth day without food and water, Kainan strode down the stairs, his usual cheery-toned greeting grating on my ears.

ASHES REMAIN

I watched him hang the oil lamp on the hook from where I laid on the floor on the far side of the room. Kainan grinned while he presented my meal to me, two boiled eggs, a handful of berries, a chunk of bread and cheese and a thick slice of meat. My belly rumbled so painfully, I doubled over.

"You're doing this to yourself, Danethrall." Kainan said – was that *disappointment* I could hear in his tone?! "All you have to do is get on your hands and knees and you will have your food and drink. Get over your pride and crawl to me."

I was desperately hungry and thirsty. At this point I didn't know if my hands and knees could support my body. Slowly I rolled onto my front and dragged my knees beneath me. Kainan cheered patronisingly as I crawled to him. My heart hammered in my chest, my joints popped and cracked as I forced myself towards him. My pride ached just as much as my body.

"Well done, Danethrall!" Kainan applauded. "Only a little further to go – come on!"

My hands curled into fists. I wanted to beat him, wanted to wrap my hands around his throat and strangle the life out of him, but I couldn't. My strength had depleted over my time locked in the cellar – the three days without food and water wrecked me worse than the whip, beatings and brand put together.

I stopped at Kainan's feet.

"I'm proud of you, Danethrall." Kainan said and proceeded to tip my food onto the floor.

My heart fell to the bottom of my chest. The food toppled to the ground, rolling across the dirt floor. I gaped up at him, tears spilling down my cheeks. Grinning from ear to ear, Kainan dropped the skin of water to the ground beside me.

"You better eat up, Danethrall. If you leave any crumbs, rats might take them."

I reached out a trembling hand and grabbed the bread. I brushed off some of the dirt and took a bite, but my mouth was so dry, I couldn't chew properly. I chomped laboriously and swallowed hard before turning to the boiled egg. It was filthy. No matter how I tried, I couldn't wipe all the dirt away and I couldn't waste my precious, limited supply of water to rinse it.

"I'm leaving soon so hurry up and eat while you have the light."

I glared at Kainan as I shoved the egg in my mouth, my teeth grating on the dirt and my stomach rumbled fiercely. I swallowed, grabbed the other filthy egg and didn't bother trying to clean it. I shoved it into my mouth, maintaining my furious stare with Kainan. His amusement dissolved as I rammed each filthy foodstuff into my mouth, conveying no shame or disgust as I did so. He grabbed the oil lamp and returned upstairs.

I scarpered across the room and searched for the skin. I gulped down the cool water, careful not to spill a drop. My stomach turned. I had eaten and drank too fast. I breathed slowly, trying to keep my meal and water down. I was far from satiated, but I couldn't vomit up the only meal I'd had in days. I sipped my water over the rest of the day and throughout the night.

The next day, Kainan entered the cellar. He hung the lamp, dropped the full skin of water onto the floor and tipped my meal onto the ground.

"Crawl." He said – no morning greeting, just that one word.

"*Nei.*"

I didn't crawl. I stepped towards him, picked up a handful of the dirty berries and shoved them into my mouth, scowling at him as I chewed. At first, Kainan chuckled, biting the nail of his thumb as he watched me defy him.

Whack!

Kainan cracked me across the face with his hand. Surprised by his strike, I staggered backwards. He didn't give me a chance to take a breath before he struck me again – I toppled to my hands and knees. Kainan grabbed a fistful of my hair with one hand and a handful of dirty food with his other.

"Don't disobey me!" He hissed, ramming food into my mouth.

I choked on the food, swallowing it between coughs and gasping breaths. Kainan stuffed the food into my mouth until there was nothing left, but the chunk of bread on the floor. He released me, pushing my head down into the ground as he stood up.

"I won't be nice anymore, Danethrall."

***

"CRAWL." KAINAN ORDERED.

ASHES REMAIN

He hung the oil lamp, dropped the skin and tipped the food onto the floor. I didn't move a muscle. Tucked in Kainan's belt was a whip. My eyes flickered between the whip and Kainan's face. He saw me staring and grinned. Slowly he pulled the whip from his waist and unravelled it, dragging the leather knots of the long skinny lashes along the dirt.

I couldn't move.

"Crawl!" Kainan roared, cracking the whip against the floor, clumps of dirt soaring from where it had struck.

I flinched, terrified by the snap of the leather lashes. At the very sight of Kainan's whip, the scars on my back throbbed. Kainan raised it again and I dropped to the floor.

"That's it, Danethrall," Kainan jeered. "Now crawl. I'll lash you for every time you make me repeat myself."

I crawled across the floor, my body trembling.

"Excellent," Kainan said. "Crawl to the other side of the room."

My breath held in my chest, I did as he commanded.

"Well done! Now come back to me."

I returned to him, my palms and knees hurting from the hard floor. Kainan made me crawl across the room three more times before he let me eat the food off the ground.

"I didn't realise how easily you'd obey if I have this in my hand." Kainan dangled the knotted thongs of the whip over my face. "Now, let's try something else ... Eat without your hands."

I gazed at Kainan pleadingly, but he only grinned in reply. I turned to the food and ate like a dog, burning with shame. All the while, Kainan drew the thongs of the whip over my body, silently reminding me that if I disobeyed, punishment would be swift.

Kainan watched me eat every bite, he even pointed to a berry that rolled away and made me crawl to it and eat it. The food finished, I sat on my knees and wiped the dirt from my face with the back of my hand, staring at Kainan's whip.

"Tell me about your life, Danethrall." Kainan said. "What happened after I left? When did you marry the Jarl's son?"

"Many years after you went." I croaked.

"Ah, yes – you were married before him. I was still in the Danish lands when Erhardt Ketilsson attacked Roskilde. Rumour has it Erhardt married Vidar's betrothed – I assumed that was you?"

I nodded slowly.

"I was surprised Erhardt didn't kill Vidar – I heard he married Vidar to his daughter instead. Is that correct?"

I nodded again, fury boiling in the pit of my stomach every time Kainan said Vidar's name. Kainan circled me slowly, dragging the whip over my body.

"How stupid. Erhardt was asking for trouble by keeping Vidar alive."

"Vidar killed Erhardt." My words were shaking with rage.

"Erhardt deserved to be killed for letting Vidar live." Kainan replied darkly. "But what about Vidar – he's been dead for some time now, hasn't he?"

I didn't answer. Kainan prodded me in the shoulder with the hilt of the whip.

"When I ask you a question you must answer, Danethrall. How long has Vidar been dead?"

"Seven years." I murmured.

"Your friend Thóra said you were trying to steal her husband. What did she mean by that?"

"She lies. She doesn't have a husband."

"I'm more inclined to believe her than you, Danethrall." Kainan said. "When I first met you, I adored your innocence – I never thought you'd lure a husband from his wife. But you played me, you seduced Vidar and me simultaneously. You were never truly innocent – that was just an image you created for yourself. You're a liar and a whore."

"I am not!" I growled.

The whipped cracked through the air, colliding with my flesh and snapping my skin through the flax fabric. A wrenching scream ripped from my throat and my body shuddered violently.

"Do not speak back to me, Danethrall!" Kainan bellowed.

The silence that ensued was so tense, I could almost hear the blood trickle down my back. I didn't dare breathe until Kainan calmed, afraid if I moved he'd whip me again.

"You *are* a whore." Kainan's voice was low and deep. "You whored yourself to Vidar when you were *my* lover. You whored yourself to Vidar *before* you married him, and you whored yourself to Vidar *while* you were married to Erhardt Ketilsson.

ASHES REMAIN

"I've monitored you since I left, Danethrall. I made sure to find out what was happening in Roskilde no matter how far away I was. The merchants bring gossip and rumour to the marketplaces along with their wares. I know of Erhardt's attack on Roskilde, your first marriage, Vidar's revenge.

"My previous owner and his heathen friends praised Vidar for getting you with child *twice* while you were married to Erhardt, for having Erhardt raise those boys without realising they weren't his. Danes are foolish people, praising daring and trickery. They praised the jarl's son for his shameful deeds, but the bastards didn't condemn the whore who carried and birthed those children."

The knotted thongs dragged in the dirt, I didn't know if Kainan was tormenting me or if he was going to strike me again. I stayed still, bracing myself for another hit.

"I missed you, Aveline." Kainan murmured. "Word of your life disappointed me – the woman you've become disappoints me. I thought you were better than the Danes, but I was wrong."

With that, Kainan left me bleeding in the darkness alone.

***

FOURTEEN MORE DAYS went by. On each of those days, Kainan stomped down the stairs with the whip tucked behind his belt, hung the oil lamp on the hook, tipped my food on the ground and ordered me to crawl. If I didn't drop to my hands and knees the moment he told me to, he whipped me. But for that one word, 'crawl', he didn't speak to me at all.

It took three days of whipping, my back flayed bloody, before I gave up. I was grudgingly grateful for small blessings – after those three days, Kainan beat me with fists or kicks instead. His fists hurt, but they hurt a lot less than the whip. Kainan dragged the knotted thongs over my body as I ate. The whip was a threat – if he consider it warranted, Kainan could and *would* lash me.

I came to crave conversation, I yearned for Kainan to bark orders at me, but he didn't. Every few days, the female thrall came down to the cellar to clear my excrement after Kainan left for he couldn't stand the stench. I tried to speak with her, begged her to just tell me her name, but she wouldn't even look me in the eye. I didn't know if she could understand me – I tried speaking to her in Norse, Latin, Frankish and Ænglisc, but she didn't so much as lift her head. They predominantly spoke Greek here and I didn't know a single word.

I hadn't heard anything but my own voice in fourteen days …

I'd lost a lot of weight and my muscles deteriorated immensely. My bones protruded grotesquely from my flesh and my stomach bloated after every meal. I became accustomed to the dark, my eyes hurting from the glow of the oil lamp whenever Kainan or the thrall came down the stairs.

Worst yet, I lost my shame, shitting and pissing in the corner of the room and eating the filthy food Kainan dropped on the dirt floor like an animal without any embarrassment.

I became so shameless that one day Kainan stomped down the stairs and immediately I crawled to him on my hands and knees, not waiting for him to drop the food or order me to crawl.

Rather than praise me for my intuitiveness, Kainan beat me until I lost consciousness, condemning me for being presumptive. When I came to, Kainan and the oil lamp were gone. I groped around the floor for hours but couldn't find the bowl of food or water skin. I went hungry that night.

Kainan returned the next day, I was still, awaiting his order.

Kainan told me to crawl and I did.

Kainan told me to eat like a dog and I did.

Kainan beat me afterwards anyway.

ASHES REMAIN
CHAPTER THIRTY-FIVE

Late Summer, 893

"GOOD MORNING, DANETHRALL."

Kainan was cheerful. I'd been caged in his cellar for forty days based on the number of his visits. Today Kainan didn't have a water skin or food and he didn't hang the oil lamp on the hook. I stared at him, petrified of the change. He'd never done this before.

"I have a surprise for you." Kainan announced. "I'm sick of your stench – I think it's time you came upstairs and bathed."

My jaw dropped. Dirt and grease caked my skin, my hair was knotted though I'd tried hard to comb the short, wretched strands with my fingers. The very idea of sinking my aching body into a tub of water seemed preposterous and incredible.

"Come to me, Danethrall. It's time to go upstairs."

"C-crawl?" I murmured.

"You may walk." Kainan smirked.

Slowly I walked to him, flinching when he shifted much to his amusement. He let me to walk ahead of him. The muscles in my legs were stiff and sore, twinging with every step, my joints popping and cracking. But for pacing the cellar, I hadn't exercised in the forty days I'd been held captive. Climbing the stairs was a feat in of itself.

Slowly I pushed the door open and flinched at the blinding light pouring in from the kitchen windows. Kainan shoved me forwards, chuckling at my troubles. He took my hand, my other shielding my eyes, and led me through his home.

Kainan pushed me into a room and patiently waited for me to become accustomed to the brightness. It took a long time and even when I was able to open my eyes, they were narrowed. Elegant furniture was situated about the tiled room and in the centre was a large bathtub, steam dancing from the hot waters inside. I squeezed Kainan's hand, nervous, but excited to bathe for the first time in over a month.

Without saying a word, Kainan gently slipped the filthy flax dress over my head and tossed it to the ground. By the gods, how wonderful it was not to wear that itchy, horrid dress!

Kainan led me to the tub by hand, ordering me softly to climb in. Carefully I stepped inside, the hot water scolding my feet, but I didn't care – this was a luxury I'd dreamed of for weeks.

Submerged in the clear, sweet smelling water, it quickly turned foul from the filth pouring off my body, creating a disgusting film on the surface. I scrubbed my arms with my hands, wiping away the dirt and revealing my pale skin beneath. I'd once been as fair as moonlight, but now my skin was as pallid as ash.

All the while, Kainan watched me. He sank to the floor, kneeling beside the tub. He pulled up the embroidered sleeve of his tunic and dipped his hand into the water.

"I've dreamed of laying my eyes on your body." Kainan murmured, trickling the droplets of water over my scarred back. "Twice now I've seen you naked, but I have yet to enjoy you."

I shuddered, goosebumps flooding my flesh.

"I remember kissing you in Birger's farmhouse. I remember touching you ... I'm sad you made me punish you." Kainan sighed, his eyes travelling over my emaciated form. "Your breasts are so small now, your body is so thin ... You're not as pretty as you used to be. You're lucky there's no infection in your back ..."

I flinched as he wiped his wet hand over the tender scabs of my lash wounds. After the three days of whipping, he didn't send his thrall to clean my wounds, instead he left them to fester.

"You forced me to turn you into this, you wretched woman. You shouldn't have fought me ..." Kainan continued. "I want to give you a chance. I want you upstairs with me, but I *must* be able to trust you. You must promise to behave."

I remained silent. He wouldn't believe anything I said anyway.

"I want you to prove yourself to me," Kainan said. "I'll be hosting a party tonight, a small gathering with some of my closest associates. I'd like to show them the famous *female Jarl of Aros*."

I nodded slowly.

"Use your words, Danethrall."

"*Já* m-master."

ASHES REMAIN

"That's better." Kainan beamed. "If you behave, you may stay upstairs. I'll give you a room with a bed and as much food as you want as often as you want, but you *must* do everything I say, when I say it. If you try to flee, you'll be stuck in the cellar indefinitely."

"I won't flee." Those words fell from my lips before I'd even registered them in my mind.

"I know you'll do well," Kainan said warmly. "I can trust you, can't I, Aveline?"

A rush of heat filled my insides. I hadn't heard my birth name in what felt like an eternity. When Kainan said it, I felt like – like a person. Kainan chuckled, running his fingers up my arm. He traced my collarbone and brought his fingers down between my breasts, my bones hard and jutting beneath my paper-thin flesh.

"I want to help you, Aveline. I want to make you beautiful again. We'll clean you, let your hair grow long, dress you in finery, feed you until your breasts and buttocks are plump again. You look like a starved horse, your hipbones protrude so awfully … If you had obeyed me sooner, you wouldn't be in such a state."

"I'm sorry." I mumbled.

"I'm sorry, *what?*"

"I'm sorry, master." I swiftly corrected myself.

"Remember your place, Danethrall, I *own* you."

"*Já*, master. I'm sorry."

"That's better." Kainan said, stroking my hair. "Prove yourself worthy of my trust tonight and I will mend you."

"*Þakka fyrir*, master."

Kainan scrubbed my body and washed my hair with sweet-scented soap, admiring the cleanliness of my body when I climbed out of the tub. He wrapped me in a sheet and led me upstairs to a large room called the *gynaikonitis*, meaning 'women's quarters', he explained. It was the room I'd woken up in after he'd bought me.

This was where I would live now. Inside was the bed, settee and table as before, but now there was a warp-weighted loom, a spinning wheel and a chest filled with clean clothes. There was a fantastically colourful long-sleeved linen dress ornamented with pearls, long enough to brush the ground, and a patterned belt for my waist. There was also a bright silk *stola*, a long billowing rectangular fabric to wrap around my body.

"Thankfully you have enough layers on to hide your body. You won't embarrass me this way." Kainan said happily.

Though he dressed me in finery, Kainan wouldn't remove my collar. He had a thrall with big brown eyes fix my hair. Though it was still short and ragged, she combed out the knots and oiled my curls into some semblance of neatness. Once she finished, Kainan and the thrall left, locking the door behind themselves.

Never had I worn something as obscenely extravagant as this – such rich designs and expensive material. I thought of the beautiful fabric Herra gifted me … I didn't know what to think – should I be thankful to Kainan for these clothes? No! He was a monster. It didn't matter how much finery he gave me, he was still a monster.

I curled up on the settee, drew my silk *stola* around me like a blanket, and gazed out the window at the sunbathed scenery below. Thoughts of escaping drifted through my mind, punishments if I failed quickly following.

I didn't want to go back to the cellar. Upstairs, light and fresh air poured in through the arching windows, upstairs I could listen to the warble of birdsong. Upstairs, it was warm and comfortable. Upstairs I felt like a human. Upstairs, Kainan was kind …

A little while passed and Kainan and the thrall returned with trays of food, meat and fish, bread and cakes, cheese, all kinds of fruit, and a jug of wine. I gorged myself until I could eat and drink no more, drooping on the settee in a daze, my stomach distended from my gluttony. Kainan laughed and carried me to the bed, he pulled the blanket over me and I quickly fell asleep.

***

"GET UP. IT'S time for the party, Aveline." Kainan cooed.

At those words, I awoke instantly, fingers of fear scurrying up my spine. I didn't want to meet Kainan's cohorts. I looked down at my body, the fantastic fabrics draped over my skeletal frame. I felt like a dog in silk. What would Kainan's associates think of me? A short haired animal swathed in finery … I looked ridiculous.

I didn't wait for Kainan to repeat himself, however. I slipped out the bed and waited for the next order, my heart racing. Kainan's thrall fixed my hair, which had been ruffled while I slept. After that, she dabbed a sweet perfume imported from the lands to the East on my neckline, hair, wrists and the back of my knees.

Kainan took my hand and led me downstairs, the sound of cheerful conversation and music growing louder as we weaved through the house. Oil lamps and incense sticks burned, filling the house with a harmonious blend of fantastical scents.

The further into the house Kainan led me, the stronger the scents and the dizzier I became. I held his hand tightly for fear I might collapse. A small part of me missed the cellar – there was comfort in the darkness. There were no bizarre sights or smells, just blackness and the familiar stench of the earthen walls.

Kainan stopped in front of a set of double doors. I flinched at the boom of laughter, a joke I couldn't understand for it was said in Greek. There were men behind those closed doors, strangers.

Maybe the slavers were there?

I shuddered.

"Our guests await us in the *triclinium*. Are you ready, Aveline?"

Kainan didn't wait for an answer. He opened one of the doors and pulled me into the *triclinium*, a large rectangular room with mosaic floors and gorgeous frescoes painted on the walls. One of the walls had tall arched windows gazing upon a courtyard. The wall at the far end was semi-circular, filled with plush settees. Around fifteen men were sprawled across the furniture around a table, drinking freely and groping the thralls serving them.

The five female thralls were clad in sheer billowy dresses, the dark curls between their legs and the shadowed circles of their hardened nipples plain for all to see – obviously for the pleasure and enticement of Kainan's guests.

Their dark curled hair was loose, cut just above their slave collars. The women were beautiful, but obviously slaves. I was dressed elegantly, my body unseen beneath the layers of exotic fabrics. But for my short hair and collar, I didn't look like a slave.

Kainan made some kind of announcement in Greek, holding his hands out and presenting me. The men turned and ogled me, smiling wickedly. My cheeks flushed and I stared at the floor, terrified to meet their eyes. Kainan laughed with his men in their foreign tongue. He grabbed my shoulders, shoving me this way and that, displaying me to the men at all angles.

"This is the female Jarl of Aros, eh?" One of the men asked in Norse.

I stared at him, shocked to hear the Norse tongue spoken in this Mediterranean room. The man was tall, maybe as tall as Jan, slumped back on a settee, his long limbs spread out lazily. He was lithe yet broad, his long blond hair falling from his head like pale silk. His blue eyes twinkled, creased at the corners when he smiled, startlingly bright contrasted with his ruddy, sun-bronzed skin.

"And Jarl of Roskilde, too." Kainan replied in Norse. "She's quite a woman in the Norse lands."

"I've heard of her." He eyed me intently. "What's her name?"

He spoke the Norse tongue fluently, but he wasn't a Dane. There was a heavy accent to his words. He wasn't Norwegian nor was he a Swede. I couldn't place where he was from – maybe he wasn't Norse at all, maybe he just spoke the language well? But I'd never met anyone as tall and fair as him who wasn't Norse …

"Aveline the Danethrall." Kainan replied smugly.

"*Danethrall?*" One of the men remarked, eliciting laughter from them all.

"Danethrall, *Dane* for her adoption by the Danes, *thrall* for her Anglo-Saxon heritage. She was taken from her lands and adopted by the barbarians when she was a child." Kainan explained in Norse for the stranger's benefit, repeating himself in Greek afterwards for the others.

"It's nice to meet you, Danethrall." The man smirked.

"This is Rurik the Varangian," Kainan said to me. "He's a Rus from far in the north, further north than even the Danes."

I nodded, surprised Kainan was friends with a Varangian.

"You may call me Rurik." The Varangian said, to which I nodded. "Quiet one, isn't she?" He remarked to Kainan.

"She knows her place. Fetch us wine, Danethrall." Kainan said, pointing to the terracotta amphorae lined up against the wall across the room.

Trembling, I made my way to them, careful not to trip on my billowing skirts. I filled Kainan and Rurik's cups before carrying the amphora around the room and filling the other men's cups in turn, by Kainan's command. It was difficult pouring the wine with the *stola* hanging in the way, but I managed without spilling any.

ASHES REMAIN

"Get yourself a cup, too." Rurik said when I returned to them. "I must take this opportunity to drink with the Jarl of Aros."

I turned to Kainan for permission and he nodded.

"She's a lovely little thing." Rurik admired. "She'd be better if she wasn't so skinny, you must fatten her up if you hope to sell her for a decent price."

"She's not for sale," Kainan replied quickly.

"Suit yourself." Rurik shrugged. "She'd be better looking if she was plumper whether you intend to sell her or not."

"I'm still breaking her in." Kainan said, patting me on the rear as I walked by him.

I flinched at Kainan's touch and hurried to the other side of the room, my cheeks red hot. I filled a cup to the brim with wine and took a deep draught before returning to Kainan and Rurik.

"I'll work on her appearance once her behaviour is resolved." Kainan said, glaring at me – my cry had displeased him.

"She's difficult, is she?" Rurik smirked.

"Nothing a bit of starving won't fix."

"How long have you had her?"

"About a month now."

"And she's *still* giving you problems?" Rurik snickered. "Don't waste your time starving her. Physical punishment works a lot faster to correct a slave's behaviour. If you avoid the face, beating won't ugly her up too much."

"I practice a balance of physical punishment, starvation and solitary confinement. It takes more time but is far more effective than beatings alone." Kainan said knowledgeably, nausea surging up my throat at how casually they spoke of torturing their thralls. "If you beat them, they fear you, but they still dream of freedom. When you *break* them, that thought never passes through their minds. They are yours completely. You could cut off their hand and they'd thank you."

Rurik and Kainan laughed.

"She's taken a lot longer to break than any other slave I've owned," Kainan admitted. "But then, she is special."

"The Danes didn't make her a jarl for nothing." Rurik agreed. "Only a certain type of man can make it as a jarl, and for a woman to have achieved that she must be *something*."

"Exactly." Kainan nodded. "I like a challenge. She might not look like much now, but once I'm finished with her, she'll be the most obedient thrall one could ever know – she'll be perfect."

"You put a lot more effort into your thralls than I do." Rurik remarked, tossing his wine to the back of his throat.

"I sell them for a lot more money than you do, too."

Their conversation plunged deeper into business. It seemed most of the men here made their living from slave trading, a booming business worldwide, though Kainan seemed to be the wealthiest of his guests considering the vastly more sumptuous clothing he was wearing.

Kainan's guests took turns examining me and asking Kainan questions. They hung on his every word, nodding to whatever he said, agreeing with everything – even without knowing their language, I could recognise they were sucking up to him.

Everything indicated that Kainan must have been the trader Herra and Jan met before we set off back to the Danish lands. He fit Jan's description perfectly. I glanced at the thralls that fawned over Kainan's guests – yes, they were similar to me. Same curls, same faces, but none had my amber eyes.

For the most part, Kainan and his guests didn't speak to me after the initial introduction and examination of me. When they wanted more wine, they shook their cups at me and I filled them quickly. I faded into the backdrop, nothing more than Kainan's shadow, following him silently, nursing a glass of wine that the men made sure I kept topped up.

As the evening went on, my head spun and my body grew weak from drink. Laughing at the state of me, Kainan led me to a seat by the window.

"You're lucky you're here," Kainan hissed, his personality changing in a flash now we were out of earshot of his guests. "If you weren't a slave, you wouldn't be allowed to attend this party, let alone make a fool of yourself with drink!"

"I'm sorry, master." I whispered, staring into my cup.

"Stay here and get a hold of yourself. If any of my guests need something, make sure you attend to them."

"*Já*, master."

ASHES REMAIN

I stayed by the window alone for the rest of the night, thank the gods. Kainan's guests – and Kainan himself – were too preoccupied with the other thralls. Kainan settled onto a settee, a thrall draped over him, delicately feeding him grapes. Kainan grinned and kissed her.

These women were far from scared of the men and their travelling hands. They seemed to know exactly what they were doing – almost as though they enjoyed the men's lustful attention, or at least they knew better than to fight it. They danced about in their sheer gowns, smiling and giggling and twirling seductively.

A guest poured wine into a thrall's mouth. Her head tipped back and mouth wide open, she swallowed it all, giggling as the last drop slipped down her cheek and trickled down her neck. The man proceeded to lick up the red wine trial before engaging in a sloppy, wine-soaked kiss with her.

The thralls were quickly undressed by Kainan's guests, some completely naked, others with just their breasts bared. A few men shamelessly presented their cocks like delicacies to the thralls, and the women received them eagerly, bending between the men's legs or stroking their members wide-eyed with glee.

The party unravelled before my eyes. Discussion turned to debauchery, snacking and drinking became foreplay and dancing turned to lovemaking. I feared the moment I would be stripped and forced to perform on the men, too, but luckily that didn't happen. I stayed in my spot in the corner of the room, silently.

Outside the stars twinkled bright, scattered across the black sky, not a cloud to be seen. The moon was full, a great white disc, beautiful and bright. Drawn to it, I wanted to go outside, to climb a mountain and touch it. The trees, the warm breeze drifting through the windows, the endless sky sparkling over all reaches of Midgard ... By the gods I yearned to be out there. It was suffocating inside this large, airy room.

"Come to me, Aveline the Danethrall." Rurik said, snapping me from my daze. "I want to look at you."

Was I to undress now? I swallowed hard and stepped towards him, staring at the floor. Rurik towered over me. He paced around me and I quaked under his scrutinous gaze. His hands slid over my body, gathered my clothing at my sides to see the outline of my figure. Rurik ran his fingers through my hair, commenting angrily about its pitiful length. He pushed my face up with his finger beneath my chin, forcing me to meet his eyes.

"You're really the famous female Jarl?" Rurik murmured.

I gave him the smallest nod, unsure whether Kainan would punish me for speaking to this man without him beside me.

"How did you find yourself here, Jarl?" Rurik whispered. "Are the gods testing you or have they abandoned you?"

Was – was that concern in his eyes?

I had no answer for him. Rooted to the spot, I trembled before Rurik, my heart hammering in my chest. Rurik tutted sympathetically and tenderly cupped my cheek, his hand warm and rough. My eyelids fluttered closed and a soft sigh slipped through my parted lips. The moment Rurik's calloused fingers stroked my skin, all I could think of was Jan.

"Is she to your liking?" Kainan asked, appearing beside us.

"You ruined her." Rurik said, dropping his hand immediately. "She's too skinny. She does have lovely eyes, though. I've never seen such amber eyes before, not in all my travels."

"As I said before, I'm still breaking her in." Kainan replied. "When she's broken, I'll fatten her up and grow her hair."

"I will give you fifteen *nomismata* for her."

"*Fifteen*? For the female Jarl of Aros and Roskilde? You're trying to steal from me!"

"She's not in Aros or Roskilde anymore, her title means nothing. A skeleton that doesn't talk is all she is and that isn't worth much. Twenty – that's as high as I'll go." Rurik replied.

"She's worth fifty *nomismata* at the very least." Kainan argued.

"Fifty?! In *this* state? She must suck cock better than anyone in the world for that price!" Rurik exclaimed. "You can force me up to twenty, but fifty? Absolutely not!"

"This doesn't matter, she *isn't* for sale." Kainan snapped.

"But you'd consider selling her for fifty?"

"Fifty would be the *starting* bid if I did consider selling her."

"I'd want to try her out before I bought her at *that* price."

"You wouldn't buy the beast if I gave you the milk for free." Kainan said through gritted teeth. "*She is not for sale.* If you are so desperate for one of my slaves, I have others within your price range that you can view tomorrow. Tonight, you may enjoy any of the slaves in this room, just not this one. This one is *mine*."

"I have my own slaves I can enjoy for free." Rurik replied.

"Then why so eager for this one?"

The men snickered, but there was no humour in their laughter.

"I can't tell whether she is special or if you're making a song and dance about her just to up her price." Rurik said.

Kainan gazed at me almost tenderly, a small smile turning up one corner of his mouth.

"By the time I'm done, she will be my most prized possession."

***

"YOU BEHAVED WONDERFULLY this evening, Aveline." Kainan said, taking me back to the *gynaikonitis*. "I will let you sleep in the *gynaikonitis* tonight as reward for your obedience."

"*Þakka fyrir*, master." I murmured in my drunken stupor.

Kainan opened the door and let me through first, shutting it behind us. I stood waveringly in the middle of the room, waiting for him to tell me what to do. Kainan set the oil lamp on the tabletop and paused beside the bed.

"Did you enjoy yourself this evening?" Kainan asked.

"*Já, þakka fyrir*, master." I replied quietly.

"You could live like this, you know." Kainan said. "You could wear silks and fine linen every day, drink wine and eat delectable foods. You can serve me upstairs, away from that dirty, dank cellar. I'll let you stay up here and live a wonderful life with me – but you must do things in return for that privilege."

Fear gripped me. I knew what he wanted in return.

"Take off your clothes. Put them in the chest."

I slipped off my red shoes and placed them in the chest before removing the *stola* and dress. Kainan was quiet, watching me disrobe. I folded the clothing slowly and deliberately before placing them in the chest. Naked but for the collar, I turned around, staring at the floor.

"Come to me." Kainan said.

I shuffled towards him, my arms crossed over my chest and my head hanging with shame. How I missed the solitude of the cellar!

I stopped before him, my eyes welling with tears. Kainan cupped my jaw briefly, trailing his hands over my neck, chest, and breasts.

"Not tonight," Kainan murmured, grazing my nipple with his fingertip. "As much as I'd like to, not tonight."

Though I couldn't allow myself to express it, relief washed over me. Kainan pushed my face up to look at him.

"You obeyed me well. You proved I can trust you and for that I am proud of you, Aveline." Kainan said, kissing my brow. "You will begin your duties to remain upstairs another time. No, tonight we must do something else ... Regrettable because of what a lovely evening we had together, you really did do very well."

Suddenly Kainan struck me, smashing his fist into my stomach. I fell to the floor wheezing, unprepared for his attack. He grabbed my iron collar, dragged me to my feet and punched me again.

"I hate to do this, Aveline, I really do." Kainan said earnestly, dropping me on the floor. "But I can't let you get complacent so early into your release. One night will not garner you my trust. You must remember what you are – my slave."

Without another word, Kainan beat me until I lost consciousness.

ASHES REMAIN
CHAPTER THIRTY-SIX

Autumn, 893

THE *GYNAIKONITIS* WAS another cage. It was better than the cellar, with furniture, windows, a basin of warm water given me every morning to wash with, and respectable facilities in the furthest part of the room behind a screen to relieve myself in. I weaved at a loom and spun wool every day. I watched the sun mount the sky, I gazed at the moon during the night, I ate twice a day and didn't have to crawl across the floor for my meal.

It wasn't all wonderful living upstairs. Occasionally Kainan entered my room at night with a bundle of new clothes. He'd wake me and make me put them on and twirl around, all the while telling me how beautiful I was. When he was done he made me undress, pack the clothes away in the chest, then he would beat me.

I feared the nights when Kainan brought me gifts. He never struck my face, it seemed he took Rurik's advice after all, but my arms, legs and torso were blackened. By the time the bruises healed, Kainan brought me a present and new bruises with it.

The sun had sunk beneath the horizon thirty times. I'd been locked in the room for a month. Every night I dreamt of climbing out of the window, I dreamt of returning to Aros, I dreamt of how I would kill Kainan when I had my chance.

Erhardt Ketilsson, my first husband, had raped and beaten me. I thought he was the cruellest man in the world, equalled only by his vicious righthand man, Tarben the Beardless. How wrong I was ... There was always somebody crueller.

Kainan was worse than both of them. Kainan hadn't raped me, yet at least. The fear loomed over me for the day he'd ask me to pay him for the 'privilege' of living upstairs, and his random beatings set me on edge constantly. I feared when he brought my meals. I feared his gifts, I couldn't admire silk clothing anymore for finery and beauty meant beatings and pain ...

The daylight and the stars brought me hope, though.

Somewhere across the world, Jan and my children were staring at the same sky. They wouldn't rest until they found me, I knew it. Hidden beneath the earth in Kainan's cellar, I would never be found – I was practically buried alive – but in this room ... In this room there was a chance.

I gazed outside, longing for the day Jan or Young Birger or Sander would stride down the street in search of me. I would scream out to them – they would turn and see me – by the time they reached the house, Kainan would enter my room and I would fight my way passed him, bolstered by hope. I would run down the stairs, fling open the front door and let Jan and my sons into Kainan's house, I would take one of their swords and run it through Kainan, spilling his guts over the marble floor of the gilded cage he'd trapped me in for far too long.

By my estimation, I had been trapped in Kainan's house for a total of seventy days between the cellar and the *gynaikonitis*. Seventy days of abuse, thraldom and slavery. I needed Jan and my sons to find me – I didn't know if I could survive much longer.

***

"GOOD EVENING DANETHRALL." Kainan said.

As usual, Kainan set his oil lamp on the table beneath the window. A thrall followed him, carrying a silver tray on which was a jug and two cups. She set the tray on the tabletop then disappeared, shutting the door tight behind her.

"Drink with me." Kainan said, pouring wine into the cups.

I got up from the bed and sat across the table from him, following his orders immediately despite how groggy I was. It was late at night and I had been curled up in bed asleep.

I accepted the cup and took a sip. The wine was sweet. For a while we sat in silence, drinking by the glow of the oil lamp. I was more awake now, eyeing Kainan nervously. He hadn't brought me any clothes and it wasn't mealtime. He didn't usually visit but for those occasions. Kainan didn't speak until I finished my wine. He poured me a new one and urged me to drink it.

"I'm not going to beat you," Kainan said, presumably noticing the trepidation on my face. "I'd like to talk with you instead."

I nodded, but I didn't believe him.

"You've been gaining weight nicely." Kainan commented. "I'm hosting another party in a few weeks and I want you presentable. If I have to hear that damned Varangian talk about how ugly you are again, I'll slit his throat."

I gaped at him.

"See? I will defend your honour, Danethrall. It pains me to hear him make such callous remarks about your appearance. I care about you – you may not think so, but I do."

"*Þakka fyrir*, master." I mumbled.

Kainan silently watched me finish my second wine then took the cup from me and set it down on the table between us.

"Take off your clothes." Kainan ordered softly.

Nei ... Please, *nei* ...

Slowly I rose to my feet and did as he commanded. I wore a simple long-sleeved dress made of soft pale blue linen, embroidered with silver threads around the hems and the neckline. It was a gift Kainan gave me two weeks ago, along with the dark bruises scattered over my stomach and legs.

While I undressed, Kainan filled my cup yet again. Naked, I took my time folding my clothes and placing them inside the chest. Kainan was ever patient. Soon enough I was standing before him, hunched over with my arms crossed over my chest, goosebumps scattered over my flesh from the cool night air.

"Here." He gave me the cup.

I held the cup with both hands, holding it close to my chest. Kainan circled me, touching my back, making me shiver. He stopped behind me, dragging his fingers over the countless scars from the top of my back to my bottom, sighing as he did so.

"Do you remember when I showed you my scars?" He asked, his voice distant. "You cried out when you saw them."

Yes, I remembered ... Instantly, the memory of the web of scars stretched across his entire back appeared in my mind. Kainan told me he received the wounds from the Varangian captors who stole him and sold him to the Danes when he was young. I had gasped when I saw them, shocked at the gruesome tangle of leathery scars.

Now I had my own set of scars ...

Now *my* body was hideous ...

Vidar's body had been scarred by war and battle, but his had not been ugly. I had traced every cut and scar with my fingers, admiring them, asking Vidar to recount the stories behind each mark. I had kissed them, loved them. When Kainan showed me his, I had recoiled.

"I wanted to kiss you the day I showed you my scars." Kainan said. "I was stupid – too cowardly to make a move. I'm a different man now, I'm brave and strong. A lot has changed over the last two decades and I owe that all to you.

"You were the first person to treat me kindly since the Varangians kidnapped me when I was a child – everyone else treated me like an animal. You were kindly, you were loving, but you hurt me more than anyone else.

"I learned a lot from you, Aveline. You made me fall in love with you then you broke my heart. You were no better than any of the masters who'd owned me – you were worse. They hurt me, but they treated me honestly, they *hated* me honestly. You tricked me into falling in love with you, toying with me before tossing me aside in favour of a Dane."

Kainan reached around my body and forced me to bring the cup to my lips. He trickled the wine into my mouth, his lips grazing my neck as he watched over my shoulder. Warmth filled my body from my cheeks to the tips of my toes, but it was not a comforting warmth. It was the heat of the inferno that would burn me alive. Kainan was getting me drunk on purpose, to weaken me, to make me unable to fight him.

My cup empty, Kainan tossed it onto a chair then pressed the cold rim of his full cup against my lips, forcing me to consume it. Wine dribbled from the corners of my mouth, my mouth too full, but Kainan did not relent.

"That's it, drink," Kainan whispered in my ear. "It's thanks to you I am who I am today. You taught me not to trust anyone. I knew as a thrall I would fail at life, but you gave me the drive to make something of myself. I was determined to become the master – and I did." A dry laugh tumbled from his lips. "I never thought I'd become *your* master – that's just a fortunate delight."

My head spun, the heat of drunkenness coursing through me. I spluttered after draining my fourth cup of wine in such a short time. Kainan tossed his cup onto the chair, the cups clanging against each other, then coiled his arms around me and pulled me against him. I felt the hardness of his cock press against me through his clothes, making the hairs on my body stand on end.

"I've waited so long to have you." Kainan's voice was low and husky, his words dragged out slowly, almost melodically. "Do you remember when I said you could live up here, dressed in finery, eating good food and wine? I said there were things you must do in return for those privileges. Do you remember?"

"*Já.*" I whispered.

"Tonight is the night you repay your master."

Tears filled my eyes and sobs brewed in my chest, building so quickly I didn't know if I could control them. Kainan kissed my neck. He groped my breasts, tugging my nipples until I whimpered. His teeth grazed my flesh, his kisses turning into bites.

"Let's go to the bed." Kainan muttered, nibbling my earlobe.

I couldn't move. Kainan pushed me. I staggered forward, but halted again, fear stopping me. Kainan huffed irritably, losing his patience quickly.

"Move, Danethrall." Kainan growled.

"Please, *nei*!" I begged, tears spilling down my cheeks.

Kainan grabbed my collar and yanked me across the room. He shoved me face down on the mattress and smacked my rear so hard I screamed. He smacked me again and again. I wept into the mattress, covering my buttocks with my hands, listening to Kainan rip off his clothing and throw them aside.

"Please *nei*." I whimpered into the bed.

"I am your master, Danethrall! Get on your hands and knees!"

Weeping uncontrollably, my body shook as I obeyed. I howled as Kainan kicked my legs apart with his knee and shoved his cock inside me.

"*Nei*!" I screeched.

Kainan ignored me, curling his fingers around my collar, the other gripping my hip. He jerked my head back as he slammed into me with a handful of powerful thrusts.

"Who am I, Danethrall?" Kainan demanded.

"M-my m-master." I wept.

"Louder! Who am I, Danethrall?" He roared.

"My master!" I howled.

Kainan released my collar, grabbed my hips with both hands and raped me, my cries filling the air.

After what felt like an eternity, Kainan finally pulled out of me, his seed spilling down my thighs. I curled into a ball and wept. Kainan turned the oil lamp off and returned to the bed, wrapping his body around mine. He ran his hand down my leg, stroking the raised scab of the brand on my calf.

"I regret so much from the old days," Kainan murmured. "But I suppose everything was meant to be ... Look at us now – you and me, together. With Vidar dead, he can't take you away from me again."

I couldn't breathe. When Kainan said Vidar's name, spikes of fury and anguish stabbed through my heart. He tarnished Vidar's name every time he said it! He didn't deserve to say Vidar's name!

Kainan kissed my shoulder, tightening his grip around my body.

"I finally have you, Danethrall. You're finally mine!"

***

"I SAW AN associate of mine today," Kainan said, sipping his wine as he watched me eat my evening meal the following night. "He's travelling to Ribe tomorrow, possibly stopping by a few other Norse towns along the way back. We spoke about Roskilde for a little while ... Memories flooded back to me, bringing up so many questions I never received the answers to. Maybe you could enlighten me?"

"I – I'll try." I stammered.

"Maybe now you will tell me why you treated me like a fool."

I gaped at Kainan for a moment, surprised by his question.

"Treating you like a fool was never my intention."

"Then why did you?" Kainan asked. "Tell me, truthfully, when you were with me, were you sharing Vidar's bed?"

"*Nei*, I was not." I said firmly. "I didn't share his bed until long after you left. There was no romantic relationship between Vidar and me while we were together."

"Then why wouldn't you marry me?" Kainan pressed. "If you had feelings for me, why wouldn't you marry me?"

ASHES REMAIN

"Vidar swore he'd kill you if you took me from him." I mumbled, picking at the bread in my hands. "Being with you romantically ... I was risking your life."

"Why didn't you tell me this back then?" Kainan exclaimed.

"Because I didn't know what you'd do. I – I didn't want you to get hurt ..."

"I would've killed him!"

"I didn't want him dead."

"Why? Because you loved him?"

I gazed at him, silently pleading for him to calm down. Kainan glowered at me in return.

"It doesn't matter how I felt about him," I said carefully. "He was bigger – stronger. He would've killed you. You weren't as powerful as you are now. He would've hurt you – I – I didn't want that to happen."

"We could've run away together," Kainan argued. "In the dead of night, we could've left Roskilde together!"

"With no horse, no ship, no money?"

"We could have gone by foot–"

"To where?"

Tears filled my eyes, Kainan was only getting angrier.

"My lands, your lands, wherever we wanted! The world was open to us!"

"We would've *died*."

"We could've waited for Birger's permission to marry!"

Tears streamed down my face. No matter what answer I gave Kainan, truth or lie, I would upset him. I took a deep breath and chose truth.

"Do you truly believe Birger would've given his only daughter permission to marry a thrall?" I asked. "What life could you offer me? Offer our children?"

Kainan fell silent, frowning at me, his brow furrowed.

"Did you ever plan to marry me? Did you ever love me?"

"I cared for you very much, Kainan."

"But you didn't want to marry me – you didn't *love* me?"

"I never wanted you to get hurt. A life together, married – that never would've happened ... I *couldn't* love you, Kainan."

"I loved *you*, Aveline."

"Then you really were a fool." I mumbled.

Kainan threw his cup across the room. It smashed into the wall, shattering into a thousand pieces. I flinched, but didn't move, watching Kainan with trepidation. He stormed towards me – I backed away, shrinking from him. I hit the wall – trapped.

"Love blossomed between you and Vidar though, didn't it?" Kainan fumed. "You married *him* – but of course you did, he wasn't a thrall, he was the jarl's son! Remind me, how many children did you have with your precious jarl's son?"

"Five." I answered, my children's faces materialising in my mind.

"Ah, yes, five! And you were pregnant with Vidar's son when you were married off to Erhardt – *before* you were married off to anyone!" Kainan snarled. "You didn't seem to care about sharing *Vidar's* bed before marriage, but you damn well wouldn't share mine! I remember all the times you told me, *no, no, we're not married, Kainan, no, no*! And I listened to you! What a fool I was indeed! I should've taken you when I had the chance!"

"Please! It's been twenty years! Why does it matter anymore?"

"You should have been mine!" Kainan hissed.

"*You* left *me*! *You* asked Vidar to sell you!"

"Oh! I gave you to him so you became his whore?"

"Please, Kainan!" I sobbed.

"You were his whore, but now you're mine! You belong to me, I own you!" Kainan bellowed, grabbing the collar around my neck. "Damn you Aveline – we spent so much time together! Why did you prefer to be a Dane's *whore* rather than my *wife*? Why wasn't I good enough for you?"

"Please, *nei*!" I begged as he dragged me to the bed.

"Silence!" Kainan roared, smacking me across the face, holding tight to the collar. "So many times, you offered me your body only to run away before I could enjoy it. You teased me, you seduced me, you tricked me! You used me and tossed me aside in favour of the damn jarl's son!"

Kainan smacked me again. I clawed at his hand, tried to free myself from his grasp. He held tight to the slave collar around my neck. I flailed, but Kainan pulled on the collar, choking me.

"Things are very different now, Danethrall! Vidar is dead and I am here, strong, rich and powerful. I could drag you into the street and beat you and no one would bat an eye!" Kainan snarled, striking my face a third time.

The pain of Kainan's strikes burned on my face. He'd hit me so hard I was dizzy. The room span, I couldn't tell which way was up or down. Kainan dragged me across the room to the window. He ripped open the shutters and shoved me over the edge. I tried to grasp the windowsill, but Kainan shoved me further out. If he let go of my collar, I would fall. I clung to his wrist, my body trembling, sobbing uncontrollably.

"I could throw you out of this window right now if I wanted." Kainan growled. "You would crash to the ground and die – maybe not immediately, but you *would* die. You would spend your last moments of life in total agony, all of your bones broken to pieces! I could do that to you, Danethrall."

Kainan pulled me inside and let go of my collar. I fell to the floor and curled into a ball, clinging to my neck, gasping for air. Kainan boiled with fury. I heard him suck in breath between his teeth. I waited for another strike, a kick, or worse …

"Am I good enough for you now?" He spat.

I gave him no answer.

Kainan left, slamming the door shut behind himself.

He was right. Things were different. Vidar *was* dead and I was alone here, no one knew where I was, no one could save me. Kainan *could* kill me whenever he wanted. He spared me this time, but would he spare me the next time I angered him?

CHAPTER THIRTY-SEVEN

Spring, 894

THE RASP OF the key turning in the lock woke me up. Kainan entered my room, set the oil lamp on the table, threw off his clothes and crawled into my bed. I waited, still as stone. He groped me, kissed me, bit me, his hands slithering over my body. As he spread my legs, I squeezed my eyes shut and waited for it to be over. When he finished, Kainan exited my room, taking the oil lamp with him. He locked the door, leaving me alone in my gilded cage with his seed spilling down my legs.

My hope of escape dwindled to nothing, I resigned myself to my dismal fate. Autumn faded into a cold winter – though winter in Constantinople was much shorter than winter in Denmark. The snow melted weeks ago, for rain showers it was sunny and bright outside my window. During the day, the delicate scent of newly bloomed flowers drifted on the air, the freshness of the earth after winter cradling me in an evanescent peace. Fear flooded over me as the sun sank below the horizon, then I would wait.

Every night I passed out from exhaustion, unable to fall into a peaceful sleep for fear Kainan might appear in my room to defile me. I never knew when he was coming – there was no pattern to his carnal visits. He came to me sometimes four days in a row, sometimes once a week, sometimes every other day. Sometimes he wouldn't visit me for weeks. I didn't lower my guard for the moment I felt safe he would appear.

I cleaned away the mess between my legs and crept over to the window. I opened the wooden shutters, careful not to make a noise. I could never return to sleep after Kainan's visits, the respite I gained from slumber ruined by his sporadic urge to copulate. Curled up on the settee, I stared at the night sky. Clouds suffocated the stars and twisted around the moon like vines.

I couldn't feel it yet, I hoped beyond hope I'd lost track of the days and my menses would arrive any day now ... I'd hoped that

ASHES REMAIN

for thirty days now, but still nothing. It didn't matter how hard I wished otherwise, I knew inside my belly was Kainan's bastard.

My hands curled into fists, my heart splintering with anger. Already I hated the unborn child within me. I hated Kainan for putting it inside me! I could not love Kainan's bastard, despite the fact it grew inside me, despite the fact it was mine too.

Throughout my life, in the Kingdom of the East Angles and in the Danish lands, I had seen women weep at the loss of their unborn child, born well before its time in a torrent of blood and pain, its tiny body not yet formed into the proper shape of a baby.

I had seen the women's suffering. I heard their cries ... My parents had told me the stories of my mother's losses – all the daughters she'd born in various stages of pregnancy, all born too early, all born dead – yet I wished for that to happen to me, to this child inside my belly. I didn't want this child to live.

I dreaded bringing this life into the world, dreaded the fact I would have to raise it, feed it from my breast ... Most of all I dreaded the idea I might come to love it ...

I thought of my children – my darling Young Birger, Sander, Æsa and Einar. Did they still think of me? Though they were all grown, did their hearts yearn for their mother as my heart yearned for them? How were their lives now that I'd been gone for so long?

A vision of Jan materialised in my mind. We'd conceived three children in the first two years we'd shared a bed, despite the brews and seeds I ingested to prevent pregnancy. Three times I drank a brew that expelled each unborn child from my womb. I hadn't wanted to mother any more children, though I came to regret that. Would Jan and I ever have a chance to have a family together now?

I wondered whether Jan was looking at the same moon, thinking of me as I thought of him. Had Jan given up searching for me? Had my sons given up? What new lies had Thóra told them? Had she managed to seduce Jan now she had me out of the picture?

What if Thóra told them I left Storm-Serpent willingly, abandoning them all for a new life in Constantinople? They all knew how miserable I was to leave the city after all.

Did they think I had been caught in the sea goddess Ran's net and dragged to the bottom of the sea? So much time had passed and with no sign of me, perhaps they thought I was dead ...

Yet again I was held captive by a monster. I had used sex to manipulate Erhardt Ketilsson, to influence his decisions and ease the suffering of our marriage. I quickly realised that when I spread my legs for him, when I initiated intercourse or pleasured him, I gained a hold over him. Erhardt stopped beating me, stupidly thinking I'd become his loyal wife.

Erhardt's righthand man, Tarben the Beardless, had seen right through me, but by continuing my manipulation, Erhardt protected me. Tarben would not touch a hair on my head without suffering Erhardt's wrath. That helped me survive the five long years of marriage before Vidar managed to kill them both.

I couldn't manipulate Kainan. I didn't have the chance to initiate sex with him – when the urge struck him, Kainan came to my room and took me whether I was awake or sleeping. Erhardt had allowed me to wander Aros with a thrall at my side whereas Kainan didn't afford me that luxury. He didn't trust me. He kept me in the *gynaikonitis* alone, trapped like a bird in a cage.

The five years of being Erhardt's wife were terrible, but I was young then, I was strong ... I survived by my faith in Vidar and my faith in the Norse gods. But now ... Now I was old and weak. Vidar was dead and I had long since abandoned the gods.

Long ago I prayed to Frigg, my once beloved goddess, to give me strength and protect me and my children. I asked for courage and knowledge, for her to stand by me through the passing days, knowing I couldn't change what I was doomed to face. I asked her to lend me her strength to weather whatever storms the Nornir had planned out for me and she did! Frigg gave me the strength to persevere. She gave me the knowledge of manipulating Erhardt. She gave me bravery to do what I must to survive.

After Alffinna was killed, I turned my back on Frigg. She was the Allmother, she was the goddess of children, love and marriage, but she had not saved my baby daughter.

Wracked with misery, I had travelled to a powerful völva, a mysterious shaman who resided in the wetlands outside of Ribe, who had the power to speak to the gods. The völva helped me travel to the spirit realm to confront the Allfather, to demand my daughter be returned to me.

ASHES REMAIN

Though he couldn't revive my daughter, the Allfather gave me words of wisdom and made a deal with me to protect my living children. In return for nine sacrifices he would grant my children his blessings throughout their lives. Had I known Vidar was among the Allfather's list, I might not have made the deal, but the gods were tricksters, and the Allfather would've taken these lives – taken Vidar's life! – whether I agreed to give them or not.

The Allfather had since received all, but two of the lives he'd demanded, but I did not know who the remaining two were – I had not known who any of the sacrificial lives were – and I did not know the fates of my children. Anything could've happened to them since I'd been enslaved by Kainan ...

Since Vidar's death, I conducted blóts and rituals for image sake, not out of earnest. As jarl, I was the leader of religious conduct, I *had* to pray to the gods, had to sacrifice to them, honour them. Since giving my jarldoms to my sons, I gave up those duties.

I was angry at the Allfather and furious at the Nornir for weaving such an atrocious web for me and my family. I hated them for stealing the lives of my daughter and husband – the lives of my adoptive father Birger Bloody Sword, Vidar's parents, and my friends ... I even blamed them for taking my blood parents and brothers as well.

I had enough of toiling and suffering for the satisfaction of the gods. I refused to honour a pantheon of almighty beings who culled my kin for their own debauched amusement.

I hated the gods – I hated the unborn child inside me – but I couldn't help remembering the prayer I used to recite to the Allmother every night while I was married to Erhardt. It had given me – sanity and the comfort of knowing she might protect me and my children. I thought about the epiphany I had woken to after praying to Frigg for so long ... She gave me inspiration to survive – she gave me what I prayed for.

Should I turn to her again?

The gods were fickle, they held grudges, they gave aid only to those they deemed worthy, but they were impulsive. Was I worthy enough for them to throw me a bone?

A deep sigh fell from my lips and my cheeks reddened – I was ashamed of myself – embarrassed. Had it come to this? Did I really hope the gods would give me sympathy because of how pathetic I was? Was I truly hoping for their pity, was I truly hoping to receive their favour even though I had forsaken them?

I truly was a shell of the woman I used to be. Even when I was wife of Erhardt I hadn't been this wretched. I was just eighteen years old when I sought power from the gods to fight my enemy, to come out victorious from the struggles they set for me.

Now I was close to forty and snivelling like a baby. Why would the gods help me when I resigned myself to this damned existence? When I allowed this monster to defile me? When I chose not to fight?

I was a Dane. Not long ago I was once a powerful jarl! I rose to such a height because I was strong and daring! Because I was brave!

I gave in to Kainan quickly. I accepted his abuse, I accepted him as my master, I accepted my thraldom. I gave up fighting.

I hadn't given up to Erhardt – I did everything I could to turn my tribulations into steppingstones leading to my victory. Now I yielded to my suffering with no intention of conquering it. Of course the gods abandoned me, of course they closed their eyes and ears to me. If I wasn't willing to fight for myself then why should they fight for me?

There were only two options left. I could rot away here as Kainan's slave or I could escape. If I was to escape, I would have to do it myself, I would have to fight. I couldn't keep waiting for someone to save me, I had to do it on my own.

I would save myself.

I would *free* myself!

The child inside me ... I couldn't keep it, I couldn't raise it, I couldn't love the bastard of my captor. After I seized my freedom, I would expel it with Brynja's brew – if the child was born by then I would find a place for it somewhere far away from me. Could I gift it to the *landvættir*? I didn't know ...

I stood up and held the frame of the window, the night air dancing over my skin, kissing it with cold. My shoulder-length chestnut curls drifted around my face on the cool breeze. I closed my eyes and listened to the wind. It grew stronger, tugging my clothes. I listened to the calm pace of my breath, my heart steady.

ASHES REMAIN

I had survived the Great Heathen Army's attack.
I had been accepted by the warrior Danes.
I had defeated Erhardt and Tarben.
I had stormed across Denmark in blizzards.
I had drunk poisonous potions and survived.
I had travelled to the spirit realm.
I had made demands of the mighty Allfather.
I had slain warriors and soldiers.
I had conquered villages and towns.
I had become the first female jarl.
I had swayed the law, benefiting all Norse women.
I had fought.
There was power in me!

I opened my eyes and looked at the moon. The wind had batted the clouds almost completely away. And there, soaring across the silver disc was a raven, its caw distinct over the lament of the wind.

Without seeing its face, I knew exactly which raven it was – the one with the blind eye. It had followed me during my life in the Danish lands. The Allfather's companion was coursing through the Mediterranean skies, which meant only one thing, the Allfather was here, listening to me.

"Hear me, Allfather,
God of Wisdom, Magic and Death.
I open my arms to suffering,
I open my arms to toil and strife,
I open my arms to death!
I open my arms
And accept the cruelties laid out for me.
I will overcome them,
I will fight them, and I will be victorious!
Give me your blessings, Allfather,
With strength and courage,
I will face the tapestry
The Nornir have woven for me,
And I will tear it apart!"

GWENDOLINE SK TERRY
CHAPTER THIRTY-EIGHT

Summer, 894

I WAS VISIBLY with child by the time I achieved a glimpse of freedom. The infant moved inside me, pains shooting through me when the child stretched and poked my organs with its tiny limbs. I was almost two-thirds of the way through the pregnancy.

Kainan offered me no mercy during his carnal visits despite the fact I carried his child. He took me as fiercely and forcefully as before. Part of me hoped his rough handling would cause me to lose the baby, a grotesque desire to be sure, but I still hoped …

But for confirming I was with child, Kainan and I hadn't spoken about the baby. He did regard me somewhat differently, though. I still wasn't allowed outside of his home, but Kainan let me out of the *gynaikonitis*, less concerned that I would flee now, and for good reason, I supposed.

My lower back ached and my feet were constantly swollen. My stomach wasn't huge, but it bulged enough to hinder my actions. The unborn baby sapped my energy, the parasite that it was. I was too exhausted to do more than wander his house holding my stomach, flinching at the movements of the child inside me.

Released from the *gynaikonitis* was a step towards freedom, albeit a small one. Beyond the *gynaikonitis* walls, I was able to see more of what went on, gleaming knowledge of Kainan's activities when he was absent from my quarters, and I found he did not spend much time inside his home at all. Always out checking his ships, inspecting his merchandise shipments.

Kainan hosted opulent parties in his *triclinium* with the men under his employ and for his wealthy potential customers, during which I was confined to the *gynaikonitis*. There were precious moments – albeit infrequent – where I stole chances to speak to Rurik or at least catch his eye. I sought an ally in him, hoping the similarities of our cultures might persuade him to help me escape.

ASHES REMAIN

Rurik and Kainan weren't friends, but their professions kept them in close contact. Rurik, I found out, was Kainan's largest supplier of slaves from the northern lands. In return for a decent percentage, Rurik transported and sold slaves to the Varangians and Norsemen on Kainan's behalf.

Kainan refused to set foot in the Norse lands where he might be remembered as a runaway thrall so Rurik did that for him. Kainan could've found a different merchant to sell for him, but none garnered as high a profit as Rurik. Kainan was stuck working with him no matter how much he despised Varangians.

Rurik infuriated Kainan. The nights after Kainan entertained Rurik were always tumultuous. Kainan would storm into the *gynaikonitis* snapping about whatever comment Rurik had made and I would sit and listen raptly. One day I would use this information against Kainan, use it to sway Rurik to my side.

I stretched, my arms aching from weaving at the loom all day. I could hear the muffled noise of laughter downstairs. This was the second party Kainan hosted this month. He must've been doing well with his business, flaunting his money like this.

There was a chance Rurik was here. I had tried to entice Rurik to me for the last few months. But for the first time we met, I hadn't yet had a full conversation with him, just a handful of pleasantries at parties since then. I could tell he was interested in me. He smiled when I caught his eye, brushed his hand against me when he walked by me. A few times he tried to speak alone with me, but Kainan was quick to appear and thwart him.

My plan was further hindered by Kainan. About two months ago, when I started to show with child, Kainan stopped exhibiting me at his gatherings, shutting me away in the *gynaikonitis*. I tried to reason with him, the *stola* and gowns were billowy and loose, concealing my pregnant stomach, but Kainan wouldn't hear of it. If I wanted to speak with Rurik, I had to be sneaky.

My usual excuse prepared, I scurried downstairs with my jug in my arms. If I bumped into Kainan, I would simply tell him I was fetching water – the well was located near the kitchen, which was close to the *triclinium*. Hopefully Kainan would be too busy hosting his party, and if luck were on my side, I might catch Rurik and talk to him alone at last.

I leaned against the kitchen wall near the door listening to the voices in the *triclinium*, but I couldn't pick out Rurik's, they were too muffled.

Wait, what was that – footsteps?

I peered around the doorway to find out who was coming down the corridor. Luck *was* on my side! It was Rurik! He spotted me and smiled.

Forgive me, Jan. I prayed in my mind.

For my plan to work, I had to betray him. I prayed he would understand I had to do what I must to return to him, even if it meant being disloyal.

"A pleasure to see you again, Aveline." Rurik crooned. "I'm happy to see you, it's been a while."

"I must return to the *gynaikonitis* at once." I said, flickering my gaze between Rurik's brilliant blue eyes and the floor between us, pretending to be shy and demure.

"What are you doing down here then?" Rurik asked.

"Fetching water." I replied, shifting the jug in my arms. "Why aren't you in the *triclinium*?"

"A man must relieve himself sometimes." Rurik laughed. "I'm glad to bump into you though. You're not as skinny as you were when I met you."

"A welcomed change, is it?"

"It is indeed." Rurik said, running one hand lightly over my hip. His eyes widened as his fingers brushed my hard stomach.

"Ah, what's this? You're with child!" Rurik spread his hand over my belly. "Don't tell me it's *his* bastard growing inside you?"

"Fine, I won't." I replied, pursing my lips.

"He's ruining you." Rurik sighed. "This is why he's kept you locked away recently … I suppose at least he's let you grow your hair – you're far prettier now it's longer."

My hair had grown a lot in the past seven months especially since I'd become pregnant. My chestnut curls grazed my shoulders now.

"I'm pleased that at least *one* part of my appearance is to your liking." I ventured bravely, touching my hair.

"Oh *ja*?" A smirk tugged at the corner of Rurik's mouth.

"Very much so." I smiled.

ASHES REMAIN

I fluttered my eyelashes at the Varangian, watching a grin spread across his face. He stepped closer, stroking his fair beard. Rurik didn't know what to make of me. I winked at him and tried to slip passed him, but he stuck his arm out against the wall, blocking my way. I glanced at it, feigning surprise at his action. Rurik chuckled and ran his fingers through my hair.

"My master won't be happy to find us like this."

"Your master isn't happy with anything." Rurik mumbled, tucking a lock of hair behind my ear gently. "By Odin's beard, you do have the most beautiful eyes."

I gazed at him unblinking, tilting my head and pouting my lips just a little. He rested his hand on the curve of my hip, the other still playing with my hair. I settled a hand on his chest, stroking the solid muscles hidden beneath his tunic.

"What else do you like about me?" I asked quietly.

"I like your mouth ..." Rurik said softly. "And your hips ..."

Rurik stooped over me, bringing his face closer to mine, the jug wedged between us. I stood on my tiptoes and brushed my lips against his. He tried to kiss me, but I pulled away – not completely, just enough for our lips to graze. I giggled softly, feeling his mouth curve into a smile.

"You're teasing me," Rurik remarked huskily.

"I am."

"You won't give me just one kiss?"

"*Nei*," I replied, pulling myself out of his embrace. "Not yet."

"Why are you making me wait? Just one little kiss is all I want." Rurik attempted to be sly and seductive, but he did not hide his eagerness well.

"*Góða nótt*, Rurik." I smiled.

I slipped past him and returned to my room, feeling him watch me as I left. I smiled to myself. I didn't need to search him out anymore, he would come to find me.

***

FOUR WEEKS PASSED before Rurik managed to pay me a secret visit. It was evening time and I was in the *gynaikonitis* weaving at my loom when I heard a gentle knock on my door. No one tended to knock, even the thralls barged in whenever they needed to enter.

"Who is it?" I asked through the door.

"Open it and you'll find out."

I smiled and let Rurik enter.

"What are you doing here? What if my master catches you?" I gasped, adopting a worried façade.

"Don't worry, he'll be busy for a while." Rurik grinned, gripping my hips and pulling me against him. "One of the lords of Constantinople has invited Kainan to his mansion. He has expressed interest in purchasing many of Kainan's slaves. Kainan will not let anyone, but himself sell to a man of such high status, especially with such a large amount of money dangling in front of him. He should be busy for a while, which gives us a chance to enjoy each other's company."

"You seem to be enjoying my company already." I smiled, placing my hands over his.

"You've cast quite the spell on me, Aveline. I've thought of nothing, but you since we last met."

"Even though my stomach swells with Kainan's child?" I asked pushing his hands off me.

I drifted to the loom, half shrouded with shadow, watching Rurik through the corner of my eye. I ran my hand over the woollen threads, glancing over my shoulder to smile at him. He gave me a vulpine grin in return as he stroked his beard.

"What was it you said?" I paused thoughtfully. "Ah, *já*, Kainan *ruined* me by getting me with child. I'm larger now than I was then. Do you truly still want me?"

"Women are such sensitive creatures." Rurik mocked.

I rolled my eyes and turned my back on him, picking up where I'd left off on my loom.

"Your stomach isn't as big as it could be." Rurik said. "Anyway, there might be something you can do to distract me from it."

"Ignorant bastard." I muttered under my breath.

My heart leapt as Rurik's shadow cast over me. He'd crept up on me so silently! He slipped his arms around my body and stroked my stomach with both his hands.

"For a slave, you're quite brazen." Rurik smiled.

ASHES REMAIN

"You forget, I'm not a slave, I'm a jarl." I replied, leaning against him, enjoying the way he caressed me.

Rurik laughed. He trailed his hand over my breasts and slipped his fingers beneath my iron collar.

"You're not a jarl here, Aveline." He said, tugging the collar.

"But I am in my lands." I lied. "Tell me, Rurik, have you visited Aros? Have you been to Roskilde?"

"I've been to both a handful of times."

"Do you remember how beautiful they are?"

"*Já*, I do." Rurik said, releasing my collar and gliding his hand over my breast.

"If I returned to my lands, whoever aided me would be rewarded greatly." I turned in Rurik's embrace, running my hands over his chest, his muscles solid under my touch. "You're a well-travelled man. Tell me, do *you* know how I could leave Constantinople?"

"I know how dangerous this conversation is for you."

"I know how dangerous this embrace is for the both of us."

"You aren't scared?" Rurik grinned.

"I'm not afraid of anything." I whispered, tracing his bottom lip with my finger.

"You aren't as docile as Kainan claims." Rurik admired.

"No matter what *he* says I cannot be *broken* – I'm not a horse." I replied stoutly. "Will you help me, Rurik?"

"I don't know if you should trust me. If I was a good man, I would tell my associate immediately that his thrall is trying to seduce me and run away."

"I'm hoping you're *not* a good man." I stood on my tiptoes, my gaze flickering between his pale blue eyes and his full pink lips. "I'm hoping you'll fall for my wiles. I'm hoping you'll sneak behind your associate's back and help me."

"I should receive quite the reward for something so devious – you're asking me to betray my business partner." The lustful gaze Rurik looked at me with told me exactly what reward he desired.

"Help me and I'll give you what you want."

"I could just take you – you are a slave after all."

Rurik's lips grazed against mine, but I would not kiss him.

"You'd enjoy me a lot more if I gave myself to you willingly."

"You make a lot of promises, Aveline."

"Give me your word and you'll find me true to mine."

"I won't agree to anything unless I know all the details."

"Kainan told me last night you'll be sailing to Götaland in the morning. Take me to the shipyard now, let me hide with your cargo. When morning comes, take me to Aros."

"Kainan will be very upset to find his prized slave missing. I should tell him your plan and make you suffer the consequences."

"You should, but you won't, will you?" I ventured daringly.

"Won't I?" Rurik mused.

"*Nei*, you won't. You *know* I don't belong here with him."

"He bought you fairly at the market, you *are* his property. I would be *stealing* you if I got you out of here."

"I am *not* property."

I was growing impatient. I cleared my throat and tried to resume an enticing tone, but I was getting tired of my ruse, tired of trying to convince him to help me. I couldn't stop now, not when Rurik knew I was trying to escape – I *had* to make him agree.

"You're Rus, *ja*? *Varangian*, that's what they call Norsemen here. Your people worship the same gods as mine – we're similar, you and me. Why do you side with a Christian?"

"Business, my sweet. Business with Kainan is exceptionally profitable."

"Business? I see." I pulled away from Rurik, crossed the room and poured myself a cup of wine, taking a sip before continuing. "You were willing to buy me for fifteen *nomismata* when we first met. I will give you that much for my freedom."

"I also said I would've paid twenty for you, even considering the skinny waste you were back then."

"Fine, I will pay you twenty."

"Things have changed, you're with child. I don't know if I want you now you have Kainan's bastard in your belly."

"Don't haggle my worth because of this damned child, it hasn't changed the fact I'm still Jarl of Aros and Roskilde." I scolded. "Besides, I thought you could look past my stomach for a while?"

"If you were distracting me appropriately – this conversation is *not* the distraction I was insinuating."

I sat down on a chair as though it were a throne, surveying Rurik through narrowed eyes.

ASHES REMAIN

"I'll give you fifty *nomismata* for safe passage on your ship to Aros."

"Fifty?" Rurik's eyes widened. "And where is your money, Jarl?"

"It's in Aros – take me there and I'll give it to you."

"The moment we arrive in Aros, you could have me cut down by one of your men. I need something *now* – a guarantee."

"On my word–"

"Word is not enough." He interrupted. "You have no silver or gold, only words, and that is *not* enough."

"What do you want?"

"Don't act stupid, you know what I want." Rurik said, leaning over me, holding the arms of my chair. "You might be old, and the fact you're carrying Kainan's bastard *does* disgust me, but you have such pretty eyes … *You* will do nicely."

Anger boiled in the pit of my stomach. How dare the bastard insult me like this!

"If my body isn't pleasing to you, why would you want to lay with me? Surely the promise of riches is better than lying with someone *subpar* to your tastes." I said, my words dripping venom.

"I've never fucked a female jarl, this may be my only chance."

"As opposed to all the male jarls' beds you've shared?"

"Hold your tongue, viper, otherwise I'll tell your master everything we've spoken about tonight." Rurik wasn't angry – in fact, he sounded amused.

Rurik stroked my hair, letting his hand trail down to my shoulder, pulling the *stola* away to reveal the gown beneath the silk.

"You've been flaunting yourself to me every time you've come near me. Don't tell me you've suddenly become cold? You still owe me a kiss." Rurik brought his face down low to mine.

His breath danced on my lips. I glowered at him.

"Give me your word."

"On my word, *if* you share your bed with me, I'll take you to Aros. Now give me your word that when we arrive, you'll give me one hundred *nomismata*." Rurik said. "Deny me and I'll tell Kainan everything. I'm sure he'll let me and every man in *Miklagarðr* have his turn with you as punishment."

"*One hundred* nomismata?" I gasped.

Rurik nodded, took my cup from my hand and drank my wine.

Rurik was right. If Kainan found me, he would take the most extreme measures possible to punish me. If I was lucky he would just whip me half to death. If I wasn't lucky, the Varangian's suggestion was a realistic prospect, on top of a whipping no doubt. If I survived all that then Kainan would lock me in his cellar again.

I couldn't go back to that cellar. It was easier for me to pay Rurik the outrageous sum he demanded and lay with him rather than face Kainan's abuse.

"Fine. One hundred *nomismata*." I said. "I will not give myself to you here, though. Take me to the shipyard – that will prove you're being honest."

"Alright." Rurik grinned. "Wrap yourself up in my cloak. It's unseemly for a woman to be out at night unless she's searching for business – though I suppose, in a way, you *are*."

ASHES REMAIN
CHAPTER THIRTY-NINE

WE SCURRIED THROUGH the winding streets past ragged beggars and starving urchins, stumbling drunks and women of the night enticing men to employ their services. I had both my *stola* and the hood of Rurik's cloak pulled over my head, clutching the fabrics nervously. I was afraid one of Kainan's associates might be about and recognise me. Rurik didn't seem to have any fears, he strode ahead of me confidently, his head held high.

My feet slipped on the paving slabs and pebbles dug into my soles. My red leather shoes didn't protect me from the rough roads. Rurik snatched my hand, frustrated by me falling behind.

"Don't drag me!"

"Would you prefer to get caught instead?" Rurik asked, tugging me closer to his side.

"I thought you said we had time?"

"*Já*, time to enjoy each other not to scheme and dash about the streets of *Miklagarðr* all night."

Rurik pulled me the rest of the way to the harbour. We stumbled down a flight of weathered stone stairs and hugged the ships as we dashed. Though it was late, we didn't trust the darkness to conceal us. Guards patrolled the shipyard in groups, alert and beady-eyed.

With bated breath, we waited for a group of guards, all heavily armed, to pass before we slipped down a little further. Rurik's pace quickened – he must've spotted his ship. We hurried on, but rather than take me to his ship, Rurik led me to a long, tall building.

"Where are you taking me?" I demanded.

Rurik brought his finger to his lips. With one hand, he fiddled with the keys hanging from the brass ring on his belt until he found the one he was searching for. He unlocked the door to the building and shoved me inside.

It smelled of wood, tar and salt in here. In the middle of the building the skeleton of a ship perched on scaffolds, illuminated eerily by the silver-blue light pouring in from the slipway on the opposite end of the building. Along the sides of the building were workbenches with various tools, unlit oil lamps, planks and hunks of wood scattered about them.

Rurik dragged me further into the building before releasing my hand. He slipped his cloak from my shoulders and laid it on the nearest workbench. I wandered from him, examining the half-built vessel. From the looks of the ship, it would take two more years before the scaffolding would be removed and the ship would be pushed into the water for its maiden voyage.

"Where are you going, Jarl Aveline?" Rurik called.

I glanced over my shoulder and found Rurik stripping off his tunic. He tossed it onto the workbench with his cloak. I admired his long, lean body, the broadness of his shoulders, his tapered waist, and the way shadows played on his muscles as he moved.

It was a shame Rurik's personality wasn't as magnificent as his appearance ... Slowly I met Rurik's bright blue gaze and couldn't help blushing as his handsome features shifted into a telling grin.

"Am I to your liking?" Rurik asked, holding his arms out, presenting himself to me.

It didn't matter how handsome he was, I didn't trust him.

"Why did you bring me here and not to your ship?"

"Did you see how many guards were out there? There's no way we can board my ship without being spotted. You can hide here until dawn." Rurik explained as he neared me. "Anyway, don't complain. It's warmer in here than it is outside."

As much as I didn't want to admit it, Rurik was right.

"So? Shall we satisfy the obligations of our arrangement?"

"You're a romantic, I see." I rolled my eyes at him.

"Sarcasm is not an attractive feature on a woman." Rurik remarked. "That added with your belly and I'm not sure if I want to keep this arrangement after all."

"Don't try to scare me, Rurik." I scowled at the cocky Rus, my hands balled into fists at my sides. "I must gather myself to follow through with this ordeal so give me a moment."

"You hurt me with your lack of enthusiasm!" Rurik exclaimed. "What's changed? You spent months slinking around Kainan's home batting your eyelashes at me. Now I'm here at your disposal and you're acting as though I disgust you! Do you not find me attractive anymore?"

Rurik flashed me a fake pout before resuming his usual smirk.

"I sought an ally in you, Rurik, that's why I lured you to me."

"And your plan worked." Rurik smiled. "We have arranged a partnership between us, now we must do as all good associates do and follow through with what has been agreed on."

"If I'm so repulsive to you, why do you persist?"

"I've hurt your feelings, haven't I?" Rurik laughed. "In that case, I apologise, Jarl Aveline. I know it couldn't have been your choice to bare Kainan's bastard. I assure you, I *do* find you desirable otherwise I wouldn't be here."

If I'd had my precious *Úlfsblóð*, I would've run Rurik through with it, his condescension was infuriating me beyond words.

"Let me take off your clothes." Rurik said softly, drawing his hands over my shoulders. "I want to look at you."

Rurik pulled my *stola* off. I watched it drop to the floor, the sheen of moonlight on the fabric creating the illusion of a pool about my feet. Meeting Rurik's eager gaze, I slowly unbuckled the belt around my waist and tossed it to the ground, my face burning.

"Don't speak to me while we do this, I want to imagine you're somebody else."

"Now who's being callous?" Rurik said, watching me pull my arms out of the dress's tight sleeves.

"Be quiet."

I tossed the dress aside. Naked, my flesh flooded with goosebumps from the cool night air, I held my head high and scowled at Rurik. He smoothed my hair behind my shoulders.

"You will do nicely, Jarl Aveline."

Rurik pulled me against him with one hand, cupping my jaw with his other. I gasped, squeezing my eyelids shut, memories of Kainan's brutalness flashing through my mind. Rather than smashing his mouth against mine like Kainan did, Rurik stroked my bottom lip with his fingertip, his lips parting just slightly.

Rurik moved his hand from my jaw to the back of my head, his light blue eyes shining in the dim light. I slid my hands over his chest, the hairs there soft against my palms. Rurik lowered his head closer to mine. The gentleness of his touch and the sweetness of his breath dancing on my face drew me to him. Before I knew it, I rose to my tiptoes to meet his lips. It had been so long since a man was so tender with me …

At first our kiss was meek, brief. Our lips parted for just a moment before Rurik kissed me again, harder. The fullness of his lips pressed against mine sparked flames inside me. His mouth opened slightly, I met his tongue with mine, timidly grazing it. The trace of wine lingered in his mouth, I could taste the sharp flavour even now – it was delicious.

Just that small meeting of our tongues fanned the flames inside me. I wrapped my arms around his neck and kissed him deeper, our tongues clashing.

We broke apart, both of us panting. Rurik rested his brow against mine, still holding me tightly against him.

"I've wanted to kiss you for so long." His voice was low.

"Was it worth the wait?" I whispered.

"Not even Freyja could give such an exquisite kiss!"

Rurik kissed me again. I could feel his arousal, his hard cock pressing hard against me through his trousers. He caressed me as he kissed me, his touch firm, but warm. Perhaps I would enjoy this agreement after all …

My nipples tightened as Rurik flicked his thumbs over them. My breasts had increased in size over the course of my pregnancy – they'd increased in sensitivity, too. I gasped against his lips, unable to concentrate on kissing him, distracted by the delicious twinges shooting through my body from his touch.

I turned in Rurik's arms so he could play with my breasts. He stooped low to nuzzle my neck, his hands spread over my breasts, alternating between squeezing them and pinching my nipples. One of Rurik's hands travelled lower … His warm fingertips searched through the nest of curls between my legs and I gasped when he found my most sensitive spot. Rurik chuckled softly, his breath hot against my tingling flesh.

"Come with me," Rurik murmured.

Rurik led me to the nearest workbench. He cleared the workbench with one swoop of his arms, sending chisels, pots of nails, hammers and the like clattering to the floor. Rurik turned to me, his eyes flashing hungrily. I couldn't help, but smirk at the lust exuding from him. I wrapped my arms around his neck and he pulled me against him, gripping my buttocks, delicious bolts sizzling through me as he nipped the soft flesh of my shoulder.

This – our lovemaking – was *meant* to be currency. It was transactional – Rurik had my body in return for my freedom. I thought he'd only lift my skirts and take me, disaffected, detached, just a tool to reach his climax. I had been so wrong.

By the gods, I could feel how Rurik wanted to *enjoy* my body, not just use me to meet his own end like Kainan did. Worse yet, I wanted him. Rurik was tender yet passionate, rough yet warm. His touch grew wilder and I revelled in him! Every graze and caress, each squeeze and nibble – by the gods, I hadn't enjoyed being with a man like this since – since Jan.

I'm so sorry, Jan ...

Rurik lifted me from the ground. Taken by surprise, I flailed, but he put me down as quickly as he scooped me up, setting me on the worktop. Rurik cupped my breasts, clamped his mouth over one nipple and sucked it as keenly as a starving babe.

I squeezed my eyes shut and grabbed his shoulders, the warmth of his mouth and wetness of his tongue sending shudders through me. With a smack of his lips, he released my nipple and moved to the other, suckling it just as ravenously.

Rurik's hand travelled down between my legs, his other clutching my breast still. I opened my legs to him, breathy moans slipping from my lips as his fingers searched wildly through my silken hairs, quickly finding the delicate folds there. Somehow he knew just where and how to stroke me, his fingertips drawing small, firm circles over me, my bliss mounting.

Before I could meet my release, Rurik slipped his finger inside me. He eased it deep inside, pumping me slowly, deliberately, relishing each moan that fell from my lips.

"Not so bad, am I?" Rurik asked.

"Ssh." I replied, my eyes drifting half-open.

"Who are you imagining?" Rurik whispered, bringing his face close to mine.

"Kiss me, Rurik!" I breathed, clasping his face between my hands.

Rurik kissed me, smirking at my arousal, my passionate need for his kiss, his touch — he was obviously pleased with his effect on me judging by his haughty grin.

Embarrassingly, I found myself enjoying Rurik's smugness. Motivated by my appreciation of his talents, he kneeled on the ground and nibbled my thighs. I gasped and twitched at each sharp bite — he didn't hurt me, he bit just enough for me to feel the graze of his teeth.

"There are other places I can kiss. Would you like me to?"

"Don't tease me!" I groaned as he flicked his tongue against me.

"Only if you say please."

"Rurik!"

Rurik laughed against me, the heat of his breath driving me wild. Before I could bark his name again, he drew his tongue flat over me — I moaned loudly, his name trapped in my throat. I grabbed the back of his head, my fingers tangled in his long fair tresses, pinning him against me, needing him to stay where he was.

Thankfully, Rurik appeased me. He buried his head between my legs, his tongue flicking and lapping, one hand clutching my breast, the other grasping my thigh, holding my quaking legs open.

Rurik's beard tickled me as he licked me. I held onto the bench, my eyes screwed shut, focused on the sharp, delicious sensation building between my legs. Euphoria was growing inside me like a pot boiling over a fire, and my blood simmered.

Rurik pressed his tongue against me harder, his pace and pressure escalating alongside my euphoria. My legs twitched and shuddered, my body jerked uncontrollably. I slumped back against the rough wall, holding his head between my legs with both hands. Ecstasy erupted through me, flooding through my body from my centre to the tips of my fingers and toes.

Rurik stood up, victory splashed across his face. He wiped my wetness from his mouth with the back of his hand and kissed me, my flavour coating his tongue. I searched for his belt with both hands as we kissed.

"You're returning the favour, are you?" Rurik grinned, glancing down as I untied his trousers.

I grasped his cock, running my hand slowly up and down it, admiring the length and girth of it.

"You don't want me to?" I asked coyly.

"Oh, I want you too." Rurik said, helping me down from the workbench.

I sank to my knees, holding his cock in both hands. I drew my tongue over his long, thick shaft, leaving a trail of saliva glistening on it. I licked the ridge and head, all the while massaging his balls with my hand.

At first, I worked slowly, steadily, easing him further into my mouth, sucking deeply, curling my tongue around him, pulling away. I held the base of his cock with one hand, gently moving it up and down his shaft while sucking the head. Rurik gathered the hair from around my face and pulled it behind my head, compelling me to take him deeper.

I opened my mouth as wide as I could and took his cock all the way in. I pulled away slowly, allowing myself a breath through my nostrils before I repeated the process. I obeyed the pressure Rurik applied on the back of my head, made note of his groans and how his body twitched when I sucked on him at different pressures. I answered his pushes and pulls by increasing my speed, eliciting a cascade of husky moans from him.

Rurik's arousal was mounting. He grabbed my head with both hands and thrust into my mouth, shoving his cock further down my throat at such a speed, my head practically bounced between his legs. I gagged and choked, fighting for breath as I let him use me. He arched his back, groaning louder, but before he reached his climax, Rurik pulled my head away and stumbled backwards.

"I see why Kainan wants to keep you." Rurik panted. "You're talented with your mouth!"

"Then why did you make me stop?" I cocked a brow at him.

"There are other things I want to do with you yet, dear."

Rurik grabbed his cloak and laid it down on the paved floor. He pulled me into his arms, our lips colliding as we lowered to the floor. The coldness of the stone seeped through Rurik's cloak and froze my back. My blood pumping from the heat of the passion burning between us, I didn't care.

Rurik laid over me, kissing me as he pushed his cock inside me. With steady, deliberate movements, Rurik fucked me, his speed increasing as his ecstasy grew. I grabbed his waist, crying out as euphoria erupted through me a second time. Emblazoned, Rurik pounded me, roaring as he filled me with his seed.

Embraced like lovers, we panted on the floor in silence for what felt like an age, my head rested on his arm.

"Will you take me to Aros?" I murmured, kissing his chest.

"*Já*, now I know you can be trusted." Rurik said with a soft laugh, his fingertips dancing over my arm. "At daybreak I'll sneak you onto one of my ships. After unloading my wares in Götaland, I'll take you to Aros."

"I don't want to go to Götaland, I want to go straight to Aros." I sat up and glared at him.

"Beggars can't be choosers. Just be happy you're returning to Aros at all." Rurik said.

He propped himself up on his elbow and reached out to me, stroking my jaw softly, attempting to lure me back into his arms.

"What am I meant to do in the meantime?" I demanded, slapping his hand from my face.

"Wait here, rest, sleep. If you want passage to Aros, you'll stay here until daybreak."

Rurik, who obviously realised I was in no mood to snuggle him anymore, got up and searched for his clothes. I stood up and watched him dress, picking up his cloak and holding it against my chest. He turned to me, wordlessly. I offered the garment to him.

"Keep it," Rurik said. "You'll need it."

"*Nei*," I replied firmly.

He stared at the cloak for a moment before acquiescing. He slipped it about himself and fastened his brooch over his right shoulder. Ready to depart, Rurik gripped my shoulders.

"I enjoyed our time together, Jarl Aveline." Rurik said, resting his brow against mine. "I don't want to leave you angry at me."

"I look forward to your return in the morning." I said, bristling with irritation.

"I hope I might enjoy you again on our trip to Götaland."

"I'll see you in the morning." I spat through gritted teeth.

The passion was well and truly extinguished. Rurik sighed and pressed a kiss to my forehead. He turned his back and left me alone in the shipyard, locking the door behind himself.

ASHES REMAIN

I was furious Rurik wouldn't take me directly to Aros. That wasn't part of the deal! I strode to the slipway and eased myself to the ground, my legs hanging above the water. I gazed through the opening at the end of the room. The moon was much lower, soon the sun would stretch its golden fingers over the horizon and drag itself up into the sky.

As Rurik said, at least I'd be going to Aros. Directly or not, at least I was still going. The smile that spread across my face at that realisation was so big, my cheeks ached. At morning light, I would be on a ship headed far away from Constantinople and the terrors contained in this damned city.

By morning light, I would finally go home!

CHAPTER FORTY

THE CREAK OF the door woke me up – I must've fallen asleep. Footsteps echoed on the stone slabbed floor. Rurik was here! It was still dark outside, I expected him a little later, but I wasn't complaining – the sooner I was on his ship, the better. I wiped sleep from my bleary eyes and slipped down from the workbench.

"Aveline?" Rurik called out as he neared me.

"There you are!"

Vomit rose in my throat and my heart sank to the bottom of my chest. Slinking behind in Rurik's shadow was Kainan. Rurik betrayed me!

"I've been searching for you all night, Danethrall!"

Kainan was obviously trying to keep his voice calm, but it trembled with anger – the threat of danger laced his words. I staggered backwards, I couldn't let Kainan get me, not now! I glanced around the building, Rurik and Kainan crept forward, spreading out to block my way to the door.

"Be a good slave and come back to your master." Kainan growled. "Perhaps I'll show you mercy, my little runaway whore!"

There had to be another door, another way out – but where would I go? I was so pregnant, I couldn't run quickly – and there were *two* of them! There was nothing, no other ways to flee this damned building, they blocked the only way in or out! Wait – there *was* another way out. I glanced at the slipway.

"Don't even think about it, Danethrall!" Kainan spat.

With one more glance at them, I jumped into the waters – the moment I did, the men lunged after me. The water was shallower than I expected, my feet gave way beneath me when I landed. Panicked, I strode as fast as I could to the mouth of the shipyard, the sea spread out before me. My movements were slowed, working against the resistance of the water. I staggered onward, panting and panicking.

ASHES REMAIN

Two splashes echoed behind me, Kainan and Rurik jumped into the slipway, too – they were following me! I threw off my *stola*, took a breath and dove down into the water, thankful Vidar taught me to swim all those years ago.

It was faster swimming than walking, the burden of the bastard inside me alleviated by the water. I swam into the harbour, glancing at the opening between the great harbour walls.

What would I do? *Swim* to Aros? No, but hopefully Kainan and Rurik would give up and swim back to shore and jump into a boat to row after me instead. In those precious moments I could swim back to shore and flee through the city on foot. Dressed in the long gowns of a freewoman, I might have a chance at freedom, as long as I kept the brand on my calf hidden …

I glanced over my shoulder – damn it, they were gaining on me! I swam harder, gasping for breath, my arms aching. I kicked and kicked. My body was weak from being locked away in Kainan's home for so long. I'd lost all the muscle and strength I had before coming to this damned place!

A hand wrapped around my leg, pulling me under the water. I spluttered and flailed, kicking at whoever grabbed me, but I couldn't shake him. I didn't realise how fast Kainan could swim! He pulled me towards him, not caring that my head went beneath the water.

Kainan dragged me to the shore.

Coughing and choking, lying on my belly on the sands, hot tears spilled down my cheeks, imperceptible from the seawater streaming from my hair. Pain ripped through my stomach, my limbs were heavy and aching.

I forced myself onto my hands and knees, looking this way and that, searching for someone on the beach who might come to my aid, but there was no one. Only Rurik was on the shore with us. He was standing a short way in the distance, frowning. I wanted to scream out to him, wanted him to help me, but the words were lodged in my throat.

"You shouldn't have done this, Aveline."

Kainan kicked me. Wailing, I curled into a ball as he beat me. I felt the crack of my ribs as Kainan kicked me again and again. All the while, Rurik watched, not moving an inch to stop Kainan.

Kainan flipped me over and punched me, his fist slamming into my face, the hard knuckles of his hand smashing my cheekbones. Over and over, Kainan raised his arm, panting as he punched me. He staggered back and resumed kicking me in the stomach, his blows slow yet hard. The last sight I snatched before passing out was of Rurik. He just stood there and watched.

***

SHARP PAINS WRENCHED through me. My vision bleary, I peered through the narrow slits of my swollen eyes. I was in the cellar, I recognised the familiar scent of the earthen room. An oil lamp hung across the way on a hook – Kainan must've forgotten to take it after he'd dumped me in here.

How long had I been here? My clothes were still wet, the briny tang of seawater oozed from me. I couldn't tell if my flesh was covered in sand, congealed blood or the thin crust of salt from dried up seawater – most likely an amalgamation of the three. I tried to move, but my body was too stiff and swollen. I stayed curled up on the floor, every inch of me throbbing, pain tearing through my chest with each shallow breath.

Another sharp pain shot through me. I cried out, flinching and crying more from my body's reflective jerk. I clung to my stomach, feeling the child inside me move. Was it time? Had the stress of fleeing or the beating I'd received initiated labour? I forced myself to sit up, propped myself against the earthen wall, my legs splayed out in front of me. Another pain ripped through me.

"Frigg!" I wailed. "Allmother, hear me! Give me strength, Frigg! Come to my side and aid me!"

My prayer was cut short by another wrenching pain.

The child was coming.

I had no charms – no silver keys or runes to hold to aid a quick, safe birth. No thrall, healer or helping woman to sing the ritual songs or support my arms or wait ready at my knees for when the baby would appear. How was I supposed to birth a child alone?!

"Kainan!" I roared through the contractions searing through me.

I screamed for Kainan until my voice was hoarse and throat raw. He didn't come – no one did. They had to hear my cries, they had

ASHES REMAIN

to! But they ignored them, they chose not to aid me. I had to suffer this alone.

"Freyja! Help me!" I wailed, the pains growing ever closer. "Frigg, give me relief! Assist me!"

Groaning, I forced myself onto my knees, my rigid muscles quivering. I scraped at the wall, attempting to cling to it, the packed dirt crumbling in my palms and caking beneath my nails. There was hardly a breath between the pains!

I struggled to reach past the swell of my aching stomach, searching between my legs, my movements stiff and slow. Wet, slimy smoothness met my fingertips – the baby's head. I fell to the ground on my elbows and knees, screaming.

I pushed. I pushed and pushed! With all my might I tried to expel the child from inside me. By the gods, I thought my body would shatter, the child was splitting me in half as it exited my body!

"Frigg – help!" I wept, pushing one more time.

The baby fell out of me, tumbling onto the floor with a damp *thud!*, followed shortly by the slimy mass of afterbirth. With my heart pounding in my ears, I collapsed to the ground panting.

Something – something was wrong.

The baby wasn't crying.

I clawed myself around, reaching for the newborn child.

It was a boy – *a son*.

But it – it wasn't the right colour. Its – *his* – tiny thin lips were dark, almost purple, his fragile skin red – he wasn't rosy and pink like my other children had been. Was it – was *he* – a changeling? Was he something not human? And – and he didn't cry. The child was silent – he was still.

Nausea overwhelmed me as I pulled the newborn towards me and held him against my chest. He was warm and wet, covered in the slime of birth, but he didn't move.

The child wasn't a changeling … he was dead.

I leaned against the cellar wall and rested the baby on my legs. I stared at him, examining his little face. His mouth was hanging open, his closed eyes were swollen. He looked like a baby, with ten tiny fingers and ten tiny toes, but his colour was off, his nostrils were flat …

As time went by, his face became puffy and broken. I ripped his cord apart, detaching him from the afterbirth, and clutched him against my breast.

"I'm sorry, child." I whispered, tears slipping from my eyes and landing on his mop of dark, wet hair. "I'm sorry …"

My body aching, I set the child down on the floor, wishing for my *stola* to wrap him in, and crossed the room. I curled into a ball and wept.

Hours went by before Kainan appeared. He spotted the child and the afterbirth across the room from me. He quietly stepped towards the baby and scooped it up gently, staring at the tiny corpse silently for what felt like an age.

"You birthed me a son." Kainan murmured.

"You killed your son." I growled.

"We had a son …" He mumbled, ignoring me.

With one arm, he carefully held the tiny corpse against his chest as though he was sleeping and carried him up the stairs, taking the oil lamp in his empty hand. The click of the lock rang to my ears, Kainan locked the door behind himself.

Even in the darkness, I stared across the room at where the child had been. He was gone, a nameless bastard borne of my womb. Though I hadn't wanted him, though I detested the child before he was even born, I felt hollow, broken – the absence of the child tore me apart.

I clutched my empty stomach and wept.

I was completely alone.

ASHES REMAIN
CHAPTER FORTY-ONE

Late Summer, 894

IT FELT LIKE months since I last saw Kainan. He hadn't returned since he removed our dead child from the earthen cellar. The only face I saw was that of the thrall who tended my wounds, brought me food and water, and emptied the bucket I defecated in. Days after I birthed Kainan's bastard, two male thralls came down to the cellar and fit fetters about my feet.

The fact Kainan sent a thrall to tend to my wound and feed me meant he didn't intend to starve me to death in this underground prison. Why was he keeping me alive? Unless this was torture – a slow death trapped beneath the earth. A hunk of bread and skin of water would keep me alive for only so long.

My body was stiff and sore, but most of my contusions had faded and the swelling of my eyes subsided. I was lucky no bones were broken, but my ribs were bruised significantly – only in the last week or was I able to breathe normally, without pain.

The thrall visited me eighty-six times since I birthed the child. I assumed she visited once a day like when I was first imprisoned here … Perhaps she visited every other day? If so then had I been locked down here for one hundred and seventy-two days. What if she came twice a day – then it had been forty-three days?

I slept a lot, sometimes willingly, other times I blacked out from the pain in my body and empty stomach. I could've been in the cellar for longer than I estimated. I couldn't know for sure.

Whether counting the days kept me from losing my mind or was actually a sign of me losing it, I didn't know. To pass the time between the thrall's visits, I sang to myself, songs I'd sung to my children when they were babies, songs we'd sing on the ships when we raided, songs Vidar would sing to me in moments of silliness. I sang ritual songs, those wordless noises, the deep Norse throat singing, those melodious animalistic growls and hisses and gasps.

I counted my bruises, examined how well they were healing. I paced the room, counting each restricted step, the fetters clanking around my ankles. At first I staggered, dragging my feet along the dirt floor leaving twisted tracks across the floor. Then I hobbled, slowly growing strength in my weakened muscles.

As time passed, I was able to walk again.

And I prayed. I prayed to all the gods, the goddesses of love and family to care for my children, grandchildren and Jan, I called on the gods of justice, war and vengeance to back me when my time for revenge arrived, and I muttered the words to Odin that had empowered me to flee from Kainan to begin with.

My recapture had not disillusioned me. No, I still planned to escape, but for now I was too weak, even the thrall could tackle me to the ground. The next time I escaped, I would have to succeed, for I knew Kainan would kill me if I didn't.

I was obsessed with freedom. With every fibre of my being, I refused to perish beneath Kainan's house, refused to rot away like a corpse in this cellar. I would *not* die as Kainan's slave!

The fear Kainan instilled in me contorted into deep, black hatred. Though I hadn't faced him in a long time, I thought of him every day, picturing his face and filling myself with anger at the sight of him. I would not quake or quail in his presence.

I will face the tapestry the Nornir have woven for me, and I will tear it apart ...

And I spoke to Vidar. I called to him, asking what he would do if he was in my position, and I knew the answer instantly. He would devise a plan and he would escape. He would fight and kill all those in his path, but he wouldn't stop there –he would hunt Kainan down and take his vengeance, slaughtering the bastard.

Other times I would just ask Vidar how he was or I would tell him how many steps I'd taken around the room that day or I would reminisce on funny moments from our past. I would speak to him, but I would never receive an answer, no matter how I longed for one.

"What about today, my love?" I whispered into the darkness. "Will I to return to you today? Or must I keep going on like this?"

Instinct and anger spurred me to survive, but part of me wished life *would* just end. My children were grown, Jan was with them to protect them and guide them ... I was old now and they'd lived so long without me. Did I need to live any longer?

Sometimes I dreamed of Vidar appearing in the cellar, his arms open wide, beckoning me into the afterlife with him. I'd wake from those dreams with an aching heart for I longed to go with Vidar as strongly as I yearned to escape.

The door opened and light poured down the stairs. I shielded my eyes, unaccustomed to the brightness. Footsteps sounded, heavier than normal. It was only a matter of time until Kainan came down here. He stomped down the stairs holding an oil lamp. Tucked behind his belt was his whip.

"Danethrall." Kainan said, his voice dripping with bitterness.

I was silent.

"You have nothing to say to your master? You have nothing to say after you made such a fool of me?" An exasperated laugh tumbled from Kainan's lips. "Imagine how I felt when I came home, eager to see you after closing an incredible sale with one of the richest lords in Constantinople and instead I found you gone. I wanted to share my good fortune with you, my *happiness* with you! And you'd vanished!

"I knew exactly where to find you. That morning I told you Rurik was going to Götaland. How stupid of me! You decided to sneak on board his ship and smuggle yourself to Aros!"

I didn't say a word, eyeing Kainan's whip, all bravado and courage expelled from me at the sight of it.

"I gave you expensive clothing, jewellery, shoes, food, wine! I only asked for one thing in return, yet you still tried to flee. Your disobedience sickens me! I haven't been able to visit you in three months because of how you disgust me, you ungrateful, despicable Dane!" Kainan roared.

He lunged at me, grabbed a fistful of fabric at the front of my dress and slapped me across the face. He swung his arm back, my arms shot up protectively over my face, but he stopped. I peeked at him, Kainan's hand trembled with fury – he looked like he was having difficulty holding back from hitting me.

Why was he stopping himself?

"Get up, I can't stand the stench in here."

I didn't move.

Kainan grabbed me by my hair and dragged me up to my feet.

"Don't make me repeat myself!" Kainan hissed, spittle flying from his mouth all over my face.

Kainan threw me to the ground. I scarpered up the stairs, wincing as the chain between the fetters struck my ankles. In the kitchen I stole a brief glance out the window. It was morning outside, the sun gleamed over the horizon, stretching lazily upwards, slicing through the deep blue remnants of night.

I didn't have long to admire the scenery before Kainan ripped my filthy clothes off my body. I was wearing the same clothes since the night I'd tried to escape. They were stiff and foul with dried seawater, sand, dirt and blood. Kainan wrinkled his nose at the disgusting garment.

A slave quickly set about cleaning me, scrubbing the filth from my body with a rag and cold water from a bucket. It was remarkable to see my flesh beneath layers upon layers of grime. As she washed the dirt from the back of my legs, the deep red brand of Kainan's initials shone like a fresh painting. I shuddered at the memory, the pain, the stench of my flesh sizzling under the scolding metal in this very room …

The slave made me kneel over the bucket so she could scrub my tresses. When the bathing was finished, Kainan made me pull on a flax dress. It was itchy and frayed, but at least it was clean.

"Despite your name, you were never truly a slave, were you Danethrall? Not even when you lived in Roskilde." Kainan sneered. "What slave duty did you perform here? What chores did I give you? I kept you in a beautiful *gynaikonitis*, kept you dressed in fine clothes and jewels – you were a pet, not a slave.

"Not anymore. You'll stay fettered indefinitely. You *will* clean my floors, fetch water from the well, wash linens and serve my guests. You *will* complete every chore I set you and you *will* do them perfectly, otherwise you *will* suffer." Kainan patted his whip. "I have no sympathy left for you, Danethrall. No second chances."

***

AT NIGHT I slept on the hard wooden floor of Kainan's room without so much as a sheet to cover me. A chain fixed to a hook in his bedpost was locked to the ring at the front of the iron collar around my neck. Kainan was confident I couldn't escape this way. It was better on the floor of his room than in the dank cellar, but most places were, even if I was tied up like a dog.

During the day, I swept and scrubbed the floors of Kainan's home and the paving slabs of his courtyard. I wiped the window shutters, cupboards and wooden furniture, cleaned the walls, and polished the vases, statues and ornaments that decorated his house. On warm, windy days, I laundered clothes and bedsheets with strong soap in a large tub of hot boiled water in the courtyard and hung them to dry on the washing line.

When I had chores that needed to be done in outside, Kainan was there with me, watching me like a hawk. The shackles around my ankles limited my movement to the point I could do no more than shuffle about. Regardless, Kainan didn't trust me. He watched me always, he never left me alone.

The other thralls took care of meal preparation, cooking and pruning the gardens. I wasn't allowed near knives or sheers. While a few of his thralls were trusted to go to the marketplace to purchase foodstuffs, I wasn't allowed to leave.

Kainan didn't let me go unmonitored in his home for a moment. He posted armed guards at the exterior doors of his home. If I tried to escape while he was out, they would stop me. He didn't even allow me to speak to the other slaves, vowing to cut out their tongues if I tried.

The solitude was difficult, but I could tolerate the chores. Nothing was worse than the nights. When the whim took him, I had to endure Kainan's carnal urges. If I refused him, I was whipped. I fought back only once and the nine slashes across my back were enough that I didn't refuse him again.

***

Early Autumn, 894

I STOOD AGAINST the wall of the *triclinium*, the five other slaves beside me. We were dressed in identical sheer white dresses, our breasts, navels and the dark curls between our legs visible through the transparent fabric. Kainan's guests were due any moment.

Rurik visited Kainan a few times over the weeks since Kainan brought me upstairs. The Rus would greet me, he would try to speak with me when I poured his wine, but I refused to even meet his gaze. How dare he lie to me – use me – betray me! When the chance presented itself, I would kill the bastard.

Rurik was not at the party yet. Of course, Rurik was never on time – he always swaggered in late. The first man to arrive this evening was a wealthy lord, the newest of Kainan's customers. He strutted into the room eyeing me and the other slaves hungrily.

As he examined us, the lord made comments to Kainan in Greek. He paused in front of me, pointing at my fettered feet. Both he and Kainan laughed at whatever answer Kainan gave him.

Soon enough, the other guests arrived. Another lord, some merchants, a few slave traders who worked for Kainan, Rurik and–

Herra?!

No, it couldn't be!

Herra Kaupmaðr sauntered into the room with his crewman, Leifr, and Rurik. He and Leifr glanced at me but didn't give any sign that he recognised me. He seated himself on a settee beside Kainan, who snapped his fingers at me for a drink. Grabbing the terracotta amphora of wine, I hurried over to them.

As I poured his drink, Herra looked me up and down and pointed to my fetters, saying something to Kainan in Greek. Kainan replied to him and together they laughed, just like every other time with every other guest.

As Herra and Kainan spoke together in Greek, Kainan signalled for me to turn in circles with a flick of his finger. He paused me occasionally, assumedly to give Herra a better look at me.

"This is Herra Kaupmaðr, a merchant from the north. In fact, he is the most famous merchant in the world." Kainan said to me in the Norse tongue. "You should be flattered he's expressed such an interest in you."

"She's Norse?" Herra asked in his native tongue, answered by a quick nod from Kainan. Herra smiled warmly at me. "Why, you *are* a pretty thing – what lovely eyes you have! I'm sure you've heard that often, haven't you? What's your name, my sweet?"

ASHES REMAIN

"I call her Danethrall." Kainan interjected. "Thank him for complimenting you, Danethrall."

"*Þakka fyrir*, Herra Kaupmaðr." I tried to keep my voice level.

"She has an accent." Herra furrowed his brow. "She doesn't sound like she's from the Norse lands at all."

"You have a keen ear, Herra Kaupmaðr! Most wouldn't have noticed. Danes took her from the Anglo-Saxon kingdoms when she was a child. They taught her to speak the Norse tongue." Kainan explained. "She spent the majority of her life in the Danish lands – she's one of them in all, but birth."

"I see. And how did you come across her, my friend?"

"Her owner brought her to Constantinople on his travels. As I'm sure you can assume by the fetters, she's a fiery thing. Her previous owner was glad to be rid of her!" Kainan lied.

"That explains the wounds on her back." Herra remarked.

"Ah, those?" Kainan laughed.

Kainan stood up, grabbed my shoulders and turned me around. Without warning, he yanked my dress down to my waist, baring my naked torso for all to see, not that the sheer fabric did much to hide my shame to begin with.

The other guests, but for Herra and Rurik, gasped in horror at the sight that met their eyes. Rather than excitedly ogling my naked body, they grimaced and cringed at the gruesome web of scabs, welts and whip lashes that marred my flesh.

"She's been difficult for you, too, I see." Herra commented, touching the most recent of my scars – one of twelve long wounds Kainan inflicted upon me just days ago.

"She came to me fierce and fighting, I did what I must to crush the hostility in her." Kainan explained. "I can't say she's been a wise acquisition – she tried to flee not long ago and she's refused my commands more often than I'd like to admit. I've tried various ways to handle her, from rewards to punishment, but she only seems to respond well to the latter."

I caught sight of Rurik in the corner of my eye. He bit his bottom lip and shook his head before turning and stepping away. Was he appalled by me? I was a damn sight worse off than when he last saw me, that was certain. Was he too guilty to look at my mutilated flesh? He *was* the reason I received these wounds!

"Why do you torture yourself by keeping her?" Herra asked.

"I don't care for her insubordination, but I *do* enjoy her looks." Kainan smiled. "The fetters and chains restrict her movements and make her more manageable."

"I've had similar thralls in my time." Herra said, nodding knowingly. "If only I had your patience, Kainan! If she were mine and caused enough trouble to warrant all of those wounds, I would've sacrificed her to the gods long ago!"

"Unfortunately, my God does not accept blood sacrifices."

Herra and Kainan laughed together. Herra turned back to me, considering me quietly as he sipped his wine.

"If she's such an inconvenience, I'll take her off your hands."

"I'd be a terrible friend if I foisted such a difficult thrall on you." Kainan replied delicately, the humour vanishing from his smile.

"Not at all! You said it yourself, she wasn't a wise acquisition. I'll give you twenty-five *nomismata* for her."

"She's not for sale my friend, but if she were, she'd be worth more than just twenty-five *nomismata*!"

"Money is no object." Herra shrugged. "Fifty? Seventy-five? How much do you want for her, my friend?"

"You'd pay *that* much for a troublesome thrall?" Kainan gaped.

"I want her, Kainan. Let me buy her off you and I'll consider contracting exclusively with you for thralls."

"After all this time, why would selling *her* to you finally convince you to do that?" Kainan asked suspiciously, his eyes narrowing.

"My gods admire those who are bold and daring like you've described her to be. If I delivered a creature like her to my jarl so that he could sacrifice her to our gods, I'd garner great standing with both him and gods." Herra replied. "This is the least I could give you for helping me so."

"I see ..." Kainan sipped his wine in silence, assumedly reflecting over Herra's enticing offer.

I tried not to show my excitement or eagerness. If Kainan sold me to Herra, I'd finally be free! He tossed the wine to the back of his throat and stared at me, his coal black eyes empty of light.

"I've wanted to be your exclusive provider of thralls for so long." Kainan said quietly. "As much as I would like to help you, unfortunately, she's not for sale."

ASHES REMAIN

I swallowed my cry, devastated by his answer.

"*Nei?*" Herra raised his brows.

"I appreciate the offer, but I'm in no need to be rid of her." Kainan mumbled, avoiding Herra's gaze.

Silence fell over the *triclinium*. It seemed that denying Herra Kaupmaðr was not a common occurrence. The guests frowned at Kainan, though they didn't speak the Norse tongue (but for Rurik) they seemed to understand what was going on.

"While you two haggle over this one, I'm going to relieve myself." Leifr said, brows raised and lips pursed – he must've recognised what a bad decision Kainan was making.

Leifr slipped out of the room. Herra didn't so much as glance at him, his eyes locked on Kainan.

"You're letting a lucrative offer pass through your fingers." Herra cautioned. "You know I won't offer this again."

Kainan's face was red. He was a fool for denying Herra's offer. All evening he tried to ingratiate himself to Herra, but he'd ruined it all by refusing to give up ownership of me. I could only hope that Kainan would change his mind, if only to save face.

"I'm sorry." Kainan mumbled.

"I'll not lie to you, Kainan, I'm disappointed with your reply." Herra said disappointedly. "Part of me hopes you're trying to swindle more out of this deal for yourself."

"I wouldn't dream of swindling you!" Kainan swore. "I *want* to come to an agreement with you, but I can't sell this particular slave to you. You can have any other – I'll give you as many as you want, whichever you want, to prove I'm not trying to cheat you! You just can't have *this* one – she isn't for sale."

"I have thralls aplenty," Herra sighed, shifting in his seat. "But a thrall with as much fire in her soul as this one? Why, you can see it in her eyes, they're like embers! It's not often one comes across such a specimen. She'd be an ideal offering to my gods."

"I'm sorry, Herra." Kainan replied sincerely. "If I change my mind, I'll give her to you happily, for no cost at all. In fact – if it pleases you, you're welcome to enjoy her while you're here."

"You'll share her?" Rurik interrupted.

"Freely to Herra – for a price to others." Kainan scowled at him.

"You don't let your friends enjoy this one?" Herra questioned.

Kainan's nostrils flared with the anger he was trying to conceal.

"I've been greedy, I admit." Kainan said through gritted teeth. "Her recent transgression has since opened my eyes. I won't hog her any longer – I hope the more men take her, the more her fiery soul will be quenched."

"It all makes sense now. You won't sell her to me because she's your concubine." Herra remarked, disapproval audible in his tone.

"There is no harm in a man keeping concubines!"

"Of course there isn't, Kainan, but you refuse to sell something of such great worth to *me*, solely because she spreads her legs for *you*." Herra scolded. "Do you know how I became renown? Because I don't keep the best spoils to myself! I sell them off – albeit at a profit. *That* is how one garners a reputation like mine. If you want buyers to seek you out like they do me, you *must* be willing to sell everything!"

"If I find another amber-eyed thrall, I'll give you her." Kainan snapped. "I appreciate your advice, but the matter is settled."

"Then how about we just take her?"

Heads spun to the doorway to the *triclinium* – Leifr held one of the doors open wide, letting Jan storm into the room, Young Birger and Sander behind him, all three men's swords drawn and bloody. My heart raced – they found me! They were here!

One of Kainan's cohorts dived towards the double doorway leading to the garden outside the *triclinium* but froze in his tracks. The garden was filled with warriors!

Mjölnir amulets hung around their necks and shining gold and silver bands jangled on their tattooed arms. Their long hair was braided back or loose like lion manes, black kohl warpaint slathered across their faces. The men descended upon the *triclinium*, their weapons doused in blood like Jan's and my sons'.

I grinned as they neared, for I knew these warriors. My beloved friends, Hallmundr, Domnall, Einarr, Yngvi, Lars and Ebbe, with Herra's crew storming up behind them!

"*Þakka* for distracting the bastards, Herra." Jan smirked.

Kainan gaped at Herra, who smiled innocently back.

"I was not entirely honest with you, Kainan." Herra said, pausing to sip his wine. "I did not intend to sacrifice her, but I did intend to impress a jarl – two of them in fact. May I introduce you to *Frú*

ASHES REMAIN

Aveline's sons, the Jarls of Roskilde and Aros, Birger and Sander Vidarsson."

All colour had drained from Kainan's face. He spun around, eyes darting about the room. In every archway, doorway and window, broad, tattooed warriors sneered, shields slung over their backs, sword, axe or *sax* in hand. Kainan had no hope of escape.

Kainan's hands flexed at his sides. They were empty, he had no weapon – unarmed, without so much as his whip, Kainan was vulnerable and he knew it.

"Guards! *Guards!*" Kainan bellowed.

"They're at Hel's mercy now!" Young Birger growled.

Before the men could say another word, with an almighty swing, I smashed the amphora against Kainan's head. The pottery shattered, shards flew, wine sprayed everywhere. Kainan toppled to the ground, blood oozing from the side of his head.

I threw the broken handles to the ground and dashed to Jan as quickly as my fetters allowed. With just a few strides, Jan met me, gripping my shoulders and pulling me against him. We didn't have time to embrace. I seized the *sax* from his belt, glancing up at him.

"Kill everyone!" I hissed. "But leave *him* for me!"

"Of course," Jan grinned.

Upon my order, Kainan's guests and thralls screeched. They tried to rush through the warriors, but they were no match for the Danes and Norsemen. Jan and our companions slaughtered them all. Shrieks filled the air, blood splashed, skin snapped, bones cracked, bodies thudded to the floor. While my friends murdered every damned person in the room, I rammed Jan's dagger into the locks of my fetters, determined to free myself.

I glanced up frequently, watching the massacre unfold. To my horror, I spotted Rurik across the room – he was armed! Not only that, but instead of attacking him, Jan, my sons and the others seemed to be fighting alongside him!

At last the fetters sprang open – I was free! I leapt to my feet, squeezing the ivory handle of Jan's *sax*, ready to plunge it into one of Kainan's despicable cohorts, but the massacre was already over. The bastards were defenceless, trapped in the *triclinium*, all their deaths were swift, masters, slavers and thralls alike.

"What of him?" I snarled, pointing the *sax* at Rurik.

"What of me? I kept my word to you. You laid with me and I freed you."

Roaring, cheeks blazing red with anger and shame, I lunged at Rurik, ready to plunge the *sax* into his chest, but Young Birger grabbed me.

"He brought us here, *móðir*!" My eldest son exclaimed.

Seething, I scowled at the Rus.

"What are we going to do with our friend, *Frú*?" Rurik asked, nodding at Kainan who was sprawled nonconscious on the floor, soaked with wine and bleeding.

Ignoring Rurik, I turned to my companions.

"Search for my things – my beads, brooches, rings – they might be here, find them!" I commanded. "Take everything of worth that you can carry – and bring me Kainan's whip!"

The men scattered, but for Rurik and Jan.

"What? You don't want to loot his home?" I snarled at the Rus.

"I have everything I need. I'd much prefer to see what you're going to do." Rurik grinned.

I stood over Kainan, hatred boiling in my veins. I tore his clothes from his unconscious body, whacking his head against the tiled floor carelessly as I yanked his tunic over his head. An arm's length away was a dead thrall, blood oozing from her wounds. I took her bloodied *stola* and hurriedly fashioned it into a rope, binding Kainan's feet together like mine had been in the fetters. As I bound him, Hallmundr arrived, Kainan's whip in his hands.

"*Þakka fyrir*, my friend." I said, accepting the whip.

"Now what?" Rurik asked, amusement alight in his words.

"Carry him to the cellar."

***

IT DIDN'T TAKE long for Kainan to wake up. I sat on the bottom step of the stairs, watching him. Kainan groaned, clinging to his head, his movements slow and stiff. He was obviously in great pain – I couldn't help but smile. He writhed on the floor, glancing panicked about the room, realising where he was, realising he was naked. The oil lamp hung on the hook, offering an orange glow for us to see by.

"Good morning, Kainan." I said softly. "You told me about a lot during my time here. Now it's time for you to listen."

"You whore! You bitch! I'll kill you!" Kainan hissed.

"*Nei*, you won't." I replied, unwinding the whip slowly before Kainan's petrified stare. "Things have changed, Kainan. Why, look at our situation – before it was me lying bound and naked on the cellar floor." My voice tailed off, letting the tense silence hang in the air.

In one fierce movement, I jumped to my feet and swung the whip, striking Kainan with such force, blood sprayed the moment the leather thongs collided with his flesh. Kainan roared in agony, writhing like a worm doused in vinegar.

"Does it feel good?" I murmured. "Perhaps you forgot the pain over the years since you were a thrall."

Kainan continued to moan and thrash on the floor.

"Do you remember when you were a thrall, Kainan? Do you remember the abuse you suffered at the hands of your masters? I remember you telling me about it, I remember the darkness whirling in your eyes as you told me." I paced around Kainan, watching the blood trickle down his body. "So many years ago ..."

I dragged the whip over his head, down his scarred back, through the lashes, leaving bloody streaks along his buttocks and thighs.

"Before you were sold, when you and I were still – well, *whatever we were* – Vidar and I spent a lot of time together. He fell in love with me and asked me to marry him." I said softly, crouching down beside Kainan's head. "Do you know what my reply was?"

Kainan struggled to lift his head and meet my gaze. He glowered at me, loathing and venom dripping from his tear-filled eyes. For the first time since Kainan bought me, I felt nothing towards him. No anger, no hate. A bizarre calmness had taken over me – no, an *emptiness*. I felt no remorse or uncertainty – I felt no pleasure – for what I was about to. This was more than revenge. This was justice.

"I refused him. Do you know what Vidar did when I rejected him? He respected my answer." I smiled, the memory flashing in my mind. "He didn't pressure me or try to force me to change my mind, he just accepted my choice."

"He's better than me because I persevered where he gave up?" Kainan demanded.

"Vidar won me for many reasons." I replied, watching Kainan drag his knees up beneath him. "The respect he had for me was just one of them. You never respected me, you never loved me, you just wanted to *own* me! Well, you've owned me, Kainan, and now it's time to pay the price."

I brought the whip down on him again. Shrieking, he collapsed.

"It's been over twenty years, Kainan. Your bitterness spurred you to become a wealthy man, but it turned you into a monster.

"You were correct when you said a lot has changed over the last two decades. I *have* changed – I *am* a Dane, not the meek little Anglo-Saxon girl you knew, nor that ridiculous evil temptress you imagined me to be … I am vengeance and justice!"

I stooped down and grabbed a fistful of Kainan's hair, yanking his head up and bringing my lips to his ear.

"Now, *crawl*."

I shoved Kainan's head into the dirt floor as I stood up. I backed away to the stairs, my sight locked on his trembling body. Slowly Kainan did as I commanded, drawing his legs beneath him, pushing himself up onto his hands, his limbs shaking violently.

"Well done, Kainan! You were much easier to break than I expected!" I applauded. "Now crawl across the room!"

Sweat poured from Kainan's flesh, his face red, blood streaming from his wounds. He crawled across the floor and paused at the wall. I barked at him to crawl again and he crossed the room, slowly, painfully, tears trickling down his face.

"Your cruelty surprised me. All those years ago you told me the Varangians took you, beat you, whipped you, starved you. Why would you do that to someone else when you know their pain?"

"Because it worked." Kainan hissed. "I was obedient! I never fled, never fought against them!"

"But you did eventually, didn't you? How else did you establish yourself as a slave trader here? And a successful one at that! I remember you bragging to Rurik about your methods of breaking slaves. You know the life and pain of a thrall yet you had no problem inflicting it on others. You became just like the Varangians who enslaved you!"

ASHES REMAIN

"Because of you!" Kainan snarled, struggling to sit back on his legs. "When I met you, I found the fight inside me again! You made me believe there was hope! I fell in love with you and the promise you inspired. You were proof there was more to life than rotting away as a Dane's slave!

"Then you broke my heart – choosing my master over me! I realised then that everyone's the same, as long as you are a thrall, people will treat you like the shit you are! Your lies and betrayal made me become the man I am now!"

"Do *not* blame me for your mistakes, Kainan!" I bellowed, cracking the whip in the air just to watch him flinch. "A young girl rejecting you *two decades ago* couldn't turn you into the wretched monster you are today. If that's all it took, then you are far more pathetic and twisted than I thought!

"*Nei*, it wasn't me who did this to you, Kainan. *Your* bitterness and loathing turned you into this vile creature. *You* made the choice! You could've become a wealthy merchant and freed thralls like yourself, but instead you became the worst master of all."

I paused, breathing deeply. Kainan's wide, terrified eyes watched the whip in my hands. He didn't know when I would strike him again. I knew exactly how he felt – I knew his terror.

"You hurt me ... You raped me – tortured me ... Do you remember loving me, Kainan? Do you remember being *happy* with me? Why didn't those memories stop you from striking me?" I didn't give him chance to answer – I didn't *want* him to answer. "I know now – truly, I understand why you did it. I remember feeling happy with you yet there is nothing I want to do more than whip you within inches of your life – just as you did me!"

I raised the whip high and struck him over and over, his shrieks and cries ripping through the air in a relentless tumult. The thongs curled around his body, slashing his sides, shredding his flesh.

After a while, Kainan's cries stopped, the only sounds were the whistle of the whip as it ripped through the air, the *snap* as it struck him and the squelch of his frayed flesh. His blood sprayed over me as refreshing as rain after a drought.

"Aveline," Jan was leaning against the wall beside the staircase beside Rurik, my beloved *Úlfsblóð* in his hands. "We need to leave before daylight comes."

GWENDOLINE SK TERRY

I turned back to Kainan, a bloodied mess before me. The skin of his back was slush, reddened bone visible in places. But for the occasional twitch, he was still. He was alive, he rasped for air in his unconscious state, his breath rattling. I crouched beside him and shoved him onto his back.

The front of his body was unmarred by the whip. I admired the deep olive tone of his skin, the broadness of his shoulders, his muscled arms. I stroked his right arm, lifting it up and examining his hand. There was the faded crescent shaped scar from when my sheep bit him all those years ago.

My lips twisted into a half-smile as I stroked the scar, the memory of that day appearing so clearly in my mind even though it had been over twenty years. I rested my cheek against the scar.

"I cared for you once, Kainan. I truly did." I murmured.

I stood up and reached out to Jan, wordlessly asking for my sword. Jan gave it to me, closing his hand over mine around the hilt. We glanced at each other, no words shared, but we didn't need to speak. Jan was with me, he supported me, he would be here with me, to see my revenge through to the very end.

"Nothing can kill a man if his time hasn't come, and nothing can save one doomed to die." I said, holding my sword over Kainan's stomach. "Your time has come, Kainan. Nothing will save you. I hope you get what you deserve in your afterlife."

I plunged *Úlfsblóð* into Kainan's stomach. Groans gurgled in his throat, but still he didn't move. Kainan would die soon enough.

"Let's go." I turned to Jan.

Jan nodded and climbed the stairs ahead of me.

"Well done, *Frú*." Rurik crooned.

"Leave." I spat.

Rurik climbed the stairs. I took the oil lamp from the hook, glancing at Kainan a final time. I climbed a few steps then threw the oil lamp at the bottom step. The lamp smashed, splashing flaming oil all over the wooden stairs. Kainan wouldn't survive his wounds, but I would not let him have a way out of the cellar – he would die trapped, his only exit consumed by flames.

Kainan would suffer here, just as I had.

ASHES REMAIN
CHAPTER FORTY-TWO

IN THE KITCHEN, I slammed the cellar door shut and rammed the table against it, the wooden legs screeching over the tile. No one questioned me, they let me do what I wanted. The fire was growing quickly, black ribbons of smoke were already slipping through the cracks around the door.

"Do you have your loot?" I asked.

"*Já, Frú* Aveline." My men nodded.

"To the harbour. Storm-Serpent awaits." Jan smiled.

We dashed through the night, my men carrying chests of gold and silver, jewels and chains, bundles of silks and clothing, whatever they seized while I was torturing Kainan.

Morning would arrive soon, we had to get ourselves and our loot onto the ship before anyone woke and spotted us. We would be imprisoned or possibly lose a hand each for theft, but the moment they found Kainan's house ablaze, Kainan's burned, mutilated corpse and the charred bodies of his guests and thralls, we would be put to death.

The gods looked favourably upon us, however, and we made it to the harbour without issue. My heart raced at the sight of Storm-Serpent, the symbol of my freedom. Upon my ship, the rest of my crew waited, lowering the gangplank upon sight of us. Grins spread across their faces, they waved to me and shouted their thanks to the gods for my return.

Domnall and the others carried their plunder aboard the ship, leaving me, Jan, my sons, and Rurik on the shore.

"I suppose it's time for us to say *far vel*." Rurik said. "I'm glad to have met you, Aveline."

I drew *Úlfsblóð* so quickly Rurik didn't have a chance to defend himself. The pointed end of my double-edged blade pressed under his chin, I glared at the Rus with fury and contempt.

"Why didn't you stop him?" I hissed through gritted teeth "You could've killed Kainan on the beach and ended this long ago!"

"*Nei*, I couldn't." Rurik replied matter-of-factly. "The guards would've caught me, and we both would've been killed on the spot. The best thing was to have Kainan believe you concocted this plan on your own."

"Rurik came to Aros. He ran into my hall and told me he knew where you were." Sander said, moving to stand beside Rurik protectively. "It's thanks to him you're alive, *móðir*."

"Did you go to Götaland first?" I demanded.

"Of course, my ship was weighed down with wares." The corner of his mouth lifted in a half-smile. "But that was my plan all along, remember, *Frú*? I always said I would go there first."

"Even while my life was at stake?!"

"I promised to go to Aros *after* Götaland. I didn't lie to you, did I, *Frú*? That's more than I can say for you – you aren't even a jarl!"

"*That's* what's important to you?"

"*Frú*, I didn't *need* to go to Aros. I didn't *need* to tell anyone where you were." Rurik said. "If I were as cruel as you're insinuating, I would've left you as Kainan's slave. I could've had you as often as I wanted that way, but instead I brought help to you. *I saved you!* You should be grateful!"

My hands trembled. I wanted to kill him! Instead I sheathed my sword, snarling with frustration. Rurik smiled at me with that irritating, smarmy grin.

"If I ever see you again, I *will* kill you." I spat.

"You're welcome, *Frú* Aveline." Rurik winked. "When I see a shipyard, I'll think of you and our time together. What an honour, bedding the only woman-jarl of the Danish lands!"

"Leave!" I roared.

Jan grabbed Rurik's shoulders and pushed him towards his ship. I didn't know how he managed to keep calm, listening to the Rus brag about bedding me – listening to my betrayal. Somehow he did – though I could tell from the glance I stole, I was not the only person who wanted to run Rurik through with a sword.

Young Birger and Sander stared at me, both of them wearing identical expressions. Their brows were furrowed and lips rolled together, and stray blond hairs drifted about their handsome faces.

ASHES REMAIN

At that moment, my anger disappeared, replaced by a strange mix of relief and regret – I was so thankful to lay my eyes on my sons again, so much time had been stolen from us.

With tear filled eyes, I held out my arms and together we embraced. I squeezed them, weeping uncontrollably. They were so different to when I last saw them. They were so tall ...

"I missed you desperately!"

"We missed you, too, *móðir*." Young Birger murmured. "We came here multiple times, but we couldn't find you!"

"We never gave up, *móðir*! I wish we found you sooner." Sander lamented, his head rested against mine. "What they did to you – I- I'm so sorry, *móðir*."

I sniffed hard, my voice thick with emotion.

"It's over now ... Let's go home." I smiled.

We boarded Storm-Serpent, Jan quickly joining us.

"Would you take the rudder, *Frú*?" Jan beamed at me.

"*Já, þakka fyrir*." I grinned.

***

NIGHT ENVELOPED US like a blanket studded with diamonds. I couldn't remember seeing the stars and moon glow so brightly before. We sailed swiftly through the day, Storm-Serpent cutting through the waves, the strong wind propelling us home. The sparkling city of Constantinople was far behind us, vanished from sight, a lifetime away. Unlike before, my heart didn't ache for the place anymore.

It was finally over.

"You should rest," Jan said, slipping past the crewmen, most of them asleep on their benches. "Let me relieve you."

I watched him remove his cloak and smiled as he draped it about my shoulders. I grasped it tightly and shuffled over for him to sit, unable to stop smiling at him. Jan grinned in return, stars captured in the sapphire depths of his eyes.

Time had taken its toll on Jan. Even in the dark, the lines etched around his mouth and across his brow were clearly visible, as were the dark smudges beneath his eyes. Silver streaked his long tawny hair and speckled his beard. I curled up against his body and he wrapped his arm around me, holding me close against him.

"I don't want to sleep. I'm afraid when I wake this will all have been a dream." I mumbled, my words muffled by his clothes.

"On all nine realms, I swear this is real."

"That's what you'd say if this was a dream."

Jan laughed. He lowered his head and I cupped his jaw, the coarse hairs of his beard tickling the palm of my hand. Our lips met in the sweetest, softest of kisses. Tingles surged through my body like lightning, warming me through.

"I knew you'd come." I said. "I didn't doubt you for a moment."

"I'm sorry it took so long," Jan's voice was low, laden with regret. "I never stopped searching for you. I–"

"Ssh," I whispered. "I'm here now – with you. That's all I wanted for so long – that's *all* I want."

"I saw what he did to you." Jan murmured, the guilt in his voice shattering my heart. "Your back, your leg ... I should've–"

"*Nei*, Jan." I said firmly, staring at him fiercely. "None of us could control what happened. It doesn't matter anymore – I had my revenge ... All that's left is Thóra."

"Thóra?"

I stared ahead, watching the waves, anger brewing in my stomach, bile rising in my throat. Her image appeared in my mind, her vicious grin as she shoved me overboard ... Thóra would pay for what she did to me.

"Kainan was the man we hit with the apple in the marketplace." I explained. "He saw us – he saw *her* with us. When we ran off, he approached her and asked who I was and she told him. She told him she wanted me gone – she said I was stealing *you* from her."

"What?!"

"They planned this all. Thóra pushed me off Storm-Serpent, Jan. I don't know what she told you, but she pushed me! Kainan's men were ready to seize me and take me to him – the merchant ships behind us on the waters belonged to him."

"She didn't say a thing." Jan growled, his hands curling into fists. "She – she was sleeping – she said she hadn't seen you –you were on the ship when she fell asleep and gone when she woke."

ASHES REMAIN

"She's a filthy liar!" I spat. "I *will* have my revenge on her, Jan. I know you care about her—"

"I stopped caring for her when she took my son away." The harshness of Jan's tone took me by surprise.

I gazed up at him and he glared down at me.

"By the gods, I don't know how to convince you that she's nothing to me!" Jan cried out, clearly exasperated. "My heart belongs to *you*. Whether you accept it or not, I will love *only* you long after my body has rotted into the damned earth!"

My expression softened. With brows raised and lips parted, I gazed at Jan, shocked by the passion in his words, but heartened by them, too. There were so many things I wanted to tell him, but I couldn't, so surprised by his declaration of his love. Of course, Jan had told me he loved me many times in the past, but this ...

I felt his words to my very bones.

"If you loved him, you'd know it in your bones, as I know in mine that I love you."

Vidar's words echoed in my mind. He said that to me when he'd announced his love for me, when he'd asked me to marry him for the first time, years ago, and I stupidly rejected him because of my relationship with Kainan.

I loved Vidar with every inch of my mind, body and soul, feeling love for him in my very bones, just as he said. It was a feeling I'd never felt for any other man ... Until Jan. It was not just Jan's love for me that I felt in my bones, but my own love for him as well.

"Do what you must to Thóra." Jan said. "She deserves to be outlawed for what she did to you. I only ask that you don't banish Thórvar. He's my only living child."

"I'll spare him." I nodded.

Jan kissed the top of my head. In the jumble of emotions spinning inside me, I didn't have the heart to tell Jan that I wasn't going to just outlaw Thóra, I was going to kill her.

GWENDOLINE SK TERRY
CHAPTER FORTY-THREE

I STEPPED OFF Storm-Serpent, grasping *Úlfsblóð* tight. As I marched through the harbour, townspeople gasped at the sight of me – I must've looked like a corpse dragged from a battlefield.

After weeks on the sea, unable to change my clothing or bathe (though I'd scrubbed my body as best I could with a rag and bucket of seawater), I was still wearing the sheer thrall dress Kainan had me dressed in, only Jan's cloak around my shoulders to conceal my body. Dried blood stained my clothing and I stank of sweat, saltwater and death.

Fenja, Rowena and Melisende, who I assumed came to the harbour the moment they'd heard our horn blast through the air, grimaced at the sight of me. Regardless, the three women dashed towards me and hugged me, tears streaming down their faces.

"Go to the hall and draw a bath for *móðir*." Fenja ordered.

Rowena and Melisende nodded, wiping their eyes with their sleeves as they scurried back to our home. While Fenja embraced her husband, greeting Sander with kisses and tears of happiness, I continued towards the hall, adrenalin coursing through my veins.

Townspeople gathered in front of the hall, hailing the gods and thanking them for returning me to them. Chewing my lips, I scoured the crowd.

Someone was missing – Thóra.

Anger boiled inside me. After all she'd done, Thóra was too cowardly to face me. I threw down my sword, ripped Jan's cloak from my shoulders and tore the dress from my body.

"Look at me!" I thundered, spittle flying from my lips. "Look upon my suffering!"

I snatched my hair over one shoulder and turned to show the lash wounds. Every person before me was stunned into silence. Women clapped their hands to their mouths or shielded their children's eyes. Men swore, curling their hands into fists.

ASHES REMAIN

"*I was a thrall!*" I boomed. "I was hurled off my ship and forced into thraldom! I suffered every day of my captivity! I was raped! Beaten! Lashed! But I survived – and with his own whip, I killed the man who enslaved me!"

The crowd cheered and whooped. I examined every face, noticed every grimace at my appearance and the anger that curled their lips as they heard the mistreatment I endured. I was bolstered by their joy, heartened as their chests swelled with pride when I declared my victory.

"But I am not yet done with my vengeance! There is still one person left with my blood on their hands." I announced, silencing the crowd. "Bring me Thóra Arnsteinsdóttir!"

The crowds searched for the woman. As they hunted Thóra down, I hauled the cloak around my shoulders and seized *Úlfsblóð*. Soon enough, Thóra was dragged to me, thrown at my feet, tears pouring down her face. She snivelled and begged, but I held my hand up, silencing her instantly.

"I did not whimper or cry when you threw me off my own ship!" I snarled. "You sealed your fate when you struck a deal with Kainan! Face your death with dignity!"

I drew *Úlfsblóð* from its sheath. She shrieked, her face ruddy and dripping, but there wasn't an ounce of mercy left in me. She tried to scramble to her feet and run, but Domnall grabbed her. She flailed in his grip, but he kicked the back of her legs and she fell to her knees. Domnall and Hallmundr pinned her to the ground by her arms. She wouldn't get away.

In the corner of my eye, I spotted Jan. Beside him, Thórvar was pale-faced and panicked, his eyes round as coins.

"Stop her! Jan! *Stop her!*" Thórvar howled, glancing between Jan and his mother.

Jan was a statue, his arms folded over his chest, his eyes locked on me. He supported me. He would see my revenge to the end.

"This woman came to Aros seeking protection against her husband – a man who beat her ruthlessly!" I roared. "I granted her that protection! When Kveldúlfr arrived in Aros with his army, demanding she be returned to him, I led our army against him! We defeated him for her! We *bled* for her! Our men *died* to defend her! This woman had our protection and what did she do in thanks?

She struck a deal with my enemy! She plotted against me and sent me to my doom! For her betrayal, I condemn Thóra Arnsteinsdóttir to death!"

"*Móðir! Nei!*" Thórvar screeched.

Thórvar's eyes, filled with tears, found mine. Gripping the antler hilt with both hands, I raised *Úlfsblóð* over his mother, the fatally sharp tip aimed between her shoulders. She wailed at me to stop, begged me to show mercy. I turned away from Thórvar, his cries – like hers – falling on deaf ears.

Without guilt, I brought my sword down, plunging it through Thóra's flesh. A mighty crack shook the air as the metal crunched her bone, accompanied by Thóra's final shriek. I wrenched my sword from her body, the blade scarlet with her blood, and Domnall and Hallmundr released her. She dropped to the ground.

Thóra was dead.

I found Thórvar in the crowd. His face was screwed up in heartbreak and fury, tears glistening on his cheeks. He ripped his hate-filled eyes from me, turned and ran. To my surprise, Jan didn't follow him, but Galinn Johansson did.

"Whoever betrays me faces my blade!" I bellowed, watching Galinn turn to me briefly. "Whoever betrays me faces death!"

Galinn scowled before chasing after Thórvar.

ASHES REMAIN
CHAPTER FORTY-FOUR

AROS, DENMARK
Late Autumn, 894

JAN AND I had laid in bed for hours, but neither of us could fall asleep. Jan had been up since sunrise searching for his missing son, arriving home late in the evening for a bath and a meal. In the morning he intended to get up and begin the search again, with Galinn's wife, Sibba, at his side. They wanted to visit the neighbouring towns and gather information on Thórvar and Galinn's whereabouts.

They had done the same thing for weeks – sometimes they would be gone for days at a time. I sent men to different towns to aid their search, but so far we'd heard nothing. It was as though Thórvar and Galinn had disappeared from the face of the earth.

Jan hadn't slept well since Thórvar left. Jan supported me killing Thóra, but he didn't hate me for Thórvar running away. By killing his mother, I'd run Thórvar out of town. Privately, I knew that might happen before I killed Thóra, but I was willing to take the risk. Nothing could stop me from punishing Thóra for everything I suffered in Constantinople.

Galinn's mother, Ósk, and his wife, Sibba, were a different story. They loathed me with every fibre of their beings. I didn't realise Ósk could despise me and my family more than before, but Galinn's disappearance revealed a new level of hostility from the old woman.

Usually she kept her thoughts to herself and avoided me and my kin, but now she scorned me to anyone who would listen. Her husband had abandoned her and Galinn when Vidar overthrew Erhardt Ketilsson and took Aros. Now her son disappeared and her daughter-in-law left to search for him because of me.

"We were meant to be married a year ago." Jan said, his voice cutting through the night and tearing me from my thoughts. "We were meant to marry the moment we returned from *Miklagarðr*."

"*Já*, we were," I murmured.

"We've been home for six weeks. Why haven't we married yet?"

I rolled onto my side and stared at him, puzzled. Through the darkness I discerned his solemn expression. Was he serious? What made him suddenly ask this?

"We've been busy, there have been more important concerns." I said, tactfully referring to Thórvar's disappearance.

"Isn't our marriage an important concern?"

"I-it is," I replied, my brows shooting up my head.

"Then *why* aren't we married yet?"

I let his question hang in the air. The truth was all our time was spent fruitlessly searching for Thórvar. I hadn't brought up marriage because I didn't want to appear like I didn't care about Thórvar. Despite not feeling guilty for being the reason he ran away, I *was* concerned about him. He was not guilty of his mother's sins, he was a victim of her actions and lies.

"I assumed we'd marry after we found Thórvar." I said at last.

"And if we never find him? Will we never marry?"

I had no answer.

"I've been waiting to marry you since the day I met you, Aveline. I don't want to wait any longer."

"Then let's not."

"Aveline?"

Jan rolled onto his side, his eyes locked on mine. He seemed to know what I was thinking before I'd even said it, judging by the excitement dancing in his eyes.

"Why not? It *is* Frigg's day."

"Right now?"

"You said you don't want to wait any longer."

"I don't."

"Come on then! I'll wake the children while you go to the *goði* and find sacrifices." I leapt out of bed and pulled my boots over my bare feet. "I'll have Einar, Æsa and Sander gather Domnall, Ebbe and the others – we'll meet at the altar."

"We'll marry in our nightclothes?"

"Why not? They're just as good as anything else." I shrugged.

Jan beamed at me through the darkness.

"Let's do it! Let's get married!"

"Wait–" I froze. "What about rings?"

ASHES REMAIN

Jan paused, thinking furiously. With a grin and a flash of realisation across his face, he lunged to his chest across the room and shuffled through it, tossing items to the floor. Within moments he cheered victoriously and returned to me with a small wooden box in his hands.

"I've been waiting to give this to you since the day we met." Jan said, watching me open the box.

Inside was a gorgeous silver ring. It was plain, simple, delicate.

"It's the ring my *faðir* gave my *móðir* when they wed." Jan announced proudly.

"It's perfect!" I whispered. Struck by guilt, I frowned, my heart racing in my chest. "But I have nothing for you!"

Jan returned to his chest, shuffling through it yet again, until he found whatever he was searching for.

"You gave this ring to me on an expedition years ago." Jan beamed, holding out a thick silver band. "It was part of my lot from a monastery we raided. As stupid as it sounds, I never had the heart to sell it or melt it and cut it up … It fits me perfectly."

Jan's scarlet blush was visible even though the darkness. I crossed the room, wrapped my arms around his neck and kissed him deeply.

"It will make a fine wedding band!"

***

ASSEMBLED AT THE stone altar, excitement sizzled through the air like lightning. Huddled in their cloaks, Jan, the *goði* and I were surrounded by Sander, Fenja, Æsa, Einar, and our thralls, Melisende and Rowena, as well as our friends Lars, Einar, Ebbe, Guðrin and Domnall, Ebbe and Borghildr, and their three raven-haired sons and daughter, Borgunna, Æsa's beloved friend.

Though they shivered in the frigid night, their breath hanging in clouds about their faces, they beamed at us, excited to watch us marry at last. Jan and I were standing before the *goði* in front of them, all nineteen of us dressed in nought but our boots, nightclothes and cloaks.

I wished Young Birger, Signý and Ísarr, and our dear friends Hallmundr, and Yngvi, Domnall and Guðrin's son, were there, but we could not wait any longer. My time as Kainan's captive had proven if waited too long we'd have nothing left but regret. Jan suffered throughout his life – death stole his first wife, his children, his kin, Vidar. I knew that, like me, he feared if we didn't marry that very night, fate might never offer us the chance again.

It took some convincing for the *goði* to agree to forgo the majority of the wedding rituals, but thankfully he was persuaded – at least we had a goat and sow to sacrifice and wedding bands to give each other.

Sander (as the eldest male of my family since Young Birger wasn't with us) and Jan negotiated the marriage with the *goði*, making their agreement before us all as witnesses. With that, all we had to do was invoke the gods, sacrifice the animals, make our vows to each other and swap rings.

"Neither of you would rather wait to conduct the ceremony properly?" The *goði* asked a final time, stifling a yawn with his fist.

"*Nei*," Jan and I replied in unison, grinning at each other.

"I've waited twenty-three years to do this." Jan said. "If I have to wait another day, I'll go mad."

"Fine," the *goði* sighed. "Have it your way."

As the *goði* invoked the gods, I clutched my wedding and engagement rings from Vidar, both hanging from a leather thong around my neck. The metal was cold and hard against my palm. As the *goði* invoked the gods, I silently prayed to Vidar.

I would never forget him. No man – not even Jan – would ever replace him. A piece of my heart would always be missing without Vidar, but I knew he would be relieved to know I'd found happiness again.

Before he died, Vidar made Jan vow to protect me and our children. Jan kept his vows to my late husband and the wedding ring he slipped on my finger was proof.

ASHES REMAIN
CHAPTER FORTY-FIVE

Late Summer, 895

"WHERE ARE THEY?" Jan fumed, five months after Thórvar and Galinn disappeared. "I've searched every corner of the Danish lands! How in Hel's name has no one seen them?"

Over the last few months, Jan spent most of his time scouring the Danish lands for the young men, but he couldn't ignore his duties on his farm forever. I understood – if it was my child I would do the same, but after so long with not so much as a glimpse of them, I was starting to believe Galinn and Thórvar were hiding from us.

Since they left, we searched nonstop without any luck. We were hindered in autumn by harvest and winter preparations. Winter slowed us, too, for it was too treacherous a time to travel. In just a few months, spring would bring a multitude of farming responsibilities that would impede our search as well.

"Jan ... What if they don't want to be found?" I asked carefully, watching him pace up and down the middle of his farmhouse.

"It doesn't matter if they don't want to be—"

"But it *does*."

Jan stopped and glowered at me.

"Thórvar and Galinn are *men*. They might be young, but they can hold their own. They're not helpless children. At some point we have to stop treating them like they are and respect their decision."

"I can't just stop looking for my son." Jan shot back.

"Jan, they'll return when they're ready. I know it."

"How can you be so sure?"

"I killed his mother, Jan – and you didn't stop me." I said, lifting an eyebrow at him. "He *hates* me, and in his mind you betrayed him by not stopping me. He'll be back for revenge if nothing else."

A mournful frown replaced Jan's frustrated glare. He slumped into a chair and released a soft, humourless laugh.

"My son – my only living child wants vengeance against me ... By the gods, I wish I understood the Nornir's humour."

Jan's words hung heavily in the air. I wasn't the one who crafted Jan's fate, but I was responsible, too. If Thórvar was alive, he wanted my blood, I was certain of that. Did he want Jan's blood, too? His father let his lover murder his mother ... Yes, Thórvar probably wanted to kill Jan as well.

"I'm sorry, Jan ..." I mumbled. "I-I'm sorry this happened."

"So am I ..." Jan sighed, rubbing his face in both hands. "I understand you needed to punish Thóra for what she did to you, but I can't pretend I didn't wish you outlawed her instead ..."

"Thórvar wouldn't be here now even if I *had* outlawed her – you know he would've left with her."

Jan said nothing. He stared solemnly at the flames dancing in the firepit, the orange light glinting on the white hairs in his unkempt beard. Usually Jan was tidy and well-groomed, his hair silken and beard neatly trimmed and plaited at the front. Since Thórvar vanished, Jan did nothing more than bathe, tear a brush through his hair and tie it back carelessly.

Nothing we spoke about mattered – none of it changed the fact his son was missing and nothing I did would ease Jan's worry. The Nornir had laid out a merciless plan when they wove Jan's life tapestry. All he could do was suffer it bravely.

***

SEVEN MONTHS PASSED since our conversation that cold winter afternoon. An entire year had gone by since I returned from Constantinople and killed Thóra Arnsteinsdóttir, and, by the gods, so much had happened.

On top of searching for Thórvar and Galinn with Jan, I worked hard to gain back the muscle I'd lost over the year I was captured. I practiced both armed and unarmed fighting every day with Jan, Sander, Lars and our other friends, for hours at a time. I was stronger than ever before.

Soon after our wedding, Jan and I travelled to Roskilde to announce our marriage to Young Birger (he and Signý were elated for us). We informed him of Thórvar and Galinn's disappearances, hoping against hope they might have come to Roskilde, but we were met with disappointing news. It seemed not a soul in either of my sons' jarldoms had seen them.

It was not all disappointment in Roskilde, however. While there, we met our beautiful granddaughter, Solfager, whom Ísarr guarded fiercely, taking his role as older brother seriously indeed.

Solfager was born while I was trapped in Constantinople. She was now two years old, could say an astounding number of words, and ran more often than she walked.

Not only had Birger and Signý welcomed another child to their growing family, but a few months ago, Fenja gave birth to her and Sander's first child, a sweet golden-haired son they named Hjarnar.

I mourned the time Kainan stole from me. I held my grandchildren tight and kissed them often, thankful that I had survived to meet Solfager and Hjarnar and embrace my darling Ísarr once again.

I gazed at Æsa, who was weaving at the loom across the room from me. Despite her age and the many suitors offered her, my daughter was still unmarried. I was once concerned by indulging in her refusal to marry, but I didn't care anymore. She had a family who loved her, she had brothers who protected her. If she didn't want to marry, I wouldn't force her. All I wanted was for Æsa to be happy – and she was.

"Where's Jarl Sander?" A man exclaimed, bursting into the hall.

"I'm here, calm yourself man!" Sander replied, sauntering out of the kitchen with his mouth full of food, holding dried sausage slices in one hand.

"There are ships in the harbour! They bare Túnsberg banners!"

Jan and Sander glanced at each other. In an instant, Sander threw the sausage onto the table before both men snatched up their swords and shields and sprinted out of the hall.

"*Móðir?*" Æsa whispered, her face deathly pale.

My body trembled. Had Kveldúlfr returned? I thought he had died – how in Hel's name did he survive his wounds? What about the grand funeral – was it a ploy after all? Did he have an heir seeking vengeance for his death? Damn it! Damn Túnsberg! Damn the gods and damn the Nornir!

"Stay here – shut the doors and arm yourselves." I ordered, snatching up *Úlfsblóð* and slinging my shield over my back. "Einar, guard the hall – protect our family!"

***

THIRTEEN SHIPS FROM Túnsberg bobbed on the waters, filled with warriors visibly itching for battle. It didn't matter that the ships were packed with men, it was an unimpressive amount of warriors to lead against Aros's army. Regardless, a chill ran through me, worsened by the ravens soaring overhead.

Our warriors lined the harbour, shields and weapons at the ready. Archers knelt in front of them, their arrows trained on the ten or so men from Túnsberg who bravely stepped foot on our shore. Sander and Jan were speaking with them.

I swallowed hard as I neared them, my fears proven true.

Kveldúlfr was alive.

"Jarl Aveline, how nice of you to join us." Kveldúlfr called, beaming at me as I took my place between Jan and Sander.

"I'm not jarl anymore, Kveldúlfr." I replied calmly.

The Norwegian's weapons were sheathed – he wanted to talk.

"That's what I've just been told." Kveldúlfr said, sneering at Jan and Sander. "Unfortunately for your son, I don't negotiate with children."

In the corner of my eye, I noticed Sander tighten his grip on the hilt of his sword. Thankfully, he didn't react rashly, though I knew he was insulted beyond measure. I don't know what Kveldúlfr was saying before I arrived, but Sander's temper was already hot.

"There's nothing for you and Jarl Sander to negotiate, Kveldúlfr." I said coolly.

"You're correct – there isn't. I'm here for you, Aveline Birgersdóttir. No one else."

"Oh *já*? Don't tell me you're here for my life again? You saw how well that went last time." I mocked, leaning on one leg and rolling my eyes at the Norwegian.

"I'm not the only one who wants your head this time, *Frú*." Kveldúlfr grinned, baring his fangs like a wolf. "There are others who seek vengeance against you and your family."

ASHES REMAIN

"And who might they be?" I asked indifferently.

Kveldúlfr turned and watched his warriors separate, allowing two young men passage–

"Thórvar!" Jan exclaimed. "Galinn!"

Galinn Johansson and Thórvar stopped either side of the Norwegian jarl, their chests puffed out, scowls fixed to their faces. Thórvar glanced proudly at Kveldúlfr who rested his hand on Thórvar's shoulder, before turning to glare at Jan and me.

Upon sight of them, I straightened my stance and grabbed the hilt of my sword.

"Get away from my son!" Jan snarled, ripping his sword from his scabbard and pointing it at Kveldúlfr.

"I see there is much you still don't know. I won't take your lives without you all knowing why." Kveldúlfr smirked, studying Jan briefly, unphased by his blade. "*Frú* Aveline, do you why I'm called 'Kveldúlfr'?"

"*Nei*, nor do I care." I spat. "What are you doing with them?!"

"I earned the byname *Kveldúlfr* during my time fighting with the Great Army in Britain." He said, ignoring my question. "Some say for my stealth, some for my viciousness and determination in battle, others say for my temper."

Kveldúlfr shrugged, his lips twisted into a dark smile.

"And here I assumed it was because you prey on the weak."

"You're funny, *Frú*. I do appreciate a good jest."

"Am I laughing?"

Kveldúlfr licked his lips, his eyes locked on mine.

"Do you know what my true name is, Jarl Aveline?" Kveldúlfr pressed, pausing briefly. "My *móðir* named me 'Thórvar' after my true *faðir*, and so Thóra named our son after me."

My jaw dropped. My gaze shot to Jan. For the briefest moment he gaped at Kveldúlfr and Thórvar in horror, both men smiling smugly in return. Quickly Jan's expression returned to that of fury.

"You lie!" Jan hissed.

"*Frú*, would you control your dog while we're speaking?"

Jan stepped forward, but I reached out and touched his wrist, halting him. Darkness roiled in Jan's sapphire eyes as he turned his frightening scowl to me. I swallowed, shook my head slowly and turned back to Kveldúlfr and Thórvar.

"I can't say I'm surprised by your reaction, Thóra had a penchant for lying. My son told me all the tales she spun – he also said she didn't have much to say about the first female jarl of the Danish lands either." Kveldúlfr chuckled. "My son is a good man, he's loyal. He weathered all his *móðir*'s stories and lies. After you killed her, he returned to where he belonged – at his *faðir*'s side.

"Which is why I'm here, Aveline Birgersdóttir. To avenge Thóra Arnsteinsdóttir."

"Why do you seek to avenge a woman who wanted *you* dead?"

"For my son." Kveldúlfr said simply. "Thórvar loved his *móðir*. Despite her faults, I loved her, too."

"If you want to die needlessly that's your decision to make. I'll defeat you, as I did before."

Kveldúlfr rubbed his jaw, a wry smile twisting his lips.

"Things are different, Aveline." Kveldúlfr said. "Your warriors might have defeated my army before, but they won't this time. For the last few years I travelled the Norse lands and amassed a force of *berserkir*, *úlfhéðnar* and *svinfylking*."

Bear warriors, wolf warriors and boar warriors. Aided by the magic and potions of *völvur* and *spákonas*, they were the strongest, most formidable warriors in the Norse lands – I'd wager the most fearsome in the world.

I swallowed hard.

"Galinn, why do you side with this fiend?" Sander demanded, eyeing the silver-haired youth. "You stand there silent while this wolf threatens to attack Aros – your wife and *móðir*'s home!"

"It hasn't been our home since your damned *faðir* became jarl." Galinn spat. "I've waited years to kill you, Sander Vidarsson! Jarl Kveldúlfr has offered me my chance!"

"What of Ósk? What of Sibba? Are you prepared to fight her *faðir*? Her uncles? *Your* kin through marriage?" Sander pressed.

"If it means killing you, I will burn the Danish lands to cinders – Sibba and her family with it." Galinn replied, venom dripping from his every word.

"We can settle this in battle, *Frú* Aveline, I have no qualm about that – but there *is* another way." Kveldúlfr interjected. "Rather than send your people to slaughter, you can give me your life and give your son's life to Galinn–"

ASHES REMAIN

"And give me Æsa as peace-bride." Thórvar added, much to Kveldúlfr's amusement. "The feud between my family and yours will end when we are wed, you have my word."

"Your word means nothing!" I spat at Thórvar.

"Think about it, *Frú* Aveline." Kveldúlfr said, that sickening smirk twisted around his fangs. "Your farmers can't defeat my *berserkir*, *úlfhéðnar* and *svinfylking*. Accept our offer and no one else will be hurt. If you refuse, my army will cut down every man, woman and child in Aros and leave their corpses for the ravens. Are you selfish enough to risk them all? You and Sander will die and my son will have your daughter as his bride either way."

"Leave!" I hissed.

"I'll see you in the morning, *Frú*. For your people's sake, I hope you will have changed your mind."

***

"THEY WILL NOT have my children!" I snarled, thundering up and down the hall. "Galinn can eat shit if he thinks he can touch a hair on Sander's head, let alone take his life! And demanding Æsa! The fucking gall of those bastards!"

When Kveldúlfr returned to his ship, I turned on my heel and stormed up the shore with tears burning in my eyes. There was no way in any of the nine realms that I would let them kill my son nor give my daughter as peace-bride to Thórvar, like I had been given to Erhardt. I would cut out Galinn, Thórvar and Kveldúlfr's hearts for daring to make such demands!

"Nor will I let him kill you, Aveline." Jan replied.

"If Kveldúlfr is anything like his reputation – which I have no doubt he is – it wouldn't matter if we did agree to his terms, he'd destroy Aros anyway." Domnall nodded, a scowl fixed to his face.

"There isn't a man in Aros who would give you, Sander and Æsa to those bastards." Lars said, his arms crossed over his chest.

Exclamations of agreement rumbled through the hall.

"We're going to fight, then," Sander said. "We have to get the women and children to safety, first. I've sent groups of scouts to survey Kveldúlfr's camp in the north and kill any of his spies in the west so we can smuggle the vulnerable out tonight. I'd prefer to have them leave by water, but I can't spare enough men to row that many ships. I'll spare as many men as I can to protect them while they evacuate Aros by foot.

"Einarr, Lars, Domnall – visit every home and tell them they need to be ready by nightfall. They can take nothing, but the clothes on their backs. When darkness falls, I want everyone at the west gate – they must travel as far from the waters as possible, Kveldúlfr might have archers posted on boats along the fjord.

"I will have a single *karve* sail to Roskilde. That's where you come in Einar." Sander said, turning to his younger brother.

"What?" Einar barked, furrowing his brow at his older sibling.

"I need you to be on the *karve* with *móðir*, Æsa, Fenja and Hjarnar. When you get to Roskilde, you must tell Birger to assemble is army and sail to us. You must–"

"I'm staying here." I interrupted.

Sander glanced at me long enough to roll his eyes and sigh exasperatedly. He turned back to his brother and tried to continue.

"Einar, I need–"

"I need to stay here and fight with you!"

"Who will defend our sister? Who will defend my wife and son? Who will gather the reinforcements?" Sander pressed.

"Any other man in Aros can do that!" Einar argued, his hands balled into fists. "Literally any other man!"

"*Nei*, Einar. There is no man in Aros I trust more than you. It *must* be you! You *must* see our family to Roskilde and you *must* bring Birger to us. You are the key to our success, Einar!"

Einar shook his head, visibly torn. Of course he wanted to see his family to safety, but he wanted to stay and fight like the rest of the men, not flee with the women, children and elderly. Jan grabbed Einar by his shoulders to face him.

"Einar, I understand what you're feeling, but your duty to your people is just as important as honour in battle." Jan advised, his sapphire eyes boring into Einar's icy blues. "You must know when to fight and when to stand back.

"Do you think your *faðir* wanted to remain in Roskilde when Alvar the First One led his army across the seas to fight with the Great Army? Vidar was left out of the war to protect his people from Erhardt Ketilsson! And he did that willingly – forgoing whatever glory he could seize in Britain because protecting his *móðir* and townspeople was more important!

"You *must* decide what's more important now – glory or protecting Æsa, Fenja, Hjarnar and the townspeople of Aros. You must make your decision now, you don't have time to think!"

"What of *móðir*?" Einar argued.

"We both know how obstinate she is – neither of us will convince her to change her mind once she's made it. She'll stay here and fight with us, and as her husband, it's my duty to defend her and support her. And Einar, as her son, it is your job to avenge us should you need to."

Einar gazed at me mournfully, chewing his bottom lip.

"Fine," Einar said at last, tears filling his eyes though he refused to let them fall. "But you must promise me you'll die if it means protecting my *móðir*! Promise me, Jan! Now!"

Einar thrust his arm forward. Jan gazed at it for only a moment before grabbing it and squeezing Einar's forearm tight.

"I vow to give my life to protect Aveline Birgersdóttir! I will die before any harm befalls her, I promise you, Einar Vidarsson!"

"May the gods hold you to your vow," Einar mumbled. "And may the Allfather grant you victory. Should you die, Jan Jarlufson, I will avenge you – I love you, *faðir*!"

Einar released Jan's arm and embraced him, tears slipping down his cheeks. Jan squeezed Einar, tears tumbling down his own face.

"I love you too, *sonr*."

***

I EMBRACED Einar, Æsa, Fenja and Hjarnar. I wept with them and kissed them, declaring my love for them endlessly. I wished them luck and safety and they wished me the same. I bade farewell to Rowena, Melisende, Guðrin, Borghildr and Borgunna, my heart breaking to say goodbye to my beloved friends. They needed to get as far from Aros as possible, they needed to get to safety.

After kissing my cheek, Einar climbed onto the little warship.

"There's still time to go with them." Jan said softly. "It isn't dishonourable for you to go, Aveline."

"Part of me wants to go," I admitted, dabbing my eyes with my sleeve. "But I refuse to sit idly by while you fight. If I'm to die, it will be at my husband's side."

"You'll be taking our family to safety!"

"I will fight and die at my husband's side." I repeated firmly. "Don't try to change my mind – you know how *obstinate* I am."

Jan sighed exasperatedly as he pulled me against his chest.

"I will fight and die at my wife's side." Jan said, kissing me softly. "For she's an obstinate woman even in the face of death."

"You remember that." I managed to smile despite the emotion lodged in my throat and the tears streaming down my face.

The few scouts Kveldúlfr sent out were slaughtered. We slipped the women, elderly and children out of Aros by foot before sending Einar, Æsa and the others away by ship.

My family, Guðrin, Borghildr, Borgunna, Rowena and Melisende held out for as long as they could, but the time had come. I'd wanted them to leave Aros, to get as far from the battle as they could quickly, but they stayed until the very last moment.

I was thankful.

Come morning, war would erupt throughout Aros. Lives would be slain, homes destroyed, families ripped apart. All I could hope for was victory so I could see my loved ones again – or an honourable death on the battlefield at the very least.

Archers lined the centre of the ship, bows in hand and quivers filled with arrows. At Sander's order, rowers dipped their oars into the water, propelling the ship away from the harbour.

I watched my family until darkness swallowed them completely.

The day passed in a storm of preparation, fear and adrenalin crackling throughout Aros like lightning. Children cried as they were carried from their fathers, mothers and wives wept as they left their sons and husbands. Some women stayed, taking up farming tools to defend their homes, refusing to leave their men.

The balmy night air kissed my skin, contrasted by the coolness of Vidar's runestone against my back. It was hard to sleep after saying goodbye to my family and friends. I slipped out of the hall, leaving Jan, Sander, Lars, Einarr and Domnall in the hall where they were drinking mead by the fire. They couldn't sleep either.

ASHES REMAIN

The coldness of the runestone seeped through my dress and chilled me, but I didn't mind. I'd been slumped against it for what felt like hours, lost in thought.

If Kveldúlfr truly had assembled an army of *berserkir*, *úlfheðnar* and *svinfylking* we would struggle for victory even with their lesser numbers. Sander had proven himself to be a talented strategist, but privately I wondered whether his plan would be enough to defeat the most vicious warriors in the Norse lands.

A yawn escaped my lips, so deep it made my body shudder. I didn't try to stifle it – I stretched my arms out in front of me, my joints popping and crackling.

Maybe I would get some sleep that night after all … What a blessing that would be. Between my time incarcerated in Constantinople and the nightmares that haunted me since, I hadn't had a full, uninterrupted night's sleep in years.

The moon was gradually descending, closer to the horizon than I wanted it to be. In just a few hours we would wake up and dress for battle. If I was to be victorious, I needed to get some sleep. I staggered to my feet, using Vidar's runestone to aid me.

"I'll be victorious whether I live or die, I promise you." I murmured.

***

JAN WAS THE only person awake in the hall when I crept through the door. The others were curled up beneath woollen blankets around the main room. Jan was sitting by the fire. He glanced up when I neared him, offering me the warmest smile I'd seen on his face all day.

"Are you ready for bed?" Jan asked.

"*Já*, I am now."

Jan set his cup on the edge of the fire and wrapped an arm around me. I slipped my arm about his waist and we ambled toward the sleeping area. Sander had fallen asleep in the main room – Jan and I had the entire sleeping area to ourselves.

We'd taken just a step inside the room when Jan began pulling off his clothes. I watched him remove his belt and tunic, tilting my head and admiring his plump bottom as he slipped off his trousers. Jan caught me peeking, grinning as he neared me.

"It's your turn – take off your clothes and come to bed." Jan murmured, grasping my shoulders and pulling me against him.

I stood on my tiptoes and snaked my arms around Jan's neck, our lips meeting in a tender kiss.

"Mmm …" I purred, resting my head against his chest, his hands dancing over me. "Undress me, I'm too tired to do it myself."

I didn't need to tell him twice. Jan unpinned my brooches and let my apron drop and pool about my feet. He placed my brooches and beads on a chest before sliding his hands down my back, my ribs, my hips, gathering my skirts and pulling my dress off me.

All that was left was my *hustrulinet*, the white kerchief I pinned over my hair that proclaimed my status as a married woman. Tenderly, Jan pulled the pins from the *hustrulinet* and wrapped them in the fabric. He placed the items with my brooches before running his fingers through my curls. I felt suddenly insecure about the strands of silver gleaming among my long chestnut tresses.

Jan wiped my mind clean of all thought when he pulled me against him, our naked bodies pressed together, his lips grazing mine. Goosebumps flooded my body and heat smouldered in the pit of my stomach, fanned by each delicate kiss.

We climbed into bed together. Jan drew my body against his, his hard cock trapped between us, but he didn't try to initiate lovemaking. Our limbs tangled, Jan's heartbeat hammered against my ear and his breath danced in my hair. This might be the last time we would hug each other – the last time we'd share a bed. I wondered if Jan felt as afraid as I did …

"No matter how hard I tried to form a bond with Thórvar, I couldn't." Jan said suddenly, his voice low and distant. "I thought he just didn't trust me, which I understood, he didn't remember me, he didn't know who I was. After eight years apart, who could blame him? He was so young when she took him away.

"I thought by living together, we could work through it, but he always kept me at a distance – as though he *refused* to be my son. Now I know why … Thórvar knew he was Kveldúlfr's son all along – he *knew* Thóra was using me to protect her from Kveldúlfr so he played along."

ASHES REMAIN

I listened to Jan without saying a word.

"I remember the *hólmganga* with her brother, Thorn. After I defeated him, he kept accusing me of murdering Thóra. I told him I didn't kill Thóra and Thórvar just before he cut down Caterine and little Alffinna …"

Jan squeezed me. He didn't need to remind me – the moment I heard the word '*hólmganga*' that day replayed in my mind vividly – it was the day my daughter was killed.

"It was strange – Thorn … Thorn gaped at me as though he'd made a horrible mistake." Jan said. "He demanded I repeat the name of my child, and I did. I'd never seen such a look of horror. I didn't take any notice of it at first, but after Kveldúlfr … I think Thorn knew Kveldúlfr's real name. At that moment, Thorn knew the child wasn't mine – he knew Thóra lied. It all makes sense …

"I don't think her family knew she was pregnant with Kveldúlfr's child when her *faðir* sent her to Roskilde. I think she was sent there just to keep her away from the fiend … I was stupid and married her quickly at her behest – she wouldn't share my bed otherwise and I was hopelessly infatuated with her so I agreed …"

"Jarl Halvard Sturluson, Kveldúlfr's *faðir*, died around the time Thora left you …" The realisation struck me like a lightning bolt.

"*Já*, he did." Jan nodded. "I think Thóra left me to reunite with Kveldúlfr. When he got violent and threatened her life, she came back. Thórvar knew the truth – he went along with Thóra's lies. He did everything to protect his *móðir* until the day she died."

"And now he's out for revenge." I whispered.

Silence settled over us, the moments and stories and lies and sorrows that led to this very night weighing heavily on us. Jan must've been thinking about this all day – he'd figured it all out.

"*Berserkir, úlfhéðnar* and *svinfylking* …" Jan murmured.

"We won't survive." I breathed, the wretched reality of what the morning would bring turning my stomach.

"I'm an old man, Aveline. I've lived far longer than I ever imagined I would." Jan said softly. "I'm glad I've lived my long life with you. Through all we've faced, the good and the terrible, you've made me happy … I'm ready for death."

"Stay close to me tomorrow," I replied. "If we're to die, I want to die with you."

"I'll hold you until my last breath." Jan vowed.

A few tears spilled down my cheeks as Jan brought his mouth to mine. Our tongues danced as his hands explored my body, caressing and stroking me with such reverence – as though this was the first time he'd ever touched me.

With every fibre of my being, I prayed it wouldn't be the last.

ASHES REMAIN
CHAPTER FORTY-SIX

MIST HUNG LOW and thick, as though the clouds had fallen from the sky. From my vantage point on an archer tower near the northern gate, I peered at Kveldúlfr's camp on the mainland. Just like Aros, the camp was humming with preparation since the first pale sunbeams stretched up from the horizon.

Kveldúlfr's army dispersed around the palisade surrounding Aros. We outnumbered them by at least five or six hundred warriors. Once Einar and the others rallied Young Birger and his army, we would squash Kveldúlfr easily. I only hoped we survived long enough for them to arrive.

Though we outnumbered them, the sight of so many *berserkir*, *úlfheðnar* and *svinfylking* made me shudder. They were the strongest, hardest warriors in the world – champions, elite soldiers. We might defeat them by the skin of our teeth if we were lucky.

"So many are wearing furs for armour." Sander remarked.

"They're the ones you must watch out for." I eyed the hulking warriors dressed in bear, wolf or boar skins.

"Animal warriors ..." A solemn stare replaced Sander's sneer.

I watched Sander's icy eyes travel over our enemies, his lips moving wordlessly. He was counting them. How had Kveldúlfr gathered so many of these infamous warriors?

Sander chewed his bottom lip, his brows knitted.

"I heard their strength is enhanced by magical potions and they can shapeshift into bears, wolves or boars ..." The confidence in Sander's voice wavered. "I heard they're immune to fire and iron, and they can rip a man apart with their bare hands."

"In all my years, I've *never* seen a man transform into an animal and *nothing* is immune to iron or fire." I said firmly, hoping to quell not just Sander's fears, but my own as well. "Pay no mind to stories. This is going to be a hard battle, but honour and glory *will* be yours. Fight with all your strength and courage and you *will* defeat them."

"We'll kill them all, *móðir*." Sander nodded. "I promise."

"I know you will, my love." I smiled.

I rested my head on my son's shoulder. Sander wrapped his arm around me and leaned his head against mine. For the briefest moment my heart swelled, and my eyelids fluttered shut. I almost forgot we were about to go to war – almost.

"What are they doing over there?"

Sander stepped closer to the wall and pointed toward the mainland to the west where our largest fields of crops were situated, watched over by a few farmhouses. A group of enemy warriors skulked through the low mists towards one of the houses on the edge of a barley field.

We squinted at the figures in the distance and watched them enter the home. A while later they emerged from the house, carrying logs, clothing, wooden furniture and what seemed to be rushes they'd assumedly collected from the floor.

Cracks echoed from the mainland as the men destroyed the furniture and piled it against the farmhouse. Sander swore under his breath. I clutched Vidar's rings hanging around my neck, watching the fiends set the pile on fire. Over and over, the buildings were engulfed in flames. Not only did the fiends burn the structures, but they set fire to the barley, rye and oat fields too.

We expected this. The homes were undefended, of course they would attack them first. The day Kveldúlfr arrived Sander had the women and children evacuated and took the men into Aros's walls. Though we knew it would happen, molten fury roiled through my veins at the destruction his warriors wrought.

If we survived the battle, we might starve this coming winter.

"Bastards." Sander cursed, descending the stairs of the tower.

It didn't take long for our warriors to notice the bitter stench of the burning buildings and fields and spot the dark plumes of smoke filling the sky.

Men froze where they stood, staring.

The battle had begun.

ASHES REMAIN

Warriors assembled in front of the hall armed with spears and axes, swords and bows. Some were wealthy enough to own chainmail, others wore lamellar. Most wore layers of quilted cloth.

Sander surveyed them all, gripping his helmet under one arm.

"It's time." Sander announced, his voice loud and level, clear for every warrior in his army to hear. "I made enough riveting speeches last night to last me a lifetime, so I won't make another. Get ready. It's time to kill Kveldúlfr once and for all."

Archers and men equipped with slings and baskets heavy with rocks lined up in neat rows along the harbour or streamed to the walls, filling the archer towers and the platforms between them. Warriors assembled at the gates, all our exits defended.

Unlike the big cities in Francia or the Anglo-Saxon lands, we had no stone walls nor any siege weapons to protect us from invaders. We had nothing more than a palisade protecting our town. We would defend Aros with only the weapons in our hands. If our enemies brought down our wooden walls, we would meet them head on and stare into their eyes as we killed them.

With my bow at the ready, I stood between Sander and Jan on one of the raised platforms between two archer towers. Together we watched a group of men ride towards our northern gate.

Kveldúlfr was coming for my answer.

The men stopped at the edge of the bridge, their horses snorting and thumping the ground with their hooves. Galinn and Thórvar were among the men, wearing fine armour and weapons at their hips. Kveldúlfr had dressed them up like dolls in chainmail and shiny helmets. Galinn carried an axe while Thórvar had a sword.

"I heard the women and children fled in the night." Kveldúlfr smiled up at me. "I assume you've made your decision?"

"Did you kill them?" I spat.

"How dare you ask me that!" Kveldúlfr barked. "My men and I aren't cowards! I would never kill women or children."

"Unless that woman is Aveline." Jan remarked.

"Or any woman with the misfortune of marrying you." I added.

"There is no justice or honour in killing Norse women and children *fleeing from battle*." Kveldúlfr replied, ignoring my loud snort at his statement.

Kveldúlfr's eyes glinted with amusement. He and I both knew he was spouting shit. If rumour was true – and so far it had been in every way – why would he suddenly change a lifelong habit? The honourless bastard would slaughter every man, woman and child opposing him, fleeing from battle or not.

"As for you, Aveline, an eye for an eye. You murdered Thórvar's mother – *my wife*. You deserve what you get."

"What's your excuse for beating and killing your other wives?"

"Is your sword as sharp as your tongue, *Frú*?"

"You'll find out when I kill you with it."

Kveldúlfr laughed deeply and heartily.

"*You* will kill me? Ha! We shall see!"

As Kveldúlfr and his men turned their horses and started back towards their lines, I lifted my bow, nocked an arrow and aimed at Kveldúlfr's head.

"Aveline, what are you–"

Before Jan could finish, I released my arrow. It sliced through the air, hurtling towards my enemy. It whistled past Kveldúlfr's ear, piercing the ground a few paces in front of him. His horse lurched, but Kveldúlfr jerked the reins and quickly controlled his mare. He glared at me from over his shoulder.

I smiled.

Every fibre of my being wanted to kill Kveldúlfr then and there, but I missed on purpose. When the time came I would watch the life fade from his eyes and feel his last breath dance on my skin.

***

THE BATTLE RAGED like a monstrous pulsating heart, chaos followed by fleeting moments of calm until pandemonium erupted again. Kveldúlfr's lines tightened around us, drawing dangerously nearer. We shot down some of their men, their corpses littered the fields behind their army, but the Norwegians moved ever forward, protected by their shield wall and leagues of archers.

Surrounded, our exits blocked, arrows hailed down on us from all sides in smothering waves. We were trapped. Our warriors ached to escape the confines of our palisade and charge towards the Norwegian army, but Sander refused to open the gates. If our men surged through them, they'd be funnelled across the bridges to the mainland and picked off by our enemies with ease.

"Fire!" One of our warriors yelled. "The houses are burning!"

Heads spun. Burning arrows soared through the air, stabbing into walls and doors, plunging deep into thatched rooves. Most of the fiery arrows went out the moment they struck, but the few that continued to burn wrought havoc.

Clouds of smoke and flame erupted everywhere. The conflagration swiftly spread, devouring rafters until the rooves caved in. Embers drifted like scarlet and gold snowflakes, setting fire to rushes or straw or bags of flour and grain scattered inside and around the exteriors of the homes.

"How in Hel's name–" Sander swore, interrupted by an arrow whistling dangerously close to him.

My heart pounded in my throat. They may not have brought siege weapons, but they had brought the next best thing.

"Fuck!" Sander hissed.

"We need to put out the fires!" Jan said.

"They're just trying to distract us!" Sander growled.

"We can't let the fires spread, Sander!"

"I know, *móðir*!" Sander fumed, chewing his bottom lip. "Both of you, gather men to put out the fires as best you can. Don't take too many, I need as many warriors as possible to defend the walls."

"*Já*, Jarl!" Jan and I nodded in unison.

We ran to the harbour, snatching buckets from a garden as we went. As we passed, we ordered men to the palisades and others to fetch water. Some seized water from wells or dashed to the harbour with buckets to fill.

We splashed smouldering thatch rooves, stomped on burning arrows that missed their mark, drenched smoking bales of hay and straw, dodging yet more arrows as we dashed between the buildings. To our dismay, the fires spread faster than we could collect water.

Our archers plucked at Kveldúlfr's shield walls as they steadily advanced towards us. The Norwegian army would be at our doorstep soon enough. If the fires continued to spread, would the palisade be protecting us or keeping us contained to burn to death? Anyone who attempted to flee through the exits would be slaughtered by the Norwegians. If it came to it, we could escape on the ships – Aros would be taken, but we could save most of our army that way–

I shook my head. Einar, Æsa and the others should've made it to Roskilde by now. They set sail at midnight, at least fifteen hours has passed since then. Usually it would take us thirteen hours to sail there – they *had* to be in Roskilde by now. Young Birger would assemble his army and sail to Aros as soon as possible – once they arrived we would slaughter the Norwegians, we just had to survive until Young Birger and his army arrived.

"Shields up! Shields up!" Domnall boomed.

I glanced up. In the chaos we hadn't noticed part of Kveldúlfr's fleet appear in the harbour, archers shooting from the vessels at those of us collecting water. We sprinted to the safety of the marketplace palisade, covered by a blanket of arrows shot from our archers lining the shore.

"A few of the bastards are dead in the water, but most have their shields raised." Domnall spat, crouched beside me.

"There's what – five ships? That's six hundred men at most. They can't risk so few entering the city." Jan remarked.

"They're distracting us like Sander said." I growled, flinching as an arrow struck the palisade in front of me. "It doesn't matter how few enter the city – the moment they're in, we'll turn our focus onto them, then the rest can enter Aros with ease."

"What do you suggest, *Frú*?" Domnall asked.

"Let the houses burn."

I tore my bow from across my body and, in one swift movement, nocked an arrow, slipped out from behind the palisade, took aim at the nearest ship and released. My arrow whistled through the air and struck one of the warriors in the throat. He plunged into the water, dead.

"May Ullr guide all our arrows as he guides yours!" Jan grinned, readying his own bow.

"Drop your buckets!" I roared at the warriors near me. "Focus on the ships – let the houses burn!"

***

ASHES REMAIN

NIGHT WAS FALLING. Deterred by our arrows, Kveldúlfr's ships loomed at the edge of the harbour, too far to hit, but near enough to intimidate us. Thankfully the encroaching darkness forced the Norwegian army to disengage. Battling at night was a futile endeavour.

I was thankful the combat was calming. We had the night to recuperate. The realisation of how many lives were lost shook me to the core. Bitterly, I wondered if Ullr, the deity associated with archery, had given his blessings to our enemy instead of us.

"Aveline, you *must* rest." Jan said yet again.

The wounded were taken to the hall where the few women who remained in Aros tended to their injuries. Since Kveldúlfr's men retreated, I checked on the injured warriors and helped carry the dead to a barn while other warriors put out the remaining fires and smouldering wreckage of our burned homes.

Inside the barn, bodies were laid side-by-side, their shields and weapons set on top of their stationary chests. There was honour in dying in battle, but that didn't diminish the sadness of seeing so many killed.

Jan had found me in the barn kneeling beside the corpse of a young man named Orvar, an oil lamp set on a stool beside me lighting the corpse in a warm orange glow.

Orvar was perhaps fourteen years of age – a year older than my youngest son, Einar. An arrow had struck Orvar in the face, it had entered through his eye and lodged in the back of his skull. He must've been staring at the arrow as it hurtled towards him.

I wasn't the one to pull the arrow from Orvar's corpse, but I had cleaned the blood and fluid of his ruptured eyeball from his face with a wet rag and bandaged his empty socket.

I stroked Orvar's hair, the light brown strands stringy and filthy with dried blood and sweat. The poor young man wasn't even old enough to marry …

"Come and eat," Jan pleaded. "There's stew at the hall."

"We should've slaughtered half their army today." I murmured – the first words I'd said to Jan since he found me. "The odds were in our favour."

"Aveline–" Jan started, but he stopped abruptly.

"Their formations were too tight, their shields too thick." I released a hollow laugh, smoothing Orvar's tousled hair over his shoulders. "Domnall was wrong ... Ullr didn't side with us today."

"Stop." Jan said firmly, striding toward me.

Jan grabbed me by my shoulders, jerking my hand away from Orvar's corpse. Reluctantly I turned to him. The light from my oil lamp illuminated half of Jan's face, the other half was swathed in shadow. With firelight smouldering in only one of his eyes, he reminded me of how Hel, Loki's daughter and ruler of the underworld, was described in tales told to children.

"*Men die*, Aveline." Jan stated, his brows knitted, and mouth turned in a stern frown. "You know this! This is not the first war you've ever seen – and, by the gods, it won't be the last."

I shrugged Jan's hands from my arms and rubbed my face with my hands. Sighing, I settled my gaze back on Orvar, folding my arms tightly across my chest.

There was a part of me that was surprised by how dazed I was from the ceaseless brutality of the day. This was normal – fighting, killing, death – nothing that happened today was anything I hadn't witnessed or participated in before. Though Aros had never been besieged before, I'd experienced situations a lot worse than this many times in the past. Why was I so shaken now?

"*Deyr fé, deyja frændr, deyr sjalfr it sama ...*" I mumbled.

Cattle die, kinsmen die, and so shall you die too ...

"*En orðstírr deyr aldregi, hveim er sér góðan getr.*" Jan replied.

But one thing I know that never dies, the fame of a dead man's deeds.

I leaned over Orvar's corpse and pressed a tender kiss to his brow before standing up and turning to Jan. He offered me his hand, but rather than accept it, I leaned against his chest, burying my face in his tunic.

"Let's get some stew." I conceded.

***

CRAZED HOWLS STARTLED us from our brief slumber. Banging boomed around us, matched by the clang of metal on metal. Jan and I snatched our shields and weapons and sprinted out of the hall on Sander's heels. In the dim grey light, Kveldúlfr's warriors were shadows in the mist, looming from the shoreline.

What happened to the archers guarding the harbour? Did the Norwegians sneak into the camp and assassinate them so the ships could dock? How had they entered our fucking town?!

"The harbour's breached!" Sander bellowed.

It didn't matter how they entered – they were here. We had no time to call on the gods, to make sacrifices to sway their favour to our advantage. It was time to fight – time to kill – time to die.

The Norwegians had already slaughtered many of our warriors, their bodies discarded, stepped over or kicked aside as our enemies paraded up the shore and through the palisade. At the front of the procession was a *berserkr*, huge and ugly as a troll. As our warriors stormed towards them, the *berserkr* roared with delight, veins like ropes protruding from his thick neck.

One of our warriors lunged at the *berserkr*, his axe raised high. In one swift movement, the brute dodged the axe and grabbed our warrior by his shoulders. He lifted our warrior from his feet, smashed his head into his face then dropped his limp body.

The Norwegian army walked around the *berserkr* and our unconscious comrade like a stream cutting around a boulder. Vomit surged up my throat as I watched the *berserkr* stomp on our warrior. Blood sprayed, bone crunched, until his head was nothing more than mush, squelching sickeningly with every stamp of the *berserkr*'s boot.

Over the heads of his men, I spotted Kveldúlfr in the distance, his fangs bared in a wolfish grin, surveying my people with hungry eyes. He paused beside the *berserkr* and clapped him on the back proudly, laughing with the troll.

Loathing and fury blazed like black fire inside me. They would die – they would *all* die! Every Norwegian who dared to step foot in Aros would fucking die, and the *berserkr*'s head would be mounted on a pike.

I would kill Kveldúlfr.

I would kill them all!

***

GWENDOLINE SK TERRY

THE PUNGENT, METALLIC stench of blood filled my nostrils – intoxicating – delicious. More than an instinctual need to survive, I slashed through my enemies, my heart pounding in my ears, euphoric and insatiable. The wet snap of flesh, the splatter of blood, the thud of bodies tumbling to the ground – I *needed* them to die – I *needed* to kill them.

I danced about my enemies, dipping, twirling and leaping around their attacks. My sword sang through their bodies, glided through their skin and organs like a knife through butter. When my blade collided with their bones, the ricochet shuddered up my arm, prickling my flesh with goosebumps.

Beneath the coat of foreign blood I wore, I knew my body was bruised and broken, but I felt no pain. My lungs seared, my throat was raw, but my screams and roars were strong and clear, and my throbbing eyes eagerly searched for new foes.

Then I saw him.

Kveldúlfr and Einarr were locked in battle before Vidar's towering runestone, both men filthy with dirt and blood. Kveldúlfr bore down on Einarr with his sword, shattering the musician's shield into splinters.

I ran.

Einarr dodged and dived out of Kveldúlfr's way, narrowly escaping the mighty blade that shrieked for his blood. He managed to swipe a shield from a nearby corpse, withstanding blow after blow from the relentless Norwegian jarl.

Stabbing and cutting, pushing and shoving, I barged my way through the throng of fighting, leaving behind me a slew of injured and dead. I arrived at the edge of the battle just in time to watch Kveldúlfr bury his sword in Einarr's skull. Blood poured like tears down Einarr's cheeks as he tumbled to the ground.

"Kveldúlfr!" I bellowed.

"Friend of yours?" He replied casually, nudging Einarr's corpse with his foot.

"Fuck you!" I snarled.

"This is all your fault, you know." Kveldúlfr said matter-of-factly. "This could've been avoided if you'd agreed to my terms. It's your fault he's dead – why all of them are dead." He gestured to the corpses of my warriors strewn all around.

ASHES REMAIN

"I'll rip your fucking throat out!"

"Don't be ridiculous, *Frú.*" Kveldúlfr chuckled. "I'll have what I came here for – *your life.*"

My skin crawled. Venomous rage like snakes writhed beneath my flesh. The very sight of Kveldúlfr brought vomit to my throat.

"I will do whatever it takes to kill you," I vowed, my voice low and deep. "And I will take *pleasure* doing it!"

"Dear *Frú*, I was about to say the very same thing to you!" Kveldúlfr cackled.

With *Úlfsblóð* and my shield at the ready, I stepped towards Kveldúlfr, glowering at the troll. He was huge. His cobalt eyes followed me, that smirk twisting his lips. For a second I remembered my fight against Háken Tarbenson, another monstrously tall man. If I could defeat him, I could defeat Kveldúlfr.

Háken had been blinded by anger, young and inexperienced.

I had been young, spry and skilled in battle.

Kveldúlfr was a strong, violent jarl with many successful battles under his belt and countless victims' blood on his hands.

I was old and broken, but, hopefully, still competent enough to defeat him. I didn't have to live as long as Kveldúlfr died.

Kveldúlfr launched himself forward, blade baring down on me. Instinct lifted my shield-arm as I narrowly sidestepped his strike, breath held, heart racing.

In a blink, Kveldúlfr spun, arcing around with his sword. I threw myself to the ground, rolled across the grass and leapt to my feet, evading the edge of his blade by the skin of my teeth. In that same swift movement, Kveldúlfr slashed at me again. I caught his weapon with my shield, my arm rattling from the force.

Shoving his sword aside with my shield, I thrust *Úlfsblóð* towards Kveldúlfr's ribs, but the bastard leapt backwards. Kveldúlfr advanced tirelessly, swinging, sweeping, slashing. I parried every blow, my muscles screaming.

Kveldúlfr's bloodied blade glinted in the grey sunlight as he brought it down on me. Parrying it with my blade, I gasped as Kveldúlfr rammed me backwards, forcing me against the runestone. My teeth clenched, I dug my heels into the ground and desperately tried to fight against Kveldúlfr's blade.

In the corner of my eye, I noticed Einarr's dead eyes watching me in permanent horror, red tears sliding down his cheeks, skull cracked down the middle, flies gathering on his brains.

"All your warriors are dying because of your selfishness." Kveldúlfr leered, rivulets of sweat cutting through the blood, dirt and warpaint plastered to his face. "You were always going to die, Aveline. Why would you drag them down with you? There's no honour here, dying for *you*."

Kveldúlfr carried on as though it didn't take him any effort to pin me against Vidar's runestone with his blade. I struggled against him with all my might, focussed on keeping his sword away from my throat.

"If only you'd given yourself up, none of them would've died. I would've even let you watch your daughter marry my son."

"She'll never marry your fucking son!" I spat through gritted teeth.

"Oh, how I would've killed you!" Kveldúlfr growled, a dark lust glinting in his deep blue eyes, ignoring my insult. "It wouldn't be quick like this – I would've taken it slowly, enjoyed every moment of it. You stole that from me, you selfish bitch."

Kveldúlfr forced our blades closer to my neck. My arms trembled with exhaustion, every muscle throbbing and searing. I couldn't keep this up much longer – Kveldúlfr was too strong!

"Since the first time I wrapped my hands around your throat, I've dreamt of strangling you. To crush your neck in my hands and feel your pulse hammer until it stops – by the gods, there's nothing more intimate or sensual than that! Have you ever choked someone to death, *Frú*? There's nothing better than feeling the life of your victim slip away beneath your palms, like extinguishing a candle flame with your fingertips!"

I gathered every ounce of strength inside me and brought my knee up between his legs. With a strangled howl, Kveldúlfr staggered back, dropping his blade and clutching his bollocks.

I fell to the floor, panting. I couldn't rest – I had to get to my feet – if I stayed prone, Kveldúlfr would kill me! I forced myself up, falling against Vidar's runestone, my arms burning.

"*Móðir!*" Sander roared.

ASHES REMAIN

I had no idea where they'd come from, but I'd never been more thankful to see Sander and Jan. I shot them a feeble smile.

Distracted for just a moment, I didn't see Kveldúlfr lunge at me, his arm swung back. His fist slammed against my cheek, his knuckles like steel colliding with my bone. My vision temporarily vanished, I flew to the ground gasping, my head reeling.

"Aveline!" Jan bellowed.

"You arrived just in time to watch her die!" Kveldúlfr sneered.

Kveldúlfr didn't have a chance to strike me again. Jan pounced on him like a giant wild cat, knocking the Norwegian to the ground. Sander shot towards me and dropped to my side, his soothing words difficult to hear over the ringing in my ears.

"Come on, *móðir*, we have to get you to safety!" Sander's voice trembled. "Get up, come on! Take your shield, hold it close!"

"Are we winning?" I wheezed, clutching the shield's leather strap, allowing Sander to drag me away.

"We are, *móðir*!" Sander beamed. "You'll live to celebrate our victory if you leave now! Come on – I saw a horse across the way! You can ride to safety, just hold your shield!"

The sickening thump of fist pounding flesh and bone was almost deafening. As Sander tried to lead me away, I glanced over my shoulder at Jan and Kveldúlfr brutally beating each other. Lumps and bruises sprang from their blood stained flesh as they brought their fists down on each other like hammers on anvils.

Jan's bloodcurdling wail stopped us in our tracks.

"Jan?" I whispered.

Jan's legs crumpled beneath him, Kveldúlfr's *sax* stuck in his gut. Kveldúlfr stumbled backwards, laughing.

"Jan!" I shrieked.

Kveldúlfr sneered at me. I ripped myself from Sander's grasp, drew Vidar's utility knife from my belt and flew at Kveldúlfr. Bolstered by fury, a second wind filled my body with all the strength I needed, the pain of my wounds ignored.

The Norwegian was bigger and stronger, but I was faster. Twisting about Kveldúlfr's body like smoke, I evaded his attacks. In the corner of my eye, I saw Sander drag Jan to the foot of Vidar's runestone, pressing some bloodied fabric over Jan's stomach.

Jan was speaking to Sander – he was still alive!

Parrying Kveldúlfr's strikes with my shield, I darted around him, slitting his flesh with thousands of shallow cuts from my blade. They weren't enough to kill him but kept his attention on me.

Sander left Jan's side and darted towards Kveldúlfr and me silently. My enemy didn't notice my son stealth up behind him, his *sax* gripped between both hands and raised over his head.

"Argh!" Kveldúlfr howled, falling to his knees, my son's blade buried in his spine.

I tossed down my shield and buried Vidar's utility knife into the side of Kveldúlfr's neck, opening his throat and dousing myself in his blood. I closed my eyes, the slick liquid spraying my face with an almost comforting warmth. Splatters covered my lips and trickled over my tongue – copper, salt and honey.

Blood and saliva gurgled in the gaping wound in Kveldúlfr's neck and scarlet blood vessels knotted in the whites of his bulging eyes. Despite the morbidity of his expression frozen on his face by death, I couldn't help admiring the pretty blue of his irises.

"*Far vel*, Kveldúlfr." I muttered, pulling my blade from his throat and letting his body crumple to the ground.

Sander bellowed with triumph and adrenalin – we killed him! We killed Kveldúlfr! We defeated our enemy – we won!

We dashed to Jan, crouching down on either side of him.

"He's definitely dead," Sander grinned. "*Móðir* made sure of it this time."

"When his men see his corpse, they'll flee." Jan panted, grimacing from the pain of his wound.

"Hold on, my love. Let's get you to the hall." I said, stroking away the hair stuck to his face by sweat and blood.

"*Ledrhals kerling*! *Halftroll beiskaldi*!"
Leather neck old hag – half troll bitch?

"Is that aimed at one of you?" Sander flashed us a brief smirk.

I glanced about to see who was hurling insults. Thórvar was across the way, his face red, tears streaming down his cheeks. I wiped his father's blood from my eyes.

It was time to finish this feud once and for all.

"You've caused a lot of trouble, boy." I growled, seizing *Úlfsblóð* from the ground.

ASHES REMAIN

"I'll cleave your head from your neck for what you've done to my family!" Thórvar thundered.

Thórvar bore down on me with his sword, hatred burning in his eyes. I slammed my shield against his blade and slashed at his belly, grazing his abdomen. His armour protected him. Sander lunged toward him, but Galinn appeared out of nowhere and intercepted, batting my son's sword with his shield. Sander caught Galinn's axe with his own shield, the blade biting through the painted wood.

The two young men disappeared from my view. I heard them fighting, but I couldn't see them. I couldn't glance over to see how my son was faring, Thórvar didn't hesitate for even a moment.

We exchanged blows, slashing, parrying. Thórvar was taller than me so I incorrectly assumed he was slower. It took only one hit for me to realise he was just as nimble if not more than me.

Thankfully, where hatred and heartache bolstered me, they impaired him. So intent on killing me, Thórvar made mistake after mistake. His movements were swift, but his aim was sloppy and his body trembled incessantly.

I deflected his attacks but was rapidly running out of energy. Despite how quick the fight had been, Kveldúlfr had exhausted me. I needed to finish this fast.

Beneath the shadow of Vidar's runestone, Thórvar swung. I knocked his sword back with my shield and whacked his wrist with the flat of my blade.

He dropped his shield.

Our eyes connected.

Thórvar's jaw fell.

I grinned.

I raised *Úlfsblóð* – Thórvar lifted his sword – I brought my sword down upon him – blood sprayed in a hot mist, the metallic stench filling my nostrils.

It took only a moment for me to realise it was *my* blood. A piercing pain ripped through my shoulder, the bones of my collarbone and ribs shattered. In the split second it took for me to slash at Thórvar, he stabbed me.

Stunned, Thórvar and I froze, staring at each other, his hand wrapped around the hilt of his weapon. Our eyes moved to my shoulder, the tip of the blade buried deep inside me, my blood oozing around it. Thórvar stumbled backwards, eyes wide, pulling the sword out. His hands trembled and he dropped the weapon. It landed with on the ground with a dull *thud*.

Has he ever killed someone before? I wondered before my legs crumpled beneath me.

"Aveline!" Jan roared.

Blood gushed from Jan's stomach as he pounced on Thórvar. With one massive hand wrapped around the back of the boy's head, Jan smashed Thórvar's face against the runestone.

Crack! Crack! Crack!

Thórvar's face was bloody mush. Jan threw the boy's corpse aside, landing neatly beside Kveldúlfr. I turned my gaze to Sander, just in time to watch him swing Galinn's own axe square in the centre of his chest. I forced myself up and leaned against the runestone, sucking air in rasping gasps.

Jan dropped beside me and pulled me against him, kissing my brow and pressing his hand against my wound to staunch the bleeding.

"*Nei*," I murmured, taking his hand in mine and kissing it.

My eyes travelled to Jan's stomach where blood poured, soaking his clothing in red. He wouldn't survive his wound – and I didn't want to survive mine. I would die beside him, just as I vowed.

I embraced my husband. We were silent for just a moment before a sob burst from my chest and tears streamed down my cheeks. The thrill of the battle was receding now my enemies were dead. Left in the aftermath, my body trembled, nausea bubbled in my stomach and I realised just how much my body hurt.

"*Móðir*! By the gods, *nei*!" Sander panicked, his face turning grey when he spotted my shoulder.

I swallowed my sobs.

"It's alright, my heart." I smiled warmly, wincing from the pain.

"I'll get a healer – you'll be okay!"

"*Nei*, son, stay with me. It's alright."

"I won't let you die! I'll get help!"

"Sander," Jan said as firmly as he could muster.

"Sit with us, Sander." I pleaded.

"I won't let you die!" Sander vowed.

ASHES REMAIN

Sander pressed a deep, teary kiss to my brow, swiped up his sword and shield and darted towards the hall. My heart dropped in my chest – I wanted my son to stay, to hold my hand in my last moments. I called after him, but he kept running.

The deep bay of horns howled through the air.

"Young Birger's here." Jan mumbled.

We peered at the waters in the distance, watching the black silhouettes of his vast fleet appear. The wind was on their side – they soared across the waters, swiftly approaching Aros. The Norwegian warriors nearby us visibly shrank with fear as they spotted our reinforcements. Some sprinted towards the walls, fleeing like cowards, others ran to the bay either to meet their enemy or flee in their ships.

Jan and I would be avenged. Our children and grandchildren would live. The blood feud ended when we killed Thórvar and Kveldúlfr. Young Birger and Sander would slaughter the remaining enemies in retribution.

We won.

CHAPTER FORTY-SEVEN

I SURVIVED VIDAR by nine years. Nine years …

The number nine seemed to follow me, I mused as I felt my life ebb away. I was nine years old when Birger Bloody Sword took me from my homeland in the Kingdom of the East Angles and brought me to Roskilde in the land of the Danes.

Vidar and I married nine years after we first spoke together all those years ago in a woodshed in the middle of winter in Roskilde.

The Allfather had taken nine significant people of my past to grant me my life as a Dane, then a further nine from my Danish life to secure the fates of my children.

I still owed him two lives, but I knew whose lives they were now.

The number nine was significant to the Norse people and their gods. The Norse people believed there were nine worlds nestled in the roots and branches of the world tree, Yggdrasil, in Odin's self-sacrifice to attain knowledge, he hung for nine nights from one of Yggdrasil's branches. It was foretold that after Thor defeated Jörmungandr in battle at Ragnarök, he would take nine steps before he'd fall down dead, poisoned by the venom the Midgard serpent spewed on him.

Horns blazed across the fjord, the mournful howl echoing through Aros. Though I knew death in battle was glorious for a Dane, I was pleased and thankful my daughter, my youngest son, my grandchildren and daughters-in-law were far from the battlefield, the Anglo-Saxon deep inside me relieved they would live to see another day.

The Dane in me was bolstered by the knowledge my sons were fighting valiantly against our enemy – and deep inside me, I knew they would win. My body would rot away to nothingness upon the bloodstained soil of Aros, but my children, my legacy, would live on – and with them, the memories of Jan, Vidar and me.

Jan shifted, pulling me closer to him, groaning as he forced himself to move. His body was weak, but he grinned at me regardless, his sapphire eyes twinkling. I returned his smile and cupped his face, his skin clammy and damp with sweat and blood. My arm was heavy, an invisible force weighing it down, the draw of death sapping my strength away.

"Thank you for taking care of me." I whispered.

"I've enjoyed every moment of it." Jan winked.

"I'm sorry for all the times I wronged you, Jan." Tears welled in my eyes. "I wish I married you sooner – I wish I gave you the children you wanted. I wish I could turn back time and undo my actions."

"You can't, Aveline, and that's okay." Jan smiled mournfully. "Everything happens for a reason."

"If we survive this, I will give you an army of children." I vowed fiercely, but it was a hallow promise and we both knew it.

"An army of Jan's." Jan laughed. "The world would be so lucky!"

"You deserved so much more than I gave you."

"Why are you apologising, Aveline? You gave me everything I ever wanted. I'm happy. *You made me happy*! There was nothing else I needed or wanted but that."

"Y-you made me happy, t-too." I stammered through my tears.

"You made me angry and crazy and sad – but most of all you made me happy." Jan clutched his chest as he snickered, pain tearing through him.

"By the gods, even when you're dying, you're wicked!"

My laughter halted and my heart lurched in my chest. Jan was dying. We were *both* dying. The realisation struck me like a battering ram.

"By the gods, Jan, this is it." I murmured. "What about Einar and Æsa and Sander and Young Birger? What about Signý and Fenja? What about our grandchildren?"

"Sander and Birger will continue being the incredible jarls they are. Sweet Æsa will raise Einar to be the formidable warrior he is destined to be." Jan's certainty was staggering. "We are blessed that we were able to meet our grandchildren. I don't fear for their futures because I know how well their parents will raise them."

Jan was right – he was right. I knew he was right. Selfishly I wished we could've lived long enough to see our grandchildren's children – but I was greedy and spoiled. Hardly anyone lived long enough to see the birth of their first grandchild, but Jan and I met three of ours!

I watched Jan's chest rise and fall as he struggled for each rasping breath. For years I had wanted to die with Vidar. I wanted to die wrapped in the arms of the man I loved ... And I was.

Jan wasn't Vidar – I didn't love Jan as I loved Vidar, but I didn't need to. Jan wasn't Vidar, he never was and never would be. He was Jan 'Jötunnson' Jarlufson, the foster brother of my late husband, my closest companion, the man who loved me and protected me when Vidar no longer could. I loved Jan for that, but not *only* that.

I loved Jan for his wicked comments and cheeky smiles, for how he made me laugh, for how we argued over every little thing, for how he weathered every storm at my side. I loved Jan for how he loved my children, raising them like they were his own. I loved Jan for his loyalty and kindness. I loved Jan for how he loved me, for how pure his heart was. I loved Jan for never being afraid to communicate with me even if it led to arguments and hurt. I loved Jan for accepting me. I loved Jan for being him.

"I thought you'd live forever." I whispered.

"Why would I want to live forever when I've been blessed with a death like this? I fought by your side and now I get to die in your arms – I thank the Nornir for giving me a death like this!" Jan chuckled. "Besides, we'll be in Valhalla together soon enough."

"Odin would be lucky to have two mighty warriors like us."

"*Já*, he would! He best be ready for us – we're a force to be reckoned with!"

We laughed joyfully, painfully, abundantly. This would be the last time we would laugh together, the last time we would smile together in the realm of Midgard. Jan eased his head down and I stretched upwards to meet his lips, tenderly sharing our final kiss.

"I love you, Aveline Birgersdóttir. I am glad to die by your side."

"I love you, too, Jan Jötunnson Jarlufson, and I am honoured to die by yours."

Jan closed his eyes, holding me against him, my head rested on his chest. For a few quiet moments I listened to his heart beat slow, his breathing draw shallow until finally it stopped. His hand fell, his head dropped back.

ASHES REMAIN

Jan was dead.

My eighth loss ... All that was left was me.

Across the way a raven cawed. I admired the blue-black of its feathers, the sharpness of its beak, the roughness of its caw. It hopped towards me, pausing an arms-length away. A white cloud swirled in one of its eyes while the other was glossy and dark.

"Hello, my friend." I murmured, unafraid of its presence for the first time in my life. "Tell your master I'm coming."

The raven titled its head, croaking back at me. It hopped a little closer and preened its wing with its long charcoal-coloured bill, displacing a single black feather that fluttered to the ground. The raven cocked its head at me once more before taking flight.

It would relay my message to the Allfather of that I was sure.

A deep sigh fell from my lips and my eyes fell shut, my lids too heavy to keep open anymore. My heart was light and my body tired. I was ready. It was time for me to leave the confines of Midgard and find my place in the afterlife.

It was time to return to Vidar.

I pictured Vidar in my mind, his cerulean and silver eyes sparkling as he gazed at me, his skin like faded bronze, sun-kissed and glowing. Long golden tresses fell around his face and from his neatly trimmed beard his pale pink lips curved into a seductive smirk. Creases formed at the corner of his beautiful icy eyes as he smiled ... I could almost hear him speak to me.

"Hello, little fawn."

As though Vidar actually said those words, my heart swelled with happiness, with love, with warmth despite the cold that crept through my body from my fingers and toes. I felt each drop of blood trickle down my skin and puddle beneath me. Though my body was broken, my pain stopped. I hadn't expected this, but I was grateful – death was tender.

A small part of me was disappointed I wouldn't die in Roskilde, the town my new life began. Though I would've been amused by the irony, I consoled myself with the knowledge that dying in Aros was better.

A long time ago, I thought I'd die in Aros at the hand of Erhardt Ketilsson, never to see Vidar again. Instead, I ruled here beside Vidar, loyal and devoted to one another. We turned Aros, a place saturated with painful memories, into our home. We owned this town, we changed it, improved it – we made it ours.

Yes, dying in Aros was much better.

I found myself unafraid – death is only sad for those who survive. I thought of the great feast in Valhalla, the Allfather's hall, filled with an endless supply of mead and food – the reward for all his chosen warriors. I mused at the thought of thousands of ethereal warriors raising their tankards and striking up song, feasting and fighting until Ragnarök. I looked forward to meeting my fallen friends and family again.

The gods gave with one hand and took away with the other. Despite all the chaos and horrific ordeals I suffered throughout my life, I was thankful for the extraordinary children I'd been blessed with and the wonderful grandchildren they'd given me. I cherished the families I'd been lucky to be a part of and the dear friendships I'd made. I was grateful for the precious loves I'd enjoyed – the loves of both Vidar and Jan.

Despite the terrible past I'd suffered and the wonderful future I wouldn't be a part of, I thanked the gods for all they granted me, the pain and the happiness, the tears and the smiles. I knew my children and grandchildren would live long lives and revel in victory and success long after my death.

It was time for my story to end and my children's to begin. My tapestry was complete, and the time had come for the Nornir to cut the final thread. I would pay my debt to the Allfather, I would give him his final sacrifice.

The vision of Vidar continued to beam at me, gentle, welcoming, overflowing with love. A smile touched my lips and my last breath fell, and my gaze settled on the feather from the raven's wing. It was time for me to leave Midgard and let only memories and stories and ashes remain.

AUTHOR'S NOTE

ASHES REMAIN is the final instalment of the DANETHRALL series. Historically inspired, ASHES REMAIN is primarily a fiction and I hope any historical inaccuracies that may be found in these pages will be recognised as creative license, forgiven and appreciated for their use in propelling this story.

Set mainly in ninth century Denmark, I have tried to remain as faithful to the period as possible but have taken advantage of creative license to a certain degree. The language spoken in ninth century Denmark was Old East Norse, but you may find some Danish and Icelandic words amongst the Old Norse scattered throughout the book.

Most characters in this story have period-specific Old Norse names, but for a few characters I preferred to not be as strict. Therefore, in these pages you will find a handful of characters with Icelandic names, modern, traditional or Old Scandinavian names, names that weren't first used until well after the ninth century, etc. I have used the anglicized or 'younger version' of names here and there (for example, Vidar is the younger version of the old Norse Viðarr).

In a few chapters you will see the words 'seax' and 'sax' mentioned. No, there are no typos, 'seax' is the Old English word for a form of knife/dagger and 'sax' is simply the Norse version.

Regardless of inaccuracies and creative license, I do hope this story was as exciting and enjoyable for you to read, as it was for me to write.

For more information on the Old Norse, Ænglisc and Old French words used in this book, and a lot more, please visit my website, gskterry.com.

Gwendoline SK Terry